MIDNIGHT PLEASURES

AMANDA ASHLEY

SHERRILYN KENYON

MAGGIE SHAYNE

RONDA THOMPSON

St. Martin's Paperbacks

MIDNIGHT PLEASURES

ISBN: 0-312-98762-5

Printed in the United States of America

St. Martin's Paperbacks edition / November 2003

St. Martin's Paperbacks are published by St. Martin's Press, 175 Fifth Avenue, New York, NY 10010.

10 9 8 7 6 5 4 3 2 1

DARKFEST
BY AMANDA ASHLEY

The price of saving her dying mother is Channa's promise to spend a year at the castle of tormented nobleman, Lord Darkfest . . . to obey him as his servant or, as his secrets are revealed, to become his salvation. And her own.

PHANTOM LOVER
BY SHERRILYN KENYON

Haunted by recurring nightmares of terrifying beasts, Erin McDaniels is afraid to sleep—until a hero arrives in her dreams to save her . . . and makes erotic, incredible love to her. But can she find him again when she is awake?

UNDER HER SPELL
BY MAGGIE SHAYNE

A consultant for a TV series about one gorgeous witch, "white witch" Melissa St. Cloud plans to make the show authentic. But once on the set she is pulled into the arms of a man who opens up a doorway to the dark side and chilling peril.

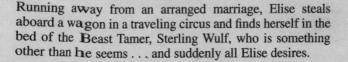

A WULF'S CURSE
BY RONDA THOMPSON

Running away from an arranged marriage, Elise steals aboard a wagon in a traveling circus and finds herself in the bed of the Beast Tamer, Sterling Wulf, who is something other than he seems . . . and suddenly all Elise desires.

CONTENTS

Darkfest 1
   by Amanda Ashley

Phantom Lover 101
   by Sherrilyn Kenyon

Under Her Spell 185
   by Maggie Shayne

A Wulf's Curse 275
   by Ronda Thompson

DARKFEST

AMANDA ASHLEY

For all those who patiently
—And not so patiently—
Urged me to finish this tale,
I hope you're as happy with
The results as I am.

And especially for
Ethan and Monique—
I couldn't have done it
Without you.

PROLOGUE

THEY were afraid of him, but then, as far back as he could remember, people had been afraid of him. Even his mother had looked upon him with a certain measure of fear. He had learned to walk when he was but six months old, could converse with his elders by the time he was two, could turn water into ale at three.

As a child, he had not understood the amazement of his elders. He had thought all males were as gifted as he. He had been well and truly surprised to discover that those he came in contact with could not read his mind as he read theirs. His playmates, though few, stood in awe of his ability to create fire and summon thunder at his will.

He had cherished his unique powers, not knowing that, as time passed, those who knew him would come to fear him, while others who were hungry for power would go to any and all lengths to learn the secret of his awesome powers, his eternal youth. Feared and held in suspicion by those who knew him, pursued by those who would steal his power, his very life, he had taken refuge inside his father's keep.

Now, three hundred years later, all those he had known in his youth were gone, and he alone remained, shut up in a prison of his own making at the top of a high mountain.

CHAPTER 1

A distant land before recorded time

IT was midnight on the Eve of First Harvest and he stood alone on a rocky pinnacle of his high mountain, watching the villagers far below as they danced around a fire blazing in the middle of the square.

No mere mortal could have discerned aught but the flames, but the wizard of Darkfest Keep could clearly see the face and form of each man, woman, and child, hear their songs of joy, their shouts of carefree laughter. He saw Adair, the cooper, flirting with a woman who was not his wife, saw young Muggins slip quietly into the shadows with the blacksmith's daughter. Old Henrew was telling ribald stories to a handful of young men, while Alys the midwife sat apart from the others telling a young maid's fortune.

Such foolishness, the wizard mused, singing and dancing during the dark of the moon. He could have told them that all the singing in the world would not protect their crops from weevils or drought, or ensure a bountiful harvest. Dancing barefoot in the dirt would not make their women fertile, but who was he to vanquish their hopes and dreams, foolish though they might be?

And when the crops failed and the clouds withheld their

moisture, the villagers would take their courage in hand and climb the narrow rocky mountain path to his door. Cowering with fear, careful not to meet his gaze, they would plead for his help. They would bring him golden ears of corn and flasks of spiced wine, a lamb without blemish, the meager contents of the town's treasury. They would grant him homage and beg for his mercy. And if it suited his mood, he would accept their offerings and grant their boon, and they would hurry away, never meeting his eyes, careful to keep him from seeing that they made the sign against evil behind his back.

Their fear amused him. He possessed many strange and wondrous powers, but, awesome as his talents might be, even he could not perform all the mystical feats of which they believed him capable.

The sound of lute and tambourine floated toward him, borne on the wings of a gentle east wind. And then he heard a voice, *her voice,* as light as morning dew, as clear as crystal ice. A lovely voice that threaded through the darkness and twined around his soul like a fine silken web.

Channa Leigh's voice.

It tugged at him, pulling him nearer the edge of the precipice on which he stood, tantalizing him, calling to something deep within his soul as it did each time he heard it. He saw her clearly, sitting on the edge of the well in the center of the village square. Her father, Dugald of Brynn, stood near her side, proud and protective, but Darkfest had eyes only for the fair Channa Leigh. She wore a white apron over a simple blue dress. Her hair, as bright as the sun on a summer day, fell in rippling waves down her back and over her shoulders, glistening in the firelight like a river of molten gold.

This night, her voice beckoned him as never before. Unable to resist, eager to more closely behold the face of the one blessed with the voice of an angel, he gathered his power close around him. He felt it coalesce and he drew it close, feeling it surround him, and then he stepped out into the darkness of space, his body falling like a leaf from a tree, changing from wizard to wolf as he drifted downward to land, as light as dandelion down, on the ground.

"SING another, Channa Leigh."

"Aye, lass, give us another!"

Channa Leigh smiled as the crowd gathered around her urged her to sing another song. Singing was her one true love, her sole reason for living. Locked in a world of darkness, she had only her music to light her days.

Hands clasped to her breast, she began to sing again, an ancient lullaby she had often heard her mother sing. A hush fell over the crowd, and even the rowdy young men near the tavern fell silent, until the only sound to be heard was her voice, the notes strong and true, blending with the whisper of the night wind and the faint crackle of the flames. The lullaby gave way to a ballad of love lost and found, the words sung with such feeling that many a woman wept silent tears, and many a man, too.

There was a moment of awed quiet as the last note fell away, and then Channa Leigh heard someone gasp, heard someone else softly exclaim, "Look at that!"

She felt the undercurrent of fear that ran through the crowd, heard their shuffling feet as they backed away from her.

"Hold still, lass," her father called softly.

Accustomed to obeying her father's every word, Channa Leigh did as she was told. And then, like a ray of brilliant sunshine penetrating a dark cloud, she felt a presence beside her.

"Dinna move, Daughter." Her father's voice trembled now. "Dinna move."

She felt a pressure against her leg, the brush of thick, soft fur against her hand. "What is it?" she whispered.

"'Tis a mountain wolf, the biggest I've ever seen."

She should have been afraid. Mountain wolves were huge beasts, some near as large as a draft pony. They were predators without equal.

She should have been afraid, yet she felt no fear at all as

the big wolf circled her, his body pressing against her legs. She felt a stirring in the air, a whisper, like the mournful sighing of the wind before dawn. A tingling on her skin, like the touch of the sun after a cold winter. Before she had time to wonder what it meant, the chains of darkness fell away from her eyes. Too stunned to speak, she stared at the creature as he rubbed his huge head against her hand, blatantly begging for her touch. What magic was this? she wondered in awe. What witchery had fallen on her to restore her sight? Hesitantly, she scratched his ears, then ran her fingertips over his head and neck. She was rewarded with a low growl that rumbled like soft thunder. Startled, she drew her hand away, and darkness descended on her once more.

The wolf whined low in his throat, his muzzle pressing against her arm. She blinked and blinked again, and as she sat there, her hand resting lightly upon the wolf's head, she realized that she was seeing the world through the wolf's eyes. Her own eyes widened with surprise as she noticed the wolf's eyes were blue. Who had ever heard of such a thing as a blue-eyed wolf?

"Be still, lass," Dugald warned softly. "Ronin has gone for his bow."

"Nay!" Channa Leigh cried. "Nay, Papa, you must not kill it!"

"Are you daft, girl? 'Tis a wild beastie, not a pet."

Slowly, her hand resting firmly on the wolf's head, she stood and turned toward the sound of her father's voice. "Papa? Papa, I can see you."

Dugald stared at his daughter in astonishment. "Channa Leigh, what are you saying?"

"I can see you."

"Channa Leigh?" A woman stepped out of the crowd, her pale blue eyes shining with tears.

"Mama? Oh, Mama, I can see."

Mara stared at her daughter. "But . . . but . . . how is that possible?"

"I dinna know." Slowly, Channa Leigh glanced around,

and she could see them all, the people she had lived with all her life, some whom she had never seen. "'Tis a miracle."

A miracle that ended when Ronin ran forward, his long-bow clutched in his hand. Ronin, who was the best hunter in the village, who provided the village folk with meat summer and winter, who found game when no one else could.

She shouted, "Nay, you must not!" as he put arrow to string and sighted down the shaft.

With a graceful leap and a roar that seemed to shake the very pillars of the earth, the big black wolf disappeared into the night, leaving her in darkness once more.

HE stood once again on the pinnacle of the mountain, shaken to the very foundation of his soul. Her spirit, as pure and clean as the light of dawn, had brushed his, and as their souls collided, the fetters of blindness had melted away and she had seen the world through his eyes. He had felt her joy as she looked upon the faces of her father and mother for the first time since an illness in childhood had stolen her sight. In those few moments, he had felt all of her pain, her sense of being shut off from the rest of the world, her yearning for a home and a family of her own.

How was this possible? In three hundred years, he had performed countless miracles, healed the sick, coaxed rain from the heavens, but never had he plumbed the depths of another soul, nor had another see the world through his eyes.

He gazed down at the villagers. They stood subdued after the incident with the wolf. Had he willed it, he could have heard their voices, read their thoughts, but he closed his mind against them, his whole being focused on the young woman who gazed sightlessly into the distance, her heart silently beseeching the great black wolf to return to her side.

CHAPTER 2

HE paced through the empty rooms of the great stone castle all that night, his mind in turmoil.

He knew so much, and yet he knew so little.

He had performed wondrous feats of magic, yet could not explain why a blind peasant girl had been able to see when she touched him.

He paused in front of the looking glass that adorned one wall of his chamber, stared at the reflection before him as though it could give him the answers he sought, but he saw only what he had always seen: a tall man, broad of chest and long of limb. His hair fell past his shoulders, long and straight and black save for a narrow streak of gray at his left temple. His eyes changed color with the seasons—cold gray in winter, pale green in spring, deep brown in the fall. This night, they were the warm blue of a summer sky.

She had touched him and seen the world through his eyes. How was that possible? Were he to touch her while in his human form, would the same miracle occur?

He walked slowly through the great stone castle that was his domain. He had lived here alone all his adult life, watching the world change, watching the people in the village below as they went through the endless cycle of life and death.

He had watched Channa Leigh grow from being a plump, pink-cheeked babe, to a long-legged girl, to a beautiful young woman. It seemed he had always watched Channa Leigh, that he had ever been drawn to the beautiful green-eyed girl who now stared at the world through sightless eyes.

He paused in the great hall to stare up at the painting of his parents. His mother was as fair as his father was dark. She had been a pale, slender creature with light brown hair and eyes as blue as a deep mountain lake. His father had been darkness itself—dark of skin and hair and eyes. Dark of soul, some had said. The people of the village had called him the Dragon Lord of Darkfest Keep.

Darkfest left the castle and wandered through the quiet night, bedeviled by questions for which he had no answers, knowing only that should he surrender to the darkness that dwelled deep within him, he would be forever lost, forever damned.

In the days that followed, he tried to put Channa Leigh out of his mind, but it was impossible. Like the ache from an old wound, she came back again and again to torment him. He felt anew the touch of her small, gentle hand on his head, relived her wonder as she saw the world through his eyes. And because he had ever been selfish when it came to satisfying his own wants, a fortnight later he again changed into the guise of a mountain wolf and made his way down the mountainside to the village.

He knew which house was hers, knew in what room she slept. But even had he not known, her warm, familiar scent would have beckoned him as surely as candlelight drew the tiny white moths.

He hesitated a moment, weighing the risk of being discovered against the prize, and then dismissed the danger. He was Darkfest, more than a match for a few lowly peasants.

Her window was open and he leaped effortlessly over the low sill, then padded soundlessly toward her narrow bed. She slept on her side, facing the window, one hand tucked, childlike, beneath her cheek. Her eyes were closed, but he knew them well, wide and innocent beneath delicately shaped brows, as green as the leaves of the pine trees that grew close together along the river. Her rich golden hair fell in a long braid over her shoulder. He lifted the heavy braid with his paw, closed his eyes, and breathed deeply. Her scent filled his nostrils, warmed every nerve.

Would she wake if he dared to lie beside her? It was a temptation he could not resist. Lightly he jumped onto her bed and stretched out beside her, his back to her front. A low growl of satisfaction rumbled in his throat as she snuggled against him.

A sigh, soft as a summer breeze, whispered past her lips, ruffling his fur.

Of what do ye dream, my Channa Leigh? he wondered, and closing his eyes, he covered her hand with his paw and let his mind meld with hers. ...

At first there was only darkness, and then, gradually, the world brightened and he saw her walking along the riverbank, one hand resting on the head of a huge wolf. And she saw the world through his eyes. He experienced her wonder as she watched a gray squirrel run up a tree. She stopped to touch the soft pink petals of a brier rose, stooped to run her hands over the green velvet grass. Now and then she paused and gazed up at the sky, and then she moved on, her head turning slowly from side to side, examining everything she passed—flowers, leaves, rocks, a fat brown caterpillar.

He felt her fingers in his hair as her hand stroked the dream wolf's head. He had thought to change into his true form but decided against it now, afraid she might sense the change and awaken.

In her dream, she sat down in the shade of a flowering oak, and the big wolf stretched out beside her, his head in her lap.

As she stroked the dream wolf, he felt his own body tingle, his skin ripple with pleasure, as though she were caressing him and not the wolf in her dream.

"Isn't the world a wondrous place, my dark one?" she said. *"I had forgotten how beautiful it all was."* She ran one hand over the grass. *"This is green. 'Tis a glorious color.*

And the earth. 'Tis brown, like Papa's cow. Oh, and look at the sky. 'Tis a wondrous shade of blue. As blue as your eyes."

Time passed. An hour, a day . . . in a dream, time had no meaning, not that it mattered. He had all the time in the world. Man or beast, in this world or in the world of Channa Leigh's dreams, he was content to rest there, by her side, to feel her fingers stroke his fur, to breathe in her scent, to imagine himself as a man at her side, his head cradled in her lap, his lips tasting hers. . . .

As if she knew his thoughts, the dreaming Channa Leigh pressed her fingertips to her lips. *"Tell me, dark one, do you think I shall ever find a man to love?"* She laughed softly, sadly. *"I think Ronin has feelings for me, though he has never spoken them aloud."* She breathed a heavy sigh. *"But even should he care, what man would want one such as I?"*

What man, indeed, he mused. Just lying beside her, watching her sleep, made him ache with a need he had never indulged.

In her dream, the big wolf rolled onto his back.

He sucked in a deep breath, felt his desire stir to vigorous life, as she began to scratch the dream wolf's stomach. In three hundred years, he had never known a woman, never felt such a sharp stab of desire. . .

A low growl rumbled in his throat as he took his paw from her hand, severing the bond between them. The dream dissolved, like a shadow running from the sun.

Witch woman, he thought. *What are ye doing to me?*

With a start, he realized she was awake.

"Oh!" Channa Leigh exclaimed. Her fear quickly turned to pleasure as she saw a ray of silvery moonlight filtering through her window, saw the huge wolf stretched out beside her. "What are you doing here?"

He growled softly, then licked her hand.

She shivered with delight at the touch of his tongue, warm and rough against her palm. Sitting up, she glanced around her room, one hand clutching the wolf's fur. There was her chair. Mama had made the cover in shades of blue,

because blue had always been Channa Leigh's favorite
color. The cross above her bed was delicately carved from
dark wood. Black, she thought. The color was black, like
the wolf. The quilt on her bed was dark blue; the curtains at
the window were white with tiny red flowers. Colors. So
many colors. She had learned them early and never forgotten them.

She glanced out the window, her hand still stroking the
wolf's coat. There was so much to see. "Would you like to
go for a walk?"

As if he understood, the big wolf leaped to the floor,
stretched, then moved to her side of the bed, waiting patiently as she stood up and drew on her wrapper. Then, one hand
fisted in the long fur at his neck, she tiptoed quietly out of
the house lest she wake her parents, who would certainly
object to her taking a walk in the moonlight with the wolf.

The night was bright beneath a full lover's moon. Awed
by the beauty of it, Channa Leigh walked through the village, stopping at each cottage, each shop. As a child she
had been inside most of them, but the memory of how they
looked had been lost.

The big wolf paced slowly at her side, stopping when
she stopped, sitting patiently while she stared in wonder at
the small stained-glass window set high in the wall of the
church. Lit by the lamp that burned from within, she recit-
ed the colors.

"Red. Blue. Green. Yellow. So beautiful." She paused to
study the summer roses that grew alongside the midwife's
house, ran her fingertips over the petals. They were soft, so
soft.

"'Tis just as I always dreamed it," she mused as they
walked on, leaving the town behind, "and it's all so beautiful."

She paused atop a grassy hill and sat down on a log, her
hand stroking the wolf's fur. "Have you a name, I wonder?"
She tilted her head to one side, and her braid fell over her
shoulder. "What shall I call you, hmm?" She cradled his
big head in her hands. "Magick," she decided. "I shall call
you Magick, for truly, that is what you are."

He growled softly and licked her hand.

"Like it, do you?" she asked, and her voice was like music in his ears.

He laid his head in her lap, inviting her touch.

"Ah, Magick, isn't it a wonderful world? Look at the stars, shining so brightly. And our village, there, below. See now, there is the house of Lazlo, the baker. He has a son, you know." She sighed softly. "I've not seen his face since I was a small child, of course, but he has a lovely voice. And he has ever been kind to me."

He licked her hand in an effort to draw her thoughts away from the son of Lazlo the baker. He knew the boy. Tall and lanky, with a shock of wheat-blond hair and guileless brown eyes. It startled him to realize he was jealous of her affection for that callow youth.

"Papa says there is a pool up here. Shall we find it?"

She stood up, and he stood beside her. He knew where the pool was. When she had a firm hold on his fur, he led her farther up the hill.

"Are you sure 'tis this way?" Channa Leigh asked. She spoke to him as if was the most natural thing in the world, as if she expected a reply.

A low rumble in his throat was her answer.

And then, as they topped the rise, she saw the pool, shining like a crystal placed in a bed of green velvet. The surface of the pool shone like a mirror, reflecting the light of the moon and stars.

"Oh, Magick," she murmured, "have you ever seen anything so beautiful in all your life?"

And the big wolf, looking at the wonder in her face, the radiance in her eyes, knew he had not.

HE stood before the hearth, gazing into the flames. The fire was his to command. It had no power over him; he could walk through it unharmed, call it forth from darkness. He could command the wind, call lightning from the sky.

His powers were many and awesome to behold, yet in

Channa Leigh's presence he had felt weak, defenseless, as vulnerable as a suckling babe. They had walked until dawn came to steal the darkness, and then he had taken her back home and seen her safely tucked into bed.

Channa Leigh. Leaving her had made him ache deep inside, as if some vital part of his being had been cut away and left behind.

He raised his hands and a small ball of fire leaped from the center of the hearth into his cupped palms.

"I am Darkfest," he said, his voice echoing like thunder off the stone walls that surrounded him. "Master of fire and flame. Show me the woman, Channa Leigh by name."

The fire danced in his hands, became a shimmering sheet of flame, and there, like starlight reflected on the face of a still pool, he saw Channa Leigh's image.

She sat at a rough-hewn table in her small kitchen, singing as she peeled potatoes and dropped them into a pot of water. He watched and listened, mesmerized by the sound of her voice, the quiet beauty of her face, the soft womanly curves evident beneath her coarse clothing. He had a sudden urge to see her clad in silks and satins, with gems the color of her eyes at her throat and ropes of diamonds woven into the golden strands of her hair.

"Mama," she said, "do you think the wolf will ever come back?"

"I dinna know, child," her mother replied. "Perhaps we could send Ronin to hunt for it."

Hope brightened Channa Leigh's face; then, with a sigh, she shook her head. "No. The beast would surely die in captivity. Sure and it would be cruel to keep it caged."

"But, child, if we could capture the beast, and tame it, think what it would mean to you."

"No, Mama . . . it wouldna be right. Besides, Ronin would probably kill it, don't you know, for the wolf has a fine pelt that would surely bring a good price . . ."

"Flame, begone." He could look at her no longer, could not see the yearning in her face, hear the resignation in her voice. Nor did he understand such sweetness, such tenderness, that would make a blind girl choose to remain blind rather than keep a wild beast against his will.

Using all his considerable self-control, he banished her from his mind, determined to think of her no more.

For three hundred years he had lived alone, complacent in his solitude, content with his magic. He would not let one evening in a woman's presence shatter his hard-won tranquillity.

He would not.

CHAPTER 3

CHANNA Leigh walked at Ronin's side, her hand resting lightly on his arm. She had been surprised the first time he had come to call, but she had soon come to look forward to his company. Now, he described what he saw as they walked . . . the colors of the leaves changing on the trees, a red fox scurrying for its hole, the fluffy white clouds drifting across the sky. It was pleasant, walking along the river, the leaves crunching cheerfully beneath her feet, but she couldn't help wishing it were the wolf at her side, allowing her to see the world for herself.

Ronin patted Channa Leigh's hand. Her skin was smooth, soft. A fortnight had passed since he had first found the courage to call on her. In truth, he had not given her much thought at all until Merick, the baker's son, chanced to remark that she was passing fair. Ronin had noticed her comeliness for himself on the night of First Harvest. The beauty of her voice was something all those in the village took for granted, but that night he had seen her as a woman. For the first time, he had noticed the way the firelight played over her face. Her skin was smooth and clear, her body nicely rounded; her hair was the color of sun-ripened corn. And so he had taken his courage in hand and asked her father if he might take her walking. Since that time, they had spent every evening together. It pleased him, not only because he had truly come to care for the fragile creature at his side, but also because he had bested his childhood rival, Merick, yet again.

They had been walking for quite some time when they came to a fallen log and he suggested they sit awhile.

"Channa Leigh?"

She turned toward the sound of his voice. "Yes, Ronin?"

He cleared his throat. "In this past fortnight, I have come to care for you. . . ." He cleared his throat again, glad that she could not see the blush staining his cheeks. "What I mean is, I think I love you, Channa Leigh. Will you marry me? I swear I'll make you a good husband. You'll want for nothing."

A soft sigh escaped Channa Leigh's lips. She was not in love with Ronin. He was a kind man, a good man, and she knew he would care for her and provide for her. But she did not love him. She did not love anyone. She thought fleetingly of Merick, the baker's son, but he had never shown any interest in her, and she feared he never would.

"Please, Channa Leigh," Ronin murmured.

"Ronin . . ."

He lifted her hand and she felt the brush of his lips on her fingertips. "Say yes, Channa Leigh."

Why not say yes? It seemed no one else wanted her. She was far past the age when most girls were married. But would it be fair to marry Ronin when she did not love him?

"Channa Leigh, what say you?"

Honesty compelled her to say, "Ronin, you know I am fond of you, but I dinna love you."

"But you may come to love me, in time."

"Perhaps."

"You'll marry me, then?"

She sighed, a soft sigh tinged with resignation. "Aye, Ronin, I will marry you. In the spring." She lifted a hand to his face, let her fingertips trace his features. She had seen him only once since childhood, and that very briefly the night the wolf appeared in the village square. Ronin was a handsome young man, with light brown hair and brown eyes and, yes, a cleft in his chin, she recalled, running her finger over the gentle dip in his skin.

"Channa Leigh." He took her hand and gave it a gentle squeeze. "Might I . . ." He swallowed hard. "Might I kiss you?"

She nodded, her heart pounding with trepidation. She had seen two and twenty summers and never had she been kissed by a man.

His lips were warm on hers, his touch as light as dandelion fluff. It was pleasant, she thought, quite pleasant.

"Come," Ronin said, suddenly exuberant. "Let us go back and tell yer kinfolk."

DUGALD and Mara were pleased by the news of their daughter's betrothal. They had long hoped for just this match for their daughter, for Ronin was a kind man, one who would be patient with her affliction. As he was a strong hunter, she would never lack for meat at her table.

"Aye, you'll make a beautiful bride," Mara remarked, beaming.

Dugald brought out a flask and they toasted the young couple. Ronin stayed to take supper with them, and they made plans for the wedding. Mara would begin weaving the material for Channa Leigh's dress on the morrow; Ronin would begin looking for a suitable place to build their house; Dugald would gather the best of his flock for her dowry.

Later that night, still caught up in the excitement of the evening's events and unable to sleep, Channa Leigh gazed sightlessly into the darkness and wondered where the wolf had gone and if he would ever come to her again.

CHAPTER 4

HE heard of Channa Leigh's betrothal, as he heard of everything that happened in the village. He had shunned her presence and now she was betrothed to another. Stricken by the news, he shut himself away in his castle. He felt the changing seasons in the chill within the castle's cold stone walls, saw it in the changing color of his eyes as fall's brown turned to winter gray. He had ever hated winter. Below, the villagers gathered their children close. Huddled around their cozy hearth fires, fathers told and retold the ancient stories and legends of their people, while mothers sang songs and lullabies.

Sometimes, when it seemed the long winter nights would never pass, when the loneliness grew more than he could bear, he took on the wolf form and ran with the pack that dwelled high in the mountains behind the castle. They accepted him as one of them, and he found solace in their company.

Often, he felt compelled to go to Channa Leigh, but it was too painful to be close to her. Had he been less selfish, he would have sought her out so that she might again see the world through his eyes, but being near her only emphasized his loneliness, his separateness from those in the village.

Now, he stood before the hearth, the light from the fire playing hide-and-seek with the shadows that lurked in the corners. He held his hands out to the flames, felt the warmth seep into him, but all the fire in the world could not ease his loneliness or chase the darkness from his heart and soul.

He was like the shadows, he thought, torn between light and dark, between good and evil. There had been times, though rare, when he had refused to grant a boon to one of the villagers simply because it pleased him to refuse, because it gave him a perverse sense of power to know that he held the fate of the supplicant in his hands. There were times, when he stood within the cold stone walls of the dungeon where he practiced his magic, that he felt the darkness rise up within him. At those times, he felt the promise, the insidious lure, of the Dark Arts.

Other times, when he had granted a boon to one who sought his help, he was filled with an inner light, with the satisfaction that came from helping one in need.

But he had no thought for goodness or kindness this night. The Darkness rose up within him, thick and black and smothering. Turning away from the fire, he left the dungeon to stalk the dusky corridors of the castle, his long black cloak floating behind him like the smoky gray mists that sometimes covered the land near the sea.

He caught a glimpse of himself in one of the windows, a tall, dark silhouette moving swiftly, silently. A solitary creature who belonged to no one, belonged nowhere but here, in a castle that was as cold and empty as his heart.

He paused in midstride, nostrils flaring. Someone was coming.

Descending the long spiral staircase, he crossed the great hall and flung open the door.

Dugald of Brynn reeled back, his eyes growing wide. One hand, lifted to pull the bell, remained frozen in midair.

Darkfest glared at the man. "What brings ye here at this hour, Dugald?"

"'Tis my wife," the man said. Lowering his arm, he took a deep breath, shoved his hands into the pockets of his trousers to still their trembling. "She's sick with a fever. Three days now."

Darkfest grunted softly. "So, what is that to me?"

"Our healer has been unable to help. I thought . . ." Dugald took a deep breath. "I thought perhaps you might come and have a look at her."

"Did ye?"

"Please, my lord. I'll give you anything you ask."

"Indeed? And what if the price is dear?"

"Only name it, and if it's in my power to give, it will be yours."

Channa Leigh's image rose in his mind. At last, a way to claim that which he desired. He shook off an unwelcome sense of guilt. Surely he deserved a special gift for the healing Dugald required.

"In time," Darkfest replied softly. "In time."

HE caught her scent even before he entered the cottage, felt a warmth spread through him that had nothing to do with the heat of the fire radiating from the hearth in the corner and everything to do with her presence. She was sitting at her mother's bedside, singing softly.

"For the land that's most fair, 'tis where I shall fly,
For my true love lies there, in a glen wild and high,
And if I but wait, and yield not to despair,
I know, by and by, my love will find me
Waiting there,
Waiting there . . ."

The pure, clear notes trailed off as they entered the room.

She turned toward the door, head cocked to one side. "Papa?"

"Yes, child."

Darkfest stood silent behind Dugald. Channa Leigh had not asked if he had come in answer to her father's summons, but there was no need. She sensed his presence in the room. He knew it without doubt.

Channa Leigh clutched her mother's hand. "Her fever is worse."

Dugald laid a callused hand on his wife's brow. Her breathing was labored, shallow. Dark circles of pain shadowed her eyes.

"Can you heal her?" Channa Leigh asked, tears evident in her voice. "Can you?"

"If I cannot," Darkfest replied arrogantly, "then no one can."

Dugald cleared his throat, afraid to ask the question that must be asked. "And what payment will you require?"

Darkfest did not look at her, only spoke her name. "Your daughter, Channa Leigh."

Dugald blinked at him. "What?"

"I will require yer daughter."

Dugald stared at him in blatant disbelief. "My daughter!" A look of horror washed over the man's face. "But . . . but . . . she is not chattel, to be bartered back and forth like a lamb."

" 'Tis my price."

"But she is betrothed to another."

Almost, he relented. But then he recalled the loneliness of the keep, the warmth of Channa Leigh's smile. It strengthened his resolve. "I will have the girl for one year. When winter comes again, she may return home and take her vows."

Dugald shook his head. Not even to save his wife could he allow his daughter to go off with the dark wizard of the mountain.

"It canna be done," Dugald said. And then he glanced at his wife, lying so still and pale upon the bed they had shared for over thirty years. How could he abandon her now? Without the wizard's help, she would surely die.

Swallowing hard, he looked back at the man standing tall and still, waiting for his decision. "Please, my lord, have mercy on us. My wife will nae forgive me if I trade our only child for her life."

Darkfest shrugged. " 'Tis yer decision."

"I have a fine ram, and a wee bit of gold."

"I have no need of a ram," Darkfest replied brusquely. "And no need for gold."

"Please," Dugald begged, wringing his callused hands. "Be merciful."

Channa Leigh squared her shoulders. She knew what had to be done. Taking a deep breath, she said, "Papa, dinna fret. I'm not afraid. I will go with him and gladly, if it will help Mama."

"Nay, child. Yer mother would not hear of it."

"I have yer word, Channa Leigh?" Darkfest asked. "Ye will come with me, of yer own free will, and stay with me for one year?"

"Aye."

Dugald looked at his daughter as if seeing her for the first time. "Nay, Channa Leigh," he said sternly. "I forbid it."

" 'Tis done, Papa."

"Leave me," Darkfest said. "Both of ye."

Channa Leigh shook her head. "Nay, I wish to stay."

"Come, Daughter," her father said.

He reached for her hand, but she shook him off. "Nay, I will not leave Mama."

Dugald looked at the wizard. " 'Tis sorry I am," he said apologetically. "She can be most stubborn at times."

Darkfest nodded. "Let her stay."

Dugald pressed a kiss to his wife's brow, glanced fleetingly at the wizard, who loomed like a tall dark cloud at the foot of the bed, then left the room, quietly closing the rough-hewn wooden door behind him.

Darkfest moved to the side of the bed and took the woman's hand in his. Her skin was hot and dry, her breathing labored. Why did they always wait until the soul was on the brink of flight to call him? Were they so afraid of him, so afraid of his power, his wrath? Well, they were right to fear him.

He closed his eyes and summoned his power, felt it crawl over his skin as it gathered and coalesced, felt it swell and grow until it thundered within him, until he was aware of nothing else, only the power thrumming through every fiber of his being.

He placed both hands on the woman's head, and then,

channeling his strength into his hands, he began to chant softly.

"I am Darkfest, master of fire and flame. Spirit of evil, depart in my name."

He felt the fever leave the woman, felt it burn through his hands, felt the weakness that had engulfed her as the sickness left her body and entered his, to be devoured by his strength.

He took a deep breath, exhaling it in a long, slow sigh as he removed his hands from the woman. "'Tis done."

Channa Leigh stared at him through sightless eyes. "She's healed?" A wealth of hope lay in those two words.

"Aye. She will sleep through the night and when she wakes on the morrow, she will be well."

Tears sparkled in Channa Leigh's eyes. "Thank you, my lord," she whispered tremulously.

"I have done my part." He clenched his hands at his sides, wondering if she would keep her word. Wondering what he would do if she did not. Did she but realize the power she held over him, she could have easily refused without fear of retribution. But she did not know. "Will ye now do yours?" he asked, and waited, hardly daring to breathe, for her answer.

"Aye, my lord," she said tremulously. "I will come to you whenever you say."

"Tomorrow morn."

She crossed her arms over her breasts, a shiver of unease shaking her slight shoulders. "As you will."

"Exactly as I will," he said curtly, and left the room in search of her father.

Dugald was standing near the hearth, head hanging, eyes closed. He looked up, a glimmer of hope in his deep-set eyes, as the wizard entered the room.

"'Tis done," Darkfest said.

"You give me my wife, and take my daughter," Dugald said bitterly. He took a deep breath, and only his love for his offspring gave him courage to speak. "What will you do with her, with my Channa Leigh?"

"Whatever pleases me, old man."

Dugald's eyes widened in horror as he imagined his only child at the mercy of the wizard's every whim. "She is but a child, innocent in the ways of men."

"She is no longer your concern."

"You will not . . . harm her?"

"I shall expect her on the morrow." Darkfest rose to his full height. "Do not think to betray our bargain, Dugald," he warned, his voice like frost on a winter's morn, "lest a worse fate befall your woman."

"She will be there," Dugald vowed, his voice hoarse. "On the morrow."

Darkfest nodded once, and then he was gone.

CHANNA Leigh sat at her mother's bedside all through the night, her thoughts in turmoil as she tried to control the fear that engulfed her. All her life, she had heard tales of the master of Darkfest Castle. He was feared by all, for his powers were great. Some said he was the spawn of the Dark One. Some said he *was* the Dark One.

Why did he want her?

What would he do to her, with her?

Would she be enslaved in his castle, forced to serve the Dark One?

Growing up, she had heard many tales of the wizard, each more frightening than the last. Shuddering, she wrapped her arms tightly around her waist. It was said he drank the blood of children, that he sacrificed virgins to his Master. Was she, then, to be the next sacrifice? Her mouth went dry at the thought. But no. He had promised to return her to her home the following winter. And yet of what value was the word of a man who served the Dark One?

Slipping from her chair, she knelt at her mother's bedside and prayed for the courage to fulfill her promise, for the strength to withstand whatever evil awaited her at the wizard's hands.

HE did not sleep that night but spent the dark empty hours till dawn pacing from one end of his dreary castle to the other. Soon. Soon, she would be here. What madness had made him demand Channa Leigh in payment? What was he to do with a blind girl? How could he endure her nearness day after day? Hear her voice, see her face, and know she was there only because of a vow made in exchange for her mother's life?

A harsh laugh tinged with bitterness rose in his throat. In three hundred years he had never lain with a woman, nor felt a woman's hand upon his flesh. He could have demanded any woman in the village, but he had recoiled from the idea of bedding a woman who had no affection for him, nor did he wish to embrace a woman who did not want him in return. Better to remain alone than take a woman by force and see the revulsion in her eyes. No, he had never wanted a woman who had no true affection for him.

Until now. Until Channa Leigh. What foolishness, what arrogance, had made him think he could be near her day after day without touching her? He doubted even his monumental self-control, forged through centuries of self-denial, would be enough to protect her from his lust.

A knock at the door. Though faint, it echoed like thunder in his mind.

She was here.

CHAPTER 5

CHANNA Leigh couldn't stop shaking. At home, at her mother's bedside, she would have said anything, promised anything, to see her mother well again. But now, standing here on Darkfest's doorstep, it was time to make good upon her promise.

"What is he like, Papa, this wizard?"

"I dinna know, Channa Leigh. No one really knows."

"What does he look like? Is his face cruel?"

Dugald frowned. "He is a tall man, with long black hair. His eyes are as changeable as the seasons. As for his face . . . 'tis a hard face, to be sure. I dinna know if you would call it cruel, but . . . 'tis hard. He is never seen without a cloak. A long black cloak that billows behind him like the hounds of hell."

"Papa, do you think—?" She bit off the words as the door opened with a faint creak.

The wizard stood in the doorway, towering over them.

He wore a loose-fitting white shirt, black breeches, and supple black leather boots. A long black cloak fell from his shoulders to ward off the chill of early morning. His eyes burned with an intensity that Dugald found unsettling. Fear for himself and his daughter turned his blood to ice.

Dugald took an involuntary step backward. "I have brought my daughter, as promised." He studied the wizard's face. Was it cruel? The eyes seemed dark and cold; the mouth was set in a firm line; the jaw was firm and square and well defined, the cheekbones high and proud, the nose straight and sharp as the blade of an ax. "We . . ." He swallowed hard, unsettled by the wizard's unwavering stare. "We will expect her back in one year."

"Aye, old man, that was the bargain."

"You do not ask about my woman."

One dark brow rose slightly. "She is well, is she not?"

"Aye," Dugald replied. Mara was well enough, though she had been inconsolable upon hearing that her dear Channa Leigh had to leave them for a time. *You should have let me die,* Mara had raged at him. *Better that I should be dead than our daughter be at his mercy.*

Channa Leigh drew in a sharp breath as a large unfamiliar hand closed over her arm.

"Come," said the wizard.

"Fare thee well, Channa Leigh," Dugald said. He handed the wizard the small cloth bag that held his daughter's few belongings. "I will come for you when the year is up."

"Fare thee well, Papa," she replied tremulously. "Will you not hug me good-bye?"

She felt the wizard's hand fall away from her arm as her father stepped forward to embrace her.

"Be a good lass," her father admonished softly, and she heard the unshed tears in his voice. "Remember yer prayers, at daybreak and eventide."

"I will, Papa."

He hugged her, hard and quick, and then he was gone, and she was alone with a stranger. Once again she felt the wizard's hand upon her arm as he guided her into the castle.

She had never heard anything so frightening, or so final, as the sound of the heavy door closing behind her.

He released her, and she stood there, lost and alone in the darkness. She knew he was still there. She could feel his presence looming over her. Hands clasped, she waited, wondering what was expected of her.

Darkfest dropped the girl's belongings on the floor beside the door. "Can ye cook?" he asked.

"Aye."

"That will be one of your chores on the morrow. Today, I will prepare our meals."

"Have you no servants?" she asked, thinking it strange that such a powerful wizard had no one to look after him.

"No."

A sliver of fear ran down her spine. She had not realized she would be alone in the keep with him. "I can prepare a meal," she said. "I enjoy cooking." It was something she did well, something that she had struggled hard to learn. Something that gave her a sense of accomplishment and self-worth.

"Come along then," he said. He walked slowly toward the kitchen, and she followed the sound of his footsteps, her feet learning the shape and feel of the cold stones.

In the kitchen, he took her hand, wondering if his touch would enable her to see, but she continued to stare ahead, looking at nothing. Odd that in his wolf form, his touch granted her sight. What was it, he mused, that made the difference?

Holding her by the hand, he guided her to the pantry and to the hearth, showed her where the cook pots were, the shelves that held the pewter plates and cups and bowls, the drawer that held the utensils and the linen. He guided her hand to the pump.

"Where do you keep the wood and the flint, my lord?" she asked.

He blinked at her. He was master of fire and flame; he had no need of flint.

"Ye will have no need of them," he replied. "The fire burns day and night."

She gazed in his direction, unseeing, unblinking.

"Is there anything ye need?" he asked.

She shook her head. She had been blessed with a quick mind, a good memory. It would take her but a little while to learn her way around the kitchen; until she did, she would rather stumble around on her own than ask for his help.

"Call me when the meal is ready."

"Aye, my lord."

With a grunt, he left the kitchen; then, on silent feet, he returned to stand in the doorway, watching her. She moved slowly about the kitchen, one hand out in front of her. He was tempted to go to her aid as she ran her hands over the pans, looking for a particular size, but he stayed where he was, curious to see if she would call for help.

She had the patience of a saint, he mused, as he watched her. By smell and by touch, she found the ingredients she desired. His amazement grew as he watched her prepare a pot of porridge, boil half a dozen eggs, and brew a pot of tea.

He backed away from the door as she walked toward him.

"My lord Darkfest," she called. " 'Tis ready."

He waited a moment, then moved toward the kitchen, making certain she could hear his footsteps.

He approached the table and sat down. He waited for her to join him, and when she did not, he cleared his throat and said, "Come, eat with me."

"I'd rather not."

"I would rather ye did."

She hesitated a moment, then made her way to the table and sat down in the chair across from him. "Shall I serve you, my lord?"

"I can do it," he said gruffly.

He watched her while he ate, studying her face, the rich golden color of her hair, the delicate shape of her brows. She ate very little. Her hands trembled slightly. Did she fear him so much then? Ha! He knew the stories they told of him down in the village, that he drank blood and devoured children, that he sacrificed virgins to the Dark One. That he was the misbegotten son of the Dark One.

He would have renounced it all as nonsense save for the fact that he did not know who his father was. Perhaps he *was* the son of the Dark One. Perhaps that was why he had lived so long, why he did not grow old; perhaps it explained his supernatural powers.

Darkfest stood up when the meal was over. "Would ye like me to show ye the rest of the castle now?"

She stood up. "Aye, I would."

Taking her by the hand, he led her through each of the rooms on the castle's main floor.

"This is the great hall." He led her around the room, describing the huge stone fireplace that took up the entire west wall, letting her touch the long trestle tables where no one had eaten as long as he could remember. He led her to the raised dais situated near the east wall. Two chairs were located on the dais; a thick carpet was spread before the heavy oak chairs. She ran her hands over the heavy draperies that covered the windows.

There were tapestries on the walls, three of which were embroidered with scenes he was glad Channa Leigh could not see. They had troubled him all his life. The first depicted a large black wolf being pursued by hunters. A spear protruded from the wolf's back; blood stained his fur, trailed behind him in the snow.

The second tapestry showed a tall man clad in a flowing black cloak. Behind him, the dark sky was growing light as the sun rose over a craggy cliff. Surrounding the man were a dozen hunters armed with spears. Apart from the hunters stood a priest, a large silver cross raised over his head. Teeth bared, the man in the cloak faced his pursuers. It was the eyes that troubled Darkfest. Red eyes alight with defiance. The wolf's eyes.

The third tapestry portrayed either a victory or a defeat, depending on one's point of view. A black wolf lay dead in the snow, surrounded by the hunters and the priest. A hooded man stood at the wolf's side, an ax poised to sever the wolf's head from his body.

Darkfest guided her into the library, felt his face grow hot as he realized she would have no need of this room.

He took her to the solarium, watched her smile as she took a deep breath, her nostrils filling with the scents of the hardy mountain flowers that bloomed and thrived even in the midst of winter.

He bypassed his bedchamber and led her into the room that connected to his. It was a large square room. Once, it had belonged to his mother.

Step by step, he guided Channa Leigh to the huge canopy bed, the table that held ewer and basin. There were two large chests in the room, one for her clothing, he explained, and one for extra bedding.

A smaller room opened off this room. It had been his mother's sewing room.

He escorted Channa Leigh down the narrow corridor to the garderobe, saw the color bloom in her cheeks as he told her what it was.

When the tour was complete, he took her back to her own room. "I will get yer belongings," he said, and left her there.

Channa Leigh made her way to the bed and sat down. 'Twas a huge place. She would not have been surprised to learn that the whole of her village could fit inside the main hall. She ran her hands over the mattress. The bed itself was bigger than her room at home.

Home. A single tear slipped down her cheek. A year away from her mother and father, from Ronin, seemed a terribly long time, and yet it was a small price to pay for her mother's life.

She shook off her melancholy and thought about the wizard instead. What did he want of her?

Frightened and restless, she stood up and began to pace the room, her feet moving slowly over the floor as she memorized the dimensions of her chamber, her hands exploring every object within the room, running over the window ledge, touching the glass.

She whirled around at the sound of the door opening.

"'Tis I," Darkfest said. "I have brought yer things."

She heard his footsteps as he crossed the floor.

"I have put yer bag on the foot of the bed."

"Thank you, my lord." She clasped her hands to still their trembling, took a deep breath. "I would like to know, my lord, what it is you expect of me."

"I should like ye to prepare my meals and wash my clothes, and clean the castle, as best ye can."

"Aye, my lord. Is that all?"

"It is."

"I do not mean to be impudent, my lord, but surely you could have hired a girl from the village to serve you. One who could see."

"Aye, Channa Leigh."

"Then why . . ."

"Why did I want ye?"

She nodded, certain she had angered him.

"I want ye to sing for me in the evening, Channa Leigh. For me, and for no one else. Is there anything else ye wish to know?"

"Nay, my lord. I shall do whatever you wish."

"Then we shall get on well together, the two of us."

She heard his footsteps move toward the door.

"I shall see ye this evening. The larder is well stocked with meat. Prepare whatever ye wish for supper."

"Aye, my lord."

She breathed a sigh of relief when she heard the door close. She would cook for him and sing for him, and at the end of a year she would go home.

DARKFEST cursed softly as he left the girl's room. He should not have brought her here. What folly had possessed him to do so, to think he could look at her every day and not want her, to think he could remember the touch of her hand upon his wolf self and not take her to his bed? Even now, he burned for her, for the touch of her hand, the sound of her voice rising in ecstasy, sobbing his name.

With a harsh laugh, he plunged down the stairs to the dungeon room where he practiced his sorcery. What did he know of women? Of ecstasy? No doubt she knew more of the carnal nature of what went on between a man and a woman than he did. His only experience in coupling had been in his wolf form with a she-wolf late one moonlit night. It had left him feeling satisfied and confused and frightened.

A wave of his hand, and a dozen candles sprang to life, illuminating the room where he kept the ingredients he used in his magic. Powdered horn of a unicorn. Saint-John's-wort. Crushed rosemary and thyme, vervain and yarrow and lavender, garlic and sage and rue, mugwort and cinquefoil and hyssop. He kept a large supply of tree bark and leaves: birch for cleansing and to expel evil; hazel for wisdom and the divining of water; yew, the tree of death; rowan for life and healing; ash for power and absorbing illness; pine for rejuvenation; willow for enchantment; hawthorn for male potency; holly for beauty; the apple for fertility; mistletoe for love and peace. And the alder, said to be the tree of fire, the wood of witches and wizards. He carried a whistle made of alder in his pocket for use in summoning and controlling the four winds.

He needed but little help in conjuring or making spells. The power was within him, within his hands, within his heart and mind. His, for good or for evil.

But it was not power or magic that concerned him this night. It was a fair lass by name of Channa Leigh. What was he to do with her, now that she was here?

DINNER was a silent affair. He could think of nothing to say to her, the beautiful young woman who sat across from him, her head bowed, the shimmering curtain of her hair concealing her face from his prying eyes.

The meal she had prepared was fit for a liege lord: the roasted venison succulent and swimming in a rich sauce, the vegetables sweet, the bread still warm from the oven. And yet he would have traded it all for a plate of cold ashes to see her smile.

When the meal was over, he thanked her, curtly, and left the room.

He took refuge in the high-ceilinged library that was his favorite room in the castle. It was a large chamber, with a cozy hearth and leaded windows. A bearskin rug was spread before the fireplace; curtains of so deep a blue as to be almost black hung at the windows. An enormous overstuffed chair, large enough to seat two comfortably, was angled toward the fire. A heavy oak table stood beside it. Two walls were lined with shelves that were crammed with ancient books and scrolls that held the wisdom of the known world. He had read them all many times over.

He whirled around, his gaze going to the door, which he had left open. He heard her footsteps in the corridor, hesitant, barely audible, and yet they echoed in his mind like thunder.

"My lord?" She stood in the doorway, her head cocked to one side. "Are you here?"

"Aye, lass. What is it ye want?"

"You said you wished me to sing for you."

He grunted softly. "Come in," he invited, and then, remembering that she could not see, he went to her. Taking her by the hand, he led her into the room, bid her sit down in his chair.

"I would rather stand," she said, "if you dinna mind."

"As ye wish."

"What will you have me sing, my lord?"

"Whatever pleases ye."

She hesitated a moment, and then she began to sing the lullaby he had heard her sing on the night of First Harvest. Hands clasped to her breasts, head high, eyes closed, her voice filled the room, soft and sweet and filled with yearning, and he knew in that moment that she dreamed of marriage, that she hungered for a babe of her own.

> *"My sweet bonnie lass,*
> *A boon from heaven above,*
> *I cradle you to my heart*
> *And pray you know my love.*

> *"Sweet bonnie lass,*
> *My sweet bonnie lass,*

Heaven sent you to me.
Heaven sent you to me.

"My sweet bonnie lass
So young and fair of face,
May you ever walk in sunshine
And be blessed with God's good grace."

She sang to him for an hour, and he felt her words twine around his heart, as delicate as a silken web, as binding as silver chains.

How beautiful she was, this woman known as Channa Leigh. There was magic in her voice, a mystical power equal to his own as she sang of a maiden's dreams and a mother's love and a warrior's heart.

"Enough," he said, his voice hoarse, his mind reeling from the images her songs had planted within his mind.

"As you wish, my lord," she said, and with a curtsey she left the room, leaving him awash in darkness though the room glowed with the warm rosy light of the fire.

And he knew, as he listened to her footsteps fade away, that he was totally, irrevocably, lost.

CHAPTER 6

IN her room, as she undressed for bed, she resolved to be brave and strong. A year was not so very long, after all, and when it was over, she would go home and marry Ronin.

She found her bag at the foot of the bed and dug through its meager contents for her nightgown. Slipping it over her head, she crawled under the covers. The mattress was soft, the sheets wondrously clean. And warm. They were not made of the coarse cotton she was used to, but some soft material that seemed to enfold her. Her pillow, too, was softer than what she was used to. Filled with down, she thought.

Lying on her side, one hand beneath her cheek, she stared sightlessly into the darkness, a single tear slipping down her cheek.

"Mama's life is worth it," she whispered. But it didn't stop the tears.

DARKFEST stood before the hearth in the great hall, listening to the sound of her tears. She was lonely and homesick and afraid. Why had he brought her here?

Why, indeed?

Without conscious thought, her image danced across his mind—her body supple, her hair like sunlight, her skin the color of the wild peaches that grew to the north. Oh, yes, he knew why he had brought her here, knew it with every breath, knew it in the deepest region of his heart and soul.

But he could not admit it. Neither could he stay away from her side.

He changed to wolf form as he made his way down the corridor. A thought opened the door and he padded into her room. For a time, he stood beside the bed, watching her, and then he licked her arm.

She woke with a start, her sightless eyes wide, her mouth open in a silent cry.

A low rumble rose from his throat as he leaned forward and licked her arm again.

"Magick? Is that you?"

He growled softly in reply.

"But . . . how did you get in here?"

With eager hands she reached for him, her fingers gently grasping his fur. And he felt the darkness leave her eyes, saw her smile as the shadowy room became visible. She gasped as the candle at her bedside sprang to life.

"Oh, my," she murmured, glancing around. " 'Tis even bigger than I thought."

She swung her legs over the side of the bed and sat up, one hand still clinging to his fur. "Look how high the ceilings are. Oh! Magick, look."

He heard the wonder in her voice as she stared at the painting on the ceiling. It had been done hundreds of years ago. He had stopped seeing it long ago; now, as he looked at it through her eyes, it was like seeing it for the first time. Fluffy white clouds were scattered against a pale blue sky. Turtledoves nested within the branches of a tree. A fawn slept in a thicket. A handful of sheep grazed in green pastures. It was a lovely mural, meant to lull one into peaceful slumber.

She ruffled his fur, and then she frowned. Leaning forward, she cradled his head in her hands. "Your eyes," she murmured. "They were blue before, and now they are gray. How is that possible?"

The wolf's tail thumped on the floor.

" 'Tis very strange," she said, and then laughed softly. "But no more strange than the way my sight returns when you are here."

Slipping out of bed, she crossed the room, opened the door, and peered up and down the corridor. "Where do you suppose *he* is?" she asked. "Do you think he's asleep?"

The wolf gave a low bark.

"Come," she said, and with a firm grip on his fur she left her chamber. The wolf padded quietly beside her.

She paused when she reached the bedchamber where Darkfest slept. Pressing her ear to the door, she listened for a moment, then looked down at the wolf. "I dinna hear anything." She giggled behind her hand. "I thought he would snore loudly, like Papa."

The wolf looked up at her, tail wagging.

They explored the main floor of the castle. She thought it odd that candles burned in every room even after the lord of the castle had retired for the night. He must be rich indeed, she thought, to incur such waste.

She ran her hands over the rich green velvet that covered the thronelike chairs in the great hall. An enormous carpet, woven in muted shades of green and blue, was spread before the chairs; another was spread before the hearth. She ran her fingertips over the exquisite tapestries that covered the cold stone walls, paused in front of a painting that hung from a gold cord. "They are a handsome couple, are they not?" she mused, and smiled when the wolf thumped his tail on the floor.

She touched everything she saw. Several long tables and benches lined two walls. All were covered with a fine layer of dust. She trailed her finger over one of the tables, leaving a clean streak behind.

" 'Tis a great deal of work to be done," she remarked.

She paused at the great stone hearth and stared up at the sword that hung above the mantel. It was a large, heavy weapon. The hilt was set with sapphires and emeralds that winked a bright blue and green in the candlelight.

"Is that *his* sword, do you think?" she mused. "Looks very sharp."

Leaving the hall, they went into the solarium. There were a myriad of flowers and other plants growing there and she touched them all, stopping to smell the flowers, marveling at the silky feel of one of the blossoms, amazed that there were flowers at all when winter winds blew.

"Do you think he knows the names of all these flowers?" she wondered aloud. She stooped to smell a delicate bloom.

The next room was filled with books, more books than she had ever dreamed existed in all the world. Shelves of books, of scrolls covered with strange lines and symbols. Surely it would take several lifetimes to read so many books.

She picked one up and turned the pages. The words meant nothing, but there were pictures on some of the pages—pictures of animals and plants and people. A storybook, perhaps.

They left the library and went into the kitchen and she studied the pots and pans, the knives, the placement of the dishes and cups in the cupboard, so she could better remember them tomorrow. She lifted the lid on the bread box, cut a thick slice from a loaf of crusty brown bread, and covered it with butter and honey.

"Hmm," she said. She looked down at the wolf as she licked a drop of honey from her lips. "Would you care for a taste?"

The wolf wagged his tail, so she broke off a corner of the bread and offered it to him. He took it gently from her hand, then licked the crumbs from her fingertips. The rough velvet of his tongue sent a shiver down her spine.

It was near dawn by the time she returned to her own chamber. Yawning, she climbed up on the big bed, then patted the mattress beside her.

With a low *woof,* the wolf leaped up beside her. "Oh, Magick, I wish you could stay with me always," she said wistfully. She slid under the covers, and the wolf stretched out beside her. "Are you really here?" she asked, her voice low and dreamy and sleep-edged. "Or am I just dreaming?"

Perhaps I am the one dreaming, the wolf thought as her

breasts pressed against his back. Her arms wrapped around him and she rested her chin on the top of his head. *If so, I hope I never awake.*

He lay there, her warm body pressed against his own, feeling her fingers stroke his head. Eyes closed with pleasure, he remained at her side until sleep claimed her. And then, unable to resist, he took on his own shape, his body humming with desire as he felt her soft curves pressed against his back.

He stayed there, unmoving, until the torment grew unbearable. And then, muttering an oath, he left her bed without a backward glance.

HE woke to the tantalizing aroma of sausage and fresh-baked biscuits. A word brought the fireplace to life, the flames quickly chasing the chill from the air.

He slid from his bed, naked, to stand before the hearth, all thought coming to a halt as the heavenly sound of Channa Leigh's voice filled the air. She sang a cheerful morning song, praising the God of heaven for the beauty of the new day, for home and family and friends.

Darkfest stood there, mesmerized by the pure, sweet notes, by the knowledge that, for the first time in hundreds of years, he was not alone in the house. A year, he thought. She would be here for only one year. And already one day was gone.

He closed his eyes, letting the music caress him, feeling it move over him and through him. He was startled to find himself smiling.

When the song ended, he pulled on a pair of woolen trousers, a heavy shirt, thick stockings, his boots. And then, wondering if she would tell him of her adventure with the wolf, he went downstairs.

CHANNA Leigh sensed his presence even before she heard his footsteps. Though she had never seen him, she knew he was a big man, tall and broad. His voice was rich and resonant; sometimes it seemed to reach deep down inside her.

His nearness, the way she trembled whenever he was close by, frightened her.

She heard the scrape of wood as he pulled a chair out from the kitchen table. Surely he didn't mean to eat in here, with her?

"My lord," she stammered, "if you will wait in the dining hall, I shall serve your meal."

He grunted softly. "'Tis cold and drafty in that great dungeon of a room. I shall eat in here."

"Yes, my lord. Very well, my lord."

She filled a plate and placed it before him, along with a mug of black tea, then went to stand by the stove while he ate.

"Here now," he said gruffly. "Why are ye not eating?"

"I . . . I'll eat later."

"Cease this foolishness. Come, sit with me."

"My lord?"

"I wish yer company."

"But . . ."

"Do not argue with me, lass."

Biting down on her lower lip, she filled a plate for herself, walked carefully to the table, and sat down. She felt terribly self-conscious, sitting there, eating in front of him. It was one thing to eat with her parents. There were times, however few and far between, when she spilled a cup of milk or dropped food on the floor. At home, such incidents were of little consequence, but here . . .

Trying to be extra careful only made her clumsy and uncertain. To her horror, she misjudged the placement of her cup and knocked it over. Her cheeks burned with humiliation as she heard it hit the floor.

"I'm sorry, my lord," she said hastily. "I am not usually so clumsy."

She had started to stand up when she felt his hand on her arm, staying her.

"'Tis nothing to fret over, Channa Leigh; 'tis only a bit of a spill." Rising, he took a clean mug from the shelf and poured her another cup of tea. Then, very gently, he placed the cup in her hand.

"Thank you, my lord," she said.

He shrugged; then, realizing she could not see him, he sat down, muttering, "Yer welcome."

It was the longest meal of her life. Once, he complimented her on her cooking. She murmured her thanks, pleased and embarrassed by his praise. She would have to take his word for the quality of the meal; she might have been eating dirt for all the notice she took of the food, so disconcerted was she by his nearness.

"Did ye sleep well?" he asked.

Channa Leigh nodded. "'Tis a very fine chamber, my lord. The painting on the ceiling is—" As soon as she realized what she'd said, she clapped her hand over her mouth. She was blind. How could she explain that she had seen the ceiling?

"Go on," he said quietly. "Tell me about the ceiling."

"I . . ."

"Yes?"

Her fingers worried a fold in her skirt. What should she say? If she told him about the wolf, would be believe her? She could scarcely believe it herself.

"I know about the wolf," he said, his voice carefully neutral.

"Do you? But how?"

"I am Darkfest," he said, a touch of arrogance in his tone. "I know all."

"'Tis most amazing, my lord," Channa Leigh said, her excitement momentarily chasing away her awe at being in his presence. "When I touch him, I can see. Oh, my lord, 'tis a miracle."

"Aye," he agreed. "A miracle." And knew in that moment that he would not rest until he had found a way to cure Channa Leigh's blindness.

LATER, alone in his workshop, he pored through his books, looking for a spell that would restore Channa Leigh's sight. Her lack of vision was not a sickness that he could absorb into himself or heal with a bit of magic, but the result of an accident sustained in childhood.

He spent hours searching through every book, every manuscript, every scroll, and then, at last, he found it:

> *From dark to light,*
> *The trail is trod,*
> *With faith, hope, and courage*
> *And a dark dragon's blood.*

He stood up, stretching. A dark dragon's blood. There were no dragons in the mountains of Krendall and few in the lands beyond. Their numbers grew less with each passing century, for they were solitary beasts who had been hunted to near extinction. But he knew of one. Far to the north, in an enchanted valley, lived an ancient dragon known as Blackencrill. He was rumored to be a fearsome beast, friend to none and enemy to all. A powerful beast, it was said he was subject to no magic but his own. All who dared enter his valley did so at their own peril.

Going to the room's single window, Darkfest stared at the gardens beyond. Tonight, at dinner, he would tell Channa Leigh of his discovery. The decision, of course, must be hers.

"MAGIC? You think you can restore my sight through magic?" Hope exploded through Channa Leigh's heart. To see again. It was a dream come true, an answered prayer. "How soon can we leave?"

He glanced out the window. There were only a few weeks of winter left. "Soon. There are preparations I must make."

"Thank you, my lord."

She held out her hand. It took him a moment to realize she wanted to touch him. He drew a deep breath, then took her hand in his. *Opposites,* he thought. *Large and small. Dark and light.* Her skin was warm, her palms lightly callused from years of hard work.

His gaze moved over her face.

She was so lovely, so innocent. It grieved him to think of her locked in darkness, unable to see the people she loved, the beauty of a summer's day, the glory of autumn's changing leaves, the flowers that bloomed in rainbow colors on the hillsides in the spring, winter's first snowfall.

Before he quite knew what he was doing, he changed into the wolf and laid his head in her lap.

"Magick!" she exclaimed softly. "You're here." She cocked her head to one side. "Lord Darkfest? My lord, are you here?" She stroked the wolf's head, her brow furrowed. "Where do you suppose he's gone?"

Rising, one hand firmly grasping the wolf's ruff, she left the kitchen and walked through the castle, looking for Darkfest, but he was nowhere to be found. Strange, she thought, how quickly he had disappeared. But perhaps not. He was a wizard, after all. Those in the village said he could appear and disappear at will, that he could fly or dissolve into mist. 'Twas foolishness, of course. No man could do those things. And, wizard or not, he was still a man.

"I wish I could find him," she said. "I should very much like to see if he is as fearsome to look upon as everyone says. Ah, well," she sighed, "another time, perhaps."

Turning back toward the kitchen, she filled a pan with water, put it on the stove to heat. The wolf stood beside her as she washed and dried the dishes. She found, to her delight, that as long as he was touching her or she was touching him, she was able to see.

Washing the dishes, usually a chore, was now a delight. With the wolf standing close to her side, she lifted her hand and watched the water drip from her fingers. She studied the soapsuds, noticed the way the lamplight made the bubbles sparkle and shimmer with all the colors of the rainbow. She picked up a goblet made of red glass and held it in front of her eyes, laughing as the world turned a rosy red.

How much easier to wash and dry the dishes when she could see what she was doing! She rearranged the shelves, putting the items used most frequently within easy reach.

She set the table for the morning meal; then, one hand tangled in the wolf's fur, she left the kitchen and went into the great hall.

There was a large curved settee before the huge stone fireplace. Channa Leigh stared at it, wondering where it had come from. It hadn't been there before.

Crossing the room, she sat down, her fingers caressing the velvet cloth. A furry robe was folded over the back of the settee, and she drew it over her, then settled back, her gaze drawn to the flames dancing in the hearth, one hand lightly stroking the wolf.

"I love this room," she remarked. "'Tis so big. So majestic. I've never seen anything like it." She looked at the wolf, lying on the sofa beside her, and grinned. "But then, I've never seen much of anything."

The wolf seemed to be smiling at her, she thought, but of course, it was just her imagination.

Warmed by the fire, she closed her eyes, a soft sigh of pleasure escaping her lips as the wolf licked her hand.

A moment later, she was asleep.

CHAPTER 7

"Not here?" Ronin frowned. "Where has she gone?"

Dugald and Mara exchanged worried looks.

"She's not ill?"

"Nay, nay," Dugald said quickly. "She's not ill."

"Then where is she? I promised to take her walking this forenoon."

"You might as well tell him the way of it," Mara said, her tone laced with anger. "Sure and he'll find out sooner or later."

"Tell me what?" Ronin asked sharply. He looked from Dugald to Mara, his concern growing. "Has aught befallen her?"

Mara blew out a sigh of exasperation. "I was ill, as you know," she said, her words falling hard and quick. "Dugald summoned the wizard to heal me."

Ronin nodded. It was obvious that Mara was now enjoying good health. "What has this to do with my Channa Leigh?"

"The wizard demanded her company for one year in exchange for my healing."

Ronin's eyes grew wide. "She's there, with *him*?" he exclaimed. "In the castle? Alone?"

Dugald nodded.

"You let her go?" Ronin asked in disbelief. "Did you not think to consider my feelings?"

"Of course I did," Dugald replied. " 'Twas Channa Leigh's decision to go."

Ronin blinked, and blinked again. "I dinna believe you."

" 'Tis true nonetheless. I forbade it, but she vowed she would go. The wizard would accept nothing else."

"But . . . what will he do to her?"

Mara shook her head. Tears glistened in her eyes. "Sure and it would have been better that I died than she go with the lord of Darkfest Castle."

"Nay," Dugald said, quickly crossing himself. "Dinna speak of death."

"I canna help it," Mara said, and as if a dam had burst deep inside her, tears flooded her eyes and ran down her cheeks. She looked at the two men, no longer trying to hide her sorrow or her fear for her daughter's life.

"I'm sure she's well," Dugald said, discomfited, as always, by his wife's tears.

Ronin nodded. "Of course she is," he said hastily.

"But the stories. . . ." Mara sobbed, unable to go on.

"Well, 'tis sure I am that they're naught but tales told to frighten children," Dugald said.

Ronin nodded again. "Aye, my mother told them to me oft enough when I was a lad."

Mara collapsed into a chair, her face buried in her apron.

Dugald looked at Ronin and shrugged.

"What do you really think he'll do to her?" Ronin asked, keeping his voice low so Mara could not hear.

"I dinna know. There have always been tales told of the lord of Darkfest Castle, but I've never known anyone who has actually come to harm at his hands."

With that dubious bit of comfort Ronin took his leave, determined to find out for himself how Channa Leigh fared at the hands of the wizard. She had been promised to him, and that made her his, as his horse and his crossbow were his. And he kept what was his.

IT was a long walk up the mountainside. Time and again, Ronin ran his hand over the hilt of his sword. No man he had ever met could best him with bow or blade. No man would take Channa Leigh. She had sworn to be his wife, and a betrothal was as binding as a marriage; he would not share her with another, not even with the wizard of Darkfest Keep.

The castle rose like a sleeping beast at the top of the mountain. Hewn of gray stone, it was a forbidding place, surrounded by tall trees.

Ronin paused when he reached the door, some of his courage deserting him as he gazed at the life-size wolf's head carved into the dark wood. It was remarkably lifelike, so much so that he wouldn't have been surprised if the creature had growled at him.

Chiding himself for his foolishness, he rang the bellpull, heard the sound echo and re-echo through the interior of the castle.

Moments passed. Impatient, he rang the bell again.

And then the door opened, and he found himself looking up into the face of the lord of Darkfest Castle.

"What do ye want?" the wizard demanded, his voice brusque.

"I've come for Channa Leigh."

"Indeed? Who are ye?" Darkfest asked, though he knew full well who the boy was.

"I'm Ronin the hunter," he replied, his voice overloud. "Channa Leigh is my betrothed."

"Come back in a year."

"Nay. I will take her away with me now." Ronin met the older man's gaze, refusing to be intimidated by the wizard's size and reputation.

"She is to be mine for this year," Darkfest said, his voice implacable. "I willna release her one day sooner." He made a dismissive gesture with his hand. "Be gone now, lest I turn ye into a newt."

A shiver of unease slithered down Ronin's spine, but he had come too far to turn tail and run. He was a hunter, a warrior, with a warrior's pride. Better to die with honor than be branded a coward.

Darkfest smiled faintly as he read the younger man's thoughts. *Foolish youth,* he thought, *ready to die rather than surrender.* Almost, he felt sorry for the boy. He could extinguish his life with the wave of his hand. It was a tempting thought, more so when he imagined the boy wed to Channa Leigh, taking her to his bed, planting his seed within her.

A wave of jealousy swept over him. Hardly aware of what he was doing, he had lifted his hand, ready to strike the boy down, when he heard Channa Leigh's footfalls on the floor.

He took a deep breath, willing himself to be calm.

"Channa Leigh!" Ronin called. "Are you all right?"

She moved unerringly toward the open door, causing Darkfest to marvel at her ability to get around the castle unaided. She had a remarkable memory, he thought, that she should so quickly have memorized the design of the place.

"Ronin," she said, her voice warm with welcome. "What brings you here?"

"I've come to fetch you home."

"Home?" she asked, alarmed. "Why? Is something wrong?" Her hand went to her throat. "Mama's not sick again?"

"Nay," Ronin said quickly. "All is well. 'Tis only that I've come to claim what is mine."

"I dinna understand."

"You dinna belong here," Ronin said, his courage asserting itself once more.

"Oh, but I do," she said softly. "For one year, I belong to Lord Darkfest."

"Nay! I'll not have you staying here, alone with him."

"I gave him my word, Ronin," she said. "Would you have me break it?"

"Ye have yer answer," Darkfest said, his voice like the rumble of a coming storm. "Go home."

"Fare thee well, Ronin," Channa Leigh said.

He stared at her a moment, wanting to argue, wanting to rush in and take her away by force, but he knew about honor and, in the end, he turned and started back down the path that led to the village.

Darkfest closed the door, then turned and faced Channa Leigh. "So," he said, "is that the boy yer going to wed?"

"He's no a boy," Channa Leigh said defensively. "He's a man full-grown, and a brave hunter."

Darkfest scowled, annoyed by the note of admiration in Channa Leigh's voice, jealous at the way she jumped to the boy's defense.

"'Tis a beautiful day," he growled. "Would ye care to go outside?"

"Oh, yes."

"Come, then." He took her hand, noting the way she flinched at his touch. Did she flinch when that boy touched her, or did she fall into his arms, eager and ready for his caresses?

Jealousy was an emotion he had not known before; the depth of it surprised him as much as the source. To think that he, the lord of Darkfest Keep, was jealous of a callow youth. It was unthinkable, and yet it was true.

He guided her through the castle toward the door that led into the rear yard. Tall trees cut in fanciful shapes grew along the high stone wall. Plants and flowers bloomed here in rich abundance, nourished by the strength of his power. He had fresh fruit and vegetables the year round. He raised no animals, ate little meat save that which the villagers brought him.

Peacocks strutted in the sunlight; turtledoves nested in the tops of the trees.

Holding Channa Leigh's hand, he walked her through the yard, describing the trees, the plants, the flowers, the birds. She listened intently and he saw the yearning in her face, the desire to see it for herself.

"I have business to attend to," he said, his voice curt. "Will ye be all right out here alone for a time?"

"Yes."

He led her to a low bench beneath a flowering tree. "Sit here," he said, "until I return."

With a nod, she sat down, her skirts spread around her.

Darkfest moved away a few steps, his shape changing, his muscles rippling, and then, in the guise of the wolf, he returned to her side.

"Magick!" Channa Leigh exclaimed as he pressed himself against her leg. "What are you doing here?" Smiling happily, she wrapped her arms around his neck and hugged him. "I am so glad to see you."

Rising, one hand grasping his fur, she stood up, her head turning from side to side as she tried to see everything at once.

"Oh, look!" she said, pointing at a peacock with feathers spread wide. "Isn't it beautiful? Oh, and look at that, and that."

The garden was like a fairyland, filled with plants in myriad shades of green and flowers in all the colors of the rainbow—bright reds and blues, violet and lavender, yellow and orange and pink. She walked through the flowers, pausing to touch this one, to smell that one, to stare in wonder at a tall plant with brilliant white flowers and sharp black thorns.

When she reached out to touch it, the wolf growled and pushed himself between her and the plant.

"Stop that," she said, and reached for the flower again, giving a little shriek when the wolf rose up on his hind legs and caught her hand in his mouth.

Channa Leigh frowned at Magick. "Why can I not touch it?"

Releasing her hand, the wolf shook his head.

"Is it poison?"

The wolf barked once, sharply.

"Very well." She turned away from the white flower, the forbidden plant quickly forgotten. There were birds everywhere, their feathers as colorful as the flowers.

"'Tis amazing, that he has flowers in wintertime," she mused aloud.

Lost in the wonder and beauty of the yard, she walked on until she came to a very large, very deep pond surrounded by green grass and lacy ferns. Colorful fish swam in the clear water. A bridge made of white stone spanned the pool.

Stretching out on her stomach, one arm draped over the wolf's back, she gazed into the water, content to watch the fish and the frogs and the dragonflies.

"I should probably go back to the bench," she remarked after a while, "before he comes back and finds me gone, but 'tis so pretty here." She looked at the wolf and smiled. "Do you not think so?"

He barked softly, then licked her cheek.

"I wish I knew where you come from," she said, giggling as his warm pink tongue caressed her face. "And why I can see when we touch. 'Tis the strangest thing." She gazed deep into the wolf's eyes. "Sometimes I think you can understand everything I say." She frowned. "Sometimes I think you can read my mind. Can you? It wouldna surprise me if you could. In fact, I dinna think anything will ever surprise me again."

His eyes were dark gray, familiar somehow. She knew it was only her foolish imagination, but sometimes he seemed almost human. She ran her hands over the wolf's coat, loving the rich texture of his fur.

With a low whine of pleasure, Magick stretched out beside her, basking in her touch, until the pleasure became pain and the pain became desire. Growling softly, he stood up and moved away from her before she could see his beastly desire. A few minutes alone, he thought, that was what he needed, time to vanquish his desire, time to regain his self-control.

"Magick! Magick, come back!"

She scrambled to her hands and knees, reaching blindly for the wolf, shrieking as she tumbled headfirst into the pond.

Her skirts, sodden and heavy, quickly dragged her down to the bottom. Her mouth filled with water. Panic surged through her as, arms flailing, she tried to rise to the surface. Something slimy brushed her face and a silent scream rose in her throat.

And then she felt a pair of strong hands close around her waist. Moments later, she was lying on the ground and someone was thumping her on the back. Her stomach heaved as she coughed up a mouthful of water, then lay there, cold and wet and panting for air.

Muttering an oath, Darkfest gathered Channa Leigh into his arms and carried her back to the castle. In her room, he waved the hearth to life; then, ignoring her shocked protests, he stripped off her clothing, and after swaddling her in a heavy woolen blanket, he pulled a chair in front of the fire and sat down, cradling her on his lap.

"Put me down," Channa Leigh said, her teeth chattering more from fear than the cold.

"Nay." He wrapped his arms around her and held her close.

She remained stiff in his arms, shivering from his nearness. She felt small and helpless in his embrace. It was frightening, to be held by this stranger, to know she was alone in his house, totally at his mercy. He had told her he wanted her there to sing for him, but what if it was a lie? She knew little of men, but she knew there were some who were cruel, who took women by force. Was that why Darkfest had brought her here? Should he decide to ravish her, what defense would she have?

"Ye have nothing to fear from me, Channa Leigh," he said, and his voice was low, almost like a growl. "I mean ye no harm."

His voice moved over her, easing her tension, making her feel safe and drowsy. Her head felt suddenly heavy and she rested it on his shoulder. His hand stroked her back, gentling her. His hair brushed her cheek; it was thick and silky, like the wolf's fur. A distant part of her mind noticed that she fit in his lap quite nicely, that his hands, though twice the size of hers, were gentle.

For a moment, just before sleep claimed her, she thought he licked her cheek.

CHAPTER 8

"WE leave in the morning."

"Do you mean it?" She turned toward the sound of his voice. She had been counting the days, almost the hours, waiting for this moment.

"Aye. 'Twill be a dangerous journey. And long."

"Yes, my lord."

"Ye are not afraid?"

"Oh, aye, a little. But sure and I would do anything to have my sight back."

"I will do my best to protect ye," he said. "We leave at first light."

She nodded, her smile brighter than the sun at midday.

He left the room, pausing just outside the door to watch her.

Thinking herself alone, she clasped her hands to her breasts and lifted her face upward in an attitude of prayer.

He did not have to divine her thoughts to know what it was she prayed for.

THEY left early the following morning.

Excitement rippled through Channa Leigh as Darkfest lifted her onto the back of a horse. Leaning forward, she patted the animal on the neck, loving the silky feel of the horse's coat.

"Have ye ridden before?" Darkfest asked, adjusting her stirrups.

"Never anything so large."

"Well, dinna worry. Clover is a fine beastie, well trained. She will carry ye safely."

He gazed up at Channa Leigh. She was prettier than a fresh spring morn. Sitting there, with her skirts spread over the mare's rump, a midnight-blue fur-lined cloak around her shoulders, she looked like a fairy queen going calling.

Gathering up the reins to his own great stallion, he swung into the saddle and settled his own cloak about his shoulders. He clucked to the stallion, and the horse moved forward with a shake of his great shaggy head. The mare moved up beside the stallion. A pretty little gray pack mule followed the horses, the bell around her neck tinkling softly.

The path that led down from the castle was a long and winding one, the narrow road lined by windblown trees and squat shrubs.

He watched Channa Leigh carefully. She held the reins lightly in one hand, the other hand resting on the pommel. She seemed at ease in the saddle, her body swaying with the movement of the mare. The early-morning sun danced in Channa Leigh's hair, making it glisten like spun gold. His gaze moved over her face and form, delighting in the line of her profile, the sweet curve of her breast.

He shifted uncomfortably in the saddle as his body responded to his lustful thoughts. With an oath he looked away. This journey was a mistake, he mused ruefully. In the castle, he could leave her alone when he needed to escape from the havoc she played on his senses. There was nothing within its walls that could do her harm. But out here . . . there were wild animals that could tear her to shreds, deep ravines she could stumble into, rivers that could sweep her away. He would have to keep her in his sight every moment.

He headed east when they reached the bottom of the trail.

The land stretched ahead of them, gently rolling hills and shallow valleys all covered in a sea of deep green grass. Tall trees garbed in the bright emerald green of early spring grew in scattered clusters. Large birds soared across the sky. He saw a small herd of deer grazing in the shade of a stand of timber. A speck of blue far off in the distance promised a water hole.

For a time, he lost himself in the rocking chair movement of his horse. He seldom found time to ride, seldom left his mountaintop. He had forgotten how beautiful the countryside was, the sense of freedom horseback riding afforded. He looked back from time to time to check on Channa Leigh. She rode with her face lifted to the sun, drinking in its warmth, her head turning at the sound of a flock of black-headed geese winging their way south.

He and Channa Leigh rode all that day, stopping now and then to rest the horses or to get something to eat or drink.

Channa Leigh rode without complaint, her eagerness at being outside evident in her expression. Though she could not see, she used her other senses to the fullest, running her hands over the thick velvety grass when they stopped near a river, listening to the birds as they chirped in the treetops, picking a handful of sweet-smelling flowers.

At dusk, he reined his horse to a halt. Dismounting, he lifted Channa Leigh from the back of the mare.

"Wait here," he said, and when he was certain she would obey, he unsaddled the horses and turned them loose. Next, he spread a blanket on the ground and bid Channa Leigh sit down.

When she was comfortable, he drew a circle on a small, barren patch of ground. A few words, and a fire sprang to life, crackling cheerfully in the gathering dusk.

He pulled the ingredients for dinner from his saddlebags, filled a pot with water to warm for tea. And all the while, he watched her, becoming more and more enchanted with her nearness, more and more drawn to her beauty of face and form and spirit.

She sighed, a soft sound, yet he heard it clearly.

"What is it, lass?" he asked.

"I was just wondering. . . ."

"Wondering?"

"About Magick."

"What kind of magic?"

She laughed softly. "Not sorcery. Magick, the wolf."

He grunted softly. "What were you wondering?"

"If he would come to me if I called."

"What need have you of the wolf?"

"I . . ." She chewed on her lower lip a moment. "I was wondering . . . that is, I should very much like to see your face."

His eyes widened in surprise. Of all the things she might have said, that was the furthest from his mind. He wondered if he should tell her that he was the wolf. He knew she was a little afraid of the master of Darkfest Castle. Would she be less afraid of him if she knew he was the wolf? Or more?

The wolf. What was there about his being the wolf that restored her sight? In wolf form, his own form, or any other, he was still Darkfest. He frowned. Was it the fur?

A bit of magic made quick work of cleaning up after dinner. He fixed a bed for Channa Leigh and one for himself, assured her that the fire would burn all through the night, keeping wild animals at bay.

He sat by the fire long after she was asleep, his gaze returning time and again to her face. A sigh escaped her lips, and then she smiled. It took all his self-control to keep from stealing into her dreams to see what it was that made her smile.

IT was nearing midday when he realized they were being followed. Reining his horse to a halt, he turned in the saddle. Summoning his wizard's vision, he scanned their back trail, his gaze narrowing when he saw Ronin the hunter in the distance.

Darkfest cursed under his breath.

"What is it?" Channa Leigh asked. "Is something amiss?"

"Your betrothed is following us."

"Ronin? But how . . . ?"

Darkfest shook his head; then, realizing she could not see, he said, "I dinna know, the fool."

"You will not harm him?" she asked, her voice tinged with alarm.

"Nay, I will not harm him," he muttered, "but I may change him into a toadstool."

"What?"

"I said I will not harm him." *At least not permanently.*

Darkfest watched the boy ride toward them, then rein his horse to an abrupt halt when he saw Darkfest waiting for him. The boy looked around, as though seeking a place of concealment, even though he had no hope of hiding now that he had been seen. He might be a mighty hunter, Darkfest mused, but he was not a warrior.

"Ride on," Darkfest commanded. "There is no place for ye to hide."

Squaring his shoulders, Ronin urged his horse onward.

"Why are ye following us?" Darkfest demanded.

"Why are you taking Channa Leigh away?"

"'Tis my own business and none of yours. Be gone with ye before I turn ye into a croaking toad."

The boy's eyes widened, and then he sat up tall and straight in the saddle. "I fear you not, wizard."

"Do ye not?"

The boy shook his head bravely.

Darkfest lifted his right hand. Felt the air crackle around him as he summoned his power, shaping it in his mind.

"I am Darkfest, master of fire and flame; change this mortal to a creature new; frog be now his name."

Amid a shower of green and silver sparks, the boy was transformed into a large green bullfrog. Sitting on the horse, the frog stared at Darkfest through bulging eyes, the croak that erupted from his throat filled with panic.

"Are ye still unafraid, hunter?"

Though the hunter now wore the guise of a frog, his awareness was that of the boy. The frog croaked again and again, louder each time.

With a wave of his hand, Darkfest returned the boy to his own shape.

Ronin stared at him, unable to disguise the fear in his eyes.

"Go home, hunter," Darkfest said, "lest a worst fate befall ye."

Ronin glanced at Channa Leigh. "May the gods protect you, girl, for you'll see me no more."

"Ronin!" She called his name but heard only the sound of his horse's hooves galloping away. "What did you do to Ronin? I heard the croaking of a frog. You didn't turn him . . ."

He turned in the saddle to face her. "I did, but only for a moment. He doubted my power. He doubts no more."

"And wishes to wed me no more."

"Does that sadden ye?"

She searched her heart, then shook her head. "Still, it was cruel to treat him thus."

"Would ye rather I had left him that way? I canna have him following us, and I willna be responsible for his safety. And there's an end to it."

And so saying, he urged his horse forward.

The mare trotted obediently behind.

CHAPTER 9

BECAUSE it grieved him to think of her being in darkness, because he longed to feel her touch upon him once more, he gathered his power around him and transformed into the wolf that night.

"Magick!" Her voice was filled with joy when he laid his head in her lap. "What are you doing here? How did you know where I was?"

He growled low in his throat as he felt his energy flow out of him. Out of him and into her as her hands fisted in the fur at his neck.

"Sure and you are a magic wolf!" she exclaimed softly. "For your eyes have changed color again!" They were green now, as green as new grass. She ran her hands over his head and neck as she glanced at her surroundings. They were in a small dell surrounded by lacy ferns and night-blooming flowers that filled the air with a sweet perfume. Overhead, a million stars twinkled on a bed of indigo velvet. A small fire burned nearby, fingers of orange and crimson dancing brightly in the darkness.

"But where is he?" she wondered aloud. "The wizard? Do you know where he goes? I think he worked mischief upon Ronin this very day." She smiled wistfully. "'Twas brave of Ronin to come after me."

The wolf growled low in his throat.

She looked down at the wolf. "You disagree?"

The wolf barked once.

"Well, 'tis no matter now. My lord Darkfest frightened Ronin away. I doubt he shall ever find the courage to face my lord Darkfest again. Nor can I blame him. The wizard is a powerful man, and though I fear him greatly, I shall never forget how he saved my mother's life."

The wolf licked her hand, his tail thumping against the ground.

"Dare we go for a walk?" she asked.

The wolf stood, his tail wagging. Thrusting her hand into the thick ruff at his neck, she walked away from the fire and into the darkness. The grass beneath her feet was a thick deep green.

"I wonder where he is," she mused again. "Do you know him? I should very much like to know what he looks like. I can tell he is a tall man, for when he speaks to me, his voice is above my head. His voice is rich and deep, but not unkind, though I sense a great sadness there. Perhaps because he lives alone?" She walked a few moments in silence. "I wonder why he lives alone. He seems of an age to have a wife."

She gasped with pleasure when she came to a small moonlit pool. Kneeling, she put her hand in the water. "A hot spring," she said. "It feels heavenly." She glanced around. "Do I dare . . . ? Will you guard me if I slip into the water?"

The wolf barked, his eyes bright as she removed her shoes and stockings, unbraided her hair, undressed quickly, and slid into the warm water.

"Magick? Are you there?"

The wolf moved to the edge of the water, stretched out on his belly, and pushed his head against her shoulder. Her fingers immediately delved into his fur. She sighed with pleasure as she relaxed in the effervescent water. Leaning her head back, she gazed up at the stars.

"Aren't they beautiful? They shine so. Do you see?"

The wolf whined softly.

"I was to wed Ronin next year," she said with a sigh.

"And though I did not love him, he was my only hope for marriage. Ah, well, perhaps someday another will want me. I hope so, for I should dearly love to have a child of my own." Tears thickened her voice. "Will you come to me, then, Magick? Will you be my eyes so I can see my child's face?"

The wolf licked her cheek.

"I shall take that for a yes."

She lingered there a moment more, until the wolf took her hand in his mouth and gave a gentle tug.

"Right you are," she said. "Sure and we'd best go back."

The wolf watched her as she rose from the pool, the water dripping down her skin like dewdrops. The moonlight danced in her hair, making silver highlights in the thick golden mass that fell past her hips. Her body was slender and perfect, her buttocks gently rounded, her legs long and coltish, her breasts small, the tips a dusky rose.

She stood there a moment, letting the warm breeze dry her skin, and then quickly pulled on her dress. Sitting down, she put on her stockings and her shoes, then stood once more.

"Magick?"

The wolf moved up beside her and she took hold of his fur. Moments later, they returned to the site of their camp.

Sitting down on her bedroll, Channa Leigh removed her shoes, then slid under the covers.

"Come," she said to the wolf, patting the ground beside her.

The wolf stretched out beside her. With a sigh, Channa Leigh draped her arm over his neck. Stroking his soft fur, she stared up at the stars. How beautiful they were, sparkling like dewdrops against the dark sky. A butter-yellow sickle moon hung low in the heavens. Smiling faintly, she began to count the stars.

A short time later, her soft, even breathing told the wolf she was asleep.

Easing out from under her arm, Darkfest took on his own shape. "Sweet dreams to ye, my sweet Channa Leigh," he whispered. Seeking out his lonely bed, he stared up at the dark sky, but it was Channa Leigh's image rising from the waters of the hot spring that followed him to sleep.

THE next day they traveled through a deep valley. As they rode on, Darkfest was overwhelmed with a sense of evil. The horses felt it, too. It could be seen in the way their ears twitched, in the way they picked up their feet, the way they sidled close together.

As they moved deeper into the valley, Darkfest reached inside his shirt and withdrew a small leather pouch. Inside were bits of birch, hazel, rowan, ash, and willow. And a large piece of alder. He also wore a bracelet of carved alder on his left wrist.

He saw Channa Leigh lift her head. "Where are we?" she asked.

"The valley of Madrigale."

"Something is amiss."

"Aye. I sense evil here."

She shivered and drew her cloak more tightly around her. "What kind of evil?"

"I know not."

They rode onward, and the sense of evil grew stronger.

Darkfest reined his mount to a halt, and the mare drew up alongside. His gaze moved over the valley before them. At first, he saw nothing and then, gradually, a dull shimmer, like moonlight on water, rose up before him, changing, twisting, taking on solid form and shape, until a figure with wrinkled gray skin and white hair stood before him. She wore a long black robe decorated with skulls and exploding comets.

"Who dares to cross my valley?" she demanded, her voice dry and brittle, like old bones.

"I am Darkfest, crone. Let us pass."

"Nay. Be gone!"

"I mean you no harm," he said quietly. "I seek the dragon Blackencrill."

"Then you are twice a fool," she said, cackling. Her

deep-set yellow eyes narrowed as her gaze shifted to Channa Leigh. "Leave the girl and you may cross my valley in peace."

"Nay. The girl is mine." And even as he spoke the words, he regretted they were only partly true. She was his for this year only, no more.

The witch lifted a skeletal hand. He heard her mumbling something under her breath, felt an increase in the energy arcing between them.

He reacted instinctively, his right hand tingling as he summoned his power. There was no time to invoke a spell. He flung his own energy out to block her incantation. Power flowed from deep within him, racing down his arm, shooting blue fire through the tips of his fingers. There was a sudden crackling, like ice breaking, as blue flame met the black lightning hurled by the crone. A sharp whoosh of air flattened the grass and bent the trees. The crone screamed, a high-pitched cry of outrage and pain, as blue fire engulfed her. And then, abruptly, there was silence.

"Darkfest? Darkfest!"

Channa Leigh's frightened cry brought him back to himself. "I am here." He stared at the blackened patch of ground where the crone had stood. A faint wisp of black smoke rose skyward. "The danger is past."

They camped that night near a narrow stream bordered by slender willows. After supper, Channa Leigh sat beside the fire, staring broodingly into the flames. The fire's light cast golden shadows on her fair skin. Desire stirred within him, a hunger for the touch of her hand, the taste of her lips.

She turned as he came up behind her. "My lord Darkfest, is that you?"

"Aye." He sat down beside her, his insides quivering. "Channa Leigh, would you grant me a boon?"

"If I can, my lord. What is it you wish of me?"

"A kiss," he replied, chagrined at the unexpected quiver in his voice. "Would you grant me a kiss?"

She hesitated a moment. Was she repulsed by his request?

Or was it only maidenly modesty that made her delay before answering?

"And would you grant me a boon in return?" she asked at last.

"If I can."

"I should like to see your face," she said.

"'Tis a bargain then. The wolf will come to you later." He drew his knife and placed it in her hand. "When he comes to you, cut off a bit of his hair and place it in this pouch."

"Will he let me?"

"Aye."

"Will you collect your boon now?" she asked, her fingers closing around the small leather sack.

"Nay. On the morrow, when the sun is new, we shall look upon each other. For now, I bid you good night."

"Good night, my lord."

She did not hear his footsteps, but she knew that he had left, knew she was there alone.

She sat by the fire until her eyelids grew heavy, and then she sought her blankets.

She was on the brink of sleep when a cold nose pushed against her hand. "Magick, is that you?"

The wolf whined softly as he stretched out beside her.

Channa Leigh sat up, her fingers searching for the knife she had placed nearby. "I need a bit of your fur," she said as her hand closed over the blade. She let out a soft cry of pain as the sharp blade pricked her palm. Taking hold of the handle with one hand, she gathered a bit of the wolf's fur in the other. Able to see now, she cut off some of the wolf's fur and placed it in the leather pouch.

"Thank you, Magick."

The wolf whined softly and licked her cheek.

"Tomorrow I am to see his face," she remarked, stroking the wolf's neck. "Will I find it frightening, do you think? Sometimes, when he is near, I feel so strange. Not afraid, exactly," she mused, and then paused. "I don't know how to explain it. Maybe a little of what I feel is fear," she admitted.

"He is so powerful. I felt it today, in the valley. I was glad I could not see then."

The wolf looked up at her expectantly.

"No walk tonight." She slid under the covers and the wolf stretched out beside her.

He watched her steadily until she fell asleep; then he transformed into his own shape. Picking up the pouch, he walked away into the darkness.

CHAPTER 10

SHE woke with the warmth of the sun on her face and a sense of anticipation. *On the morrow,* he had said, *when the sun is new, we shall look upon each other.*

Throwing the covers aside, she sat up. "My lord?"

"I am here, Channa Leigh."

" 'Tis dawn."

"Aye. Are ye ready?"

"Aye," she replied tremulously. "I am."

"Hold out your hand."

She did as he asked, her fingers closing over something soft. She started to ask what it was, but then she knew. It was the wolf's fur, twisted into a tight braid.

She felt his hand close over hers.

"I am Darkfest," he said, his voice soft yet ringing with power. "Master of fire and light. Believe, Channa Leigh, and receive thy sight."

Heat flowed into her hand, raced up her arm. She trembled as his power poured into her, as warm as the sunlight on her face. She blinked and blinked again as her vision cleared. Looking up, she saw him watching her.

He wore a black shirt open at the throat and black trousers tucked into supple black boots. A long black cloak fell from his broad shoulders. She had not expected him to be handsome, but he was. Undeniably so. Why hadn't her father told her? Darkfest's hair fell past his shoulders, thick and black. His brows were slightly arched, his nose straight, his lips full. His expression was stern but not cruel. But it was his eyes that held her gaze. Green eyes that were familiar somehow. He was tall, as she had expected. She was sorely tempted to run her hands over his shoulders, to press her palms to his chest. She folded her arms tightly over her breasts to keep from reaching for him. His arms were long and well muscled, his hands large and capable-looking.

"How is it possible that I can see?" She glanced at the bit of braided fur in her hand. "How long will it last?"

"Until sundown."

"No longer?"

He shook his head. The power in the cuttings of the wolf's fur grew weaker with time.

"What sort of magic is it that grants me my sight?"

"The power that lies in the hair of the wolf." Odd, he thought, that in his human form he lacked the same ability. "The power within your own blood. I wove the two of them together, then cast a spell upon it, to quicken it."

"My blood? Where did you get my blood?"

"It was on the blade of the knife." He did not tell her how tantalizing he had found the scent of her blood or how frightened he had been at the way it called to him. Nor did he tell her that he had licked her blood from the knife. It had sizzled through him like the purest fire. The memory of it thrilled him even as it repulsed him, and he shook it from his mind to examine more closely later, when he was alone.

"And now, Channa Leigh," he said quietly. "Will ye now grant me my boon?"

She nodded, not trusting herself to speak as he sat down beside her. Moving slowly, he slipped his arm around her waist, his hand splayed over her stomach.

Her heartbeat grew rapid. Her mouth grew dry. Every nerve in her body seemed to come alive as she waited for his kiss. He lowered his head toward hers. He kept his eyes open, and so did she. His eyes were as green as the leaves on the trees. They drew her in, made her think of cool

spring nights under starry skies. His kiss was light, his lips
warm and firm. He demanded nothing of her, only the
touch of her lips against his. But it wasn't enough. She
wanted more. She deepened the kiss. His eyes grew darker.
His arm tightened around her waist, drawing her closer.

With a sigh, her eyelids fluttered down and she leaned in
to him, her hands spreading across his back, her fingers
kneading his flesh.

He groaned softly. Lifting her onto his lap, he kissed her
again, his tongue stroking her lower lip, sending waves of
pleasure rippling through her.

It was a kiss unlike any she had ever known. It burned
away the memory of Ronin's chaste kiss and forever after
spoiled her for any other.

She was breathless when they parted. Feeling bereft, she
stared into his eyes, felt herself falling into the clear emerald depths. She felt the whisper of his power slide over her
skin, heard the echoes of his lonely childhood, saw the
small Cimmerian corner of his soul where his uncertainty
lived, but before she could explore it further he drew his
gaze away from hers.

"Something troubles you," she said, her voice tinged
with amazement.

He looked at her, his eyes narrowed. "What makes ye
say that?"

"I saw it when I looked into your eyes. There is a dark
place deep within you."

He did not deny it.

"What is it that troubles you?"

Lifting her from his lap, he stood and began to pace.

She sat down on her blankets and looked up at him, her
brow furrowed. "Will you not tell me?"

"There is a darkness within me," he admitted. "More
than the darkness of uncertainty. It is a love for the shadows
of the night, for the dark magic that lingers just below my
awareness." He held out his hands, palms up, and stared
down at them. "The darkness calls to something within me

that I do not understand. Sometimes . . ." He dragged his hand over his jaw, wondering how to explain the unexplainable.

"You are tempted by dark powers?"

"Aye."

"But why?"

He shook his head. "In here," he placed his hand over his heart, "I know that good is more powerful than evil, but still the darkness calls to me, tempting me to do that which can only be done through the power of darkness, to rise up and unleash the full power within me, the consequences to others be damned. I could destroy the village with the wave of my hand, enslave its people, cause famine and flood."

He dragged his hand over his face as if to block out the images his words had conjured. "I have ever used my powers for good, for healing. But there is another power, a dark power that tempts me. It calls to me in the lonely hours before the dawn, when goodness lies weak and vulnerable within me and evil rides the wings of the night."

"Virtue and vice," she said. "Truth and error. 'Tis a choice we all must make."

"Aye."

"You must not choose the darkness, my lord, you must not give in to it, else you be lost."

HE thought of her words later that day as they left the valley behind and entered a stand of thick timber. She was wise beyond her years, he thought. Knowing but little of him or his past, she nevertheless sensed the danger that lay before him if he succumbed to the darkness that beckoned him, tempting him with powers beyond imagining. The darkness. More and more he was drawn to the night. The light of the sun made his skin tingle oddly; sometimes it burned his eyes. His taste in food was also changing; where once he had preferred his meat well done, he now liked it rare and dripping with blood.

The leafy branches overhead grew thick, so thick in

some places that they shut out the light of the sun. The shade was a welcome break from the touch of the sun. The sounds of their horses' hooves were muted in the thick leaf mold and vegetation that covered the ground. Here and there he saw the glow of slanted yellow eyes observing their passing.

He watched Channa Leigh. Blessed with sight for this day, she looked at everything carefully, exclaiming softly when she saw a stag bound across their path. She remarked on the beauty of the trees, the eerie shadows beneath the branches.

Leaving the timber, they found themselves in a broad meadow.

"Oh, 'tis lovely!" Channa Leigh murmured.

And, indeed, it was. The grass was a thick blue-green. The trees wore gowns of green and gold, amber and ocher. Sweet-smelling flowers grew in clumps of bright pink and lavender, pale blue and purest white.

He heard the sound of a waterfall and turned his horse toward it, thinking to quench their thirst and refill their water flasks.

The falls were a beautiful sight—crystal clear water cascaded down the side of an onyx mountain, splashing over huge boulders to gather in a deep turquoise blue pool.

It wasn't until they were kneeling at the water's edge that he felt it, a ripple in the air, like the static before a storm.

He rose quickly to his feet, all his senses alert. He saw nothing out of the ordinary, heard nothing, and yet every instinct he possessed warned of danger. The horses stirred restlessly.

"What is it?" Channa Leigh asked. She came to stand beside him, her hand on his arm.

He shook his head. "There is something amiss. Can ye not feel it?"

She glanced around, her brow furrowed. "I feel . . . a stirring in the air."

"Aye, that's it." Gathering his power around him, he flung his senses out as a fisherman might cast a net.

There was a faint sizzle as his power came up against another force. There was a blinding flash and then a creature stood before them the likes of which Channa Leigh had never seen. It was as tall as the trees, covered with a slimy gray skin. Its eyes were close set. Its mouth was open, revealing jagged yellow teeth.

She took a step backward, repelled by the hideous creature. "What is it?"

Darkfest shook his head. He had no idea what kind of beast it was, only that it had been born of evil. He extended his arm toward the creature. "Begone!"

With a mighty roar, the beast shook its massive head.

Jerking free of their tethers, the animals bolted.

Darkfest straightened to his full height. "Begone, I say!"

The creature took a step forward, one hand reaching toward Channa Leigh. The air around it shimmered. The smell of brimstone filled the air. The grass beneath its feet withered and died.

Darkfest reacted instinctively. Thrusting Channa Leigh behind him, he lifted his hand. There was no time for words, no time to refine his magic. He gathered his power around him and hurled it at the creature.

Channa Leigh gasped and reeled backward as a ball of crimson fire flew from the wizard's fingers.

The creature screamed as its body burst into flame.

Channa Leigh covered her face with her hands, unable to watch as the leathery gray skin began to blister and melt.

There was an obscene popping sound, and then she felt Darkfest's hand on her shoulder. " 'Tis over, Channa Leigh."

Slowly, she lowered her hands and glanced around. Nothing remained of the creature but a small pile of gray ash.

She looked around, her eyes wide and scared. "Are there more of them?"

He closed his eyes a moment, then shook his head. "I think not."

"But what was it?"

"A minion of the dragon, perhaps, sent to frighten us away. No matter, 'tis over now. Come, let us go after the horses. They will not have gone far."

CHAPTER 11

CHANNA Leigh's gaze swept the land around them. She was all too conscious of time passing, all too aware that soon she would be trapped in darkness again. But for now, she delighted in everything she saw.

As Darkfest had predicted, their animals had not gone far. He lifted her onto the back of her mount, swung agilely onto the back of his own.

When they stopped to rest the horses later that day, she saw a spiderweb stretched between two bushes. She watched, fascinated, as a spotted spider slowly and carefully cocooned its unwitting prey in white silk.

They stopped again several hours later, this time near a river teeming with dozens of silver fish. Darkfest dropped down beside her. Stretching out on his stomach, he plunged his hands into the water up to his elbows and, to her delight, caught six fat fish with his bare hands.

Wrapping them in leaves, he put them in his saddlebags. "Dinner," he explained.

They rode until dusk, then made camp near a small blue pool surrounded by pale lavender ferns, flowering vines and tall slender trees with silver-blue leaves. It looked like a fairyland. She would not have been surprised to see unicorns peeking through the bushes.

She watched Darkfest unsaddle the horses and hobble

them nearby and then, with a wave of his hand and a muttered incantation, a small fire sprang to life.

Needing to feel useful, she spread the bedrolls on either side of the fire, filled their water skins. She had never cooked fish over an open fire, but when she offered, he told her there was no need. He took care of it quickly and efficiently. He cut off the heads and tails, gutted the fish, removed the bones, then cut the fish up into chunks, which he put on sticks to roast over the fire.

The meat was juicy and tender. "Delicious!" she exclaimed. "Where did you learn to do that?"

He shrugged. "I dinna recall."

"That seems passing strange."

He nodded. There were many things he could do that he had no memory of knowing or learning. The knowledge simply came to him as needed. Some of what he knew he had learned from books, but some of his magic seemed inborn. His power over fire and the elements was simply there, a part of him for as far back as he could remember.

A heaviness fell over Channa Leigh's mood as the sun began to set. She stared at Darkfest, wanting to imprint his image on her mind.

"Thank you for this day, my lord," she said, and even as she spoke, her vision began to fade, to darken, until blackness descended on her once again.

"Channa Leigh?"

She turned her face away lest he see the tears forming in her eyes. She was grateful to have been able to see for one whole day, and yet having seen the beauty of the world around her only made the darkness that engulfed her seem all the worse.

She stiffened as she felt his arm slide around her shoulders.

"Channa Leigh, why do ye weep?"

"I'm not," she said, sniffing.

"No?" His finger lifted a fat teardrop from her cheek.

"'Tis . . . 'tis only a . . . bit of dew."

He closed his eyes, overwhelmed by her tears, her nearness. All too clearly he recalled the kiss they had shared, and hungered for more. Just one more taste of her honeyed lips.

It was a temptation beyond resistance. Drawing her closer, he lowered his head and covered her mouth with his.

He felt her surprise and then her surrender as she leaned in to him, her arms twining around his neck.

He was breathless when he drew back, his body hard with wanting.

"My lord," she whispered.

"Forgive me."

"You must not kiss me so," she said, her voice as breathless as his. " 'Tis not right."

"Aye," he said, and kissed her again.

'Twas only a kiss, she thought. *How could it have such power?* It moved through her like sunlight and lightning, driving away the darkness. Her blindness no longer mattered. Nothing mattered but the touch of his lips on hers, the feel of his arms strong and sure around her, the heat that flowed through her, the little shivers of pleasure that made her press her body closer to his.

She ached deep inside, ached for something unknown, something she had never felt before. The intensity of it frightened her.

"Channa Leigh." His voice was thick and ragged, and in some way she didn't understand, it magnified the ache deep inside her, left her clinging to him in hopes that he could somehow ease the ache that throbbed in the very core of her being.

With a muttered oath, he put her away from him.

"My lord?" Confused, she reached out for him. She could hear the sound of his breathing. It came in quick gasps, as if he had run a very long way. "My lord, are you unwell?"

Unwell? He burned as with a fever. "Go to bed, Channa Leigh."

"But . . ."

"Do as I say!"

At the tone of his voice, she scrambled under the covers

and pulled the blankets up to her chin, only to lie there, her heart pounding. What had she done to anger him so? One minute he was kissing her sweetly and the next he was pushing her away.

She tried not to cry, but the tears came anyway.

And then she felt a warm tongue lave her cheek.

"Magick!" Wrapping her arms around the wolf's neck, she buried her face in his thick fur. "I'm so glad you're here."

The wolf dropped down beside her, a low whine rising in his throat.

"I don't understand him," she wailed softly. "I don't understand myself, what I'm feeling. He makes me feel so . . . strange." She stroked the wolf's fur. "He gave me my sight today. It was so wonderful. I saw the sky and the trees. And grass, and a waterfall. And his face . . . Oh, Magick, I saw his face. And he's so handsome. And his eyes, they seemed so familiar, as if I'd seen them before. . . ."

Her words trailed off and she frowned. "His eyes." Her fingertips slid up the wolf's neck to his head. "His eyes are your eyes," she mused. "The same shape, the very same color. How is that possible, unless . . . Of course! You're him, aren't you?"

The wolf whined low in his throat.

She felt her cheeks grow warm as she remembered what she had confided to the wolf, and suddenly she hoped she was wrong, hoped that the wolf was just a wolf, hoped if he was indeed Darkfest, he would not remember her words when he shed the guise of the wolf.

WHEN she woke in the morning, her world was dark again, and she was alone. Her first thought was for the wolf. Was he a magical wolf, or was he the wizard? Why did touching the wolf restore her vision when touching the wizard did not?

Darkfest. Sitting up, she folded her arms over her breasts. He had kissed her and she had reveled in it.

Where was he?

And then she felt a stirring inside her and knew, knew, that he was nearby.

"Good morrow, Channa Leigh."

The sound of his voice moved over her, low and husky and strangely melodic. She felt her cheeks grow warm as she remembered the touch of his lips on hers, the way she had melted against him. Was he remembering, too?

"Good morrow," she replied tremulously.

"I've brought breakfast."

His voice was closer now. He was near, she thought, near enough to touch if she but had the courage to reach out.

He touched her shoulder. "Here," he said, and placed a plate in her lap. "There is bread and fresh berries."

"Thank you, my lord."

He sat down across from her, watching her eat, his breath catching in his throat as she licked a drop of bright purple juice from the corner of her mouth. Desire flamed within him as he imagined drawing her into his arms. What a rare and wondrous pleasure it would be to kiss her now, when her lips were moist and sweet with berry juice.

He swore softly. Would she resist his embrace? She had not resisted yesterday. Had it been attraction she felt for him then or merely gratitude because he had not left that whelp in the guise of a toad?

He scowled into the distance. He doubted the lad possessed the courage to risk his wrath a second time. She had lost nothing when the boy turned tail and ran. Nothing but the love of a young man who obviously adored her.

His scowl deepened. Ronin could find another lass. As for himself, in three hundred years he had never seen another woman he wanted or desired. Only Channa Leigh had touched his heart, quickened his need, aroused his desire until it beat within him like the beat of his own heart.

He rose, glad, at that moment, that she could not see the clear evidence of his desire.

She lifted her head. "My lord?"

"I'm going to saddle the horses and load the mule," he said, his voice curt. " 'Tis time to go."

HE was in a foul mood the rest of the day, unable to shake off images of Channa Leigh in Ronin's arms. Channa Leigh, cleaning the hunter's house, preparing his meals, sleeping in his arms at night. Ha, the craven hunter was not worth a single hair of her head.

Hands clenched around the reins, Darkfest swore he would see the hunter dead before he would allow Channa Leigh to be his bride. And yet, if she loved Ronin, what right did he have to interfere? What right did he have to keep her from the man she loved? What right, except that he loved her himself, loved her beyond bearing. But she was his now. His until winter cast her shadow upon the land once more. In his heart, he knew it would not be long enough.

CHANNA Leigh rode beside the wizard, baffled by his silence, by the anger she had heard in his voice earlier that day. She cast back in her mind but could think of nothing she had said or done to rouse his ire. Still, he had not spoken a word to her since they left their camp that morning and she had no idea why.

Her horse came to a halt a short time later. Channa Leigh's heart began to pound when she felt Darkfest's hands at her waist as he lifted her from the saddle.

"Is everything all right?" she asked.

He grunted softly. " 'Tis time to seek shelter for the night."

"My lord?"

"Aye?"

She took a deep breath. "Are you . . . are you angry with me?"

"Nay."

"Something is amiss. Will you not tell me what it is?"

"Ye need not worry."

"Was it my kiss?" she asked, grateful that she could not see his face. "Did it not please you?"

"Is that what ye think, lass?" he asked.

She nodded, lowering her head as heat suffused her cheeks.

Whispering her name, he cupped her face in his hands and kissed her ever so gently. "Sweet," he murmured. "So sweet."

She swayed toward him, her hands resting on his chest. "More."

He willingly obliged her, his arms wrapping around her waist to draw her closer as he slanted his mouth over hers. Where his last kiss had been gentle, this one was filled with all the yearning in his soul. His tongue plundered her mouth, tasting the berries she had eaten earlier.

She boldly returned his kiss, made a soft sound of protest when he took his mouth from hers.

"Do ye love him?" Darkfest asked.

"Who?"

"The hunter, Ronin."

"Nay, my lord."

"And ye do not wish to marry him?"

"Nay, my lord, though he was my only hope."

"Another will wed ye."

She smiled up at him. "Know you who this stranger might be?"

"Ye will belong to me, lass," he said, the husky note of possession in his voice leaving no doubt that it would be so, "and to no one else."

"Are you asking me to marry you, my lord Darkfest?"

"Aye," he growled. "I'm asking." Pausing, he took a deep breath. When he spoke again, his voice had gentled. "Will ye let me love ye all the days of your life? Will ye share your happiness with me, and yer sorrows? Will ye help me to turn away the darkness? What be yer answer, lass?"

There was nothing to think about. There could only be one answer. No one else stirred her the way he did. No one else ever would. Her memory of Ronin burned away to ash in the fire that was Darkfest.

"I should be honored to be your wife, my lord," she murmured. "You will not harm Ronin?"

"There be no need now."

"You will not turn him into a newt should we meet in the square?"

"Nay, lass," he said, grinning.

"Nor a gopher?"

He laughed softly, charmed by her gentle humor and her genuine concern for the hunter.

"Think no more of him," he said, and drawing her into his arms once again, he kissed her, long and strong, driving everything else from her mind but the wonder of his kiss.

This was right, she thought. This was where she longed to be, where she was meant to be.

That night, when it was time for bed, she slept in his arms.

DARKFEST groaned softly as the light of the morning sun played over his face. Opening his eyes, he squinted against the brightness. More and more these last days, he had been bothered by the sun's glare. It made his skin feel strange, as if it was shrinking.

He had rarely spent so much time out-of-doors. At home, his days were spent within the thick gray walls of his castle. When he felt the need to go out, it was usually long after sunset. He stayed up long past midnight, preferring to sleep the day away.

Beside him, Channa Leigh slept peacefully, her cheek resting on one hand, her mouth curved in a mysterious smile. Was she dreaming of him? Did he dare walk in her dream? If she was dreaming of another, did he want to know?

He shook off his jealousy. She had said she loved him and he believed her. Deceit was unknown to Channa Leigh.

The curve of her cheek drew his hand. Lightly, so lightly, he brushed his fingertips against her skin. So soft. So warm. His gaze moved over her face, slid down the slender column of her throat to rest on the pulse beating there.

Almost, he could hear the beat of her heart, hear the blood thrumming through her veins.

With a shake of his head, he rolled to his feet, troubled by the dark thoughts rising up within him.

As if bereft of his company, Channa Leigh awoke. "My lord?"

"I am here."

She sat, one hand reaching out for him.

Hunkering down on his heels, he took her hand in his. "Something troubles ye?"

"I . . . I dinna know. I was dreaming. It was a lovely dream, at first. And then . . ." She frowned. "I dinna know what happened, but suddenly the world was dark and I was afraid."

"Dark?" He frowned. She was always in darkness.

"I dinna know how to explain it. It was not a lack of vision, but a lack of light. Do you understand?"

"Aye, lass." He understood all too well. The darkness she spoke of was the darkness that dwelled within him, but how did she know of it? If she stayed with him, would it begin to overshadow her, as well? Troubled by that thought, he released her hand and rose to his feet.

"My lord?"

"Dinna fret, lass. All is well. We will reach the valley of the dragon on the morrow."

CHAPTER 12

THEY reached the home of the dragon late in the afternoon the following day.

Dismounting, Darkfest stared down into the valley that so many had entered and from which none had returned.

He had thought they would have to hunt for the dragon, but Blackencrill was there for all to see, his deep green scales shining iridescent in the sunlight. Small puffs of smoke wafted from his nostrils as he slept, his long body curled around a shining blue castle that shimmered like an enormous sapphire. Trees, shrubs, and grass all wore the scorch marks of the dragon's breath. The remains of charred skeletons, both man and animal alike, were scattered across the valley floor.

The dragon stirred, a low rumble of pain issuing from his throat, along with a short burst of flame. Lifting his great horned head, he took a deep breath, his nostrils flaring.

It was then that Darkfest saw the hilt of the sword protruding from the dragon's flesh. Embedded in the dragon's massive neck, the weapon looked no larger than a woman's embroidery needle.

"Who goes there?" The voice of the dragon was as the sound of a rusty saw being dragged over stone.

"My lord—"

"Be silent, Channa Leigh. Dinna move. He canna see you."

Gathering his courage, Darkfest moved away from where she sat her horse. Walking slowly, he descended several yards, then came to a stop. The scent of smoke and charred flesh filled the air.

"I am Darkfest, master of fire and flame."

What might have been a laugh filled the valley, followed by a great *whoosh* of orange flame that incinerated a nearby tree. "Thou? Master of fire and flame?" Another laugh as the dragon sent a tongue of flame arcing toward him.

Gathering his power around him, Darkfest summoned a ball of dark blue fire and flung it out to meet that of the dragon. There was a great fiery explosion as the flames met in midair. Sparks of blue and orange rained down on the ground.

"Who art thou?" demanded the dragon. His tone now carried a faint note of respect.

"I am Darkfest, wizard of the north. The name of Blackencrill is known throughout the land and I have come seeking a boon at thy hand."

"A boon? Of me? What is it you seek?"

"A drop of thy blood."

"And what will you give me in return?"

"I will remove that sword from thy flesh and heal thy wound."

"Who is the woman that awaits thee?"

"My betrothed."

"And if I want the woman?"

"Ye cannot have her. She is mine."

"What need have you of my blood?"

"It is to restore her sight."

"You intrigue me, wizard of the north. Come closer."

"Do I look a fool?"

"You fear me?"

Darkfest let his gaze wander slowly over the charred skeletons scattered on the valley floor. "Aye."

"I give you my word you may enter my valley in safety."

"And my woman?"

"And the woman."

"Did these others also have thy word?"

"They did not think to ask."

"And when we wish to leave?"

A low rumble of laughter rocked the valley floor. "You are a wise wizard. I shall do nothing to harm you or the woman."

"ARE you sure 'tis safe?" Channa Leigh asked, trepidation clear in her voice. "How do you know you can trust this dragon?"

" 'Tis a chance we'll have to take."

She lifted her head as they rode across the charred valley floor. "I smell . . . death."

"Aye, lass," Darkfest replied, and for once he was glad she could not see the destruction that surrounded them. What he had seen at a distance was far worse seen up close. Skulls leered at him, their mouths open in screams of terror.

The dragon awaited them, an enormous beast with thick scales and feet armed with claws as long as battle lances. His eyes were large and black, and watched, unblinking, as they approached.

Dismounting, Darkfest lifted Channa Leigh from the saddle. He could feel her trembling.

"My woman is weary from the journey."

The dragon nodded in the direction of the castle. "You may refresh yourselves inside."

With a nod, Darkfest led Channa Leigh into the castle. It was bigger than any dwelling he had ever seen, with ceilings a hundred feet high. The floors were made of translucent crystal, the walls of jade. The hearth was large enough to roast a dozen oxen at one time. The furniture was of gigantic proportions.

The first door off the main hall was a bedchamber. A wave of his hand brought a fire to life in the hearth. He settled Channa Leigh in a chair, removed her shoes.

He found a ewer filled with water, as well as a bar of

fragrant soap and a bit of toweling. He warmed the water in the ewer with a glance.

"There is water to bathe with," he told her. "Have ye need of anything else?"

"Nay, my lord."

"I will return as soon as I can."

"You will be careful!"

"Aye, lass."

"I dinna trust that dragon."

"Nor I." Placing his hands on her shoulders, he drew her up against him. "I will not be long," he promised, and kissed her gently.

Her arms went round his neck and she pressed herself to him. "Hurry back to me, my lord."

With a nod, he kissed her again. Then, taking a cup he found next to the bed, he went out to gather the dragon's blood.

"THE castle is to your liking?" the dragon asked as Darkfest emerged.

"Aye. Who dwells there?"

"Only the memory of the creature who once tried to enslave me."

"What happened to him?"

The dragon flashed a smile amid a mouthful of razor-sharp teeth. "What think you?"

"I think I would rather not know." He looked up, his gaze meeting that of Blackencrill. "Will ye now keep your word?"

"Think you I would not?"

"I think I would not like to meet the fate of the giant."

A low chuckle stirred the air above Darkfest's head. "Indeed, you would not." The dragon lowered his head, putting the hilt of the sword within Darkfest's reach. "Pull it out."

Darkfest wiped his hands on his trousers. The sword had obviously been embedded in the dragon's flesh for some time. The skin around the blade was black and putrid, the smell overwhelming.

" 'Tis likely to hurt."

"Do you think it doesn't hurt now?" the dragon roared. "Remove it!"

Wrapping both hands around the hilt of the sword, Darkfest gave a mighty tug. The blade tore free with a sickly wet sound. Blood oozed from the wound. It sizzled on the ground; the grass withered and died wherever it touched.

A drop landed on Darkfest's cheek and he howled with pain as it seared his flesh. He glared up at the dragon. "Ye might have warned me!" he exclaimed, tossing the sword aside. "How is she to drink this vile stuff?"

"You are the wizard."

"Aye. Be still now." Closing his eyes, Darkfest gathered his power. It grew within him, refining his senses, racing like quicksilver through his veins, dancing over his skin. He placed his hands over the wound in the dragon's neck, the power thrumming through him erecting a barrier of protection between the dragon's blood and the wizard's flesh.

"I am Darkfest," he murmured, his voice like the roar of the wind. "Master of fire and land. Be healed now, dragon, by the power of my hand!"

He felt the power flow down his arms and out through his hands, felt it spread over the dragon's flesh, burning away the foul infection with the clarity of healing fire. When he stepped back, all trace of the wound was gone.

Darkfest pulled the cup from inside his shirt. "Will ye now fulfill your part of the bargain?"

"Aye. A single drop, no more."

Darkfest nodded.

Using one of his fearsome claws, the dragon made a small scratch in his chest. Lifting the cup, Darkfest caught a single drop of glittering bright red blood. It landed in the cup with a soft sizzle.

"My thanks, my lord dragon."

"And mine," Blackencrill replied. "I have carried that sword in my flesh for a decade and more."

Darkfest gestured at a nearby skeleton. "Perhaps ye should have asked one of these to remove it for ye instead of burning the meat from their bones."

"They came to rob and to plunder," the dragon replied scornfully.

With a flick of his mighty tail, he gained his feet and stretched his wings. Such wondrous wings, pale green and gold streaked with crimson. Seeming light as thistledown, the dragon rose in the air.

"Be gone before sunrise, wizard," he called, and with a stroke of his powerful wings, the dragon left the valley.

Darkfest stared after the creature. The dragon had promised he would do them no harm; still, though mystified by the warning, he took it to heart. They would be away from the valley before dawn.

CHANNA Leigh stood at the window, letting the evening breeze waft across her face, letting its warmth dry her hair. She had bathed and washed her hair. When she went to put on her dress, she was surprised to find her old dress gone and a new one in its place. Now, waiting for Darkfest to return, she wondered if the blood of the dragon could indeed restore her sight.

She sensed the wizard's presence even before he spoke her name. She turned toward the sound of his voice. "My lord?"

"I have conjured a potion made from the dragon's blood," he said, entering the room.

A shudder escaped her at the thought of partaking of another creature's life force. "Is it . . . does it taste . . . vile?"

"Nay, beloved. It tastes of peppermint and honey."

"How can that be?"

"A bit of wizardry," he replied, and she heard the smile in his voice. "A lovely potion for a lovely maid."

She flushed, pleased by his flattery.

He closed the distance between them and placed the crystal goblet in her hand. "I am Darkfest," he intoned.

"Master of fire and light. Drink, Channa Leigh, and receive thy sight."

With hands that trembled, she lifted the goblet to her lips and drank. It did, indeed, taste of peppermint and honey.

Darkfest watched her carefully, his heart pounding with anticipation as she drank the last of the brew.

He took the cup from her hand and set it aside. "Channa Leigh?"

She followed the sound of his voice. "Perhaps it takes a bit of time for the magic to work."

"Nay. I must have mixed it wrong." He paced the floor, going over the spell in his mind, and then he shook his head. "No, I did everything that was to be done, as it was meant to be done."

"My lord . . ."

"Forgive me, Channa Leigh."

"There is nothing to forgive." But he heard the disappointment in her voice. It was like a knife slicing through his heart. He had given her hope, and now that hope was gone.

He paced the floor, muttering to himself, as night flung her cloak across the sky. Channa Leigh slept, her head pillowed on her arm, and still he paced until he felt the breath of the sun warm the land.

In an instant, he recalled the dragon's warning. Lifting Channa Leigh from the bed, he draped her over his shoulder and bolted out of the castle even as it began to dissolve.

Their horses waited outside. Grabbing the reins, he closed his eyes, a distant part of his mind wondering why Channa Leigh did not wake up.

In desperation, he summoned his power, uncertain of the danger that stalked them. And even as he felt it slither up his spine, he saw it take shape, moving like a long black shadow around the edge of the valley, and everywhere it touched, thorns sprang in its wake. A dull roar filled the air, as if the very earth cried out in pain.

"I am Darkfest," he shouted, "master of fire and tide. Thou wicked dragon, I summon thee to my side!"

There was a mighty beating of wings, a blast of furnace heat, and Blackencrill descended to stand beside him.

Darkfest glared at the beast. "Foul dragon, you will take us from this place now, or your flesh will rot from your bones."

The dragon snorted, an oddly delicate sound coming from so large a creature. "I but promised I would not harm you," he said. "In return for your kindness, I warned you to leave the valley before the sun's rising." He glanced at the sky. "I fear you did not listen."

Channa Leigh stirred in his arms. "My lord?"

"All is well, beloved," Darkfest said. "Fear not. The dragon will see us to safety."

"Very well," Blackencrill said. "Hurry."

Darkfest settled Channa Leigh on the dragon's back. "Wait," he said, and lifting his hands, he summoned his power once more. "I am Darkfest, master of fire and ice. Horses and mule now become mice."

A rush of power flowed from his hands and a trio of mice stood where his and Channa Leigh's mounts and the mule had been. Gathering the creatures up, he dropped them into his pocket. Climbing onto the dragon's back, he put his arms around Channa Leigh and held her close. "Away, dragon!"

With a powerful thrumming of his wings, the dragon soared above the valley. Looking down, Darkfest saw that the valley was now surrounded by a tall hedge of briers and thorns. He could only wonder what might have awaited them if they had remained.

"Thy blood, dragon, why did it not work?"

Blackencrill shook his head. "You are the wizard, not I." And so saying, he landed in a broad meadow. "Perhaps you sought the wrong dragon. Be off now and begone. I want no more of your magic."

CHAPTER 13

THE trip home was uneventful. Channa Leigh hid her disappointment well, but Darkfest could not shake off the sense of failure. It weighed like a millstone round his neck. Why had he failed?

The question plagued him long after they returned home. Even Channa Leigh's sweet voice could not ease his troubled mind.

Late one night as he wandered through the castle, he found himself standing in front of the painting of his parents. His gaze settled on his father's face. The Dragon Lord of Darkfest Castle.

Darkfest swore a short, pithy oath, then turned and went to his chamber. He worked all through the night, and as dawn rose in the sky, he held up a small vial of ruby-colored liquid. It held three drops of his own blood and the ashes of four of the wolf's hairs mixed with the juice of wild berries to make it palatable. He stared at the vial a long moment, wondering if he had at last discovered the secret to restore Channa Leigh's sight.

Unable to wait a moment longer, he ran up the stairs to her bedchamber and rushed inside.

Kneeling beside her bed, he shook her shoulder lightly. "Channa Leigh! Wake up, lass."

She woke with a start. "Is something wrong, my lord?"

"Drink this." He thrust the vial into her hand. "Quickly now."

"What is it?"

"Drink!"

Compelled by the tone of his voice, she downed the contents in a single swallow, gasping as the fiery liquid burned its way down her throat.

He watched her carefully, his heart pounding with excitement and trepidation.

And then, slowly, she turned to face him. "My lord," she breathed, and there was a wealth of wonder in her voice. "Truly thou art the most handsome of men."

"Channa Leigh!"

"I can see you." A smile as bright as summer sun curved her lips and lit her eyes. "I can see you!"

With a glad cry, he drew her into his arms, their tears mingling as he held her close.

"But how?" she asked. "How did you do it?"

"The dragon's blood," he replied with a rueful grin.

"What dragon? Not Blackencrill?"

"No. This dragon," he said, thumping himself on the chest.

"You, my lord?"

"Aye. My father was known as the Dragon Lord of Darkfest Castle. I dinna know why I did not recall that sooner. For some reason I canna understand, there is magic in the wolf's hair, so I combined that with my blood. The dragon's blood." He frowned, wondering if his human hair would have worked as well.

"And will it last?" she asked.

"Only time will tell."

She looked up at him, her eyes shining. And then she jumped to her feet. "Come," she said, holding out her hand. "We must go and tell my mama and papa."

Grinning, Darkfest gained his feet. "Mayhap you should dress first."

She looked down at her nightgown and then back at him, her cheeks pink. "I think you may be right, my lord."

THE sun was still climbing in the sky when they made their way to Channa Leigh's home.

She burst inside, calling, "Mama, Mama!"

Her mother rushed into the room, wiping her hands on a towel, her brow lined with worry. "Channa Leigh! Child, what is wrong?"

"Mama. Oh, Mama." She flung herself into her mother's arms and hugged her tightly.

Mara looked into her daughter's face, her eyes widening in disbelief. "Can it be?" She glanced at Darkfest and took a step backward, drawing Channa Leigh with her. "What dark magic is this?"

"'Tis magic indeed, Mama!" Channa Leigh cried. "Is Papa here?"

"What's all the ruckus?" Her father's voice preceded him into the room.

"Papa!" She threw her arms around his neck and hugged him. "'Tis a miracle, Papa."

He hugged her back. "A miracle?"

She drew away a little and looked into his eyes. "I can see, Papa!"

Taking her mother and father by the hand, she pulled them into the kitchen and sat down at the table. They took their places, glancing over their shoulders as Darkfest followed them into the room.

He stood in the doorway, his arms folded over his chest, while Channa Leigh told all that had happened since she had gone to live in the wizard's castle.

There were tears in Mara's eyes when the tale was told.

Dugald rose to his feet and faced Darkfest. "And so you mean to marry my daughter, do you?"

"Aye."

"And if I say nay, what then?"

"If Channa Leigh refuses me of her own free will, I will never see her again. But if she wishes to be my wife, as she said, then I will have her, with or without your blessing."

Dugald turned his gaze to his daughter. "Do you truly wish to marry this man?"

"Aye, Papa, with all my heart."

Dugald looked to his wife. "And what say you?"

"She loves him, old man. You can see it in her eyes."

AND so it was that the fair maiden in the valley married the dark wizard upon the hill.

Darkfest stood beneath a canopy of tree boughs, waiting for his bride, felt his breath catch in his throat when he saw her walking toward him on her father's arm.

Never, in all his long life, had Darkfest seen anything to equal the beauty of Channa Leigh as she moved gracefully toward him. He gazed deep into her eyes, eyes filled with a love so deep and pure and true that it filled his heart with a sweet agony. The light in her eyes forever burned away the darkness that had ever been a part of him, banishing it from the depths of his heart and soul as if it had never existed.

It took but a few words spoken by the priest to make her his wife, to bind her to him for so long as she lived. And, thanks to his blood, she would have a long life indeed.

"I love ye, my lady of light," he murmured as he drew her into his arms.

"And I love you, my lord," she replied, and standing on her tiptoes, she claimed her first kiss as his wife.

The first, dear reader, but not the last.

PHANTOM LOVER

SHERRILYN KENYON

CHAPTER 1

"MEN are the scourge of the universe. I say we line them all up along the highway and then mow them down with big trucks." Chrissy paused as her light blue eyes widened with a new thought. "No, wait. Steamrollers! Yeah, let's steamroll them all until they're nothing more than slimy wet spots on the road."

Arching a brow at the rancor, Erin McDaniels looked up from her desk to see her co-worker Chrissy Phelps gripping the edge of Erin's tan cubicle wall. The large brunette's eyes were flashing mad and Chrissy had the look of a woman one step away from the edge.

"Having trouble with the boyfriend again, eh, Chrissy?"

"Actually, it's my younger brother who has me ticked, but since you brought up the boyfriend thing, take my advice: Be the black widow. Find a guy, have fun with him, then eviscerate him in the morning before he can brag about it to his friends."

"Okay," Erin said stretching the word out. "I think someone needs a time-out."

"Someone needs a two-month vacation in the Bahamas without her boyfriend along." Chrissy's eyes brightened. "Oooh, hey, sex camp. Yeah. That's the ticket. We need to start a sex camp where women can tell their hubbies they're going to a fat farm and instead of the boot camp diet with Nazi dieticians, they go to the beach and have hot men treat them like goddesses!"

Erin laughed.

"No, I'm serious. We'd be rich."

Erin laughed even harder. "You'd better get back to work before Lord King Bad Mood catches you over here again."

"Yeah, I know. See, proves my point. All men should be shot."

Erin was still laughing as Chrissy returned to her desk. Two seconds later, Chrissy was back, peeking over the cube wall again. "Hey, are you still having those nightmares?"

Erin's humor fled as she remembered the horrendous nightmare she'd had last night where she'd been cornered in a dark cave by an unseen force that seemed to want to feed off her terror. For the last three weeks she'd barely slept a wink. Her exhaustion was getting so bad that she was even having dizzy spells.

"Yes," Erin said.

"Did that medicine the doctor gave you help?"

"No. If anything, I think it made the dreams worse."

"Oh, man, I'm sorry."

Erin was, too. She'd hoped for at least one good night's sleep. But that no longer seemed possible.

Their boss's door opened.

Chrissy dodged off as their rotund, militant boss left his office in a huff and headed toward the coffeepot with his extra large coffee mug in hand. Oh, yeah, like that man needed any more caffeine to add to his jittery crankiness.

Erin sighed as John filled his mug to the brim and her thoughts turned back to her nightmares.

Honestly, she no longer knew what to do about them. They were just so bizarre, and every night the dreams seemed to worsen. At the rate she was going, she figured she'd be a raving lunatic by the end of the month.

Rubbing her eyes, she focused on her computer screen. She had to get her marketing report in by Friday, but all she really wanted to do was sleep.

In the back of her mind she kept seeing that huge, snarling monster that came for her. Hearing him call her name as he reached his taloned hand out, trying to claim her. Like some bad horror movie, the scenes kept haunting her, whispering through her thoughts during any unguarded moment.

Shaking her head, she dispelled the images and focused on her computer screen. But as she read, Erin felt her eyelids getting heavy again. She blinked fast and widened her eyes in an effort to stay awake.

Marketing report, marketing report . . .

Oh, yeah, like that was a good way to stay awake! Why not down a couple of sleeping pills and drink a glass of warm milk while she was at it?

What she needed was more caffeine, and since she couldn't stand coffee, she'd have to go to the Coke machine. Maybe the walk down the hall would help revive her, too.

She slid her chair back and opened her desk drawer to get her change, then rose to her feet.

As soon as she was upright, a strange buzzing began in her head. The world tilted.

And in one heartbeat everything went black and her body froze. . . .

Erin felt herself falling down a deep, dark hole. All around her, winds rushed and howled in her ears, sounding like huge, frightening beasts trying to shred her.

They were hungry. They were desperate, and they wanted *her*.

They whispered her name on breaths of fire. Told her they waited only for her.

Not again! She couldn't take any more of this horrible nightmare.

Wake up, wake up!

But she couldn't.

Erin reached out to grab anything in the darkness to stop herself from falling. There was nothing to hold on to. Nothing to save her.

"Help!" she screamed, knowing it was futile but needing to try.

Still, she fell.

She didn't stop falling until she reached the cavern she knew all too well. Dark and dank, it smelled of rotting decay. She heard the hissing and screams, the absolute agony of souls in torment.

Run away!

Her heart pounded as she stumbled in the dark, over the rough floor that seemed to grab on to her feet with rocky fingers as she tried to find an exit. She struggled to see, but the oppressive darkness wouldn't let her. All it did was stab at her eyes like tiny needles.

She reached out with her hands and touched a slimy wall that slithered and moved under her fingers. Disgusting though it was, at least it gave her some support, something tangible that might lead her home.

And she had to find a way home. The frightened voice in her head told her that if she didn't get out of this now, she'd never be able to escape it.

Panicked, she saw a dim light flickering up ahead. She ran toward it as fast as her legs would carry her.

The light. It would save her. She was sure of it.

She ran into a large cave where the light was shining over the veined and broken walls that oozed some kind of gelatinous muck. The smell of sulphur burned her nose and the screams grew louder.

Erin skidded to a halt. If she had been terrified before, it was nothing compared to what she felt now.

The dragonlike monster, with shimmery blood red scales and jet-black wings, rose up in front of her, snarling. His long teeth snapped as he eyed her hungrily.

He moved closer to her, lulling her with his eerie silver-blue eyes. Eyes that seemed to see more than just her physical self. It was as if they saw all the way into her mind, her soul.

And she knew the beast wanted her. That he longed to possess her with a fevered madness.

Oh God, this was it. The beast was here to take her. To consume her.

There was no escape.

Erin stumbled back, toward the entrance. She wouldn't just lie down and die. It wasn't in her. She was a fighter. And she would fight until the last breath left her body.

Turning around, she ran to the opening, but before she could escape, it closed up, sealing her in.

"You're not going to leave me so soon, Erin," the scaly dragon lisped, his talons scraping the floor as he drew closer. "I need the light inside you. Your thoughts. Your feelings. Your goodness. Come to me, and let me feel the warmth of you wash over me."

He lunged for her.

Erin closed her eyes and imagined a sword in her hands to fight him.

She got a tree limb. Not her weapon of choice, but it was better than nothing. She swung it at him, catching him hard across the face.

Laughing, he shook his scaly head as if he didn't feel the blow at all. "Such spirit. Such intelligence and ingenuity. And you wonder why I want you so. Show me more, Erin. Show me what else you can come up with."

She forced him to step back while she wielded her tree limb. It was a stupid weapon, but it was all she had for the moment.

As if growing bored, the dragon jerked the limb from her hands. "I want your mind, Erin. I want to feel your fear of me."

He moved even closer.

Before the beast could reach her, a bright light flashed between them, stinging her eyes even more. It grew in intensity until it appeared brighter than the sun. When it finally faded, it revealed another monster.

Erin swallowed in terror. Why couldn't she control this dream? Ever since she'd been a child, she'd been able to wish herself out of bad dreams. But for some reason, she had no control in these nightmares.

It was as if something other than her was directing them. As if she were nothing more than a marionette whose strings were being pulled by the monster.

The newest monster appeared in the form of a giant snake. Only in place of a head, she had a woman's upper body. Her scaly green complexion looked craggy, and her bluish eyes glowed.

The she-snake slithered toward her, smiling a fanged smile as she raked her eerie gaze over Erin's body. "What a tasty little morsel she is."

"She is mine!" the dragon roared. "I will not share her."

The she-snake licked her lips as her long tail slithered across the floor. "She is strong enough for us both." Then she turned toward the dragon, her hideous face a mask of rage. "Besides, I saw her first and well you know it. You found her through me and I won't let you have her."

The dragon attacked the snake.

Terrified beyond belief, Erin took advantage of their combat to pick up a rock and pound at the cave's opening. "Let me out," she demanded between clenched teeth.

She closed her eyes and tried to imagine the wall opening and her running through it.

It got her nowhere. Not until the tail of the dragon whipped around trying to sting the snake. The snake ducked, as did Erin, and in one resounding crash, the tail splintered the wall.

Trembling, Erin ran out into the darkness again. The screaming howls intensified.

"Please," she begged out loud, "please wake up! C'mon, Erin, you can do it." She pinched herself and slapped her own face as she ran, and did everything she could think of to make herself come out of this nightmare.

Nothing worked. It was as if the monsters wouldn't let her go.

She rounded a corner and found herself sliding down a small slope. At the bottom was a boiling pit where the snake-woman waited. The heat of the pit burned Erin as golden-red lava percolated.

The snake rose up before her, smiling. Those demonic eyes with their diamond-shaped pupils watched her eerily. "That's it, little prize. Come to me. It's my turn to feed off you."

Erin turned to run again, but her feet were locked to the ground. They wouldn't move at all.

The snake drew closer.

Closer.

So close Erin could feel the flick of the snake's tongue. Smell the greasy slime of her body and hear the rasping of her scales moving against the rock floor.

Defenseless, Erin closed her eyes and called out with her mind for help. She tried to summon a protector. Tried to imagine a champion who could come and defeat her monsters.

Just as the snake reached her, the cavern shook.

The snake pulled back an instant before a man appeared between Erin and the beast.

And he wasn't just any man. Clad in a suit of black armor, he had incredibly broad shoulders and long jet hair. Erin couldn't see his face, but she could feel the power of his presence. Feel the warrior essence of him as he prepared to fight the demon.

The snake shrieked in outrage, "Stand down, V'Aidan. Or perish from your stupidity!"

Erin's summoned champion laughed out loud at the she-snake's anger. "I'd perish from your breath long before my stupidity killed me, Krysti'Ana."

Screaming in outrage, the she-snake increased to ten times her size. Her massive jowls snapped and she hissed as the cavern walls around them shook even harder than before. Loud crashes sounded as pieces of stone broke free of the cavern and formed into stone men.

Erin's savior turned to her, and her breath caught at the sight of his face. More handsome than anything imaginable, he held eyes that were so clear and blue, they seemed to glow. A shock of jet-black hair fell over his forehead and contrasted sharply with his tawny skin.

Before she could move, he wrapped his lean, muscular body around hers in a protective cloak, shielding her as the monsters attacked en masse.

Erin could feel the blows he took as they vibrated from

his body into hers. She didn't know how he stood the pain of it. How he maintained his hold on her.

All she knew was, she was grateful for it. Grateful for the power and strength of his presence. Grateful that he cradled her so gently and that she was no longer alone to face her nightmare.

The warm, spicy scent of his skin soothed her. Instinctively she wrapped her arms around his lean armored waist and held on to him, afraid of letting him go. "Thank you," she breathed, shaking. "Thank you for coming."

She saw the confusion in his gaze as he frowned down at her. Then his face hardened, his eyes turned icy.

"I have you, *akribos*," he whispered quietly, and yet his deep, accented voice rolled over her senses like a powerful tidal wave. Soothing, warming. "I won't let the snake Skotos take you."

She believed that, until one of the new monsters seized her about the waist with a stone tentacle. She screamed as it tore her from her savior's grasp.

The dark knight created a sword out of air and pursued them through the dark cavern. She watched as he dodged the other stone monsters, as he literally ran down the walls themselves to get to her. He jumped over the thing carrying her, to land before them and cut off the monster's escape.

The creature caught him about the waist with a hard kick and sent him slamming high into the wall.

V'Aidan didn't seem to feel the pain at all as he slid down the wall to the floor. More monsters swarmed over him, but he fought them down. His face was a mask of determination until he stood strong and victorious over their broken bodies.

He narrowed his eyes on the thing holding her, then held his hand out, and a red glow blasted the monster, splintering it.

The knight grabbed Erin then, scooped her up in his arms, and ran with her through the darkness.

Erin wrapped her arms around his neck and held on for dear life. She could still hear the snake calling out.

"I will have her, V'Aidan. I will have both of you!"

"Don't listen," V'Aidan said. "Close your eyes. Think of something soothing. Think of a happy memory."

She did and, oddly enough, the most comforting thing she could imagine was the sound of his heart pounding under her cheek. The deep accent of his voice.

"V'Aidan!" the she-snake's voice echoed in the cavern. "Return her to me or I will make you wish you had never been born."

He laughed bitterly. "When have I ever wished otherwise?" he mumbled under his breath.

Suddenly the wall before them burst open, spilling more monsters into their path.

"Hand her over to us, V'Aidan," a large gray lizard-man demanded. "Or we will see you pay with the flesh off your back."

Still holding her close, V'Aidan spun around to flee but couldn't.

They were surrounded.

"Give her to us," an old dragon croaked, reaching out its claws. "She can feed us all."

Erin held her breath as she saw the indecision in her dark knight's eyes.

Dear Lord, he was going to hand her over.

Her heart pounding, she touched his face, her fingers brushing against his hard, sculpted jaw. Erin didn't want the monsters to have her, but inside she understood his reluctance to help her any further. He didn't know her at all. There was no reason for him to endanger himself.

He's not real.

It's a dream.

The words whispered through her mind. But like so many dreams, this one felt so real. *He* felt real.

And she had an unnatural desire to protect him.

"It's okay," she breathed. "I don't want you hurt. I can fight them on my own."

Her words seemed to confuse and surprise him.

The monsters moved in.

"Release her or die, V'Aidan," the lizard-man hissed.

Erin felt the knight's tender touch as his fingers brushed the side of her neck, sending chills all over her.

The look in his eyes was needful and tormented.

"They will not have you," he whispered. "I will take you some place where they can't reach you." He bent his head and captured her lips.

The heated passion of his kiss stole her breath.

The dream monsters faded away into vaporous clouds until nothing was left.

Not the cave, not the screams.

Nothing.

Nothing except the two of them and the sudden need she had inside her to taste more of him.

Closing her eyes, Erin inhaled the warm, manly scent of V'Aidan's skin. He ravished her mouth with passion as his tongue swept against hers and his teeth gently nipped her lips.

Now this was a dream.

He was a dream.

A perfect, blissful moment worth savoring.

She heard him growling like a wild beast as he trailed his lips down her jaw and buried them against her throat. Licking. Teasing. Inciting her desire.

Every nerve ending in her body fired at his touch. She burned for him. Her breasts swelled, wanting to feel the strokes of his tongue across the taut peaks while his hands held her. Her core throbbed with an aching, demanding need.

He lifted his head to gaze down at her and it was then that the rest of the scene filled itself in. The two of them stood outside on a bright, moonlit knoll.

The peace of the moment comforted her. She smelled the damp pine around them, heard the bubbling of a nearby waterfall.

Their clothes melted from their bodies as he laid her down on the ground, which, oddly, wasn't hard. The moss under her was softer than a cloud, and it contrasted sharply with his hard muscles pressing down on her.

She liked this dream much, much better.

"You are gorgeous," she whispered, staring at his sleek long dark hair falling around his face. His body was lean, meticulously defined, and flawless. Never had she seen a better-looking man.

She reached up and traced the sharp arch of his dark brows over those silvery-blue eyes. The color of them was so intense, it took her breath.

Then she trailed her fingers down the stubble of his cheeks to his hard, sculpted jaw. She was so grateful to him. So happy to have him hold her after the terror the monsters had put her through.

For the first time in weeks, she felt safe. Protected.

And she owed it all to him.

V'Aidan captured her hand in his and studied her fingers as if he'd never seen anything like them. There was such a tender light in his gaze that she couldn't understand what caused it.

Moaning so deep in his throat that it vibrated through her, he led her hand to his mouth and ran his tongue over the lines on her palm. His tongue stroked her flesh with featherlike caresses while his teeth gently nipped her fingers and palm. His eyes shuttered, he seemed to savor the very essence of her skin, her touch. Her taste.

Erin shivered at the hot look on his face as he kissed her again. His hands roamed her body, stroking and delving, seeking out every part of her, and stoking her inner fire until she worried it might completely consume her.

He slid his mouth from her lips, down her body to her breast. Erin hissed in pleasure. His hand gently cupped her breast, holding the peak up so that he could take his time tasting it, rolling it over his tongue as he growled again. She'd never seen a man take such pleasure from simply tasting a woman before.

V'Aidan was heaven. Pure and simple heaven. The perfect, attentive lover. It was as if he could read her mind and know exactly where and how she wanted to be touched.

His erection pressed against her hip as his hand sought

out the fire between her legs. Spreading her legs wider for him, Erin trailed her hands over the muscles of his back, muscles that rippled and flexed with every exquisite sensual move he made.

She buried her lips against his throat, tasting the salt of his skin. Chills spread over his body, making her smile that she was giving him pleasure in turn.

Never before in her dreams had she been this at ease with a man. It was the first time she'd made love without worrying if her lover would find fault with her body. If somehow she wasn't good enough for him.

Her dream lover made her feel special. Made her feel womanly and sexy. Hot. Desirable.

She held her breath as he slid his fingers through her moist curls at the juncture of her thighs, separating the tender folds of her body until he could slide his long, tapered fingers deep inside her. Hot fire stabbed her middle.

Groaning at the exquisiteness of his touch, she ran her hands through his silken hair and held him close.

He stroked and teased her body with his fingers as his mouth worked magic on her breasts. The power of his touch, the feel of those hard, defined muscles pressing down on her . . .

It was more than she could stand.

Leaning her head back, she cried out as ribbons of ecstasy tore through her. Still he kept giving her pleasure. He didn't slow down until the last deep shudder had been wrung from her.

Breathless and weak, she wanted to please him the way he had pleased her. She wanted to look into his eyes and watch him climax, too.

Rolling him over onto his back, Erin ran her hand down the perfect tawny muscles of his shoulders, his chest, his abdomen and hips and raked her fingers slowly through the dark curls between his legs. V'Aidan sucked his breath in sharply between his teeth as she trailed her lips over the hard muscles of his chest to his rock-hard abdomen.

And as she laved his tawny flesh, she cupped his hard

shaft in her hand. V'Aidan shuddered in her arms. The look of pleasure on his face thrilled her as he slowly rocked himself against her palm.

She sheathed him with her hands, delighting in the velvety feel of him throbbing between her palms. He ran his fingers through her hair. The muscles in his jaw flexed as he gazed into her eyes while she tenderly milked his body.

"I love your hands on me," he breathed, his voice deep and ragged. "I love the way you smell. The way you feel."

He took her chin into his hand and stared at her with a look that told her he wanted her even more than the dragon had. It was primitive and hot, and it stole her breath.

In that moment, she knew he was going to take her. Take her in a way she'd never been taken before.

Burying her hands in his hair, she couldn't wait for it. She wanted him to possess her.

His eyes flashing and wild, he growled before seizing her lips with his. He kissed her so passionately that she came again as he rolled over with her in his arms and pressed her back once more against the cloudlike moss.

He brought his knee up, between her thighs, and spread her legs wide as he placed his body over hers. She shivered in anticipation.

"Yes, V'Aidan," she breathed, arching her hips in invitation. "Please fill me."

His eyes feral and possessive, he drove himself into her.

Erin moaned at his hardness inside her. She'd never felt anything better than all his strength and power surrounding her, filling her totally. As he moved against her, she feared she would pass out from the bliss of it.

He touched her in ways no man had ever touched her before. As if he truly treasured her. As if she was the only woman who existed for him.

His moves were untamed as he thrust into her. Slow. Deep. Hard.

She wrapped her legs around his, sliding them up and down to feel his leg hairs caress her.

He dipped his head and captured her breast in his mouth,

teasing it mercilessly as he stroked her with his body. She moaned deep in her throat, cupping his head to her.

Then, he leaned back on his legs so that he could stare down at her. Erin swallowed at the sight of him above her as she looked into his eerie silvery-blue eyes. He held her legs in his hands as he continued to drive himself even deeper into her.

His sublime strokes were primitive and hot and tantalizing. And they tore through her, spiking pleasure so intense it went all the way up her back and down to her toes.

V'Aidan licked his lips as he watched her watching him. Erin couldn't move. His eyes held her paralyzed. All she could do was stare at him. Feel him, deep and hard inside her.

She saw his pleasure mirrored in his eyes, saw him savoring her. And when he looked down to where they were joined, she shivered.

"You are mine, Erin," he said between clenched teeth, thrusting himself even harder and deeper into her to emphasize the words.

He took her into his arms and cradled her to his chest as if she was unspeakably precious.

Erin clung to him while she felt her pleasure building even higher. In white-hot sparks she came again in his arms. He buried his face into the crook of her neck and cried out as he joined her.

She lay perfectly still while he shuddered around and in her. His breathing heavy, he didn't move for several minutes.

Pulling back, he looked down at her. "I am with you, *akribos*," he whispered. "I will always be with you."

A strange wave of heaviness came over her. She closed her eyes. Even so, she could still feel and understand what was going on.

V'Aidan draped her over his chest as he lay on his back. She could feel his hands gliding over her while she inhaled the warm, manly scent of his skin.

Even asleep, she felt him near and knew he watched over her, protecting her from the others. And for the first time in weeks, she rested in total peace and comfort.

"Sleep, Erin," he said quietly. "The Skoti can't reach you here. I won't let them."

Erin smiled in her sleep. But as the darkness came for her again, an odd voice rang out in her head.

Now who poses the greater threat to you, Erin? Krysti'Ana or V'Aidan?

CHAPTER 2

ERIN came awake slowly to find herself flat on her back, outside her cube. For a second she couldn't move at all; then her body slowly began to function again.

The first thing she saw was Chrissy's worried frown.

The second was the two EMTs sitting next to her. Her boss, along with several other co-workers, stood off to one side frowning down at her. John's face told her the only thought in his mind was how much paperwork he'd have to fill out over this.

"What happened?" Erin asked.

"You passed out," Chrissy said. "It was like you were frozen or something."

Erin covered her face with her hands as embarrassment filled her. Just her luck to have the most erotic dream of her life witnessed by half her office.

Oh God, shoot her now!

"How do you feel?" the paramedic on her right asked as he helped her sit up.

"I feel . . ." Her voice trailed off. She felt incredible, actually. Better than she had ever felt before.

"Ma'am?" the paramedic insisted. "Are you okay?"

Erin nodded, trying desperately to hold on to the image of V'Aidan, but it faded and left her feeling oddly lonely. "I'm fine, really."

"I don't know," Chrissy said. "She's been acting weird a

lot lately. Hasn't been sleeping. Maybe a short hospital stay where she can sleep—"

"Chrissy!" Erin snapped. "What are you trying to do?"

"Get you some help. Maybe they have something that can make you sleep through the night."

"I don't need to sleep," she said, amazed at the truth of those words. "I feel completely rested."

The paramedic looked at Chrissy. "Her vitals are normal. If she says she's fine, she's fine." He handed Erin a release form. "Sign that and you're on your own, but if I were you, I would go to my doctor just to be safe."

Chrissy gave her a doubtful look.

"I'm fine, Chrissy," Erin insisted, signing the release.

Even so, John told her to go home and take the rest of the week off.

Completely embarrassed, Erin didn't argue as the EMTs left. She merely gathered her things, then headed out of the building, to the parking lot.

Chrissy followed her to the car. "Listen, what I was going to say before John went for coffee and you hit the floor is that my boyfriend is a psychologist who specializes in sleep disorders."

Erin paused at her green Escort. Strange that Chrissy hadn't mentioned that before, but it explained why she had been so interested in Erin's dreams since all this started. "Really?"

"Yeah. His name is Rick Sword and I was telling him about you. He says he thinks he can help." Chrissy handed her a crisp dark gray business card. "I really think you should give him a call."

Erin studied the card. At the moment, she'd never felt better in her life, but maybe she should give him a call just in case the nightmares returned.

"Thanks," Erin said, getting into her car. "I just might do that."

Chrissy stared at her from outside the car and mouthed the words, *Call him.*

Erin waved to her, then headed home, but as she drove

through downtown traffic she really didn't feel like going back to her apartment alone.

In all honesty, she felt rather strange. She could almost sense V'Aidan's presence. She swore she could still smell the masculine scent of sandalwood that had clung to his skin, sense him in her thoughts.

"It was just a dream," she said out loud.

Still, it had been an incredible dream. So real. So vivid and erotic.

So incredibly satisfying.

She stopped at a red light and glanced down at the card on her passenger seat. Before she could talk herself out of it, she grabbed her cell phone and called Dr. Sword.

His receptionist immediately put her through to him as she headed her car toward the expressway.

"Ms. McDaniels," he said eagerly. "Chrissy has told me so much about you. I would really like to speak to you if you have time."

Something compelled her to accept. "Okay, sure. When?"

"What are you doing for lunch?"

Erin gave a nervous laugh. "I guess 'meeting you' would be the correct answer."

His own laughter answered her. "Tell you what. Why don't we meet out in public for the first time? I find it puts people more at ease. Do you like Thompson's Restaurant at Five Points?"

"Okay. What time?"

"How about right now? It should be just opening up for the day."

"Sounds like a plan. I'll be there in about half an hour."

"Good. I'll be waiting."

Erin pulled onto the expressway and headed toward their rendezvous.

Once she reached the mall, she parked her car outside the quaint restaurant that specialized in jazz music and Bohemian food, then headed inside.

There were only a handful of people in the dark interior,

all of whom were seated at tables. It was only then she realized she'd forgotten to ask the doctor what he looked like.

"Erin?"

She turned to see a tall, distinguished-looking man in his early forties entering through the door behind her.

"Yes?"

"Rick Sword," he said, extending his hand out to her.

She shook it. "Nice to meet you."

"Yes," he said with a cool smile. "Yes, it is."

He got them a table in the back of the restaurant, and once they were seated and had placed their orders, he listened as she explained her nightmares to him.

Erin felt a little nervous at first, but as she explained it to him and he didn't appear to judge her, she went into more details.

"And then this guy, V'Aidan, was there and he called the snake monster a Skotos." She paused as she trailed her straw around her Coke. "You probably think I'm nuts by now."

"Hardly," he said, his blue eyes sincere. "In truth, I find you fascinating. Tell me, have you ever heard of the Skoti before?"

"No, never."

"Hmmm, interesting."

She frowned as he made a few notes on the pad he'd carried inside with him. "Why?"

"Well, they're part of history. Tell me, did you ever take an ancient Greek civilization or mythology course in college?"

"No, not really. I mean, we covered the basic Greek pantheon in high school and I had to read the *Odyssey* and *Oedipus Rex* in college, but that was it."

"Hmmm," he said as if he found that interesting, too.

"Why do you ask?"

"I was just wondering how the idea of the Skoti got implanted into your subconscious."

There was a peculiar note in his voice that made her

extremely apprehensive. "What are you saying, they're real?"

He laughed. "That depends on whether or not you believe in the ancient Greek gods. But they were part of that culture. They were, for lack of a better term, nightmare demons. They were said to infiltrate the dreams of humans so they could suck emotions and creativity. It made them high, if you will."

"Like energy vampires?"

"Something like that. Anyway, the legend goes that they would visit a soul a few times during its lifetime and move on. It's how the ancients explained away their nightmares. Supposedly, every so often a Skotos would latch on to a particular victim and go back over and over until the person became insane from the visits."

"Insane how?"

He took a sip of his drink. "The scientific theory behind the legend would be that the visitations, whatever they really were, disrupted normal sleep patterns, causing the victim to never really rest or rejuvenate during the night, thereby causing mental duress. If it continued long enough, it would lead to mental instability."

A shiver went down her spine. This sounded just a little too much like what had been happening to her. "So, how does someone get rid of a Skotos?"

"According to legend, you can't."

"Can I fight them?"

He shook his head. "No, but the ancient Greeks believed in perfect balance. As you have the evil Skotos, likewise you have the benevolent Oneroi who fight them for you."

"Oneroi?"

"They were believed to be the children of the dream god Morpheus. They were champions of humans and gods alike. Incapable of feeling emotions, they spend eternity protecting humans in their sleep. Whenever the Skoti latch on to a human and begin to drain too much from that person, the Oneroi come in and save the human from their clutches."

"Like V'Aidan did me."

"So it would seem."

"And the Skoti, where do they come from?"

"They were the children of Phobetor, the god of animal shapes. His name means 'frightening,' hence their dominion over nightmares."

"So the Skoti and Oneroi are related?"

He nodded.

"Fascinating," she said, mulling over her new knowledge while thinking about her dreams.

Vaguely she recalled the threats the Skoti had made against V'Aidan. Was it possible that somehow these demons had really infiltrated her sleep? Could V'Aidan and the others possibly be real?

It was ludicrous and yet . . .

Her face flamed. If they were real, then she'd just had a one-night stand with a perfect stranger.

"Dr. Sword," she asked seriously, "do you believe they exist?"

His light blue gaze bored into her. "Young lady, I have seen things in my life that would make anyone prematurely gray. I learned a long time ago not to discount any possibility. But personally, I find the idea of Greek gods infiltrating my dreams highly disturbing."

Her face burned even more. "I assure you, you don't find them half as disturbing as I do."

He smiled. "I suppose not." He reached to the small leather case on his belt and pulled out a Palm Pilot. "Tell you what. Why don't you and I schedule an appointment next week to have your dreams monitored? We can hook you up to our machines, put you under a long sleep, and watch your brain waves. Maybe that will give us a scientific clue about what's going on."

She nodded gratefully. "Now that sounds a whole lot better than Greek gods and demons running loose in my dreams."

V'AIDAN sat high above the ocean, perched on a small ledge that barely accommodated his long frame. He'd come to this place as far back as he could remember. Ever since he'd been a young child back at the dawn of time.

It was here he'd come after his ritual beatings that had been designed to strip his feelings and compassion away. Here he'd rested, waiting for the pain of his existence to lessen until he could again find the numbness he was sworn to live by.

Here on his perch he could hear the roar of the waves and stare out at the vastness of the water and feel oddly at peace.

Only now that peace was gone. Shattered.

Something strange had happened to him when he had made love to Erin. It was as if he'd left a piece of himself with her.

Even now, he could sense her. If he closed his eyes, he could even tell what she was feeling.

Worse, he craved her in a way that was all-consuming. He wanted to be with her again, to feel her soothing touch on his skin. He'd never once known such gentleness existed, and now that he did . . .

"You broke a rule, didn't you?"

He clenched his teeth at Wink's voice above him. Looking up, he met two large inquisitive silver eyes that were fastened on him with interest.

Wink was the last god he wanted to see at the moment. The son of Nyx, the night goddess, and Erebus, the embodiment of primordial darkness, Wink was technically V'Aidan's great-uncle and one of the oldest of the gods; however, he acted more like some prepubescent human. His youthful face was always beaming and bright and he wore his long brown hair braided down his back.

The most annoying thing about Wink was that he loved practical jokes and was forever making fun of the children of Myst.

"I did nothing."

"Oh, come on, 'fess up, V. I heard your siblings talking about you. They said you took a human from them and vanished. Now, give me the dirt."

"Go away."

Wink smiled at that. "Then you did do something. Oooh, and it must be good, for you to be so secretive."

V'Aidan stared at the swirling ocean below. "Don't you have something better to do? Like torment gods who can actually get irritated at you?"

Wink grinned even wider. "Sarcasm. Hmm, someone's been around humans a long time."

V'Aidan didn't respond.

He didn't have to. Wink moved toward his shoulder and sniffed like a puppy with a pair of dirty socks. Wink's eyes widened as he pulled back. "You *are* irritated at me, aren't you?"

"I can't feel irritation and well you know it."

It didn't work. Wink came around to float by V'Aidan's side, his eyes larger than saucers. He took V'Aidan's chin in his hand and studied his eyes. "I can see *emotions* in there, swirling, mixing. You're scared."

V'Aidan jerked his chin out of Wink's grasp and pushed him away. "I most certainly am not. I fear nothing. I never have and I never will."

Wink arched a brow. "Such vehement denial. Your kind never feels such passion when they speak, and yet you do."

V'Aidan looked away, his heart pounding. He felt the strangeness of panic in his chest. And he remembered a time once, aeons ago, when he'd been a child and he had dared ask the wrong question.

"Aphrodite, why can't I have love?"

The goddess had laughed at him. "You are the child of Myst, V'Aidan. She is formless, shapeless. Vacuous. The best you can hope for is to feel fleeting, muted emotions, but love . . . love is solid, eternal, and beyond your understanding or abilities."

"Then why can I feel such pain?"

"Because it, like you, is a fleeting phantom. Like the great ocean it ebbs and flows, swelling to titanic proportions, then sweeping down into nothingness. It never lasts for long."

Over the centuries, he had learned the goddess was wrong about pain. It, too, was eternal. It never went away.

Not until he had held Erin.

Closing his eyes, he didn't understand it. What had she done to him?

Wink poked him on the shoulder. "Come on, V, tell me why you are in such a state."

He looked up at his great-uncle. Trust of any kind was as alien to V'Aidan as love. Still, he needed Wink's experience. Wink had been around longer and knew more than he did. Perhaps Wink could give him an insight. "If I tell you what happened, you must swear by the River Styx to tell no one. No one."

Wink nodded. "May Hades chain me in Tartarus, I swear by Styx to never utter a single word of what you tell me."

V'Aidan took a deep breath and braced himself for betrayal. "I had sex with a mortal."

Wink arched a proud brow and smiled. "Nice, isn't it?"

"Wink!"

"Well, it is. I highly recommend it." Wink paused speculatively. "Was it a man or woman?"

"A woman, of course. What kind of question is that?"

"A very nosy one and in keeping with my charming personality."

V'Aidan rolled his eyes. Now he understood what the other gods meant when they said Wink could be a major pain in the ass.

"So," Wink continued, "was she any good?"

A wave of desire tore through V'Aidan, piercing his groin with heat at the very mention of her. Still, he refused to answer that question. It was personal and none of Wink's business.

"Judging by the look on your face, I'll take that as a yes."

V'Aidan growled at his great-uncle and sought to change the subject. "Anyway, something happened."

"Something?"

"It changed me somehow."

Wink snorted. "That's just stupid. If sleeping with a mortal changed a god, there's no telling what I'd be now. As for Zeus . . . perish the thought."

V'Aidan ignored his words. The worst part of all was this incessant need he felt to see Erin again. To feel her hands on him.

He craved her tenderness.

Craved her warmth.

He had to have her.

"V'Aidan!"

Wink paled at the sound of Hypnos's voice. Hypnos was the one god who held dominion over all the gods of sleep. Sooner or later, all of them answered to him.

"Uh-oh," Wink whispered. "He looks mad." Wink vanished, leaving V'Aidan alone to face the old god's wrath.

V'Aidan looked up over his head to see the old man's angry scowl. But since he'd never seen any other look on Hypnos's face, he couldn't judge it. "He looks the same to me."

"V'Aidan," Hypnos growled. "Don't make me come down there to get you."

V'Aidan snorted in response. If Hypnos thought to scare him, he'd have to try something new. V'Aidan had learned a long time ago not to care.

Rising up to the cliffs above, he went to meet the god who made Skoti and Oneroi alike quiver in fear. He alone could give them real emotion.

V'Aidan felt nothing as he approached the old man.

"You seduced a mortal in her sleep."

The accusation hung between them as V'Aidan stared at him.

"What have you to say for yourself?"

V'Aidan said nothing. What could he say? He had committed a forbidden act. Other gods could take humans as they wanted, but not his kind.

He wasn't the first one of his kindred to violate that mandate. However, he wasn't foolish enough to think for one minute Hypnos would be merciful toward him.

He wasn't a favored son.

"You know our code," Hypnos said. "Why did you break it?"

Because I wanted to be held. Just once.

For one moment in eternity, I wanted to pretend someone cared.

The truth tore through him. Regardless of what Hypnos did to him as punishment, it had been worth it.

He would never forget that one precious moment when he'd held Erin in his arms and she had slept peacefully on top of him. Her breath tickling his chest, she had done something no one had ever done before. She had trusted him.

Her warmth had seeped into him, and for the first time since he'd been born, if not love, he had known tenderness. And it had been enough.

Hypnos looked at him as if he were disgusting. Vile. But then, V'Aidan was used to that, too.

"Take him," the old god said, shoving him into the hands of his punishers. "Strip the human taint from his flesh and make sure that he will never forget the pain of it."

CHAPTER 3

It was after midnight before Erin finally found the courage to go to sleep. She was terrified of what her dreams might bring and yet she wanted to see V'Aidan again.

How stupid was that?

He wasn't real and there was no guarantee she'd ever have another dream with him in it.

Still, she wanted a small miracle.

Surrendering herself to the domain of Morpheus, she let her exhaustion take her.

Instead of the falling sensation she'd learned to expect from her dreams, she felt as if she were flying high above the world. For the first time in weeks, she had normal, happy dreams.

No one chased her. No one scared her.

It was heaven, except for the absence of one particular phantom lover.

Sighing in her sleep, Erin saw herself dressed in jeans and a tank top, sitting outside on the porch swing that used to hang on the patio at her Aunt Mae's house. The day was perfect, bright and pleasantly warm with fragrant air laced with honeysuckle and pine. She'd spent so many youthful summers here on this farm in the California mountains.

How she had missed it.

"What is this place?"

She started at the deep, accented voice behind her.

Turning around, she saw V'Aidan leaning against the white porch railing, his hands braced on each side of him, watching her. His long black hair was tied back into a ponytail and those clear silver eyes were guarded. His black button-down shirt only emphasized the perfect muscles of his body, and his jeans had holes in the knees.

For some reason she couldn't fathom, he looked a bit pale and tired, his features pinched. Even so, she was glad he was here.

She smiled at him. "It's one of my favorite places from childhood."

"What did you do here?"

She stood up and approached him, but he quickly moved away. "Is something wrong?"

V'Aidan shook his head. He shouldn't be here. He should have stayed far away from her, and yet . . .

He couldn't.

As soon as she'd fallen asleep, he had felt her soothing presence calling out to him.

Determined, he had fought it as long as he could.

But in the end, it had been futile.

He'd come here against his will. Against his common sense. His body, even though it healed a hundred times faster than a human's, was still sore and aching from his punishment. It reminded him of the high cost he would have to pay again should anyone learn where he was.

She placed her hand on his arm. V'Aidan closed his eyes as pain swept through him. His arms were so incredibly sore, but not even the agony of his wounds could conceal the hot, intense shiver he felt at her touch.

"Come." She slid her hand down his arm to capture his hand in hers. He stared in amazement at their fingers laced together. And he tried not to feel just how soothing her touch was against his skin. How much he wanted to strip her clothes from her and make love to her for the rest of eternity.

"Let me show you," she said.

He allowed her to lead him down the porch steps and across the yard to an old barn. As they walked hand in hand, her imagination stunned him. Her dream was so vivid and vibrant. He'd never visited anyone who had created something so wonderfully detailed.

She released his hand to open the well-oiled doors of the barn and show him where three horses rested inside stalls.

V'Aidan watched her toss a horse blanket over the back of a pinto, then lead it to him. It amazed him that the horse didn't shriek at his scent. Never before had an animal tolerated his presence in a dream. But the brown-and-white pinto seemed completely at ease with him. That spoke volumes about how much power her mind held.

"Have you ever ridden?" she asked.

"No."

She showed him how to mount the horse; then she climbed up to ride in front of him. V'Aidan held on to her waist as she kicked the horse into a gallop and they rode through the fields.

The feel of the animal under him, with her in his arms as they rode, washed over him. He felt so strangely free and almost human.

She rode him out to a lake where they dismounted and the horse vanished into a brown cloud of smoke.

Erin sat on the grass and started picking wildflowers to weave into a crown. Enchanted, he watched her hands blend the stems together into an intricate piece that bore little resemblance to a simple headdress.

While she worked, he drew her back against his chest so that he could hold her.

Just for a little while.

"You are so incredibly creative," he said. "This place is so . . . you," he finished. And it was. Bright, friendly, welcoming. It was everything good.

Everything Erin.

She laughed happily and the sound of it brought a foreign comfort to his chest. "Not really."

"Yes, you are." It was what had made him seek her out originally. "Why do you suppress your creativity?"

She shrugged.

V'Aidan leaned his cheek against her brown hair and traced circles on her stomach with his hand. "Tell me."

Erin had never been the kind of person to confide in others, and yet she found herself telling V'Aidan things she'd never told another soul. "I always wanted to be creative, but I was never any good at it."

"You are."

"No. I tried to play the flute as a girl, and I remember when they were holding auditions for junior high school I went to play my scales and couldn't hit any of the lower notes."

"You were nervous."

"I was untalented."

She felt V'Aidan's breath on her neck as he nuzzled her gently. Heat coursed through her, tightening her breasts.

What was it about his touch that set her on fire? And the more she felt of his touch, the more she wanted him.

"I'll bet you would make a great artist."

Erin smiled at him and the confidence he had in her abilities. It was a nice change of pace. "I can't draw a straight line with a ruler."

He kissed her then. Deep and passionately. His tongue brushed against her lips, sending waves of desire spiraling through her. She moaned against his mouth, cupping his head as needful desire coursed through her.

He nipped her lips. "Maybe you should be a writer."

"That I most certainly can't do."

"Why?"

"I get sick at the thought of it."

He frowned. "Why?"

Erin glanced away as she remembered that horrible day. "I was in college and I wanted to be a writer so badly that I could taste it. In order to major in creative writing, we had to submit our best piece of fiction. So I came up with a short story idea that I thought was great and really different. I worked and reworked it until I was sure it was perfect. I submitted the whole packet to the head of the department and then waited to hear back."

She swallowed as she remembered how she'd learned of the professor's decision. "The *Literary Journal* came out a few weeks later, and in it were all the short stories from the students who were being admitted."

"You weren't in it?"

Her stomach tightened. "I was in it, all right. She had chosen my story to highlight what not to do if you ever wanted to be taken seriously as a writer. She ridiculed every aspect of my story."

His arms tightened around her.

"You can't imagine how humiliated I was. I swore I would never again do anything creative. That I would never put that much of myself into anything to be mocked for it."

Tears stung her eyes and she would have cried had V'Aidan not leaned her head back and run his tongue under her chin to her throat. His body soothed the pain away and she moaned at how good he felt. How safe he made her dreams.

"Why is this so important to you, that I be creative?" she asked.

He pulled back and gave her a hard stare. "Because it's your repressed creativity that is drawing out the Skoti. If you will release it, they will have no fodder for your night-mares."

That sounded wonderful until she thought about it. "And what about you?"

"What *about* me?"

"If the Skoti are gone, will you be gone, too?"

He looked away and she saw the truth of it. Her heart ached at the thought of him never coming to her again. Even though they had just met, she needed him. Liked the way he protected her. Touched her.

As a shy only child she'd lived her life with only a few friends and even fewer boyfriends. She'd never really been close to anyone. Yet she felt bonded somehow to V'Aidan. Felt a connection, a need to be with him.

"I don't want you to leave me."

V'Aidan's heart lurched at the words no one had ever

uttered to him before. He was only used to people trying to drive him away.

She leaned back against his shoulder so that she could look up at him and touch his face.

She was so beautiful there. "Why do you desire my company?" he asked.

"Because you're a champion."

"No, I'm not."

"Yes, you are. You saved me from the Skoti."

He swallowed at that. "If you ever saw the real me, you would hate me."

"How could I?"

He closed his eyes as memories surged through him. This dream with her, it was an illusion. There was no truth to it. What he heard, what they felt . . . all formless delusions.

And yet he wanted it to be real. For the first time in his life, he wanted something true.

He wanted Erin.

"You don't even know what I am," he whispered.

"Yes, I do. You're an Oneroi. You defend people from their nightmares."

V'Aidan frowned. It had been a long time since anyone knew of that term. "How do you know about the Oneroi?"

"Someone told me about them earlier today and I did some research after I got home. I know lots of things about you now."

"Such as?"

"That you can't feel any emotions whatsoever. But I don't believe that one."

"You don't?"

"No. You're too gentle."

V'Aidan was stunned by her words. Gentleness was something he had never thought to hear applied to him. Hypnos would laugh himself into a hernia at the thought.

"Hey," she said suddenly. "Let's do something I have always wanted to do but never had the guts."

"What?"

She looked over at the lake in front of them. "Let's skinny-dip." Before he could answer, she shot to her feet and pulled her top off.

His breath caught in his throat as he stared at her bared breasts. Her nipples were hard and he swore he could already taste them. His body on fire, he took a step toward her and halted only as he felt the pain of his wounds lance up his back. If he undressed, she would see the wounds. See what they had done to him. And he never wanted her to know of it.

"You go," he said. "I want to watch you."

Erin didn't know where she found the courage to undress while he watched. She'd never been so bold in real life. Yet in her dream she didn't mind. In truth she liked the hot, lustful look on his face as she stripped her jeans and panties off and headed for the water.

V'Aidan watched her swim. Watched the water lapping against her bare skin. Her breasts glistened in the light as she floated on her back, and he could see the moist tangle of curls between her legs.

He ached to go to her and spread her legs until he could . . .

He turned away then.

"V'Aidan?"

The concern in her voice tore through him. He had to leave her.

Unable to stand it, he ran through the forest, ignoring the agony of his body. It was nothing compared to what lay in his heart.

Suddenly he felt himself changing. He saw his hands losing their human form. Felt the burning sensation of his skin as his flesh transformed . . .

"V'Aidan?"

His heart pounding, he knew he couldn't stay. Not without her finding out the truth.

Closing his eyes, he teleported out of her dream.

CHAPTER 4

ERIN woke up to the sound of her phone ringing. Groaning out loud, she rolled over to answer it.

It was Chrissy. "Hiyas, chick. How are you enjoying your morning off?"

She would be enjoying it a whole lot more if someone hadn't interrupted her dream while she was trying to find V'Aidan so that she could strip him naked and drag him into the water with her.

"It's okay," Erin said, stifling her agitation.

"Did I wake you?"

"Yes, you did."

"Oh, I'm sorry. Were you having another nightmare?"

Erin smiled at the memory. "No, not a nightmare."

"Really?" Chrissy asked in disbelief. "Not a single second of one?"

"Nope. Now if you'll excuse me, I'd really like to go back to sleep."

"Yeah, sure," Chrissy said with an odd note in her voice. "Why don't you do that?"

Erin lay in bed for a solid hour, trying to go back to sleep to find V'Aidan, but it didn't work.

She felt so good from their time together that she had no choice but to get up.

Aggravated at herself for not having more control over

her ability to go back to sleep, she piddled around the house.

By late morning, she found herself at her computer, staring at her marketing report.

As she worked, V'Aidan's kind, encouraging words drifted through her mind. And before she knew what she was doing, she closed out her spreadsheet and was opening up her word processor.

Erin sat there for hours, typing furiously. It wasn't until late afternoon that she stopped.

Completely happy for the first time in years, Erin stared at what she'd done. Proud of her accomplishment, she wanted to share it with someone.

No, she corrected herself. She wanted to share it with V'Aidan.

She printed off her pages, then took them to the couch. Lying down, she clutched the papers to her chest and willed herself to sleep in hopes of seeing him again.

She found him standing in a meadow. He was dressed all in black right down to his leather biker boots. His jeans hugged his hard thighs, and his black T-shirt looked yummy as it stretched over a chest so lean and toned that it could only be real in her dreams.

The cool breeze tugged at his loose hair, and his silvery eyes shimmered in the daylight.

"I came looking for you," she said happily.

He appeared puzzled by her words. "Really?"

"Yes."

She sat down in the middle of her summer meadow with beautiful jewel-toned butterflies all around her. After their discussion last night, Erin had been trying to let her inner artist out. She wore a light peasant blouse and a loose skirt that rode up on her thighs when she sat.

Best of all, she conjured up a box of Nutter Butter Bites. V'Aidan moved closer. "What are you eating?"

"Nutter Butters. Want some?"

He dropped to his knees by her side. "What are they?"

She ran her hand through the red box and scooped out

a handful to show him the tan-colored circles. "Peanut butter cookies. They're really good, and the best part of all—in dreams, they have no calories."

He laughed at that. "Would you feed me one?"

More nervous than she could fathom, she held a cookie up for him. He licked her finger as he took the cookie into his mouth. "It's delicious. Your finger, I mean."

She smiled at him and kissed his cheek.

He looked so stunned that it was almost laughable.

"Hey," she said, putting the box aside and grabbing up the papers she'd brought with her. "You'll be proud of me."

He arched a brow.

"I wrote today. For the first time since college."

"Really?"

She nodded. "I actually finished ten pages. Want to see?"

"Of course I do." He took the pages from her hands and sat down in front of her to read them.

Erin watched his gaze sweeping over the page. She ached to reach out and run her hands over his glorious body. He was as toned as an athlete. Better still, his taste was more addictive than chocolate.

When he finished, he looked up at her and the proud, encouraging look on his face stole her breath. He was so devastatingly handsome, so warm, that it made her weak.

"Vampires?" he asked.

She grinned. "I know it's a weird topic, but I just sort of channeled them. What I like is that they're so different from other vampire stories."

"They remind me of some people I know."

Erin gaped in disbelief. "Get out! You know vampires?"

"I know lots of them."

"Are you teasing me?" she asked suspiciously, still not sure if he was serious or not. "There really is such a thing?"

He didn't answer. Instead he flipped back through the pages. "You're very talented, Erin. You shouldn't let this go to waste."

Hearing it from him, she could almost believe it. "You think so?"

"Yes, I do."

He set the pages aside and stared at her.

Erin's blouse began unlacing itself. She shivered at the dark, hungry look on V'Aidan's face as he watched it. Slowly, bit by bit, the laces came out of the holes. Her nipples hardened in expectation. Then, the opening widened, baring a single breast.

"Hey!" she teased.

He smiled unrepentantly. "My favorite part of dreams. Clothing is optional."

Erin hissed as he cupped her breast in his hand; then she gave him a whammy of her own.

He looked down at his new clothes with a frown. "What is this?"

She bit her lip at his costume. "You look *good* as a pirate."

He laughed. "Ahoy, matey," he said, laying her back against the grass. "Me cap'n's ship needs a port."

She moaned as he kissed her. "Me cap'n's port needs a ship."

They made love for an eternity. Erin had V'Aidan every way a woman could have a man. She took him under her, over her, and from behind her.

She spent hours running her hands and mouth over all that glorious tawny skin until she knew his body even better than she knew her own. In the end they soared into the sky, where they made love while the stars twinkled all around them.

Erin lay quietly in his arms, just listening to his heart beating under her cheek.

"V'Aidan?" she asked, sitting up to watch him. "Where do you go when you're not in my dreams? Do you visit other women?"

His hot look scorched her. "No. I don't want any other woman."

"Really?"

"I swear it."

She picked his hand up and kissed his palm. "Then what do you do?"

His eyes glowed. "I think up ways to make love to you."

She laughed out loud at the thought. "You know what I want to do?"

"After the night we've had, I honestly can't imagine."

"I want to show you a carnival. Have you ever been to one?"

"No."

Closing her eyes, Erin wished them to a state fair.

V'Aidan was aghast at her world. The bright lights and music . . .

Used to only visiting people in their nightmares, he'd never heard music before. The sound was wonderful and warm.

There were only a handful of people around and he let her take his hand and feed him cotton candy, candy apples, funnel cake, and corn dogs.

In between the food, they rode all kinds of rides that made his head spin. But not nearly as much as the woman herself did.

"Hey!" she said as they approached another booth. "Let's get our picture made. I've always wanted to have an old-timey photo done. What do you say?"

"Whatever makes you happy."

V'Aidan allowed her to dress him up in an Old West outfit while she dressed as a saloon girl, but his favorite part was when she sat in his lap where he could hold her. Better still, the dress she wore fell over them so that her bare thighs rested against his loins. It amazed him how fast his body leaped to life.

How could he want to make love to her when he'd already spent hours lost in her body? Yet there was no denying the fire he felt. The urge he had to free himself from his pants and press her hot, wet body down on him.

"You okay?" she asked, looking at him over her shoulder.

He nodded, even though his groin burned like an inferno.

In the first picture, they were cheek to cheek. The second was with her cradled in his arms, and for the last one she leaned over and kissed his cheek at the very last minute.

Erin took the pictures from the photographer and frowned. "Oh, good Lord," she breathed. "I look like the boobie prize."

"Excuse me?"

Her eyes sad, she handed him the pictures. "You're so incredibly handsome and I'm just a plump, round, average-looking nothing."

V'Aidan felt as though she'd slapped him. "Erin," he said, his voice thick. "You are not nothing. You are the most beautiful person I have ever known."

She smiled weakly. "You're sweet."

V'Aidan stopped her and turned her to face him. "No, I'm not. Do you want to know what I see when I look at you?"

Erin swallowed, her gaze searching his face. "Sure."

V'Aidan handed her the pictures again.

Looking at them, Erin gasped at what she saw. Her mouse-brown hair glowed with golden highlights. Her face had a perfect peachy complexion and her dark brown eyes were bright and shiny. She looked breathtaking.

And it was so *not* her.

"This is what you see?" she asked V'Aidan.

He nodded, his face grim. "That is what you are to me."

Erin reached to hug him, but before she could, a weird buzzing sounded.

V'Aidan vanished instantly.

"No!" she groaned as she woke up to the sound of someone ringing her doorbell.

Disappointed to the point of violence, she got up and answered the door.

She blinked in disbelief. Chrissy stood on the other side.

"Hey," Chrissy said brightly. "Sorry to disturb you, but John wanted me to drop off more data for the report."

Trying really hard not to be snappish, Erin opened the door and took the disks from Chrissy's hand. "Thanks.

Sorry you had to come all the way out here."

"No prob." Chrissy frowned at her. "Were you asleep again?"

Erin blushed. "Yes, I was."

"Are you sure you're okay?"

"Positive."

"Nightmares?"

"Completely gone."

"Oh," Chrissy said, her voice strangely flat. "Glad to hear it. So then, normal dreams?"

Erin frowned at how choppy and odd their conversation was. "Wonderful dreams, anyway."

Chrissy nodded. "Ah, well, that's good. I'll see you later, okay?"

"Thanks again," Erin said as she closed the door.

She leaned her head against the door and cursed. Who or what did she have to kill to have an uninterrupted day with V'Aidan?

OVER the next few days, Erin began to fear even more for her sanity. Not because of her nightmares anymore but because she no longer wanted to be awake.

Every night V'Aidan would come to her. She took him dancing and showed him all kinds of places and things he'd never seen before.

Worse, she learned that he had some degree of control over when she fell asleep. He'd told her he could borrow mist from his Uncle Wink and, much like the Sandman, Wink's mist could induce sleep.

On Friday afternoon when she felt a severe wave of tiredness come over her, she knew what V'Aidan had done.

He was becoming more and more impatient with waiting for her to fall asleep, and in the back of her mind she wondered if one day he would pull her into his realm and not let her go.

When she opened her eyes, she found him lying beside her, his eyes burning her with their intensity.

"Are you angry with me?" he asked, tracing her cheek with his hand.

"I should be. I really wanted to watch that movie."

"I'm sorry," he said, but his face told her he didn't have a smidgen of remorse.

"No, you're not."

He smiled down at her. "No, I'm not, but I don't want you to be angry with me for it."

She laughed at him. "You're evil."

His playfulness died instantly. "Why do you say that?"

She frowned at the hurt look she didn't understand. "I was joking, V'Aidan."

His jaw ticced angrily under her hand. "I never want you to think I'm truly evil."

"How could I?"

V'Aidan dipped his lips to hers, tasting her, wanting to devour her. He needed her and the more he was with her, the worse it became. He'd never known anything sweeter than those lips. Nothing more precious than her small, heart-shaped face.

Erin was overwhelmed by the passion in his kisses. Each one seemed to be even more possessive than the last.

Then he moved his lips lower, over her breasts, where he paused to take his time savoring each mound. As he teased her, white rose petals fell from the sky, covering her.

Erin laughed. "What is this?"

"My gift to you," V'Aidan said. "I want to bathe you in roses."

"Why white?"

"Because, like you, they are pure and beautiful."

Then he kissed her lower, across her stomach, her hip, down her leg, and then up her inner thigh until he kissed her where she ached.

Erin moaned at the feel of his mouth against her, his tongue sweeping across her nub, then down to where she throbbed. He growled, the sound vibrating through her.

He seemed to delight in giving her pleasure first. He

never took his own until she'd climaxed at least twice before him.

She shook in the throes of her first release. When she was finished, V'Aidan pulled back with a devilish grin that made him appear boyish. "I love the way you taste. The way you smell."

She smiled warmly at him. "I love being with you. I don't even want to wake up anymore. I just live moment to moment, wishing I were asleep and waiting until I can see you again."

A dark look crossed his features.

Had those words hurt him? She couldn't imagine how or why they would, and yet . . . "V'Aidan?"

He moved away from her and his black clothes immediately returned to cover his body.

"V'Aidan, what is it?"

V'Aidan didn't answer.

What he was doing was wrong, and not just because it was forbidden. He didn't care about rules.

What he cared about was Erin.

And every time he pulled her into his realm he was robbing her of the pleasures of her own world. Of her life.

This was wrong, and for the first time he understood exactly how wrong it was.

"V'Aidan!" the howling shout echoed through the trees surrounding them.

He knew that angry bellow. "You must leave," he said, sweeping a quick kiss across her lips.

"But—"

He gave her no time to argue before he sent her back to her world and rolled over onto his back to appear nonchalant.

She had barely vanished before M'Ordant appeared to stand over him. Dressed in the same black clothes, M'Ordant looked very similar to V'Aidan. Same black hair, same silvery-blue eyes. The only thing they differed in was height. V'Aidan stood a good four inches taller and he wore the look of a deadly predator.

M'Ordant looked like a person the humans called a Boy Scout.

"What are you doing?" M'Ordant asked.

"I am lying in the sun," V'Aidan said, placing his hands behind his head. "You?"

"Is that an attempt at humor?"

V'Aidan shrugged as he looked up at his brother. M'Ordant was one of the oldest of the Oneroi and was one of Morpheus's most favored sons. "If it were an attempt, it would be wasted on you, now wouldn't it?"

"More humor?"

V'Aidan sighed. "Why are you here?"

"I have heard distressing news about you."

"And to think I thought all news about me was distressing."

That was lost on his brother as well as M'Ordant stared down at him. "Did you learn nothing from your punishment?"

Yes, he'd learned to be more careful seeking out Erin. To tell no one of the precious time they spent together.

"You're boring me, M'Ordant. Go away."

"You can't be bored."

"And a good thing, too, since I'd no doubt perish from it while in your company."

M'Ordant stared at him blankly. "I am merely here as a courtesy. As of this moment, the woman is tagged. Summon her again, and you will deal with me."

"Well, it certainly wouldn't be the first time you and I have crossed."

"True, but I have permission from Hypnos to make it the last time if you interfere with her again."

ERIN went to sleep that night and waited for V'Aidan to show himself.

He didn't.

When she woke up in the morning, she trembled with loss and worry. Had something happened to him?

He'd acted so strangely yesterday. And that shout . . .

What could have happened? Could the Skoti have found him? Hurt him because he protected her?

"V'Aidan," she whispered. "Where are you?"

V'AIDAN ached as he heard the plea in Erin's voice. He stood at her side, so close all he had to do was shift slightly and he would touch her. "I'm here, Erin," he whispered. "I've been here all night."

She didn't hear him.

He'd stayed by her bed the entire time she slept, watching her. Making sure none of the Skoti found her. He was sure Krysti'Ana was behind M'Ordant's appearance.

V'Aidan was all that stood between Erin and Krysti'Ana. So long as he visited her dreams and they were together, his sister would never be able to claim Erin.

Erin's mind was ripe with happiness and creativity. Her dreams were vivid and warm and bubbling over with emotions. Any Skotos would be attracted to her.

And now he could neither protect her nor . . .

His thoughts scattered as she wept.

Pain lacerated his chest at the sight of her grief. She sobbed as if her heart were broken.

Why?

But worse was the helplessness he felt. He hurt for her. "Please don't cry, *akribos,*" he whispered, trying to gather her into his arms.

It didn't work.

He wasn't of her world. He could never be part of her world. Grinding his teeth, he cursed his formless existence.

Erin wept until her eyes grew heavy. Until she was spent and so tired, she couldn't move.

And as she slipped back into sleep, she thought for an instant that she caught a glimpse of V'Aidan in her room.

The next thing she knew, she found herself high on a mountaintop, looking out on the ocean.

The grass caressed her bare feet as the waves crashed on the surf far below. Wind whipped through her hair, plastering her white sundress to her body.

She breathed in the crisp, clean air and listened to the gulls cawing. How peaceful.

Just when she thought her dream couldn't improve, she felt two strong arms wrap around her. "Do you like it here?"

She shivered at the deep accent of V'Aidan's voice in her ear. "Yes, I do."

She turned in his arms to see his hot gaze staring down at her. She trembled at his concerned look, at the handsome lines of his face.

"Tell me why you were crying," he demanded.

"I was afraid something had happened to you."

"And it made you sad?"

She nodded.

V'Aidan shook with the knowledge. He leaned down and rested his chin against her shoulder and inhaled the sweet scent of her skin. She felt so incredible in his arms.

She had worried over him. It was unbelievable.

"Where were you?"

"I was with you," he breathed. "I just thought you'd want a night off."

She laughed at that. "You say that as if being around you is a trial."

"Isn't it?"

She looked aghast at the very idea. "No. Never."

"Why do you like being around me?"

"You make me happy."

He frowned. "I made you cry."

"Only a little."

"And still you want to be with me?"

"Of course I do."

The woman was the greatest fool in history.

He knew he didn't have long before M'Ordant would find them. He'd brought her to his land to help mask what he'd done, but it wouldn't shield the tag permanently.

But before he returned her, he wanted to share one last piece of himself with her before he said good-bye to her forever.

V'Aidan moved away and pointed out to the horizon

that his special perch looked out onto. "Did you know you can see the edge of the world from here?"

"Excuse me?"

He smiled. "It's true. See that gold glinting in the sunlight? That's where the human world begins."

"Where are we?"

"This is the Vanishing Isle. Greek sailors used to believe they would come here when they died so that they could always be near the ocean."

"And why do they call it the Vanishing Isle?" she asked.

"Because you can only see it for a few minutes at sunup and sundown. Much like the pot of gold at the end of a rainbow, you can try to reach it, but you never will."

She looked up at him. "Are you really a Greek god?"

"Would it scare you if I were?"

"Do you want me to fear you?"

V'Aidan hesitated at her question. It was the answer that truly surprised him. "No, I don't."

She smiled a smile that shook him all the way to his heart. "Is this where you live?"

"Sometimes."

"Why only sometimes?"

"There are certain times of the year when I am banned from here."

Her brows drew together into a concerned frown. "Why?"

"The other gods don't like my kind. I am a pariah to all."

"Why would they feel that way? You are a champion."

"Not really. I'm a dream master and not what you see. I'm nothing more than the image you have made for me, but in reality I have no substance. No feelings."

"I don't believe that. A man without feelings would never have helped me the way you have."

He fingered her cheek. "You are so naive. Are all women like you?"

"No," she said with a devilish gleam in her eyes. "I've been told many times that I am highly unusual."

V'Aidan dipped his head down and took possession of her mouth. Erin sighed as she fisted her hands in the folds of his black shirt. "You taste like heaven," she breathed.

He needed to let her go. It was time.

But . . .

He couldn't do it.

Zeus have mercy on him, he couldn't send her back. Not when all he really wanted to do was hold on to her for the rest of eternity.

The air around them sizzled with electricity as the sky above turned dark. Erin trembled in his arms.

"What is that?" she whispered.

It was his death.

"Don't worry, *akribos*," he said, "I will protect you." The emotion behind the words stunned him most of all. He meant them, and for the first time ever he understood them.

Suddenly one of Zeus's lightning bolts hit the ground, driving them apart.

Erin fell several yards from V'Aidan.

V'Aidan tried to reach her, but before he could, ten demon Skoti appeared and surrounded her.

In her snake form, Krysti'Ana laughed, the sound cackling louder than thunder. "Tell me, human," she lisped. "What do you fear more? Dying yourself or seeing him die in your place?"

"Let her go," V'Aidan said, rising to his feet. He summoned his black armor to shield him and he pulled his sword from the air around them.

"Never," Krysti'Ana said with a laugh. "I need her ideas. I need her mind. Look at you. Look at me. See what she has done to us? You didn't make her weaker by releasing her creativity. You made her stronger. I have never been so powerful."

It was true. Erin's mind, her depth of spirit, was a treasure. One he had sworn to himself that he would protect at any cost. "Release her, or I will kill you." He pierced each of the Skoti with a murderous glance. "*All* of you."

Krysti'Ana laughed even harder at that. "You are forbidden to take my life."

"Forbidden or not, I will kill you before I see her harmed."

Erin watched in terror as the Skoti attacked V'Aidan. He fought them with his sword and arms, but he was outnumbered. It was futile. They flew at him, tearing his skin with their claws, shredding his armor.

The she-snake caught him with her tail and slammed him into a tree.

V'Aidan's entire body throbbed as he tried to push himself to his feet. In his human form, he didn't stand a chance against so many of them. He couldn't teleport out and leave Erin behind, and without touching her he couldn't teleport out with her.

"What's the matter, little brother?" Krysti'Ana taunted. "Why do you not change to fight me?"

V'Aidan glanced to Erin and he knew why. He didn't want to frighten her. He only wanted . . .

He only wanted her love.

The thought tore through him. He was to never know such. Was beyond it. But still the need was there. Aching. Yearning.

V'Aidan struggled to breathe. He could live and lose the possibility of her love forever or he could be what she thought he was and die in this human form.

If he died, she would have no one to protect her. . . .

Lost and unsure, he did what he'd never done before.

He called for help. "Hypnos!"

The god's reply came in the form of M'Ordant.

The Skoti backed down, circling back to Erin and Krysti'Ana in a protective circle.

M'Ordant approached him slowly, his face completely void of any emotion. "What would you have Hypnos do, V'Aidan? Would you have him offer you mercy for your crimes? Tell me, is there any rule made which you have not broken?"

"I . . ." He looked to Erin as she struggled against the Skotos holding her. Deep in his heart he had known what

Hypnos's answer would be. He was nothing to the gods. Nothing to anyone.

But at least this way, Erin would be returned to her world and she would be free of the Skoti forever. "Protect her for me."

M'Ordant arched a brow at that. "For you? My job is to protect her *from* you." M'Ordant turned to face the Skoti. "He is yours to do with as you please. The woman, however, belongs to me."

V'Aidan felt the foreign sensation of tears in his eyes as he looked at Erin.

She was safe.

As for him . . .

He didn't want to live without her anyway.

Sinking to his knees, he dropped his sword and waited for the Skoti to carry out his sentence.

Erin screamed as she realized the monsters intended to kill V'Aidan. They circled around him like hungry lions stalking prey.

"Come," the unknown man said, taking her by the arm.

"They're going to kill him."

"If they don't kill him, I will."

"Why?"

He didn't answer. Erin felt the familiar pull of the Oneroi trying to send her home.

But she wouldn't go. She wouldn't leave V'Aidan alone to face the monsters.

Twisting out of M'Ordant's hold, she ran toward the Skoti and shoved her way through them.

She found V'Aidan on the ground, covered in blood. His armor in pieces around him, he lay helpless.

V'AIDAN felt someone tugging at him. The desperate, grasping hands hurt him even more as they rolled him to his back. He looked up, expecting to see Krysti'Ana poised to end his life, but instead he met the dark brown eyes of heaven.

Erin wrapped herself around him, shielded him with her body as she willed herself to wake up. He heard her loud thoughts screaming in his head.

He wanted to tell her to go but couldn't.

His strength gone, V'Aidan could do nothing more than wrap his arms around her and cradle her gently. Her tears stung his wounds and he wanted to tell her not to cry for him. He wasn't worth it.

He'd never been worth anything until she had taught him kindness.

He heard M'Ordant trying to get through the Skoti to pull Erin back, but the Skoti refused.

"I'll have them both," Krysti'Ana snarled. "His life and her mind."

Closing his eyes, V'Aidan summoned the last of his powers. He kissed Erin on the lips, then sent her home.

As she shimmered out of his world, V'Aidan felt himself slipping, sliding down a deep hole. The world shifted and spun. Too weak to fight it, he allowed himself to go wherever it took him, and he was sure that place would be Tartarus.

Not that it mattered. Any day without Erin in his life was hell.

ERIN woke up from her nightmare with a jerk and a scream lodged in her throat. She couldn't be back, not without V'Aidan. She had reached down deep inside her and had fastened on to him with all she possessed.

Her eyes were clenched shut. She didn't want to open them yet.

Didn't want to know that she had left him behind to die.

There had to be some way back to him. Some way to save him.

Her heart pounding, she felt something shift beneath her.

Opening her eyes, she realized she was back in her bed . . . and lying draped over a naked and bleeding V'Aidan.

CHAPTER 5

"Ow," V'Aidan said as he lay in stunned disbelief. His entire being ached from his wounds, but then, he'd suffered a lot worse beatings than this.

Still, in this "real" physical body it hurt so much that he could do nothing more than shake from the weight of the pain.

The only thing that made it bearable was Erin's presence. The softness of her body on his.

And quick on the heels of that thought came the one that if she had managed to bring him here, the others would follow to reclaim him.

V'Aidan had no fear for himself, only that they would come while he was too weak to protect her.

"Oh my gosh, it's you. It's *really* you!"

Erin reached up and touched his swollen jaw where one of the creatures had struck him hard. She brushed his hair back from his forehead and caught the panicked look in his eyes before he shielded it.

Even though bruises and cuts marred his face, she'd never seen anything more spectacular than V'Aidan alive and in her bed.

He was human.

She didn't know how she had managed it. Maybe it was her determination combined with his powers that had been forcing her away from him. Maybe it was a lot of things.

But all that mattered right now was that he was here with her. He wasn't a dream.

V'Aidan was a real-life man.

"I have to get out of here," he said, trying to get up. "I don't belong here."

No, he belonged to her dreams, and yet . . .

He was actually here. With her.

"I'm bleeding?" he asked, looking at his arm in disbelief. "Is this blood? This is blood. I'm bleeding."

She nodded, torn between the desire to cry for his wounds and to laugh out loud that she had somehow managed to bring him back with her.

"I need to get you to a doctor."

"No!" He winced. "I'm not supposed to be here. I'm not . . ."

V'Aidan paused. "I'm not human." He closed his eyes to teleport himself home. It didn't work.

Over and over he tried, and over and over he failed.

His heart pounded. It had been untold millennia since he had walked the mortal realm.

He'd forgotten the vividness of this world. The brightness of the colors and sharpness of sounds and smells.

Erin slid off the bed and disappeared while he tried to sort through it. How could he be here where she could see him?

How could he bleed real blood?

It had to be the fact that his demigod essence had been drained out of him during his beating.

The only way to kill a god was to remove all powers from him, which was what the Skoti had been doing. Erin's mind must have found some way to bring him over the threshold in that last moment before he died.

He should be in Tartarus by now, paying for his crimes for the rest of eternity. But somehow she had saved him. Somehow she had brought him here. There was no other explanation.

The power of her mind and spirit was phenomenal.

Erin returned with a damp washcloth. Carefully she wiped the blood from his face and body.

V'Aidan trembled at the softness of her hand and the way the cloth felt gliding over his flesh. She was always so kind. Until her, he had never understood that concept. Never known what it was to help someone else.

Before he realized what he was doing, he captured her lips, then winced as pain swept along his swollen jaw.

"Ow," he said again, pulling back.

Erin slid her hands over his chest as she inspected his wounds. In dreams, her touch had been muted; now it possessed a tender heat unimaginable. It left him breathless and raw.

V'Aidan reached out and cupped her face so that he could study her beautiful features. "Why are you helping me?"

"Because you need it."

He couldn't fathom such an unselfish reason. Such things didn't exist in his realm.

"You need to rest."

"I need clothes," he said.

"I will have to buy you some."

"Buy?"

"Purchase. You don't just walk into a store and have them give you what you need."

V'Aidan listened to the patience in her voice. Patience he wasn't used to. He knew so little about her human world. He'd been relegated to viewing it through the distortions of dreams and nightmares.

The pain inside him, he did know. It was the only emotion left to his kind. It was why they invaded human sleep. There they could feel other things. Even muted emotions were better than none at all.

"Would you . . . please," he forced the foreign word out, "get me some clothes?"

"Yes."

Incredible. She was so willing to help him. He was baffled by it. Slowly, carefully, he left the bed and walked around her room.

Erin's entire body shook as she left him to fetch a tape measure. How could this be real?

Was she still dreaming? There was a surrealness to this that made it seem like fantasy, and yet . . .

She cursed as she stubbed her toe against the plant stand in her living room.

No, that pain was real.

This wasn't a dream. V'Aidan was really in her world, and if she had pulled him here, maybe, just maybe, she could keep him here.

Erin! What are you thinking? A man like V'Aidan doesn't belong here. He's not even human.

And yet he was more human, more man, than anyone else she'd ever known.

She didn't want him to leave. And that thought frightened her most of all.

V'AIDAN looked up as Erin returned a few minutes later with a strange cloth coil. "What is that?" he asked as she approached him while unwinding it.

"It's a tape measure. I need to know your size to buy your pants."

She wrapped a portion of it around his waist, her hands raising chills on his body, her touch raising another part of him as well.

"Thirty-three waist," she said, her breath falling on his chest.

She sank to her knees before him.

V'Aidan shivered at the sight of her brown hair between his knees as she bent to place one edge of the tape on the floor by his foot. She ran it up the inside of his leg.

Erin swallowed at the strength of his body. And when she reached his groin, her heart pounded. He was rigid and hard, and when her hand lightly brushed his sac, he hissed sharply.

"Thirty-six," she said absently, her gaze catching his.

The heat there was intense, and for the first time, she was actually afraid of him. He was a living man now, one who could possess who knew what strengths and powers in this world.

And they were alone in her house.

V'Aidan took her hand in his and led it to his erection. "I need you to touch me, Erin," he whispered, trailing her hand down the length of his shaft. He shivered from her softness. "I need to know that this is real and not . . . not a dream."

Because deep in his heart he was afraid this was nothing more than Hades tormenting him already. Perhaps he was dead and this was the way they intended to torture him.

Erin quivered at the sensation of his hard, hot manhood in her palm, and his strong, tapered hand leading her strokes. In her dreams, she'd always been uninhibited with him. Her phantom lover had never been real, only a figment of her imagination.

But it was a living, warm body she touched now. One of flesh and blood. A beautiful, masculine body that made her quiver and burn with something more than lust.

The look in his eyes scorched her. And she knew what he wanted. He wanted comfort. He needed to know that she still cared for him. Even in this world that was alien to him.

Was he as afraid of all this as she was?

How long could they be together before their respective worlds tore them apart?

V'Aidan knew he should release her, yet he couldn't bring himself to do it. He needed her. Needed her touch in a way that defied explanation.

She rose up on her knees and, to his utter shock, placed her mouth on him. He moaned at the feeling of her lips against the tip of his shaft, of her hot tongue stroking him. She cupped him gently with one hand, stroking his sac in time with the flicks of her tongue against him.

Never had anyone touched him like this. He felt weak before her. Powerless against her.

And in that moment, he knew he would never again be able to let her go.

Dear Zeus, what was he to do?

She was mortal and he . . .

He was cursed.

Erin stroked and soothed him, and when he released himself she didn't pull away.

Only when he was drained and weak did she pull back and look up at him. Then slowly, meticulously, she kissed her way up his body until she stood before him.

"It'll all be okay, V'Aidan," she whispered. "I promise."

No, it wouldn't. He knew better. There was no way to hide from the others. Sooner or later, they would come.

But he didn't want to scare her. Someway, he would protect her. No matter the cost to him.

He gathered her into his arms and held her close. If he could, he would fly her away from here. Take her back to the Vanishing Isle and keep her forever.

And then he felt it. Felt the evil presence of his sister. The hairs on the back of his neck rose. In this condition he would never be able to stop Krysti'Ana.

The phone rang.

"I'll be right back."

He released her; all the while he looked around trying to find Krysti'Ana. Her malevolence washed over him. Somehow she knew he was here.

He reached out with his thoughts, but in his weakened, wounded state he couldn't contact her.

It didn't matter.

He knew his sister's unspoken promise. She would be coming soon and he would have to find some way to protect Erin from her clutches.

Erin returned. "Sorry about that. It was a friend from work." She headed toward her bathroom. "I'm going to take a quick shower, then buy your clothes, okay?"

He nodded but didn't speak. He couldn't. Not when thoughts of his siblings occupied his mind.

He walked around Erin's small apartment, trying to find where his sister could be hiding. He found nothing, and as the minutes went by, his sense of her grew weaker, though whether from her leaving or from his own diminishing powers, he wasn't sure.

Erin left the bathroom, her face bright and rosy. "I can't

believe I have you here." She threw herself into his arms and held him tight. "Oh, V'Aidan, tell me they can't get you here."

He opened his mouth to answer her honestly, then stopped himself. He didn't want to steal the happiness from her bright brown eyes.

"We're safe," he said, the word sticking in his throat.

She kissed him then, hot and passionately, then left him alone while she went for his clothing.

V'Aidan returned to lie on the bed and rest himself. If he could sleep, he could replenish his strength a lot faster, but he didn't dare close his eyes. Didn't dare fall asleep where he could reenter his world.

They would be waiting for him. With Erin's help, he had escaped them before. But he was sure there wouldn't be a second escape.

Sooner or later, they would take him; then Erin would be alone.

A little while later, V'Aidan heard Erin enter the apartment. Her shoes made the lightest of noises on the carpet; even so, he knew her distinctive walk. Knew her scent, her sound. Knew things about her he'd never known about anyone else.

He turned over in the bed as she entered the room with a bag in her hands.

"I didn't mean to wake you," she said.

"I wasn't sleeping."

She moved forward and set the bag on the foot of the bed, then came to rest beside him. She placed her hand against his brow, then frowned.

"How do you feel?" she asked gently.

"Like I've been beaten."

She rolled her eyes at his blasé tone. "You have a pretty bad fever there. Maybe I should—"

"You can't call a doctor, Erin. Just because I appear human, it doesn't make me one of you."

"I know." She sat by his side and brushed his hair back from his damp brow. "So what are we going to do?"

He took her hand in his and ran the backs of her knuckles along his jaw, which had already begun to heal. Her touch was sublime. He'd never known such a thing existed. "I don't know."

"I was thinking while I was out that maybe we could find a ceremony or something to make you human. Some kind of ritual."

He smiled at the idea. "It's a good thought, love, but there's no such thing."

V'Aidan watched her then, and it was on the tip of his tongue to explain to her exactly what he was. But he couldn't bring himself to do it. Not after they had been through so much.

All he wanted was to enjoy what little time they had, and with that thought, he forced himself to get up.

Erin protested his movements as he dressed. "You're still hurt."

"I'll be fine," he said dismissively. "My kind heals fast."

Erin growled low in her throat as she watched him dress. The man wouldn't listen.

Insufferably male, he refused to relax for the rest of the day. He wouldn't even stay behind and rest while she went to the grocery store.

But she had to admit she really did like having him along. She'd lived alone for so long that she hadn't realized just how much fun someone could have in the produce department.

"So," V'Aidan said as she thumped a cantaloupe, "what are you listening for?"

She held it up to his ear and thumped. "This one is too ripe." Then she held up another one and let him hear the difference. "This one isn't."

She put the good cantaloupe in the cart, then turned around to catch him thumping bananas. Erin quickly grabbed them away from him. "We don't thump those."

"Why?"

"It'll bruise them."

"Oh." He looked around, then paused. "What about those?"

She turned to see the grapes. "Only thump if you want to turn them into wine."

He pulled her into his arms. "What about if I thump you?"

She smiled. "I'd probably make all kinds of interesting noises if you did."

He grinned at that and gave her a quick, scorching kiss that sent heat throughout her entire body.

As they walked through the store, Erin couldn't help noticing the stares V'Aidan collected. She became aware again of just how different the two of them were. He was tall, sexy, and gorgeous and she was plain and simple.

She'd only had a few boyfriends and most of them had been as average-looking as she was. But V'Aidan . . .

He deserved a beautiful woman.

"Hey?" he asked as they reached the dairy section. "Are you all right?"

"I'm fine."

"You look sad."

"Just tired."

She saw the concern in his celestial eyes. "How tired?"

It was then she caught his meaning. "They'll be after us again when we sleep, won't they?"

He looked away and she had her answer.

"If they don't kill him, I will." M'Ordant's words echoed in her head.

"I won't let them have you," she said, taking V'Aidan's arm. "There has to be some way we can fight them."

He draped his arm over her shoulders and held her close. "You would fight for me?"

"Yes."

"Then I am the luckiest being in the universe."

V'Aidan gave her a tight squeeze as he inhaled the scent of her hair. And he wondered morbidly if she would feel that way if she knew the truth of his past.

If she ever knew the truth of him . . .

He wanted to tell her. But he didn't dare.

V'Aidan clenched his teeth. She would never know, any

more than he would let her be harmed because of him. He would fight this battle, all right. Fight until either he won or they killed him. But he would do it the way he had lived since the dawn of time.

Alone.

He and Erin finished shopping and were putting their items in the car when V'Aidan heard a woman shrieking in the dark parking lot.

He saw a man running away.

"Oh, no," Erin breathed. "He stole her purse."

Without thinking, V'Aidan took off after the man. He caught up to him at the alley beside the grocery store.

The man turned on him with a gun and aimed it straight at his heart. "Don't mess with me, man. I'm your worst friggin' nightmare."

V'Aidan couldn't help laughing at his words. "You have no idea."

The man fired the gun. V'Aidan ignored the bullet that entered his chest without pain or blood. He took the purse from the man, then caught the thief by his throat and held him back against the wall.

It was then V'Aidan felt himself slipping. He felt his true form welling up. His hand went from that of a human to—

"V'Aidan?"

Erin's voice brought him back. He recovered himself and stared at the thief, who was now ghostly pale from having witnessed the changes on V'Aidan's face.

"The next time you want to steal from someone, think of me waiting for you every time you close your eyes."

The thief quietly wet himself.

Erin ran up behind him with a security officer in tow. V'Aidan released the thief into the officer's custody, then handed him the woman's purse.

"Are you all right?" Erin asked, her eyes falling to the hole in V'Aidan's shirt where the bullet had entered his flesh. Mortal weapons couldn't harm an immortal being.

V'Aidan nodded. His powers were returning.

"Take me home, Erin," he said, his heart tugging at the word. He'd never had a home before. Never really understood the meaning of the word and what it entailed.

Until now.

He followed her to her car and they drove back to her apartment in silence.

In fact, they spoke very little as Erin made their dinner and they ate it.

Afterward, he helped her clean up and watched her closely. What would it be like to stay here, like this? To have this woman by his side every night? If he had such, he would never make her hurt. Never let her want. He would do anything in his power to shelter and comfort her.

But all the wishing in the world couldn't make it real.

It was only a dream. . . .

Once they were finished cleaning up their dinner, they lay entwined on the couch while she watched television.

V'Aidan watched her. He held her cradled to his chest, feeling her breath fall on his skin.

Love me, Erin.

The words hung in his heart, unspoken as he ran his hand through her hair. He had no right to ask for her love. Had no right to ask anything of her.

"You are a scourge, boy. Despicable. Unsightly and cold. No one will ever welcome something like you. It's why you have to creep into their dreams. It's the only way anyone will ever have anything to do with you."

All too well he knew the truth of Hypnos's words.

Over the centuries, he had hardened his heart to the world. To everything. He'd shut himself off completely until the night when a pair of fear-filled brown eyes had looked up at him with kindness and hope.

Now, he just wanted a way to live out his life staring into those eyes. Feeling her tiny hands on his skin.

Erin listened to V'Aidan's heart beating under her cheek. He smelled of warm sandalwood and spice. She ran her hand over where the thief had shot him, still amazed that no scar or wound remained. It was an awful reminder of the fact that her entire day with V'Aidan had been an illusion.

He wasn't born of her world. And no doubt tonight they would be parted for eternity.

The thought broke her heart. She couldn't stand the thought of not seeing him again.

If this was her last night with him, then she wanted it to last.

Crawling up his body, she met his gaze and saw the hunger in the crystal silver gaze. She cupped his cheek in her hand and kissed him.

V'Aidan growled at the taste of her as his body roared to life. He tore the shirt from her as he rolled to press her down into the couch.

Erin heard the cotton fabric tear but didn't care. She wanted him with the same desperation. She pulled his shirt over his head and feasted on the sight of his bare chest. Only scars remained of the wounds he'd suffered, and he'd told her that, by tomorrow, if he survived tonight, even those would be gone.

He removed their clothes so fast that she could barely follow his moves. He leaned her up against the back of the sofa arm and drove himself deep into her.

They moaned in unison.

She wished she could keep him inside her forever. She never wanted another day without him in it.

V'Aidan made love to her feverishly, savoring every deep stroke. He caressed her breasts as he kissed her, felt her from the top of his head all the way to his toes.

Her warm body surrounded his, fit him to perfection. And the feel of her hands on his back . . .

It was bliss. Pure bliss. He closed his eyes and delighted in the feel of her breasts on his chest, her tongue on his throat. Oh, yes, he wanted to stay here with her.

Forever.

Erin ran her hand through his long hair, her fingers

clenched as pleasure ripped through her, each thrust deeper and harder than the last. She wrapped her legs around his waist, bucking her hips in time to him. Drawing him into her body even deeper. She clung to him as she came, crying out his name.

He kissed her lips and quickened his pace until he released himself inside her.

Erin lay still, feeling his essence fill her. She didn't want to move, didn't want to feel him leave her.

"I love you, V'Aidan," she said before she could stop herself.

V'Aidan froze at the words. Pulling back, he stared at her in disbelief. "What?"

Her cheeks turned pink as her brown gaze shredded what was left of his heart. "I love you."

"You can't. It's not possible."

"Possible or not, I do."

V'Aidan gathered her into his arms and held on to her desperately. He shook from the force of what he felt for her. So powerful, so overwhelming.

Sated to a depth he'd never known before, he pulled her on top of him and listened to her even breaths as her sleep took her.

He wanted to wake her up but knew better. Unlike him, she had to have her sleep.

"Erin," he whispered softly as he stroked her hair. "I promise you, I'll always be what you think I am."

Resigned to the inevitable, he closed his eyes and waited for M'Ordant and Krysti'Ana to come for them.

CHAPTER 6

V'AIDAN woke up to a piercing screech that felt as if it would shatter his eardrums.

He groaned at the awful sound as Erin stirred on top of him.

"What is that?" he asked.

"My alarm clock," she said, rising from him to rush to her bedroom.

It wasn't until her return that they both realized what had happened.

Nothing.

"Did you have any dreams?" he asked.

She shook her head. "You?"

"No," he said, smiling.

"Do you think . . ."

His smile faded. "No. They can find us. Sooner or later, they will."

Erin closed her eyes and cursed the thought of it. "Maybe they won't bother." She saw the doubt in V'Aidan's eyes.

Wanting to cheer his dour mood, she pulled him up by his arm. "C'mon. Let's take a shower and then I'll call in sick to work."

"You can't. What if you get fired?"

She shrugged. "I'll find another job."

He shook his head at her. "You are amazing."

She smiled at him.

Erin called into work only to be reminded of the marketing report that had been due on Friday, which she had forgotten to drop off.

"The meeting is at noon," John told her.

"Okay, I'm on my way up there with it."

"Is something wrong?" V'Aidan asked as she hung up the phone.

She shook her head. "I just have to take something to the office. Want to come with me?"

"Sure."

They didn't speak much as she drove across town. V'Aidan held her hand the entire time and Erin had to admit she liked the strength of his hand wrapped around hers.

Once they reached her building, Erin led V'Aidan into the maze where her cubicle was. He watched the hustle and bustle of corporate life with a dispassionate stare.

Erin went to John's office, only to find it empty.

With V'Aidan directly behind her, she dropped the report in John's in-box, then turned to leave.

Chrissy stood in the doorway with Rick Sword behind her. The two of them stepped into the office and closed the door.

Erin heard V'Aidan curse.

What the devil was going on?

"What are you doing here?" V'Aidan asked, his voice laced with anger.

"Waiting for you." Chrissy stepped around them and pulled the blinds closed. "You won't dare fight us in her workplace, will you, V'Aidan? All we have to do is make ourselves invisible to the humans and they won't see or hear anything but her. And *her* they'll lock up in an asylum as soon as we're gone."

Erin still didn't understand what was going on. But she had a sick feeling that she had been duped from the very beginning by all of this.

If V'Aidan could be real, then so could they.

"What is this?" Erin demanded.

Chrissy's eyes flashed to yellow and it was then Erin knew the truth.

Chrissy was the she-snake from her nightmares.

"Stay out of it, human," Rick said. "We will deal with you after we finish with him."

V'Aidan pulled Erin behind him.

"How very sweet." Chrissy's tone was mocking. "One would think you were Oneroi they way you coddle her."

"He *is* Oneroi," Erin shot back, her entire body shaking from panic. How could she and V'Aidan fight them here? Like this?

Rick laughed at her words. "Is that the lie you told her?"

V'Aidan held his breath. He didn't want her to find out like this. "Erin, I . . ." His words faltered as he turned to see the confused look on her face.

He didn't want to tell her the truth. He didn't want to be what he was anymore. She had shown him something better and he didn't want to go back to the way he'd been.

"What does she mean?" Erin asked.

"He's your dragon," Krysti'Ana said mercilessly. "The thing I fought the first night we met in your dreams."

"No." Erin shook her head. "It's a lie. V'Aidan, tell me it's a lie."

He wanted to, but he couldn't. He'd lied so many times that it shouldn't have mattered to him. Yet it did.

"I'm a Skotos, Erin."

Her eyes filled with tears. "It was you! You who made me so terrified I couldn't sleep? You who chased me and . . . and . . ." She couldn't even begin to recount the torture he had put her through during those first few weeks. She had thought she was losing her mind. "Why did you trick me into thinking you were Oneroi? Was it just so you could feed from me?"

"At first, I only wanted to get you away from Krysti'Ana. I knew you wouldn't go with the dragon, so I appeared to you as a man. And then later . . ." His voice trailed off as his eyes went dead.

"You lied to me."

"I know."

She backed away from him. The agony in her eyes sliced him.

V'Aidan clenched his teeth as grief washed over him. "I needed you, Erin. And I didn't know how else to keep you with me." He reached for her.

She cringed and the gesture tore through him. She no longer wanted his touch.

Like all the others, she, too, rejected him.

The hurt betrayal on her face made him feel lower than any of the insults the others had ever dealt him.

"I should have known," she whispered, "someone like you pretended to be could never really want someone like me."

V'Aidan winced at the pain in her voice. "Erin, don't say that. You are the most wonderful person who has ever been born."

"Is that another of your lies?"

V'Aidan closed his eyes. There was nothing he could say to make this right. He'd been wrong from the very beginning.

All he could do now was make sure no other of his kind hurt her.

"M'Ordant!" he called, summoning his brother to him.

The Oneroi appeared between Krysti'Ana and Rec'Sord.

V'Aidan took a deep breath. "I will go with them peacefully if you will keep them from her."

"It is my job, is it not?"

V'Aidan nodded. It was the job of the Oneroi to help. It was the job of the Skotos to use and destroy.

He turned to look at Erin, but she refused to meet his gaze. Judging by the tears she fought, he would say he'd done his job very well this time.

His last view of her was when M'Ordant wrapped his arm around her the way he yearned to.

Krysti'Ana and Rec'Sord grabbed him to take him home.

"I'm sorry, Erin," V'Aidan whispered as they shimmered from her realm into his. "I'm so very sorry."

Erin didn't move. She knew V'Aidan was gone. She'd heard the sincerity of his apology as he vanished. But inside she was all raw emotions. Raw betrayal. She kept seeing the horrible dragon in the cave. Feeling the scaly talons on her.

How could that be the same man who had made love to her? The same man who had made her love *him*?

The betrayal of it lacerated her heart. Why? Why had he made her believe in him?

"I don't understand any of this," she said to M'Ordant.

"Sh," he said, brushing her hair back from her face. "Krysti'Ana and Rec'Sord wanted you for their own, but V'Aidan got to you first. When she found out he'd beat her to you, she was livid."

"But how did he find me?"

"Something in your subconscious called out to him. He was only supposed to give you a single nightmare and move on, but he didn't."

"And Chrissy?"

"When she couldn't take you from him, she called in her mate, Rec'Sord. I was alerted shortly thereafter to protect you. I told V'Aidan to leave you. He refused."

Her head swam from M'Ordant's information and from the pain and hurt inside her. "Why did he refuse to leave me?"

"I don't know. I guess it's just what he is. The Skoti suck the hopes and dreams out of others. I suppose he got a kick out of playing the hero with you. Building you up so he could hurt you more."

Erin felt so foolish. So betrayed. How could she have been so blind?

The eyes, she thought with a start. She should have realized the eyes were the same color.

Was she really that desperate for a hero that she would accept a demon in disguise?

Suddenly, she felt ill.

Heartbroken, she headed home, wanting to forget she had ever heard of V'Aidan.

ERIN sat alone for the rest of the day, thinking, remembering.

"You should be a writer." V'Aidan's kind voice echoed through her head.

It wasn't the demon she remembered as she sat on her couch, clutching a pillow to her middle; it was the man. And as she sat alone in her apartment, she realized she would never again see him.

Never be able to share her day or her thoughts.

Most of all, she couldn't tell him her dreams. V'Aidan might have started off by feeding from her, but in the end he had given her so much more.

He had been her friend as much as he had been her lover.

The loss tore through her.

But what could she do? He was back in his world and she was in hers. It was over.

There was nothing left.

In the end, the Skotos had won after all. V'Aidan had drained all her happiness, all her hopes, all her dreams. What was left was an aching, empty shell that wanted nothing more of this world or the other.

As the days went by, the pain of betrayal began to lessen and Erin remembered more of her dreams.

The more she remembered, the more she wanted to see V'Aidan one last time. Could she have been so stupid as to let him completely fool her?

She didn't think so.

V'Aidan wasn't that cruel. She'd seen things in him that defied what she knew him to be. His words came back to her. Words of protection. He had taught her to release her creativity to keep the Skoti away.

And there at the end . . .

"I will go with them peacefully if you will keep them from her."

No, those weren't the words of a monster. Those were the words of a man who cared more for her safety than for his own. Such a man, regardless of what M'Ordant had told her, was not all evil.

Desperate, Erin went to sleep, trying to find V'Aidan again. It didn't work.

Erin woke up in the middle of the night, terrified. Where was V'Aidan and why wouldn't he come to her?

For more than a week she tried everything she could think of to reach V'Aidan. Nothing worked. And as every day passed, she hurt more.

There had to be some way to contact him.

DISCOURAGED and heartbroken, Erin sat at her desk, dazed. She'd barely slept in days and she was so weary.

"V'Aidan," she whispered. "Why won't you talk to me?"

"Erin," John said from his doorway. "In my office. Now."

By the tone of his voice she figured she was in serious trouble. No doubt he was going to fire her for missing so much work.

What did she care anyway? At this point, she was only going through the motions of life. Nothing was important to her now. She'd lost the only thing that gave her life meaning. The only one who had ever believed in her.

Soul-sick, she got up and walked the short distance to John's office.

"Close the door. Sit down."

She did as he commanded.

He sat there for several minutes, sipping his coffee, reading his E-mail.

She wondered if he had forgotten her. Then he turned, pulled his glasses down the bridge of his nose, and stared at her. "It's awful, isn't it?"

"What?"

"Loving an immortal."

Erin had a sudden urge to clean out her ear. "Excuse me?"

"Oh, come on, don't play innocent with me. Why do you think Chrissy was working here?" He pointed to the dolphin tattoo on his left forearm. "I'm an oracle for the Greek gods. Which is why I'm so damned tired and cranky all the time. They have the most annoying habit of bursting in when you least expect it." He sighed disgustedly. "The least they could do is pay me, but oh no, I was lucky enough to be born into this. And benefits . . ." He snorted. "No sleep, no pay, no peace. Got to love it."

She disregarded his tirade. "So, you're like the Oracle of Delphi? I thought they were all women."

"Those particular oracles are, but not all of us are female. Obviously. We are merely human channels to the various gods."

Totally baffled, she stared at him, wondering if maybe this was a dream, too, or if the Big Guy had lost *his* mind. Something wasn't right, at any rate.

"Okay, so you're an oracle. Want to tell me why you hired Chrissy if you knew she was a dream-sucking monster?"

He shrugged. "She is a god and I have no choice except to serve her. She wanted a chance to scope out human targets. I merely provided her a safe cover."

"You sold me out?"

"No," he said, his stern look turning gentle. "They weren't supposed to drain you the way V'Aidan did. Trust me. What he did was wrong. And you can rest assured he is being adequately punished for it."

Her heart stopped at the forbidding note in his voice. "Punished how?"

"What do you care?" he asked, pushing the glasses back up on his nose. "You're rid of him. Right? No more Skoti in your dreams. You have your life back to yourself."

"I want to know." No, she *needed* to know what had happened to him.

John took a drink of coffee. "Why, they sent him to Tartarus, of course."

Erin didn't understand the term, and at the moment she wished she'd paid more attention in school. "Is that like jail?"

"Oh, no, hon. It's hell. They killed him the minute they took him back to his realm."

Erin couldn't breathe as tears welled up in her eyes. The weight in her chest was excruciating. It wasn't true. It couldn't be true. "They killed him?"

"Didn't you know?" he asked simply. "Didn't he tell you what they were going to do to him? V'Aidan was never one who played by the rules. He'd already been banned centuries ago from taking human form and banished from this realm."

"Why?"

"Because he would pretend to be human. Skoti are not supposed to have any creativity of their own. They're not supposed to want love. Not supposed to want anything except a single night of dream surfing, hopping from one person to the next. He'd behaved for centuries, until he found you. Even after they stripped all his skin from his immortal body, he couldn't stay away from you."

John sighed. "Hypnos had already banned his transformation powers, so he decided there was nothing more to be done with him. Since V'Aidan wouldn't obey him, they sent him to Tartarus for the rest of eternity."

"But he didn't hurt me. Not really."

"Didn't he? You look awful from here. Like you've been crying for months. And I swear you've lost at least ten pounds since all this started."

"That's not his fault."

"No?"

"No. I don't want him to suffer because of me."

His gaze searching hers, John pulled an envelope out of his desk drawer and handed it to her.

"What's this?"

"Open it."

Frowning, Erin did as he said and saw the three pictures of her and V'Aidan at the carnival. Her hand shook as grief and agony swirled in her heart. "Where did you get these?"

"M'Ordant sent them to you. He thought you might like them as a souvenir."

She stared at V'Aidan's handsome face. At the love in his eyes.

"I have to see him," she insisted.

John shook his head and sighed again. "Well, I'm afraid it's too late now."

"It can't be. Please. I need to see him again. Please, tell me there's some way I can reach him.

John narrowed an intense gaze on her. "That depends on whether or not you really love him."

ERIN still couldn't believe what she was doing. She'd allowed John to teleport her into the Underworld, where he'd told her M'Ordant would be waiting to guide her to V'Aidan.

Not that she really believed in the Underworld, but at this point . . .

M'Ordant materialized in front of her. "Are you sure about this?"

"Yes."

Nodding, he led her through a deep, dark cavern that reminded her much of the one V'Aidan had used to torment her. They walked for what seemed like miles before they came to a small cave.

A light was shining inside and she could hear a man's voice speaking. "You're thinking of her again, aren't you?"

She looked inside and saw the once-proud dragon lying weakly on the floor with his back to her. Someone had chained his neck to a large boulder. His shoulders were slumped, his wings lying broken and useless on the earthen floor. His reddish skin had an ashen, dehydrated look and every inch of his body was covered with bleeding welts.

Erin swallowed at the sight. Could that monster really be the man she loved?

"What's her name?" the man asked. "Elise? Erika?"

"Erin," the dragon rasped, his voice both familiar and yet foreign to her. "Her name is Erin."

"Ah, yes, Erin." The man shook his head. "Tell me what kind of worthless fool gives up immortality for a woman?

Especially a woman who threw him so quickly to his death?"

"She was worth it."

"Was she? M'Ordant told me she was dreaming of a man last night. Some golden-haired type. Got to figure that if she's dreaming of someone so soon, she's probably already got him picked out and is ready to sleep with him. Bet she's giving him the high hard one even as we speak."

The dragon let out an anguished cry that tore through her.

The man didn't seem to care. He dumped food and water into two containers and moved them away from the dragon. "You'd better hurry. I don't think you've made it yet before your food evaporated." Then he vanished.

Erin watched as the dragon struggled to reach the food and water. His wounds bled anew as he limped, straining against the boulder that would only barely budge. He held one to his heart, and when she saw what it clutched, her own heart splintered apart in pain.

It was that stupid wreath of wildflowers she'd made.

V'Aidan collapsed just before the water, his claw reaching out desperately for it.

Tears streaming down her face, Erin ran to where he lay. She grabbed the water, noting half of it was already gone, and as she touched the container, she knew why. It was red-hot. It burned her hands, but she didn't care.

V'Aidan needed the water.

Kneeling down, she helped him sit up enough so he could drink.

V'Aidan gasped at the liquid as it soothed his parched throat. His eyes were so swollen from his beatings that he couldn't see who helped him. All he knew was that at last he had a moment of peace from his burning thirst.

"Thank you," he breathed, laying his head back down.

"You're welcome."

He froze at the voice that had stayed with him all these weeks. The voice that both soothed and tortured him.

It was then he felt her gentle touch against his scaly flesh.

Erin cried over what they'd done to him. She ran her hand along his rocky flesh, unable to believe they had reduced him to such a state.

He tried to push himself away from her. "Go. I don't want you to see me in this hideous form."

She laid her cheek against his and held him close. She now understood what he'd meant that night at the carnival. "I don't care what you look like, V'Aidan. I love you as you are."

Those words tore through him. "You're not real," he said, his voice ragged. "My precious Erin can't love a monster. No one can. She is goodness and light, and I . . . I am nothing."

He looked up and roared at the ceiling, "Damn you, Hades! How dare you mock me like this, you bastard! Isn't it enough for you that I ache every minute of every hour for her? Just leave me to suffer in peace."

Erin refused to let go of him. "It's not an illusion, V'Aidan. I want us to go home. Together."

Tears welled in his swollen eyes, stinging them unmercifully. It was a cruel lie. He'd never had a home. Never had love.

He pulled against the chain that choked him, wishing for one moment that he could be with Erin again in her dreams. It had been the only time in eternity he had ever known happiness. "I am damned here, Erin. I have no powers. Nothing to offer you at all. You must go. If you stay here too long, they won't let you leave."

Erin looked around his cold, dark prison that smelled and slithered. She'd never seen a more inhospitable place. Her worst fear had been being stuck in this cave with the dragon.

But if that was what it took to have V'Aidan, then she was willing to do it. "I'm not going to leave you again."

He lifted his head and she could tell he was trying to see her. "What are you saying?"

"I'm saying that if you can't go home with me, then I will stay here with you. Forever."

V'Aidan gaped at her. "You don't know what you're doing." He pushed at her with his talon. "Go!"

She didn't move. "I will not leave you."

He gathered her into his arms and held her close. "If you really love me, Erin, you won't stay. I could never stand the thought of knowing you were here because of me. Please, love, please go and never look back."

Erin sat in indecision, holding his talon in her hand. How could she leave him here, like this, knowing no one else would help him? Comfort him?

M'Ordant moved forward and pulled her away from V'Aidan, then walked her to the opening, where he kept her still.

For several minutes, V'Aidan didn't move at all. Then he lifted his head and tried to look around.

"Erin?" he asked quietly. "Are you still here?"

M'Ordant motioned for her silence. "She's gone now."

V'Aidan's lip quivered with sadness. "You sent her home?"

"Yes."

"Thank you." He lay down as if all his strength had been stripped from him.

"Tell me," M'Ordant said. "Why didn't you want her to stay with you?"

"You wouldn't understand."

"Understand what?"

"Love."

M'Ordant snorted. "What does a Skotos know of love?"

"Absolutely nothing . . ." He took a deep breath. "And everything. I couldn't ask her to stay here when I know how much this place scares her."

"But you wanted her to stay?"

V'Aidan nodded weakly. "More than I want my freedom. Now, leave me, brother."

Erin wiped the tears from her face as she stared at M'Ordant. She gave him a hopeful look.

"Can I stay?" she whispered so that V'Aidan wouldn't hear her.

His face impassive, M'Ordant shook his head and led her from the room. "It's not up to me."

"Then who?"

He refused to answer. "You have to leave."

"I won't leave him," she said, her voice firm. "And no one is going to make me."

Erin found out those were famous last words as she came awake back in her office. When dealing with Greek gods, human will didn't amount to much.

Heartbroken, she wept, thinking about V'Aidan in his hell and the fact that she was the cause of it.

Worst of all, there was absolutely nothing she could do to help him. Nothing.

"V'AIDAN."

V'Aidan clenched his teeth at Hypnos's voice. He tucked Erin's wreath under a nearby rock to keep the god from seeing it and taking it from him as he had done the pictures.

It was all V'Aidan had of her and he couldn't bear the thought of losing it.

He forced himself upright and cleared his throat of the grief that choked him. "I didn't realize it was time for more punishment."

Hypnos snorted. "I can't break you, can I?"

He sensed the god moving around him.

"You know," Hypnos said irritably, "I have tried since the dawn of time to make you fear me. And you never have. Why is that?"

"I can't feel emotion, remember?"

"No. What you are is disrespectful, irreverent, and sarcastic. You have never fit in with us. And the thing that has always made me maddest with you is that you never even tried to."

V'Aidan gave a weak laugh. "A Skotos who is evil to the bone, imagine that."

"Well, therein is your problem. Unlike the others, you never were. I never could kill that last tiny bit of goodness in you. That last bit that was capable of honor. Capable of sacrifice."

V'Aidan frowned.

"M'Ordant told me what you did with Erin. Both on earth and here. As a result, Hades has informed me that he can't keep you in Tartarus. Only souls who are completely incapable of love can stay here."

A burning sensation started in V'Aidan's body, and with every heartbeat that passed, he felt himself growing stronger.

"It seems to me, boy, you have a decision to make."

ERIN opened the door to her apartment. The familiar hole in her heart burned as she imagined what it would be like to come home, just once, and have V'Aidan here.

She'd been doing that a lot lately. Daydreaming. She'd never really daydreamed before. And she'd been writing. But there was no one to share it with.

That hurt most of all.

Toeing her shoes off, she set her keys down on the mantel and happened to see a white rose petal on the carpet. She frowned as she noticed several more.

They seemed to form a trail leading to her bedroom. She followed them.

When she got to the doorway, her heart stopped.

V'Aidan was asleep in her bed. His sleek black hair was spread out over the pillows, the covers tangled in his long, tawny limbs.

He was the most gorgeous thing she'd ever seen in her life.

Erin laughed as tears welled in her eyes. How? How could he be here?

Rushing to her bed, she dropped to her knees and tried to wake him.

He didn't budge.

No matter what she tried, he wouldn't wake.

"V'Aidan?" she said, swallowing in fear. "Please, look at me."

Nothing.

Terrified, she saw a small note card on the nightstand. Picking it up, she read it:

> *It is through true love that all miracles are performed. If you really love me, Erin, kiss my lips and I will be born into your world as a mortal man. Otherwise, I shall be waiting for you only in your dreams.*
>
> *You have until midnight to decide.*
>
> V

She didn't need until midnight to decide. Cupping his face in her hands, she kissed him with all the love in her heart.

His chest rose sharply as his arms wrapped around her and held her tight.

Erin laughed happily as V'Aidan deepened their kiss. Her head swam from his warmth, his passion, and she never wanted to let him go.

Nipping her lips, he pulled back to smile at her. The love in his silvery-blue eyes scorched her. "I take it you want to keep me?"

"Buddy, you try and leave me and I'll follow you to the ends of the earth and beyond to find you and bring you home."

V'Aidan laughed. She'd already proven that to him.

Erin shivered as he unbuttoned her shirt. "I think I know what you want to do first as a mortal man."

He ran his tongue over her throat, up to her ear, where his breath sent chills through her. "Believe me, love, you won't be sleeping tonight."

EPILOGUE

Two years later

V'AIDAN lay on the sofa with his infant daughter asleep on his chest. He stared at her mop of chestnut curls, curious about what she was dreaming.

He felt his wife standing over them.

Looking up, he caught Erin's gorgeous smile. "Hi," he said, wondering what she was up to. There was a gleam in her eye much like the one she'd had the day she'd told him she was pregnant.

"Guess what?" she asked, her voice rife with excitement.

"You're pregnant again?"

She rolled her eyes at him. "It's only been three months since we had Emma."

"It happens."

She blew him a raspberry, then brought her arm from around her back and shoved a book into his hands.

V'Aidan stared at it blankly until the name on the cover registered. "Oh my God," he breathed, "it's your novel."

"I know," she said, jumping up and down. "My editor sent me the first copy of it! They'll be shipped to the stores next week."

Careful not to wake the baby, V'Aidan shot off the couch to grab Erin into his arms.

Erin sighed at the feel of his lips on hers. Even now, those lips could incinerate her. And his smell . . . Goodness, how she loved the scent of his skin.

"Thank you, V'Aidan," she said, pulling back to stare into those hauntingly silver eyes. "I would never have written it without you."

"And I would never have lived without you."

Erin held him close, delighting in the feel of him and her daughter. The two of them were the greatest gift Erin had ever known.

And it was then she realized that even out of the darkest nightmare, something good could come. It had taken strength and courage, but in the end, it had been worth the battle.

"I love you, Erin," he whispered against her hair.

"I love you, V'Aidan, and I always will."

UNDER HER SPELL

MAGGIE SHAYNE

Dedicated with love to all
the members of RavenMyst Circle, Inc.

REDE OF THE WICCAE

by Lady Gwynne Thompson
as given by her grandmother, Adrianna Porter
(Being Known as The Counsel of the Wise Ones)

1. Bide the Wiccan laws ye must in perfect love and perfect trust.
2. Live and let live—fairly take and fairly give.
3. Cast the Circle thrice about to keep all evil spirits out.
4. To bind the spell every time, let the spell be spake in rhyme.
5. Soft of eye and light of touch—speak little, listen much.
6. Deosil go by the waxing Moon—sing and dance the Wiccan rune.
7. Widdershins go when the Moon doth wane, and the Werewolf howls by the dread Wolfsbane.
8. When the Lady's moon is new, kiss the hand to her times two.
9. When the Moon rides at her peak, then your heart's desire seek.
10. Heed the Northwind's mighty gale—lock the door and drop the sail.
11. When the wind comes from the South, love will kiss thee on the mouth.
12. When the wind blows from the East, expect the new and set the feast.
13. When the West wind blows o'er thee, departed spirits restless be.
14. Nine woods in the Cauldron go—burn them quick and burn them slow.

15. Elder be ye Lady's tree—burn it not or cursed ye'll be.

16. When the Wheel begins to turn—let the Beltane fires burn.

17. When the Wheel has turned a Yule, light the Log and let Pan rule.

18. Heed ye flower, bush and tree—by the Lady blessed be.

19. Where the rippling waters go, cast a stone an truth ye'll know.

20. When ye have need, hearken not to other's greed.

21. With the fool no season spend or be counted as his friend.

22. Merry meet an merry part—bright the cheeks and warm the heart.

23. Mind the Threefold Law ye should—three times bad and three times good.

24. When misfortune is enow, wear the blue star on thy brow.

25. True in love ever be unless thy lover's false to thee.

26. Eight words the Wiccan Rede fulfill—an it harm none, do what ye will.

CHAPTER 1

THE gorgeous brunette clenched her hands into fists at her sides, her torn blouse gaping just enough to reveal the swell of her artificially enhanced cleavage as her chest heaved in anger.

"You'll never get the best of me, you black-hearted Warlock!"

The Warlock, whose shirt had been conveniently ripped off during the struggle with the Enchantress, stood facing her, his clenched, just slightly unshaven jaw and black eyes flashing defiance. "Oh, but I already have," he said in a sexy growl.

"What are you waiting for? Vanquish him!" shouted the blonde, an innocent bystander whose bosom was also enhanced, exposed and heaving.

The Witch marched forward, clutching an ancient-looking book, which she had opened to a faded parchment page. Tossing her hair and lifting her chin, she read aloud in a rather tedious monotone, " 'By your own power of dark and fear, Warlock, you are out of here!' "

The Warlock flung his arms over his face and staggered backward, through the breakaway front door. His exit would be much more impressive once they added in the special effects, Melissa supposed. There would probably be flashes of fire, whirlwinds of smoke, and a thundering roar. She'd been watching this show for a while now. There were always flashes of fire, whirlwinds of smoke, and thundering roars.

The director yelled, "Cut!" and the others in the room broke into spontaneous applause.

Melissa pinched the bridge of her nose between her thumb and forefinger. "That was awful. It was horrible. My Goddess, where are you people *getting* this stuff?"

"From the writers," a deep voice said.

She turned and looked at the guy who, she thought vaguely, should have been playing the sexy "warlock." His eyes were as black as coal and she felt them when they touched her. They made her shiver, those eyes. She tried to look elsewhere, to notice his careless hair, a little too long, completely unstyled, or his clothes—the way the black polo shirt strained against the push of his chest or the way the jeans hugged his thighs. But no, she couldn't focus on anything but those eyes.

"Are you new on the set?" he asked.

"Um, not yet." She swallowed hard, wet her lips, told herself to work harder on forming coherent sentences, and finally thrust out a hand. "I'm Melissa St. Cloud. I have an appointment with Alexander Quinn."

He lifted his brows. "Tell me it's about the tech consultant position."

"It's about the tech consultant position."

He smiled, a slow, knowing smile. His eyes seemed unable to let go of hers.

She tipped her head to one side, wondering who the hell he was. A stand-in for the dark warlock? The actors were already heading their separate ways; the two starlets didn't speak so much as a civil word as they split. But then, never breaking eye contact, the gorgeous man yelled, "Everyone, get back here. I want you to hear this!"

Muttering, they gathered around. He nodded at Melissa. "Now, tell us what was wrong with that scene."

The brunette shot her daggers. "Who *is* this person?"

"Just be quiet and listen, Rita," he said in that deep, authoritative voice that rubbed all Melissa's nerve endings until they quivered. God, she'd never been so turned on by a man in her life. There was something about him. He looked at her, touched her with his eyes. She shivered with awareness. "Go on. What was wrong with the scene?"

She swallowed the dryness in her throat. "Well . . . that's just not how it works. Reading a line from a book, no matter how old and dusty it might be, is *not* how one casts a spell. And a warlock is *not* a male Witch."

The actresses exchanged looks of disbelief; then they turned on the man, waiting. "Alex, just what the hell is going on here?" the blonde asked.

Alex? So *he* was Alexander Quinn, the creator-slash-executive producer? Why hadn't he said so?

"This is Melissa St. Cloud," he told them. "She's our new technical consultant."

"On what?" the brunette asked.

"On Witchcraft."

All eyes turned toward Melissa. She felt herself shrinking a little. The actresses were both a good six inches taller than she was and built of little more than skin, bone, and breast implants.

"You're an *expert* on *Witchcraft*?" the brunette asked. "Isn't that kind of like being an expert on, oh, I don't know, the Tooth Fairy?"

The others laughed. Alex just watched Melissa, as if waiting to see how she would handle herself.

Melissa closed her eyes, got in touch with her inner bitch, and stood a little straighter. "I've been involved in the Pagan community and the study of Witchcraft for fifteen years," she told them. "I'm a High Priestess, a licensed minister, and I hold a Ph.D. in religious studies. I teach Alternative Religions classes at UCLA one semester a year, and I've consulted on seven books on the subject. Any more questions?"

The actresses rolled their eyes, sighed, studied their nails. They did not, however, speak up again.

"Ladies," Alex said, "the network has been inundated with mail complaining that we are getting it wrong. It seems there are a lot of people out there these days who take this kind of stuff rather seriously. In today's market, the viewers are more savvy than ever before. If we want to suspend their disbelief, we have to be as accurate as possible."

"Do you hear what you're saying?" asked the blonde. "How can you be accurate about something that doesn't exist?"

Melissa sent her a swift glance. "Oh, it exists."

"Oh, please. Fine, it exists. And you're a real-live modern-day Witch. So why don't you prove it? Levitate one of us or make something disappear." She crossed her arms under her breasts, pushing them up even higher. "Well? Go on, we're all waiting."

Melissa turned to Alex. "That," she said, "is precisely the kind of misinformation that's messing up your show." Then she glanced back at the girl. "But somehow, I don't think explaining all of this to a bunch of actors is going to get us anywhere. After all, they only recite the lines the writers give them and follow the director's orders." She returned her attention to Alex, dismissing the actresses without another word. "We should probably schedule a sit-down meeting with the writing team."

He smiled very slowly, his eyes warming. "You want it, you've got it." He nodded to the others, a signal that they could leave; then he took her arm.

When his hand closed around her elbow, she shivered with an inexplicable tingle of pure sensation. My God, she had it bad. And the guy was her new boss.

Not a good situation.

He led her to a small room on the set, created by free-standing partitions with a door in them—no ceiling. Inside was a desk strewn with piles and piles of paper, a coffeemaker, and a chair. He nodded to the chair. "Sit."

She sat.

He perched on the edge of the desk, close to her. Really close. "Those credentials you were reciting in there—they all legit?"

She blinked her eyes. "You didn't already know? It was all in my résumé—I sent it in with the job application."

"Oh. Right."

"You did read it, didn't you?"

He looked away. "I got a pile of résumés. Looked them over, but after a while they all blend together. I had my secretary set up a bunch of interviews, of which you are the first."

"But . . . you hired me."

"Yeah." Again he couldn't seem to break eye contact, though he did at length. He reached for a piece of paper and a pen. "Jot down your name, address, Social. I'll get you on the payroll this afternoon."

She jotted while he watched her every move. When she finished, he took the sheet, looked at it, then at her.

"Anything else?" she asked.

He licked his lips. "Yeah." He got up from the desk, stood next to her, and bent low to pull open several drawers. His forearm brushed her thigh and she closed her eyes and wondered if an attraction this potent could possibly be for real or if she'd accidentally eaten a dose of Spanish Fly with her morning granola. This close, she could smell him—the soap he used, no cologne. He wasn't a cologne kind of man. And she could feel him—his body heat.

He finally straightened with a six-inch-thick stack of pages, which he handed to her. "This is the story arc for the season, along with the breakdowns for each episode. You're going to need to get familiar with it. Fast."

She took the heavy stack, rose slowly to her feet.

"I'll be in touch later, to let you know when we've scheduled your meeting with the writing team. You have any questions?"

She had a thousand, but right now she just wanted to get out of there. She couldn't think straight this close to the man. So she just shook her head from side to side.

"Good. Go on home, then. Read. I'll see you later."

She turned and left the studio. And it wasn't until she was in her VW Bug and heading home that she realized she had actually landed the job of her dreams. Smiling widely, she thanked the Goddess and kept on driving.

• • •

ALEX figured his mind settled back into working order when she got about fifty yards away from him. He sank into his chair. It was still warm from her body. "What the hell was that?"

He didn't get an answer. He didn't believe in magic. And it was a good thing, or he'd have thought the woman had cast some kind of a spell on him. And yet, he had no doubt he'd chosen the right person for the job. The show—his creation—was in trouble. The ratings were dropping, the actresses were feuding, the sponsors were fading, and the right-wing zealot groups were boycotting the sponsors. He was no Hollywood insider, but he was sure as hell swimming with the sharks now.

The charm he wore around his neck burned against his skin. A deep whisper echoed in his mind.

Perfect. It'll all be perfect. You have the Midas touch, you know.

He frowned, looking around the office. But he saw no one there. It must have been a snippet of dialogue from one of the nearby soundstages. Sounded excellent. Creepy, with an otherworldly hollowness to it. They must be working on a horror flick or something.

He leaned back in his chair and turned on the radio to drown out the noise, and then he tried again to figure out what it was about the woman that had hit him so powerfully.

CHAPTER 2

MELISSA drove to the beach house, an hour away. She had rented it for the summer, with the option to buy if things worked out for her here. And it looked as if they were about to work out Big-Time.

A little voice whispered misgivings—it wasn't like her to experience such intense feelings for a man she'd just met. It was more than unlike her; it was unprecedented. And she had the niggling feeling there was something more going on with Alex than was apparent—something hidden beneath the surface. Something . . . unnatural.

Her body's reactions to him puzzled her—simultaneous chills and heat, fire and ice, assaulted her at once. She was curious, wary, and attracted.

And she knew better than to feel any of those things. The man was her employer! She had to get her head straight. She had to get to the beach.

She loved the sea, the shore. The East Coast had always beckoned her, touched something deep inside her, and been her home.

The Pacific had a different energy to it. A darker, older feel. As well it should. The sun set here. It rose in the east. The two seas were opposites and yet they were reflections of the same cosmic whole, the great pouring sea of death and rebirth.

She left her VW Bug in the driveway and hurried into the

house she was quickly coming to love, peeling off her clothes on the way through. Then she stepped into the shower to rinse away the day's stress and the distinct weight of negative energy she felt clinging to her. She scrubbed it away, along with her makeup, her hair spray, and the frustration of coming face-to-face with the stereotypes that drove her nuts; let all of that baggage swirl down the drain.

When she stepped out again she felt measurably lighter. She pulled on a loose-fitting cotton kaftan of soothing turquoise, and nothing else. Then she padded barefoot through the small house and out the sliding doors in back. There was a natural stone shelf there, almost like a home-grown patio, and at its edge, steps led down to a tiny section of private beach. The beach house was modest. It was the beach that made the place valuable—far more than she could have afforded for much longer, had it not been for this new job.

The strip of beach was secluded, with the house at its back, groups of towering boulders flanking it, and the sea creating its fourth border. That sandy enclave had become her haven, her refuge, and her temple.

Here she could work magic. And she had no need for special effects.

ALEX looked at the address he'd copied down, then up at the beach house. The numbers matched. He had the right place.

He was fascinated by the woman, the Witch. Mesmerized, maybe. He couldn't get her off his mind after she left, and though he'd fought the demanding urge for a while—a token fight, really—he'd ended up giving in and driving out here. He didn't feel as if he had much choice in the matter. And it wasn't just due to the insane events of the past few weeks of his life, either. There was something about her that lured him, pulled him, like gravity.

She lived on the beach. It seemed fitting. He thought of legends of sirens luring sailors to their doom and wondered if this was the same sort of pull those sailors felt.

He climbed the shallow landscaped steps to the front door

and knocked. Then he waited, but there was no answer. A car was in the driveway, but no one seemed to be in the house.

And then the wind picked up and he heard it: a woman's voice, lifted in an enchanting, mesmerizing, haunting song and coming from the beach around back. He followed the sound, picking up the words as he went around the beach house.

"Come, Mother Ocean; come, Lady Night; come, Warrior Woman; come, bring your might."

He found the steps in the back and stared down at the woman on the beach below. And that thing, that powerful attraction he'd felt before, washed over him again like an ocean wave washing over the shore. For a moment, he couldn't breathe. He could only stand there, looking on, wondering what it was about her that sent his head spinning and tied his stomach in knots.

She stood in the sand, arms raised high above her head, a flowing blue dress dancing around her legs in the ocean breeze. There was a small fire crackling in front of her, its light melding with the orange glow of the sun, as it set over the ocean, to paint her body and hair in brushstrokes of bronze and yellow and red.

"Come, Moonlight Maiden; come, Graveyard Crone; come, Dark Enchantress, Goddess of the Foam."

Her voice seemed to grow hypnotic, more mystical with every verse she sang. As the sun sank over the sea and darkness gathered like a blanket, surrounding the firelight and the woman in its center, he noticed for the first time other tiny lights—candles, planted in the sand. Four of them, one just ahead of her, toward the sea, one to either side of her, and one behind her. And there was something on the sand in between them, leading from one dancing candle to the next in a gentle arc so that a circle was formed. As he was drawn ever closer, he squinted. Seashells. The circle was made of seashells.

"Come to thy priestess; come, fierce and strong; come, live within me; come, we are one!"

The words wound themselves around his mind. The final

three kept echoing in an ever-fading whisper, and he found himself unsure whether it was real or some trick of the night. His knees bent, without his permission, and he sank into the sand, watching her in silence. The sun breathed its last and vanished beneath the waves at the same moment he sank down.

Slowly, she lowered her arms. Her hair danced in the wind that was suddenly more powerful than before. She stood for a long time, facing the sea, meditating or pondering in silence. Sometimes, he thought he saw her lips moving, as if she were speaking to someone. Time ticked by, but he didn't make a sound. He couldn't bring himself to interrupt, wasn't even certain he would be able to if he tried. What she was doing seemed . . . sacred. And he got the feeling he was witnessing one of the mysteries he had come here hoping to solve. So he watched as she moved around the circle, wafting incense smoke, tossing something—a glittering stone, he thought—into the sea. Finally, she straightened and lifted her arms again.

"Thank you, my lady. Merry meet and merry part. With me always, in my heart. Hail and farewell."

He could see something leave her body, perhaps just tension or tautness. Or maybe something more. The glow of the firelight seemed to dim just a little, but that could have been his imagination. She walked forward then, to one of the four candles, held her arms out wide, and slowly drew them together, as if closing a pair of curtains. She said something too softly for him to hear as she snuffed the flame, stood still for a moment, then repeated the action at the next candle, and then the next, and the last. Then she walked around the circle of seashells with her palm flat toward the sand, and finally she moved out into the foamy water that washed gently up onto the shore, knelt there, and pressed her palms into the wet sand. A wave rolled in, washing up to her elbows, soaking the dress where she knelt. Yet she remained until it seemed she had finished whatever it was she was doing. Rising, she brushed the sand away from her hands and her dress, turned, and looked him straight in the eye.

"Thank you for not interrupting."

He blinked, surprised. "You knew I was here the whole time," he said, and it wasn't really a question. He had a feeling this woman was as aware of him as he was of her.

She smiled. The firelight on her face did something to her eyes. She'd been beautiful to him when he'd seen her at the studio today. Beautiful, though it made no sense. It wasn't on the surface, certainly not when she'd stood flanked by two of the most glamorous beauties in the business, wearing a rather conservative skirt and blazer, her hair in a bun, her face lightly made up. His sense of her beauty had been based on something inside her, something not seen.

Now, it was more. Now, like this, she was stunning. Inside and out.

"You can come out by the fire, if you like. I've already taken up the circle." As she spoke, she walked back toward the fire. "Grab those two folding chairs and bring them along, will you?"

He glanced to his left, saw two beach chairs sitting there. He picked them up and carried them with him across the sand to where she waited, setting them near the fire.

She sat down, and he did the same. He couldn't seem to stop looking at her, trying to nail what it was that drew him. There was something wildly attractive about her. Forbidden and natural. Her eyebrows were fuller than most women wore them these days, and her hair—God, her hair was everywhere. Untamed, long and wavy, its color a lustrous honey-tinted brown that glowed bronze in the firelight. Her feet were bare, coated in damp sand. Her breasts were heavy and unbound underneath the loose, flowing dress she wore. He liked that best of all. The weight of them. He wanted to touch, to feel.

"I'm surprised to see you here," she said. Was she nervous? She should be. He didn't know what the hell this was, but it made him nervous, too.

"I told you I'd see you later. I always say what I mean." He reached up, impulsively, to brush a bit of sand from her cheek. But the moment his fingers touched her skin, she stiffened and pulled back, her brows drawing together in a frown.

"I'm sorry." He drew his hand away, held it in midair.

She only blinked, looking him over. "It's not you—it's . . . Stand up a second, Alex."

He was puzzled, but he rose. She did, too, going closer to the fire and bending to pick up a large shell with some dried leaves inside. She took a flaming stick from the fire and touched it to the leaves. They blazed a little. She blew gently until the flames died, and smoke billowed. Then she moved toward him, knelt in front of him, and blew the smoke at his legs and feet.

Alex closed his eyes in a mingling chaos of anguish and desire. God, she was killing him.

She moved behind him, still blowing. Then higher, her breaths pushing smoke toward his thighs and buttocks. She came around to the front of him again, blowing gently at his groin.

"Jesus," he muttered, and his hands twitched, wanting to bury themselves in her hair. He fought the urge and hoped she didn't notice how hard he was getting, but hell, he was only human, and there was an earthy wild woman kneeling in front of him blowing on his crotch.

She stood, still moving around him, still blowing gently, wafting smoke over his belly and chest, his back and sides, his arms and shoulders, his neck, face, and head.

When she finished, she blew a little smoke at his chair and the area where he'd been sitting. "Better?" she asked.

He looked down at himself, frowning. When he managed to look past the fact that he was more turned on than he'd been in a decade, he realized he felt . . . different. As if he'd just stepped out of the shower. And the dull ache that had been knotting his lower back all day was gone. "Yeah," he said. "I do feel better."

"You should. You were practically reeking with negative energy."

"Yeah?" He sniffed his shirtsleeve. "And now I'm reeking of . . . ?"

"Sage." She smiled at him, sitting down in her chair,

nodding for him to do the same. "Who have you been hanging around with lately, anyway?"

"What do you mean?"

She shrugged. "Well, I'd hate to think all that darkness in your aura was coming from you. It couldn't, or I wouldn't be so—" She bit her lip, stopped herself. "You must be picking it up somewhere else."

"You wouldn't be so . . . ?" He searched her eyes and wondered which one of them was going to be the first to admit that they were each sitting here thinking about ripping the other's clothes off.

She averted her gaze. "Nothing. I just . . . nothing."

He licked his lips. No, he wouldn't bring it up. Not just yet, he decided. "Could it be the actresses?"

"They're nasty, self-centered, and vain, but I don't think they're malicious. This feels . . . dark."

He shrugged, averting his eyes, ignoring the warning bells going off in his mind. He'd been feeling the same way himself for weeks now. As if there was some dark shadow clinging to him like a parasite. He was tired, moody, didn't feel well. He kept thinking it might be the house. But damn, he didn't *want* it to be the house.

Time to change the subject. "So what were you doing when I arrived? Magic?"

"Not really."

It was not the specific answer he would have liked. "Listen, you have the job. This isn't a test. But I want to know more."

"About what I was doing when you arrived?"

He held her eyes. "For starters." She just looked at him, waiting, as if she knew he wasn't being honest. "All right," he admitted. "What I really want is the truth. What really goes on?"

Her brows rose. He decided he liked them. You couldn't tell what a woman was thinking when her eyebrows had been reduced to a pair of plucked, waxed, colored, and extremely thin arches. Hers were expressive. Now they were expressing—what? Surprise?

"What really goes on?" she repeated.

"Not the kinds of things you would normally reveal to an outsider. I want the truth. I want to know what it's really like. Ritual magic. Covens. Spells. Curses. All of it."

She lowered her eyes. "I'm not sure you have the stomach for it, Alex."

His stomach knotted up when her lips formed his name and her voice spoke it. He tried to shake off the feeling. What he was asking her was important. More important than she could know. "I have the stomach for anything you can dish out."

She tipped her head to one side, meeting his eyes once again. Hers glittered with something close to anger. "Are you sure? We're talking about some pretty heavy stuff here. Bloodletting. Ritual orgies. Animal sacrifice. The Scourge."

He held her eyes, his own unflinching. "I can handle it."

She pursed her lips and turned her head away. "We don't do any of that stuff, Alex. My God, where do you get those ideas? This is a spiritual belief system, not a cult." Lowering her head, she shook it slowly. "You created the show—are you telling me you didn't do any research at all?"

"Of course I did. I just—lately I've learned some things that contradict what I thought I knew."

"From whom?"

He shook his head. He wasn't going there, not with her.

"Tell you what," she said. "I'll loan you a book or two, so you can read up on the subject. And then we'll talk some more. All right?"

She's lying.

He frowned, ignoring that whisper in his mind. "You're going to give me one of those light, fluffy, 'harm none' books, aren't you?"

"Harm none is one of the core values of the Craft, Alex."

"So you all keep telling me."

"We all?" she asked. Then she frowned. "You sound as if you've been doing some digging on your own."

He nodded, getting to his feet, frustrated and angry. Even

more angry that he didn't want to leave this spot, this woman. He wanted to stay. For her, not the information he sought. "I really hoped you'd be different. Willing to tell me the truth," he said. "I'm disappointed that you're only giving me the same party line as the rest of the so-called Witches in town."

"So-called?" She got up as well. "Maybe if you told me just what it is you're looking for?"

He sighed, shaking his head. "Look, Melissa, not every character in this show is a do-gooder. I mean, we need opposing forces. Villains. The polar opposite of good Witches who play around with white light and moonbeams."

She stood very still, pinning him to the spot with her eyes. "Alex, don't mess with the dark stuff. You don't want that kind of energy clinging to you, trust me on this." Then she frowned. "You've already been messing with it, haven't you? That's where all that negative energy came from."

He held her gaze. Eyes like black velvet, deep and dark and potent. "Don't be so dramatic. It's not as if any of this is for real."

She closed her eyes as if praying for patience. "It's for real." Her words emerged as a whisper, one that sent shivers of reaction creeping up his spine, into his nape, tingling along his scalp. But not so much as when she opened her eyes again and they locked onto his, held them.

Something moved between them. Some energy he couldn't have put a name to even if he'd tried. It tagged him, bodily, so much so that he swayed forward. He gripped her upper arms, and she tipped her face up. And then he lowered his head to kiss her.

She turned her face away, so his mouth only grazed her cheek.

"I don't . . . I can't . . ." She drew a breath. "Go, please," she whispered.

God, the woman pulled him in like gravity. What the hell *was* that? Since when did he hire a woman he knew nothing about and proceed to make a move on her?

He turned and hurried back up the stone steps, around

the little beach house, and to his car. He would get his answers, just apparently not from her.

He drove back to the gloomy mansion that belonged to him, pulled into the driveway, and sat there for a long moment, just staring up at the huge granite stones of the place, thinking about the events of the past several weeks, as if thinking about them, analyzing them, would cause them to make sense. They didn't. They hadn't then, and they wouldn't now.

And now there was one more inexplicable event unfolding in his life. An attraction to a woman he'd just met that felt like the most powerful force in the entire universe. God, maybe he needed therapy.

CHAPTER 3

Mists rose from the river far below, engulfing the suspension bridge and the couple who stood upon it. Melissa stared through the rising mists at the man, who bore a striking resemblance to Alexander Quinn, except that he wore black ritual robes and an inverted pentacle of solid gold with diamonds winking at each of its five points. The woman stood near the railing, her back to the man, her flowing white dress dancing in the mist-laden breeze like a living thing. Her wild golden hair was damp with the kiss of the moist air. Melissa couldn't see her face, but she knew the woman was weeping.

The man spoke, though his lips never moved. *Go on. Do it. Do it, now!* He pulled something from his pocket, a small white-robed doll with hair like the woman's. *Do it!* He shoved the doll toward the railing.

The woman climbed over it.

"No," Melissa whispered. "No, wait."

But neither of them could hear her. It was as if she weren't really there.

The man moved closer to the rail, held the doll out over the water. As he did, a pair of hands, strong astral hands, attached to nothing and no one, appeared behind the woman, hovering above her shoulders.

The woman turned, as if suddenly aware of the presence, and Melissa gasped as she saw her face. It was almost like looking into a mirror.

Do it! the man commanded, and then he flung the doll over the rail.

The hands closed on the woman and pushed her.

She fell silently, her white dress wafting behind her. Like an angel cast from heaven, she spiraled downward. The water opened where she plunged into it, then closed around her, swallowing her down.

Melissa screamed.

The sound of her own voice shocked her awake, and she found herself sitting bolt upright in her own bed. Her skin was damp with sweat, her heart pounding, as she looked around the room. But it was real. She was there, in the beach house, and the rest had just been a dream.

"No," she said softly. "Not a dream. Something else—a prophecy, or a memory, or something—it was too vivid to be just a dream."

She glanced at her nightstand. The clock read 2:00 A.M. A soft, steady beep emanated from somewhere in the living room, startling her for just a second, before she recognized the familiar sound of her answering machine. Somehow, she'd been too deep in the vision to have heard the telephone ringing. Sighing, she got out of the bed, padded into the living room, hit the playback button, and then shivered at the sound of Alexander Quinn's deep voice.

"We're meeting with the writers in the morning, Melissa. Ten A.M., my office." The machine beeped once more to signal the end of the message and then went silent.

Pushing a hand through her hair, she wondered if she should just quit now and have it over with. She wandered through the living room, toward the table in the back where she'd dropped the script he'd given her the day before. As she did, she looked up, through the glass doors.

And she saw something on the beach—a shape, with long golden hair and a flowing white gown.

Her heart tripped and she lunged forward, hands pressing to the glass, eyes straining. What the hell . . . ?

There was nothing there. Maybe it had just been a reflection, a trick of the moonlight on the water, or a stray light on her glass doors. But she couldn't quite shake the feeling that she'd just seen the woman from her dream, standing in the sacred space of Melissa's own circle.

She checked her locks, just in case. Then she picked up the manuscript and took it with her, back to her bed, where she felt safe.

She wanted to do this job right—and for more reasons than just the money. She'd made a promise to her Goddess that if she could land this job, she would do it justice, set the record straight on prime-time network television. For her Craft, for her fellow Witches, for all those who'd died due to ignorance in the past.

She couldn't quit. Maybe all of this was some kind of a test.

It was not easy, forcing Alex and that troubling dream from her mind. Something was going on with him—with the two of them, maybe. She felt it in her gut, and she never ignored her intuition. It was usually dead-on. She was as afraid of him as she was drawn to him. She knew he felt that attraction, too. The air between them practically sparked with it when he was close to her.

What was the dream then? A warning? Was Alex to become her lover or her killer? Or both? Or was the dream just a manifestation of her own fears of failure and of this sudden, potent desire?

She couldn't dismiss him or the questions from her mind, only push them to the back long enough for her to do her work. She spent the rest of the night with her copy of the season's story arc, a stack of episode-by-episode break-downs, and a red pen, which ran out of ink, so she had to finish in blue.

She wasn't exactly fresh when she finished at 7:45 A.M. She spent a half hour doing yoga, fifteen minutes in the shower, and just had time for her morning ritual before she had to begin the transformation into working-girl Melissa. The change involved taming her wild hair into a nice neat bun, corralling her breasts within the confines of a bra, putting on panties and nylons and a nice, civilized-looking outfit that included an ivory-colored silklike sleeveless blouse, a matching skirt, and a pair of pumps with two-inch heels. She flat-out refused to wear heels higher than that.

Then she drove her beloved lime-green Bug into the city, into the traffic, whispering prayers of protection to keep from being hit by the frantic driving tactics common to LA.

She made it to the meeting at one minute before ten. The others were already there, seated in comfortable over-stuffed chairs and minisofas in a room that looked more like a living room than an office. The head writer, Merl Kinney, was there, gray hair, white at the temples, three-hundred-dollar suit, way too thin for a man his age and way too tan as well. Only one of his underlings had shown up, a young, pale woman with blond curls. The two were sleeping together. Melissa wasn't sure if it was as obvious to everyone else as it was to her, but as far as she was concerned they might as well have been wearing a sign. The director, Karl Stone, was there. But one presence dominated the room. Alex.

He was as potent to her senses as a shot of adrenaline. Dark hair, killer smile, and those piercing black eyes that seemed always to be focused on her. He wore tight-fitting jeans, a tank-style undershirt, and a short-sleeved button-down shirt, unbuttoned. All black. As her gaze slid over him, it froze on his chest.

He wore a pendant that rested there. An inverted penta-cle with diamondlike stones winking at its five points.

Melissa's blood went cold. It was the same as the one from her dream.

She dragged her gaze from it, up to his eyes, and then got stuck there, captured. If he saw the fear in her eyes, he didn't show it. He smiled as if he knew something she didn't, then rose from his chair until she sat in one of her own.

Karl Stone said, "What do you want, Mel, coffee? Tea? A soft drink?"

She tried not to grimace at his calling her Mel. "Nothing,

thanks, I'm fine." She opened her briefcase, pulled out the story arc and breakdowns, and stacked them on the coffee table in front of her.

Merl Kinney leaned forward, brows drawing together at the red markings on the top page. Without asking, he drew the stacks toward him, flipping through the top several pages. "My goodness," he said. "Had I known I was in need of a ghostwriter, I'd have hired one myself."

The room went dead silent. She could hear the soft ticking of someone's wristwatch, it was so quiet.

Drawing a breath, Melissa called up her courage. "These are only suggestions. I wouldn't dream of changing your words, Mr. Kinney. I only tried to highlight the places where I found . . . technical inaccuracies. The notes in the margins are suggested corrections."

He lifted his gaze from the script pages, locking it with hers. "I've won an Oscar and three Emmys, Miss St. Cloud."

"I've worked magic, Mr. Kinney."

Their gazes held.

Alex broke the silence. "Merl, Melissa was hired to tell us where we were getting it wrong, as far as the Witchcraft stuff goes. All she's done here is exactly what I hired her to do." He drew the manuscript toward him, began flipping through. "Keep in mind, we are free to take her suggestions or leave them—"

"If you leave them, I'm going to have to quit," she said, addressing Alex now.

He blinked at her as if she'd suddenly levitated or sprouted a wart on the end of her nose. "I don't follow. . . ."

"I'd prefer not to have the entire Pagan community think of me as a traitor, much less an uninformed poser, Alex. I don't want to deal with the mail I'd get, much less the E-mail." Turning her gaze to the head writer's again, she went on. "And I don't mean to tell you what to write, or how to write. Only what's accurate. And Alex is right: you can take it or leave it."

Kinney frowned and leaned back in his chair. But the

tense, offended body language remained. "Why don't you nutshell some of these . . . inaccuracies for me?"

She nodded, licking her lips, wishing she could snatch the script back from Alex as a reference, but he was engrossed. And she found it easier to concentrate when his eyes were not on her, so she decided to let it be. God, she so wanted to keep this job. But she might very well be fired or forced to walk on her first full day.

"Just as a for-instance," she began, choosing her words carefully, "the spells. When a Witch casts a spell, there's a lot more to it than just reading a couple of lines from a book. The words aren't magic. The Witch is."

"So . . . how would *you* go about casting a spell?" Alex asked, lifting his gaze from the manuscript, pinning her with it. It burned. There was something in his eyes both attractive and intense. It shook her right to the core. And those damned stones in his necklace winked in the light, adding to her discomfort.

"First I'd determine the goal, then do a divination to determine whether I should even proceed. If I got the okay, then I'd calculate the best possible timing for the spell. Best day of the week, moon phase, other astrological correspondences, best time of day, and so on. I'd determine what herbs or scents, crystals or colors should be used, picking ones whose energies and vibrational frequencies mesh with the goal. I'd compose the words of the spell, and they would be very important, everything from the rhyme scheme to the number of syllables per stanza would have meaning. I'd decide how I wanted to raise energy. Then I'd do yet another reading to ensure every precaution had been taken."

Kinney raised his eyebrows. "It sounds like we're going to need longer episodes. This might end up being a Costner-length feature every single week."

"Even if you just refer to the preparation involved, it would help," Melissa said. "A throwaway line or two would be enough. Just acknowledge there's more to it than simply opening the book and reading the lines."

He nodded. "Doable, I suppose. But boring. This *is* entertainment, Mel. Not a documentary."

"I understand that. And naturally there will be times when your characters have an emergency situation and have to act instantly."

"What about the actual spell-casting part?" Alex asked. "I mean, all the rest is prep work, correct?"

He was on the edge of his chair, leaning forward, eyes glued to hers, except when they veered south every little while, to slide over her body, down her legs like a caress. She could *feel* his eyes when they touched her that way.

"Yes. When the time is right, I would create sacred space and cast a ritual circle. I'd invoke the forces and entities I had chosen to meld their powers with mine. Part of the spell casting would involve raising energy by dancing or chanting, drumming or rattling, clapping or whispering, or any number of other methods. When the energy reaches its peak, the Witch releases it from the circle, sending it off to do its job. Then she gives thanks and releases any forces or entities she has invoked. Finally, she takes up the circle."

"So instead of a thirty-second scene it's a half-hour scene," Kinny said, his voice dripping sarcasm.

"Sounds like a riveting scene to me," Karl Stone said. It was the first comment from the director. "Can you imagine the special effects we could put in there? Tell me, Melissa, is this magic circle visible to the naked eye?"

"Not usually. But most experienced Witches know it's there. It wouldn't be outrageous to show it, as if the Enchantress were seeing it with her inner vision."

"And the . . . forces and, uh, entities she invokes?"

"Those, too. But they would always be positive in nature, so I wouldn't make them too scary-looking."

"Because our Witches only practice white magic, right?" he asked, clearly intrigued.

Alex rolled his eyes and leaned back in his chair.

"That's not exactly true," Melissa said. "True white magic is magic designed to put the Witch more in touch with the divine, more in tune with spirit. Magic designed to help yourself or others is more accurately referred to as gray magic. Nothing wrong with it, but it's not pure, either. That's why you do the divination first, to be sure it's wise to proceed. Magic designed to cause harm to yourself or anyone else is black, and to be honest, there are times when it's called for."

"I thought the rule was 'Harm none,' " Alex said. He was watching her. She swore her blood was heating while her skin sprouted goose bumps.

"Some would say allowing evil to flourish unchecked is doing harm," she told him. "So some don't feel restricted from using magic to stop evil, or protect the innocent, or see to it that a criminal is caught. Some Witches wouldn't use it even then. Others insist on doing no more than turning the evildoer's own energy back to its source, so he ends up destroying himself. That would be the most likely course of action for your characters when they were attacked by surprise, with no time to prepare—just flinging up a reflective barrier that bounces the energy back to its source. Personally, I've never subscribed to the belief that we are given the power of the gods to wield and then expected to be victims or passive witnesses to wrongdoing."

The director was rubbing his hands together, the wheels behind his eyes turning. "This is good stuff. We can use this. We're talking about true moral conflicts here. Real soul-searching." He scribbled a note, then glanced her way. "What else have you got?"

"Oh, please," Kinney said, clearly exasperated. "Are we producing a prime-time drama here, or is this going to be a Wicca One-oh-one class?"

"Kinney, you're the head writer, not the creator," Alex said. His tone, normally firm, had gone softer, and somehow that was more intimidating. "Karl and I came up with the idea; this is our baby. Our vision. If you want to stay on as head writer, I suggest you pay attention." Then, turning to Melissa, he smiled. "Please, go on."

She went on. The meeting stretched into two hours as she did her best to give the team a crash course on magic and Witchcraft. By the time she finished, she was energized, bubbling over with enthusiasm. They were actually listening to her!

Kinney alone remained hostile, though he kept it to himself throughout the rest of the meeting. Alex seemed interested, attentive, intense—but he still exuded a sense of frustration she couldn't quite understand.

When the meeting ended, a secretary came in with a list of messages for Alex even before everyone had filed out. Melissa had hoped for a private word with him, but he was clearly too busy just now. So she headed to her Bug with a new spring in her step. She was going to keep her job and her promise. They were taking her suggestions seriously.

Maybe the dream wouldn't come back again now that she'd gained a little confidence that she could actually do this job. Maybe it was only nerves after all. If she could just keep her feelings for Alex under control, she might actually get through this.

She was unlocking the car door, trying not to dance for joy, when Alex's voice came from behind her.

"You really do know your stuff, Melissa. You blew everyone away in there."

His voice sent shivers of awareness up her spine. He moved closer, standing right behind her, invading her aura. His warmth on her back made her close her eyes briefly. Then she straightened and turned to face him, resting her back against the car door. "Thank you." Her gaze lowered to the pentacle on his neck. "I wanted to ask you . . . about the pent'."

"You like it?"

"Yeah, but why are you wearing it inverted?"

He lifted a hand to finger the five-pointed star, enclosed within a circle, with its topmost point aimed downward. "It came that way. Besides, as I told you, I need to get inside the heads of the villains this season. Isn't this the way a dark magician would wear it?"

She shrugged. "Actually, in the Craft it's the symbol of the Second Degree—the descent into the shadow-self. But it's rarely used that way in the States anymore, because of its negative connotations. I think the Satanists have adopted it as their symbol, but I didn't see any Satanists cast as villains in the breakdowns."

"Wouldn't a dark magician be the same thing as a Satanist?"

"Not at all. A dark magician would be anyone who practiced magic designed to cause harm to others, or to manipulate the free will of other people for his own interests or gain. Some Satanists might be dark magicians, but I'd bet most of them aren't."

He nodded. "I think I like the symbol, even if it's not wholly accurate. In fact, I was thinking of using it as a prop on the show. It will certainly give the viewers the right cue at the right time. They see this, and they think, 'Evil.' "

"And that's a lie you intend to perpetrate even further?" She shrugged, disappointed in him, then stared at the pent', battling a shiver. "It's really a magnificent piece," she whispered. "Where did you find it?"

"It was my father's."

She lifted her head, a frown knitting itself between her brows.

"So where would one go to find an authentic dark magician?" he asked. "I have some books, but—"

Her hand shot out to clasp his upper arm. "Who *are* you, Alex? What are you playing with here?"

His eyes seemed to darken, to intensify, and her hand tingled where she touched him. "That's what I'm trying to find out," he told her. He shook her arm off and turned to walk away.

She went after him, grabbing his arm and turning him around again. "Don't dabble in the dark side, Alex. It will pull you in like quicksand. It will destroy you."

"You think so?" He shook his head. "Look over there, you see that car?"

She did. The sleek Mercedes SL 500 convertible was silver and gleaming in the sunlight.

"And there's my house. A mansion. And money. So much money I can have anything I want."

"And you got all you have through black magic?"

He seemed to go still, confusion etching his face for just a moment. "I didn't used to think so. Now . . . I'm not so sure."

She had no idea what he was talking about. Impulsively she touched his shoulder. "You can have anything you want anyway. You don't need black magic to get it. The universe is surging with abundance; all we need to do is claim it."

He smiled slowly. "Is that why you're driving a VW Bug?"

She tilted her head, studying him. "I *love* my car. Besides, it's good on gas, and better for the environment. I try to live in harmony with nature, Alex, and nature provides everything I need."

"But not everything you want."

"You don't understand. You have to get past the mentality of a child in a toy store. When you grow spiritually, Alex, your wants and desires start to meld with the will of spirit. And when that happens, things just fall into place. I adore that little car. I smile every time I look at it. I love my little beach house. And I'm starting to love this job—or I was."

"Well, I love my mansion, and I love my Mercedes, and I love the idea that I can have anything I want." He looked at her, her eyes, her lips. "Any*one* I want."

She lifted her brows. "You think so, do you?"

"I think so." He moved closer still, closing the tiny gap between them, and his arms slid around her waist. He bent over her and covered her mouth with his. God, he knew how to kiss. His lips and tongue were talented, and he tasted good, and she was female enough to enjoy every second of it. She didn't fight him, didn't struggle. She didn't want to. Instead, she returned the kiss, but gentler, slowing the movement of her mouth beneath his, soothing him with her hands as they moved on his back and shoulders, visualizing cool blue water melding with the red-hot fire she sensed burning through him.

He responded, as she had known he would. His arms around her relaxed a little, so he held her close, but not crushingly. His mouth explored, now, rather than invading. His kiss warmed, gentled, and she felt a shudder rise up as if from somewhere deep within him, and an answering one rose within her.

When he lifted his head away, he blinked twice, and his eyes searched hers. He took a step backward, away from her, licked his lips, and then lowered his gaze. "That was . . . I was being an ass."

"Yeah, I noticed," she said.

"It's been a rough month. I'm going through some things." He turned away slowly, raking his hair with one hand.

"We all go through things, Alex. But just for the record, that kiss just now didn't happen because of any magic, black or otherwise. Or because of your money or your car. It happened because I wanted it to happen. So don't beat yourself up too much over it, okay?"

She turned back to her car while he was still standing there, in a state of—she didn't know what. Confusion, remorse? She got behind the wheel, started up the Bug. He spun around as if he hadn't realized she'd even moved, even took a few steps toward her as she drove away. Then he stood there watching her go, still looking slightly dazed.

Melissa held her hand out over the passenger seat, opened her fist, and let the gold pentacle drop onto the upholstery. Her palm still pulsed with the energy the piece held. Powerful energy, but dark. She could not wait to get home and wash her hands. She would just do a little cleansing work on Alex's jewelry tonight. He could have it back tomorrow.

It was completely against her principles to do this sort of thing—messing around with his pent' without his permission. Much less stealing from her brand-new boss. But something deep inside was telling her to do it, that she had to do it. That he needed her help. And she never ignored her intuitions.

CHAPTER 4

SHE left, and he watched her go, cussing himself for acting like an idiot and wondering what horny little demon had possessed him, just now. But no, he couldn't blame his actions on anyone but himself. He was getting cocky. Starting to buy into the bullshit his father's diaries were trying so hard to sell. No matter how ridiculous Alex told himself it was, he was falling into it. He felt himself falling into it.

Maybe he just wanted it to be true. Maybe he'd just wanted an identity so badly for so long that he was embracing his newfound heritage with a little more zeal than common sense. And maybe he ought to have listened to his first instinct and stayed the hell away from the secluded old mansion where his father had lived and died.

The thought of parting with the place, though, sent a pang through his chest. It and its musty contents were all he had of his father. All he would ever have.

Besides the genes. The blood. The power.

Part of him rolled his eyes at the latter notion. Another part of him considered hurling a lightning bolt at something, just to see.

Until recently the practical part, the skeptic, had been stronger. Lately the two seemed evenly matched, and he felt constantly torn by the struggle.

He sighed and went to his car. Everyone had gone their separate ways, but they were due to meet at the studios the next day to refilm today's scene. Karl and Merl were supposed to brainstorm changes to the script, though the actual implementation would be done by Merl's writing team, who would fax the new scripts to the actors tonight. Later Karl would head to the studio to talk special effects. Alex would have to approve all of it before they shot tomorrow, but none of it would be ready for hours yet. He had the afternoon free.

So did Melissa.

He could go out there, he thought with a stirring of hunger. But another thought, one that didn't feel like one of his own, overpowered the impulse. *Don't chase her. Let her come to you. She will, you know. If all the things your father wrote in those diaries are true, she will—simply because you want her to. Wait and see.*

He rolled his eyes at the ridiculous notion even as he wondered what a good shrink would make of the voices in his head that never sounded quite like his own inner monologue. Then he got in the Mercedes and drove to the house he couldn't quite think of as home.

MELISSA used the afternoon to bury Alex's pentacle in the sand, in a spot too high for the tide to reach it, though well outside her sacred space. She called on the energies of Earth and Sea to cleanse it of its negative vibes, sprinkled rosemary, angelica, rue, and sage into the hole with it, and sank a tall stick into the sand beside it to mark the spot.

Then she washed her hands repeatedly, first in the sea, then with soap and water in her bathroom sink, and finally with Moon Water that had been blessed and charged with lunar energy.

After that, she got on the phone with Alex's secretary and got his address from the woman. He was famous enough that Melissa expected his secretary would be extremely careful about letting the information out. It surprised her when the secretary gave her the address without even a token protest. Strange.

So it was done. She'd buried the pilfered pent' to cleanse

it, and she'd gotten the address without effort. Now all she had to do was work up the nerve to go over there and tell him what she'd done . . . and maybe why she'd felt compelled to do it.

But what was she supposed to say? Was she going to lecture him about what he'd been reading, who he'd been talking to? Grill him about who the hell this father of his was that he'd gone around with a half-pound of diamond-studded gold hanging from his neck? It was none of her business. She barely knew Alex, and she was certainly in no position to preach to him. He was wealthy, powerful, successful, and respected. How dare she presume to know what was good for him?

Even if she *did*.

She wasn't certain whether she should go over there or not, and she wasn't going to be able to come to a reasonable decision in this state. She needed to get centered.

A long hot soak in a scented bath helped. She added sandalwood and myrrh oils to the water. Very grounding. She dressed in her comfort clothes—a gray fleece warm-up suit and thickly cushioned white socks. She tied her hair in a loose ponytail and then phoned her favorite take-out place and ordered a bowl of seafood chowder. Thick and creamy. Rich and piping hot.

After she'd eaten, she went to the quietest room in the house. It had been intended as a second bedroom, but since she only needed one, it had become her temple room. Beaded curtains hung in the doorway. Goddess statues stood on pedestals, and there were shelves lined with books upon books. A small table, her working altar, stood in the center of the room.

She lit her candles, fired up her censer, then went to the west, sat on the floor on a soft cushion, and let her body relax. She focused on her breaths, rushing in and out, like waves on the sea, and she felt her mind slow and quiet. Absence of thought, stillness of the mind, that was true meditation, and it was that peace she sought.

When one didn't consciously search for an answer, that

was when the answer was free to come on its own. At least that theory had proven true for her, time and time again. So she emptied her mind and sat in silence, floating in a peaceful void, without expectations or demands.

The darkness beyond her eyes began to fill with shapes and colors. The silence came alive, very slowly, with whispers and sounds.

Gradually, the shapes and colors took on more solid form.

Alex was there. No. The man from her dream, the one who looked like Alex, only dressed in dark robes and wearing that pent'. He had blood on his hands. He stood, facing toward her but not looking at her.

Melissa, where are you? I need you.

She frowned, certain that voice was *not* Alex's. And yet the face, the eyes, of the apparition were so like his—

She shivered and realized the entire room had gone icy cold. She opened her eyes to end the vision and saw her own breath cloud in front of her face.

Melissa's alpha state faded so fast she felt as if she had literally fallen from the sky, landing solidly in her body with a jarring thud. She was still sitting on the floor, in her temple room. She rubbed her arms against the chill.

"He's in trouble," a woman's voice whispered. "Help him, my sister."

Melissa jerked her head around, searching for the owner of that soft voice. But there was nothing, no one. Rising slowly, she inspected everything in the room for some clue. The spiral of incense smoke wasn't doing anything unusual. The candles' flames were steady and strong.

Except for the one in the west. It was flickering rapidly. And now that she was looking that way, she noticed the incense smoke was sort of flowing inward from that direction as well.

"I should have cast a goddamn circle," she muttered, because it was clear *something* had come in. She hadn't imagined the woman's voice or the man in the vision. She'd been a Witch too long to doubt her own senses, even the ones most people didn't believe in. She walked to the cabinet, took out a bundle of sage, changed her mind, and reached instead for the tightly sealed jar of asafetida, devil's dung. Removing a piece, keeping her face averted, she touched it to the candle's flame. The herb blazed up, and she blew it out, then walked counterclockwise around the room, smudging it with the rancid-smelling smoke.

"Spirits, depart!" She didn't whisper or chant or intone. This was a time for a clear, firm tone, one of command. "Depart through the gate you entered. This is my home and you have not been invited here. Depart, and go your way. Go, I say!"

The only sign that anything had happened was that the incense smoke swirled in a funny little eddy for a moment and then flowed steadily in the opposite direction, outward, toward the west. Melissa went to the western quarter and used the smoldering weed to draw a banishing pentagram in the air with its foul smoke. Then she doused the devil's dung, and using her hands she mimicked closing the veil, pulling it tight. She sealed the gateway with an equal-armed cross.

"So mote it be," she muttered. Then was still for a moment, waiting, sensing. But the chill was gone, as was that sense of someone else in the room.

Sighing, she extinguished her candles and her censer. Then she opened the window, to let the disgusting smell out. She left the ritual room through the tinkling beaded curtain and wondered what sort of visitation she'd just had.

She'd seen Alex. Or a man who looked like Alex—a man with blood on his hands. But what did it mean? Whether actual or symbolic, it would mean the same thing. Alex— or whoever the apparition was—was somehow responsible for causing harm, perhaps even death. She remembered the dream she'd had the night before—the woman she'd seen pushed from a bridge. Had that other voice been hers? Or was she some version of Melissa herself?

She shouldn't meddle in Alex's life any more than she already had—especially without his consent or knowledge.

There were forces moving in his life that were beyond her depth. Things she knew she would be better off not touching.

Yet her instincts were telling her to go to him.

And she never ignored her instincts.

She took her car keys from the hook and picked up the slip of paper with Alex's address on it before she headed out the front door.

CHAPTER 5

MELISSA pulled her VW Bug to a stop on the dark, narrow unpaved road and just sat there, staring at the house.

It was a monster. That was the word that whispered through her mind. It squatted there in the darkness, a red-rock monster, glaring at her from rectangular window-eyes. The grounds around the place hadn't been tended in a very long time. Gnarly trees and twisting vines, weeds and brush, grew in a tangled mess that was as good as a moat. All except for the narrow path that led to the massive wooden front door.

A light rain fell. She could easily imagine it was always raining on this place. She could almost see the black cloud over it, and she decided to leave her car on the road, rather than pulling it into the barely discernible tire tracks that passed for a driveway. She backed up a bit, then pulled forward, parking the car on the opposite shoulder. It was far enough off the road so no one would hit it as they passed, though she doubted she would encounter another vehicle on this stretch of cow path even if she stood here for a week.

Getting out of the car, she left it unlocked. For some reason, she didn't want to do anything that would delay her getting back in. She pocketed her keys and crossed the gravel road, stepping through the iron gate that stood hanging open, slightly crooked, shiny with wetness. As soon as she set foot on the path, a full body shudder racked her to a stop. Closing her eyes, clenching her fists, she sought calm.

She felt the Earth power rising up through her feet, softly glowing green. She felt the Sky power rinsing over her in the rain, a pulsing vibrant gold. The energies met in her center, swirling and growing until they filled her to bursting. She felt the power tingling in her fingers, burning in her toes. And then it grew still bigger, until it suffused her aura, surrounding her in a sphere of white light.

Better, she thought. Lifting her chin, she continued walking the path, less fearful now, more confident. She walked up the two stone steps, stood on the top one, and rapped the brass knocker that was clasped in the teeth of a gargoyle.

The rain came down a little harder. She didn't mind it in the least. Maybe it was rinsing away some of the negativity that clung to this place like a smog cloud over a large city. When there was no response to her summons, she knocked again. She glanced toward the side of the house, spotted the shiny reflection of Alex's Mercedes gleaming there in the rain. He was home.

She rapped again.

Eventually, footsteps approached and locks turned and the large door groaned open.

Alex stood on the other side, black jeans sinfully tight, black T-shirt showing every powerful muscle in his torso. He looked irritated, then surprised when he saw who stood on his stoop.

"Melissa?"

"Hello, Alex. We need to talk. Do you mind if I come in?"

He licked his lips as if nervous but stepped aside to let her in. Melissa stepped into the foyer and felt as if she'd stepped into a pool of pure blackness. It enveloped her, and she hugged her arms and shivered. She looked around the place, disliking it more and more. It was dim, unnaturally cool, cavernous, and hollow. And there were others there, though she couldn't see them. She could feel them, their eyes watching her.

"This way," Alex said. "We'll be more comfortable in the sitting room."

She followed him, but her infallible instincts were

telling her not to. They were telling her to turn around and run. She ignored them, and she knew better. Her stomach felt queasy.

She and Alex crossed through a huge living room with a domed ceiling and a few pieces of furniture that looked antique. Almost Gothic. But they didn't stop there. Alex led her into a smaller room off the right side, where more contemporary furniture, overstuffed brown velour, and a glass-topped coffee table formed a horseshoe pattern around a marble fireplace. There was a fire in the hearth, and she welcomed the warmth, taking the chair nearest it.

Alex sat on the sofa. "What did you want to talk about?" he asked her.

She had been studying the flames, and she jumped when he spoke. "Is anyone else here?"

He shook his head. "No, we're alone. Why?"

She heard whispers, unintelligible but unmistakable. He didn't act as if he heard a thing. "I . . . I just had the feeling someone else was here."

"There's a housekeeper who keeps a room here but rarely uses it. Elizabeth was my father's nurse before he died, and she stayed on, keeping the place up until it could be sold. I couldn't see putting her out, so I kept her on. But she's off tonight."

Melissa nodded slowly. "This was your father's house."

He nodded.

"And he's passed the veil."

"Yeah."

She looked around the room. "I think he's still here." Her voice had dropped to a near whisper.

Alex glanced at her sharply, then smiled. "I like to think so."

She studied his face. "What kind of man was he, your father?"

"His name was Victor Moring. I don't know what he was like. I never met him."

She frowned, waiting for him to continue, but he didn't. She licked her lips and followed her instincts. She reached across to where his hand rested on the arm of the sofa and closed hers around it. "Tell me," she whispered.

He narrowed his eyes on her. "Why?"

"I don't know. I just . . . I have the feeling it's important."

He hesitated a moment, staring at her hand on his. Finally, he sighed and gave a slight nod. "I was raised in an orphanage," he said, and he said it so matter-of-factly that she knew this was of deep importance to him. He was trying too hard to make it seem otherwise. "St. Luke's, in Boston. The nuns there didn't know who my parents were. I was left by a young woman one night, when I was barely a week old, with just a tiny wooden box that contained a note from my mother and a hunk of quartz. She told them my name was Quinn, but I'm certain that was a lie. When I was ten, and started asking questions about my family, the sisters gave the box to me and told me what little they knew, which was just what I've told you."

She blinked rapidly, tried to calm her suddenly racing heartbeat. "Can I see it?"

"What? The box?"

She nodded.

He blinked slowly, studying her face as if trying to read her. "Did you take my pent', when I kissed you earlier, Melissa?"

She looked down, feeling guilty as hell. "Yes. It's safe, I promise. I shouldn't have taken it, I just—"

"I want it back."

She nodded. "It's at my place. I never intended to keep it, just to cleanse it and bless it for you." He lifted his brows. "It's a Witch thing. We do it with all our important ritual tools." She attempted a smile that was probably weak. "It was . . . my gift to you."

His lips thinned, but he nodded and got to his feet. "Next time, ask first, okay?"

"I should have this time," she said. "I'm sorry I didn't."

"You're right, you should have." He turned for the door. "Stay here."

She nodded, even though he couldn't see her, and he left the room. His footsteps soon vanished in the depths of the house. Melissa got up, pacing the room, brimming with nervous energy and tingling with apprehension. There was something in this house—something dark. She kept feeling as if someone was standing right at her back, only to spin around and see no one.

Finally, Alex returned. She was standing close to the fire by then, soaking up its heat, staring into its flames. She turned when he came into the room; then her breath hitched in her throat. For just an instant, she'd seen that other face, superimposed over his. The face of the man in her dream, who was like Alex but not Alex.

Then it faded.

"What's wrong? You look as if you've seen a ghost."

"I . . . nothing." She looked at the small wooden box he held. "Is that it?"

"Yeah." He held it out, and she took it from him, returned to her seat in the chair, and gently opened the lid.

A folded scrap of time-yellowed paper rested inside. She looked to Alex for permission, and when he nodded, she picked it up and noticed the glittering quartz crystal that rested underneath it. Unfolding the sheet carefully, Melissa read the note.

> *My dearest Alex,*
> *Leaving you with the sisters is the hardest thing I have ever done. But my love for you is so strong that I know it is my only choice. I fear my life in this world will soon end—for the evil that pursues me draws closer every day. The best I can do for you is to put you as far from its reach as I can, in a place where I know you'll be safe. The only thing I ask of you, my son, is that you never attempt to find the man who fathered you—for I tell you from my heart, he is evil, and he will destroy you. Know that I will always be with you, watching over you, protecting you, and loving you.*
>
> > *Always,*
> > *Your mother, Jennifer*

As she read the note, Melissa swore she could *hear* the words, spoken in a gentle, loving voice—the same voice she'd heard earlier tonight in her temple room. Blinking back tears, she refolded the note and set it in the box. As she did, her fingertips caressed the crystal and she felt a surge of warmth suffusing her hand and arm.

Her chest felt tight, her heart full, as she closed the lid.

Then she frowned, holding the box in her hands. "There was something else?"

Alex seemed startled. "Yes. How did you know?"

She only shrugged.

"Three months ago, I somehow left my bedroom window open—not here, I was living closer to LA then. It stormed that day, and a gust must have swept through. When I got home, the bedroom was wet, and things were scattered everywhere. The box had been blown off its shelf, to the floor. When it hit, a little compartment in the bottom popped open. There was a card inside."

"Your father's?" she asked.

He nodded. "By then, I'd been trying to trace my roots for years. I'd managed to learn his last name, Moring, but nothing else. The address was for this house, and when I came here, there was a real-estate sign on the lawn. Elizabeth was still here. She told me my father had passed only a few months prior. But all of his things were still here as well. And the place was for sale."

"So you bought it."

"Of course I bought it." He sighed, shaking his head. "To think I'd been in LA for so long and he was so close all that time. But I only found him after he'd died. Elizabeth said he always knew I'd come back someday. She said he'd have wanted me to have the house." He searched the depths of the fire; for what, she couldn't have said. "I thought, by being here, going through his things, I could finally get to know my father."

"And have you?"

He snapped his gaze to hers. "I don't know. He . . . he left diaries—but the entries are always addressed 'Dear

Alex,' as if he was writing them to me, knowing I'd find them and read them someday. And they're full of . . ." He stopped there, as if afraid he would reveal too much. "He was either the most powerful sorcerer I could have imagined, or he was completely insane."

She nodded slowly. "And that's why you've had all the questions about the dark side of magic."

He started to nod, but stopped halfway. "Not that I think what he practiced was black magic. Just that it—it doesn't quite mesh with the fluffy white lighter stuff you find in all the books meant for public consumption."

She drew a breath, lifted her chin. "Would you be willing to let me see them?"

His head came up fast, and again, the face of that "other" seemed to hover over his own. "No!" The word blasted from his lips in a voice like thunder, and it hit her with a force that was palpable. A force she felt might have physically harmed her, had she not taken the time to shield herself before entering this place. The air in the room turned to ice, even as she shot to her feet and backed toward the door.

Alex blinked twice, frowning as if confused. "I'm sorry, I didn't mean to shout."

She held up a hand, shook her head, tried to form words to excuse herself, but gave up. Instead she simply turned and ran. She didn't look back until she was in her car, heading away from that place.

And when she did, she saw Alex, standing in the middle of the narrow road, staring after her.

ALEX was shaking all over, couldn't seem to stop it. Hell. What in God's name had just happened to him? And how was he going to explain it to Melissa when he didn't understand it himself?

He was sweating, he realized as he ran a palm across his forehead. A cold sweat. More dampness gathered on his skin from the soft, mistlike rain that fell, and he shivered. He walked back into the house.

It's just as well. She's a Witch, and she'll ruin everything. Stay away from her from now on.

Alex frowned at the foreign voice in his mind. It wasn't his own. It wasn't his inner self expressing nervousness over the sheer power of what he felt for Melissa. Everything in him was screaming just the opposite.

"I don't want to stay away from her," he whispered. "I think . . . I think I need her." He sighed, lowering his head. It was true. He sensed it right to his soul. He needed her. He didn't know why or how or exactly what it was he needed *from* her.

The truth was, he was burning to tell her everything— everything that had happened to turn his life upside down. He had been, ever since he'd first set eyes on her. In that moment when he'd opened the door to find her standing there, it felt as if he'd been lost in the desert and finally caught sight of water. Cool, clear, life-giving water. Something inside her seemed to speak to something inside him. And just being near her felt . . . soothing. Healing. When she had walked into this godforsaken tomb of a house, he swore he could almost feel a fresh, cool breeze rushing in, blasting away the cobwebs and dust and darkness.

Absently he rubbed his hand where hers had closed around it. He wanted to touch her again.

No!

Mustering his will—and God, it was an effort—he ignored the voice in his head and walked back outside, pulling his car keys out of his pocket as he did. He had to go after her.

This wasn't over.

CHAPTER 6

HE found her sitting on the natural stone patio behind her beach house. There was a lawn swing there, made of bamboo. She sat in it, swinging gently, and she didn't look the least surprised to see him there.

"I didn't mean to scare you away."

She offered a small, if somewhat uncertain, smile. "It's not you that scares me." Drawing a breath as if drawing up courage, she patted the empty spot beside her.

He moved forward, sat down beside her. "I don't know what happened. I'm sorry."

She studied his face for a long moment. "Is it gone now? Whatever it was that came over you?"

He nodded. "I'd never hurt you, Melissa."

"I know."

She leaned back in the swing, seemingly relaxing a little. Maybe those all-seeing eyes of hers told her that he was no threat. Maybe she was just more confident on her home turf. Whatever, he was irrationally glad that his outburst back at the house hadn't made her decide to have no more to do with him.

The sea breeze rinsed over him, and it reminded him of what he felt emanating from Melissa. The woman was like the ocean: deep and full of mystery and power. Cool and soothing. Mystical. And emanating a fragrant, refreshing energy the way a tree emanates oxygen, sustaining and strengthening the life force of everyone within her orbit.

He sat there watching the waves as they rolled in, breaking into curls of white froth, hissing as they ran out of steam and retreated into the depths again.

"I won't ask you any more questions if you don't want me to," she said. "And if you just came for the pent', I'll take you to it."

It was some sort of a test, he thought. She didn't dare ask him any more questions without feeling him out first. And she wasn't sure what he was doing here.

"I didn't come for the pent'. I came . . . I don't know why I came."

She let her eyes close, lashes resting on her cheeks.

"Do you believe in luck, or coincidence, Melissa?"

"I think you make your own luck," she said, not opening her eyes. "And I don't think there's any such thing as co-incidence. Synchronicity isn't random. Why?"

He leaned back, too, trying to adopt a more relaxed pose. She looked so comfortable, so at ease. He couldn't bring himself to close his eyes, though. He couldn't look at her with his eyes closed, and he found himself compelled to look at her.

"I've always been very successful. As far back as I can remember, everything I've tried to accomplish has worked out. Grades, scholarships. My career has been one lucky break after another, one amazing success after another. Opportunities seem to line up to knock on my door."

She nodded. "You work hard at what you do. I've only worked for you for two days, and I already know that. And you're good. You have a natural talent for visual storytelling. It's a gift. Probably what you were always meant to do."

"Maybe. Or maybe it was something else."

Time ticked by, silence stretching out between them, as the gentle rush of the waves over the sand whispered like a lullaby. Finally, she said, "What else could it have been, Alex?"

It was a gentle nudge, and it made him aware that he had fallen silent before completing his thought. He credited her with having distracted him. Her and the ocean.

"According to my father's diaries, it's genetic. I inherited the ability to wield his power. Anything I want, I only have to think of it to have it come to me. He wrote that it was his gift to me, but that it would fade in time, unless I learned to appreciate it and to control it."

He pushed with his feet and long legs, moving the swing gently back and forth in perfect time with the waves, and he looked at her. Her huge brown eyes were open now, plumbing the depths of his soul. He could drown in them.

"Did he say . . . how he expected you to do this?"

He nodded. "There's . . . a ritual."

Melissa sat up a little. "What kind of ritual?"

"I haven't seen it yet, but it's supposed to transfer his power to me. So that I'm not using his, but making it my own. Elizabeth knows how it goes. I guess she worked with my father a lot when he was alive. She's supposed to assist when the time comes, and I'm not supposed to know too much about it in advance."

Melissa seemed about to say something but then stopped herself.

"I thought the entire idea was ridiculous at first. But the more time I spend in that house—I don't know. It's as if it makes more sense all the time."

She nodded. "I felt him there, Alex. Your father. I think his spirit is still in that house."

He nodded slowly. "He's trapped there, according to Elizabeth. He won't be free until I undergo this—this rite. He can't rest in peace. I know it sounds crazy, but God, I feel him there, too. Then again, he died of brain cancer. All of this might just be the crazy ramblings of a man whose mind had deteriorated to the point of madness."

"Or maybe it's a little bit of both," she told him.

He nodded. "I've thought of that, too."

"What about the pentacle?" she asked.

"It was his. He'd left it with Elizabeth with instructions to give it to me when I came—he seemed to know I would in time."

"Maybe he did. But Alex, do you really believe that you

have everything you do because of him, and not because of your own hard work and talent?"

He thought for a long moment about that. "My father . . . he was extremely wealthy. Looking over the things he writes about his life, it seems that he was a lot like me. Everything he tried turned out to be successful. His diaries claim that he used magic to make it that way—that he used that same magic to ensure my life would be that way, as well." He drew a deep breath, sighed. "That's why I wanted you to teach me about magic. So that—on the off chance it is true and this ritual does grant me some kind of . . . power . . . I will know how to use it."

She jumped to her feet. "God, Alex, you don't intend to go through with this!"

He frowned. "Why wouldn't I?"

"Alex, everything in me tells me it's black magic, and that your father has been practicing it all his adult life—he would have to have in order to be as powerful as he claims to be. Do you have any idea the kind of negativity that must be clinging to his spirit by now? Can't you *feel* the darkness in that house of his? You don't want to open yourself up and invite all that darkness to jump from his lingering spirit into you. My God, it would be like—like walking unvaccinated through a smallpox ward."

Alex shook his head slowly. "I don't think he was evil," he said. "I really don't."

She stared down at him, her eyes intense. "What about the note? What about your mother's warnings?"

He had thought of that. Over and over he had thought of that, wondered about it.

"Alex, when you work magic or do anything else that causes harm to others, or takes things that were rightly meant for others, that harm brands you. It marks your soul. And the more harm you do, the bigger the mark. That mark becomes a beacon for negative energy. So the harm you do comes back. It's impossible for it not to."

He sighed, lowering his head and running his hand over the nape of his neck. "Dammit, Melissa, I think you're making too much out of all of this. You don't know he did harm to anyone. There's no proof of that."

"No?"

He shook his head.

"What about your mother? What about the harm he did to her?"

His head came up slowly. He reached out a hand, but she backstepped just enough to avoid his touch. "We don't know he did her any harm at all."

"How did your mother die, Alex?"

He shook his head hard, instant, absolute denial. "Come on, Melissa. Don't you think you're giving in to melodrama here?"

"You don't know, do you?"

"No. I don't know. The diaries only say that she took their newborn son and left." He met her eyes. "Seems to me that she was the one who did harm to him."

"Maybe." She didn't look as if she believed it, though. "I think you should find out for sure."

He threw his hands in the air. "Why the hell did I think I could talk to you about any of this? Jesus, Melissa, I thought you would understand. I thought you would give me some practical advice, not accuse a dead man—one I spent my whole life searching for—of everything from black magic to murder."

"You want practical advice?" she asked him. And even though his voice had been rising, hers remained steady, deep, and firm. "Here it is: Get away from everything to do with that man. Get as far away as you can. Have a cleansing ritual performed on you. Get the stink of his negativity off you. Give away everything he gave you. Or share his fate."

"His fate? He died a billionaire who could have anything he wanted."

"He died an old man, without a family, without his wife or his son. He died alone, horribly. And if he got his wealth the way I think he did, his next lifetime isn't likely to be much better. That is his fate. The fate he created for himself.

The fate he wants to pass on to you from beyond the grave."

Alex sighed heavily and turned away from her.

"You're not listening, are you? You're not hearing a word I say."

"I have to go. Before I do, I want my pent' back."

"Fine." She started off down the steps that led to the beach below but didn't step into the circle area.

Sacred space, he figured. She wouldn't take his father's filth into her precious white-lighter circle. She walked along the beach a little ways, off toward the left. He saw a branch standing there, one end driven deep into the sand. That was where she stopped, and then, using the branch as a digging tool, she unearthed the pentacle.

He stood there, watching. When it was uncovered, she knelt in the sand, reached her hand toward it, but didn't touch it. The moonlight bathed her face, and the sea wind played in her hair.

She shook her head. "It's still bad," she said. "I can feel it from here. You should leave it for three nights, Alex. Even then, I'm not sure—"

He reached down, not for the pent' but for her. He couldn't stand this, couldn't stand not touching her when he wanted to so very badly. His hand closed on her upper arm, and he pulled her to her feet.

"Alex?"

He pulled her closer, gently, giving her all the time in the world to resist. But she didn't. He closed his arms around her, and he kissed her. The water washed up over their feet and the moon beamed down on them and he kissed her. He thought, vaguely, that it was magical.

When he could break contact and speak again, he cradled her head to his chest, buried his hand in her wild hair. "Why am I so drawn to you? Are you messing with my head, working your own brand of magic on me?"

"I wouldn't use magic to make you feel anything for me. It would be unethical. But I have to tell you, Alex, I've been wondering the same thing about you."

"No. I wouldn't know how."

"Then what is this?" she asked him, whispering.

"I don't know."

She drew a breath, sighed.

"I've searched for him for twenty years, Melissa. I can't just deny him what was his dying wish. Please don't ask me to."

Closing her eyes slowly, she laced her fingers through his, hands at their sides. "It's a mistake, Alex. At least . . . at least think about this some more. And promise to let me know your decision before you go ahead with it."

"That much I can do."

She nodded. "You need cleansing, and shielding. You need wards. God, the thought of you going back into that house . . ."

"I'll be fine."

She stepped back, glancing down at the pent' in the sand. "Your pent'—"

"Leave it. Three nights, like you said."

She smiled, though it was shaky. "Good. Good, it can't hurt."

He held her gaze for a long moment. "Don't give up on me, Melissa. Things are—things are so messed up right now. But for some reason, at this moment, I don't want anything in the world quite as badly as I want . . . as I want you."

He tipped her chin up with his hand, kissed her again, and buried the pentacle in the sand with his feet.

"I should go," he whispered. "Because if I don't, I'm not going to."

She kissed him again, then pushed him away. Reaching down, she picked up the branch and thrust it into the ground to mark the spot where the pent' lay buried.

They turned, and he put his arm around her shoulders, held her close beside him, and they walked back toward the little beach house. But instead of veering left, toward the house, they veered right, toward her special place on the beach.

He let her lead him, unsure why she was taking him

there. At least, he was until she stopped and turned to face him. Slowly, she tugged her fleece shirt upward, over her head, and dropped it into the sand beside her.

Alex caught his breath, his throat going dry.

She heeled off her shoes and socks, then slid the soft gray fleece down over her hips and stepped out of the pants. She stood there, naked in the moonlight. And more than ever before, she seemed like some mystical creature. The spirit of the sea itself, bathed in moonlight.

"My God, you're beautiful," he whispered.

He drew her close, his hands sliding over her warm, smooth skin, and he kissed her again. Her body felt good, pressed against his. He helped her undress him as they kissed, and they fell to their knees in the sand. She lay down, pulling him with her, opening to him, welcoming him.

When he slid inside her, his body trembled, shook, and he thought he heard thunder, but whether it was in the distant sky or only within him he couldn't be sure. He held her, she wrapped herself around him, and they moved in time with the waves washing up over the sand. And he felt it—the power building, surrounding them, heat and passion and something more. It grew higher, stronger, until it was unbearable. And then it seemed to break loose at the moment when she cried out his name and he poured his very soul, it seemed, into her. For a moment it seemed the very air around them glowed.

For a long time, they lay there, just holding each other. Alex didn't know what had just happened between them. It hadn't been just sex. It hadn't even been just lovemaking. It had been something else, something more powerful than he'd ever felt before. And he knew, somewhere down deep, that it was something he would never feel again— not with anyone but Melissa.

CHAPTER 7

MELISSA didn't sleep that night after Alex, somewhat reluctantly, went home. He had work to do tonight, he said. And deep down, she knew she needed time to digest what had just happened.

She'd never attempted sex magic before. But passion, especially the kind of passion between her and Alex, generated incredible power. And even while she'd lost her focus to the ecstasy, she'd felt the power continue building within and around the two of them, surrounding them both in protection, empowering them.

She hadn't felt drained when it was over. She'd felt energized, and she sensed he had, as well. She prayed that sense was true and not just wishful thinking on her part.

Deep into the night, she sat in the darkened living room, in a chair drawn up to face the sliding glass doors that looked out over the beach and the sea. The ocean was angry tonight. Restless and moody. It swelled and receded, swirled and spat froth at the waning, lopsided moon.

Something's coming, her instincts whispered in her mind. *Something bad.*

Melissa couldn't quite bring herself to go outside, to explore the darkness and the mood of the sky and sea. Like a child, she hid in the safety of the house, wishing for daylight, and even though she knew she would never sleep, she hugged herself all the way to her bedroom to crawl beneath the covers.

As she pulled back the blankets something thudded gently to the carpeted floor behind her. The sound made her jump at first, but as soon as she spun around and saw what it was, she relaxed. The red velvet pouch full of rune-stones. The nail from which the pouch usually hung was bent low. Maybe the weight of the stones had slowly proven too much for it . . .

. . . or maybe the stones were trying to tell her something.

Frowning, she gathered the pouch in her palms, kneading it gently, feeling and hearing the gentle *click-clack* of the stones as they moved against one another inside. She loosened the drawstring, dipped inside, and closed her hand. Two cool stones rested within her fist when she drew it out again. She opened her palm and stared down at them.

Raido, action and movement. *Kennaz,* understanding and knowledge.

She got the message. She could not huddle in her bed, hiding and waiting for the bad thing to come, thinking she'd done all she could to prepare. She had to take action, figure out what she—what they both were up against, and then proceed accordingly.

Knowledge; she needed information.

Sighing, she wrapped herself in a warm, plush robe—the next best thing to huddling in her bed—and returned to the living room to turn on her computer. Connecting to the Internet, she typed the name of Alex's father, Victor Moring, into the search box and let the machine do the rest. Alex hadn't done the research he should have done. Partly, she sensed, because he didn't want to know the truth. Maybe deep down he knew what he would find wouldn't be good.

If so, he'd been right.

There were several news articles mentioning Moring's young wife, Jennifer, who'd gone missing along with her brand-new infant son, thirty years ago. The missing-persons report had been filed, not by Jennifer Simone-Moring's husband, as one might expect, but by her mother.

There was a photo of the missing woman, and Melissa sat there, rubbing her chilled arms as she waited for it to load. Line by line, the image filled in, top to bottom, the face coming clear.

Melissa jerked back from the computer, sucking in a breath. "My Goddess," she whispered. "She looks like me." The woman stared back at her, a warning in her eyes.

A sudden chill raced up Melissa's spine, and she swung her head, searching the rooms around her, suddenly feeling as if someone was watching her, someone close.

She saw no one, though, and forced herself to return her attention to the computer screen, to click on the link to the next article about the missing woman. That one talked about the police suspecting that Victor may have been involved in her disappearance and the investigation that revealed that both the man and his young wife had ties to what the police called the occult. No details on what they meant by that were offered.

But Melissa thought she might have an inkling. Alex's mother, she sensed, had been a Witch.

The next article said that the body of a young woman had been found in a New York river and that she had later been identified as Jennifer Simone Moring. The whereabouts of her infant son were still unknown, but authorities feared the worst. Her death had been ruled a suicide.

Melissa recalled the dream vision she'd had of the young woman, standing on a suspension bridge. In the dream, she hadn't gone over the rail of her own will. She'd had help—astral help perhaps, since the hands that had seemed to push her hadn't been connected to the man in the dream. So maybe it hadn't been a flesh-and-blood human there with her. But maybe, just maybe, she'd died at the will of a powerful magician.

Something moved outside. Melissa caught it from the corner of her eye, jumped to her feet, and spun to face the sliding glass doors and the darkness beyond them. Her heart pounded and her lungs clutched every breath.

A filmy gray shape moved silently along the beach, near

where Alex's pent' was buried. Whatever it was, it was dark and malicious. Melissa gasped, and her hand flashed upward, inscribing a banishing pentacle in the air with her finger and projecting its image toward the intruder. "Evil thing, be gone!" she hissed into the night. "Be gone, I say!"

She ran into her temple room and took the tiny bottle of her most powerful Moon Water, charged during a lunar eclipse, then ran to the back doors. It chilled her to stand so close, with nothing but a thin sheet of glass between her and the blackness of the night beyond, and that shape, that being, whoever or whatever it had been, gone now from her sight. She whispered an invocation to Hecate and her hounds and wet her forefinger with the Moon Water. Then she drew the banishing pent' on the glass. "By the moon and by the tide, nothing evil comes inside."

Melissa rushed through the house, repeating the process, drawing the five-pointed stars at every window and door. She turned on every light and double-checked every lock while she was at it. When she'd covered them all, she stood in the center of the living room, focused her energies, and connected them by sending a streak of astral blue flame from one mark to the next. When the blue flame boundary was complete, she focused on widening it, deepening it, expanding it beyond the walls and ceiling and floors, until her home was enclosed within a protective bubble of astral blue light. She stomped a foot to seal the energy.

Finally, she looked at the clock and vowed she would wait until dawn before she picked up the telephone and dialed Alex's number. She would not draw him back here now, when something that felt so menacing lurked just outside. She huddled in her robe in front of her computer, gaze jumping from one door or window to another with every breeze and every sound. It was going to be a long night.

THE housekeeper wore a gray hooded cloak, which had been intended to be seen by the Witch and to scare the hell out of her. She hoped the message had been received. She peered into her employer's bedroom, saw the young man thrashing in his bed, moaning the word "no" over and over. Alex was sweating, his face beaded with it. He'd flung off the covers, and he was naked from the waist up. His father, no doubt, was providing another nightmare to keep Alex off balance, unsure of himself, vulnerable.

She moved slowly forward, obeying the voice she heard inside her mind, the voice of the man she had loved.

"I followed him earlier, just as you instructed," she whispered, though no one was in the room. "The Witch lives in a beach house, had the pentacle buried in the sand." She held the pentacle, letting it dangle and spin from its chain.

Did she see you? the voice in her mind asked.

Elizabeth nodded. "I made sure of it."

Excellent. Go now, put the pentacle on my son where it belongs.

Elizabeth did exactly as she was told. She always did exactly what he told her. She leaned over Alex, fixing the chain around his neck. It was a direct link to his father's energy. It had to remain with Alex, to prepare him and link his father to him. Otherwise, the rite would never work. She straightened again and watched Alex struggling in his sleep. "Do you want to release him from the dream now that it's done?"

No. Let it eat him alive. Let it do its work. We have to burn her out of his life or she'll ruin everything, just as my darling young wife tried to do.

The woman nodded, realizing this nightmare must be about the Witch. She disliked the woman—disliked her intensely. She reminded Elizabeth of Victor's dead wife, Jennifer. How she had suffered watching the man devote himself to that woman, relegating Elizabeth to the role of housekeeper and mistress. But it was power he sought. Jennifer had it. It would combine with Victor's own in their offspring, creating for Victor an even more powerful form than he'd had the last time around.

"I can't wait," Elizabeth whispered, her gaze sliding

over Alex's chest. "He's got a beautiful body, Victor. It's going to look so good on you."

THE telephone beside Alex's bed was ringing. He rolled to one side, opened his eyes, and felt anger surging in him, though he wasn't even sure why. He reached out and yanked up the phone.

"What?"

"Alex? Alex, it's Melissa. I need to talk with you. Something happened last night."

He felt his jaw harden, his eyes narrow, and he remembered now the source of his anger. Melissa—playing him for a fool. Seducing him in order to take everything he had, only to toss him aside when she'd finished; turning him against his father so that he would have no powers with which to fight her; and all the while sleeping with every man she had to in order to get what she wanted.

"Alex, are you there?"

"I'm here. Jesus, do you know what time it is?" He glanced at his clock as he asked the question.

"Five A.M. I haven't been to sleep yet," she told him. "Are you all right, Alex? You sound . . . strange."

"Fine." He sat up, struggling to shake away the remnants of sleep. "What do you want?"

"Someone was here last night," she told him. "Down on the beach. I saw them. God, Alex, I was so scared."

He came more fully awake. Her voice, the fear in it, got to him. And slowly, as his brain cleared and the cobwebs faded, he realized that all that other stuff had been a dream. Just a dream. God, it had seemed so real.

But it wasn't real. He knew Melissa. She was not the kind of woman who would use sex as a weapon. Sex with her was—was more like a balm. A healing, tranquil balm to his troubled soul.

"Are you all right?" he asked.

She sighed; in relief, he thought. "Yes. Just frightened."

"Who was it?"

"I don't know. I . . . when it got light out, I went out

there. There were footprints in the sand. And the . . . the pent'. It's gone."

He couldn't have explained why his hand rose to touch his chest, but it did, and he knew he would feel the cool gold weight there even before his palm found it. "Jesus."

"Alex, you have to get out of there. Your father—he's more dangerous than you think."

He closed his eyes slowly. "Look, I'm going to do what you said—check into things, look at some sources besides my father's own words. But I didn't have a chance to yet—"

"I did. I think he may have killed your mother."

"You can't know that."

"Look, there was a whole series of thirty-year-old news articles about him. His pregnant young wife, Jennifer Simone Moring, your mother, disappeared, and he didn't even report her missing. Jennifer's mother—your grandmother—called the police after being unable to reach her for several days."

There was a lead ball forming in Alex's stomach. "And then?"

"The investigation turned up what the police called 'occult connections' surrounding both your parents. That set off all kinds of alarm bells. Your father's house was searched, he was kept under surveillance for weeks. But they never found anything concrete. The investigation was closed when they found your mother's body in a New York river. A witness claimed to have seen her jump from a bridge. Her death was ruled a suicide, and the case was closed. Your father was under surveillance, a continent away, at the time of her death, so he was in the clear."

Alex sighed slowly, nodded. "The orphanage was in Boston. She must have taken me there, then started back, and killed herself along the way."

"She took you there, then she started back, probably trying to get as far from you as she could before *he* managed to track her down. To protect you from him, Alex."

He shook his head slowly. "You must be one helluva Witch, to be able to read the mind of a dead woman." He said it gently, not sarcastically. He didn't want to hurt her, but she was reaching here. "My mother said in her note she wasn't long for the world. She must have been planning to take her own life when she wrote it."

"She said the evil that was pursuing her was getting closer. I think that evil was your father. Alex, she didn't want you anywhere near him. So he used some kind of powerful black magic to push her off that bridge. I know it, I feel it in my gut."

There was a shout from the hallway in a voice he recognized. Alex said, "Hold on a second, something's up." Then he went to the door, opened it. "Elizabeth? Is that you?"

"Alex, hurry. I need your help!"

He frowned, worried, and brought the phone back to his ear. "It's Elizabeth; something's wrong. I have to go."

"Alex, don't!"

He clicked the off button, tossed the phone toward the bed, and went down the stairs.

CHAPTER 8

"ALEX? Alex, don't go!"

There was no reply, just dead air. God, what was happening over there? She could only go by her instincts—and her instincts told her it was bad.

Melissa got to her feet, raced into her temple room, snatching a sack-type shoulder bag from a hook on the way past. Inside, she yanked open the cabinet, pawing through the herbs. Sage. Bindweed. Nightshade. She even tossed in her jar of devil's dung. Rosemary, yes. Angelica. She turned to her jewelry box, tugging out and donning every protective, magically charged amulet she had. Amber and jet necklace, onyx ring, agate pendant.

Hurry, she told herself. *There can't be much time.*

You can't face him alone.

Melissa froze in place, her hands halfway into the drawer where she kept her semiprecious stones, as the gentle whisper pervaded her mind.

Blinking, she lifted her head, found herself facing her mirror, which hung in the west. There was an image there, a face beside hers, almost like a photo that had been doubly exposed. The face was so similar to her own that at first she thought she was seeing double. But it wasn't exactly like her own. And it was of no substance. And then she realized she was face-to-face with Alex's mother.

"J-Jennifer?" she whispered.

Get help. You must get help. You can't fight him alone.

Melissa spun around, shivers racing up her spine, because she swore she felt the breath of that voice on her ear, but there was no one there. "Get help?" she cried to the empty room. "Where the hell am I supposed to get help? It's not like I have a coven."

There was no answer. Melissa swallowed hard, tried to stop her heart from pounding. She quickly grabbed some crystals, quartz, more agate, turquoise. Then she hurried into the living room, feeling in her soul that she was running low on time.

Get help! This time the voice shouted, and it was accompanied by a burst of wind. Pages of the news articles she'd printed out from the Internet blew from the stack beside the computer, drifting to the floor.

The bag she carried fell from Melissa's numb hand, *thunking* when it hit, the jars of herbs and the crystals clattering against one another. Melissa tried to stop shaking as she moved forward, then bent to pick up the fallen sheet of paper that had landed faceup on top of the rest.

It was one of the news articles she'd printed out—the one that said Jennifer's mother was the person who had reported her missing.

The words stood out on the page, their type seeming darker, bolder than the rest, though she knew it wasn't really: "Marinda Simone of Gardendale . . ."

Swallowing hard, Melissa turned toward her telephone. She had no doubt she had just received a clear communication from a spirit. She knew by the way the fine mist of hairs on her forearms stood upright, as if in response to static electricity. She knew by the hollow feeling in her chest and the funny skips in her heartbeat. She knew this was for real.

She picked up the phone, dialed the operator, asked if there was a listing for Marinda Simone in the small development of Gardendale, California, asked for the number and the address. She waited a beat, then nearly fainted when the computerized voice began reciting the number and the street address.

Melissa jotted it down with hands that shook, thought about calling, but decided to drive over there instead. Not only was it on the way to Alex's gloomy mausoleum, but . . . she needed time. She needed time to figure out just what the hell she was going to say to the woman when she got there. The twenty minutes it would take to get there were not nearly enough.

The house was a small white Cape Cod, with slate blue shutters and trim, a picket fence, and an herb garden with rosemary growing at the gate. Wind chimes hung from the front porch. A broomstick stood, bristles up, to one side of the front door, and a tiny clear glass Christmas ornament, with what looked like herbs inside it, dangled from a red ribbon directly over her head when Melissa stood at the front door.

She rang the bell, wondering if she was reading the signs correctly.

The door opened. A woman stood there, smiling, mildly curious. She had long once-black hair, now streaked with silver, and deep blue eyes. Aside from the crow's-feet at the corners of her eyes and the silver in her hair, the woman showed little sign of her age, though Melissa guessed she had to be well over sixty. And she was beautiful. But then the older woman's smile died and she stared as if stunned at Melissa's face. "My Goddess," she whispered.

"I, um—I'm sorry to bother you. Are you Marinda Simone?"

The woman managed to wipe the stunned expression away. "Yes. I'm—I'm sorry for my reaction, it's just that you look so much like . . . like my daughter." She blinked again, gave her head a shake. "Who *are* you?"

Melissa licked her lips. "My name is Melissa St. Cloud. I'm a friend of—of your grandson."

The woman's eyes widened. "Alex? You—you *know* Alex?"

"Yes."

Tears rose in those blue eyes. "I think you'd better come inside, dear."

"There's no time, Ms. Simone. He's in trouble."

The woman's eyes narrowed; her jaw clenched. "Is it his father? Is it Victor?"

"Yes."

Without a word, the woman clasped Melissa's hand and pulled her inside. Marinda left the door wide open, dragging Melissa at a trot through a cozy, neat-as-a-pin house and into what Melissa assumed was a bedroom.

Only it wasn't. Melissa was left to stand by the small table in the room's center, where a black cast-iron cauldron stood on a heat-resistant ceramic square. She scanned the room, the paintings of goddesses on the walls, the sculptures of them in every corner, the unlit candles everywhere. The place smelled powerfully of sandalwood and dragon's blood, and the windowsills were lined with huge blocks of amethyst and onyx and quartz.

There was a trunk on the floor in the back of the room, and the woman had opened it. She drew out a knife, unwrapping it from its black silk bindings. It had a very long double-edged blade and black handle with symbols burned into it.

"You're a Witch," Melissa said.

"As was my daughter," the woman replied, closing the trunk, turning to face Melissa, eyeing her jewelry. "As are you."

Melissa nodded. "We have to hurry."

With a nod, Marinda kept pace as Melissa rushed through the house and out to the car. Melissa dived behind the wheel. As she drove, the woman said, "Victor Moring is dead. Tell me it wasn't a mistake or a hoax when I read that in the papers."

"It wasn't. He is dead. But before he went, he planned some kind of ritual, to pass his powers on to Alex. Alex bought the house—he's living there now. Victor's old housekeeper, Elizabeth, is somehow in charge of seeing to it that the ritual happens, and I'm afraid she'll trick Alex into going through with it, somehow, even though I've warned him not to."

Marinda lowered her head and shook it. "No, it's not his power he wants to pass. I know what he wants. That's why I promised my daughter I would never try to find Alex. Because Victor would find him through me if I did, and because his intent is so foul."

She shot Melissa a look. "He'd been experimenting, researching, planning for this for his entire life. I don't believe it could even work, but I'm damned if I'm going to stand still and let him try."

"Try . . . try what?"

"Soul transferral," Marinda said. "He's going to try to move his own soul into Alex's body, so that he can return to the world of the living in Alex's place."

Melissa shook her head hard. "It won't work. It *can't* work."

"I've seen too much in my lifetime to put my faith in something being impossible. But even if it is, it won't matter. Jennifer learned what he was up to, and it frightened her so much that she ran away with little Alex to keep him safe. Victor's theory is that the first soul has to vacate the body at the moment his own tries to enter. In order for the spell to work, he has to bring Alex to the brink of death, then push him over." She closed her eyes. "He's going to murder his son, Melissa."

CHAPTER 9

ALEX followed Elizabeth's voice but didn't find her on the ground floor as he'd expected. He did hear her, though. Footsteps from—the stairway to the basement?

"Elizabeth?"

He headed down the basement stairs, worrying about what he might find. Was Elizabeth hurt, sick?

"Elizabeth, are you there?"

"Down here, Alex. Hurry, now, there's not much time!"

Alex picked up the pace, heading into the basement, wondering what on earth was wrong with the woman. If she was hurt, why the hell was she heading into the basement?

He wished he'd had time to dress in more than the pajama bottoms he was wearing. He'd never been in the basement of this old house. Elizabeth had told him there was nothing down there but the furnace and, now that he thought about it, seemed to have actively discouraged him from poking around below. He didn't relish the idea of traipsing through the cellar shirtless and barefoot. The concrete floor, while cool under his feet, seemed clean enough, and no spiderwebs stuck to his chest as he followed the sounds of Elizabeth's footsteps, and occasionally her voice, through the basement. The lights, what few there were, were low-wattage bulbs suspended from the ceiling and covered in red glass globes that were held in place by metal frames. Odd choice for a basement. But then again, his father had been an odd man.

The basement was huge, with cinder-block sides and a concrete floor. There were a furnace, a water heater, a fuel tank, and some boxes, all the things one would expect to find in a basement. There was also a wooden door, arched at the top, painted red, and standing open, that didn't seem to belong. But it was that door through which Elizabeth had gone. Beyond it, there was only darkness. Her voice floated back as if from the bowels of hell: "Come, Alex. Hurry now."

He stepped inside, wondering when she would find the light switch and flip it on. Then he heard the door close behind him, heard a lock turn. His stomach clenched tight.

"We don't want to be interrupted," Elizabeth said. A match flared, the sudden orange light licking at her face, making her seem demonic in the darkness. But she smiled and touched the flame to a candle on the floor, and then another, and another, moving around the room, spreading the light until he could finally see. He was standing within a circle of black candles. Shapes and symbols were painted on the floor, and in the center was a stone slab that looked like a bier, waist-high, rectangular, shaped as if to support a coffin.

He lifted his gaze toward Elizabeth. "What the hell is going on?"

She met his steady look with a smile. "Hush, now, and listen. It's time. It's time for your father to pass his gift on to you."

Alex gave his head a shake. "It's *his* gift, Elizabeth. Not mine. I'm not even certain I want it."

She went still, just staring at Alex's face. Then she seemed to shake herself. "You'd deny your father's dying request? Would you, Alex, after all he's done for you?"

Alex said nothing, just pushed a hand through his hair, trying to find a way to explain.

"Never mind," Elizabeth said softly. "Never mind then. It's your decision, after all." She dabbed tears from her eyes. "At least . . . join me in a drink to your father's memory. After that, we'll go back upstairs. I won't bother you about any of this again."

She nodded toward the slab.

Alex looked at it. "Let's go upstairs now. We can toast my father's memory up there."

"Oh." She seemed disappointed. "I . . . I thought you'd want to see this place, though I admit I was saving it for this special day. Now, it doesn't matter. This was your father's sacred room, Alex. He loved this room more than any other in the house."

"Really?"

She nodded. "I'll get the lights, in a second," she said, "so you can take a look around." She came toward him, carrying a tray with two ornate goblets on it. "Just sit, for a second. Take your drink. Then we'll go upstairs."

Alex pushed himself up onto the table, his legs hanging over the side, facing Elizabeth. He had to admit, he was curious about this room. "Thank you for understanding."

She lifted a goblet and handed it to Alex and took the other for herself, lowering the tray to the floor.

"To Victor Moring," Elizabeth said, lifting her glass. "May he find his ultimate joy. And to his son, may his body retain its power, its health, and its youthfulness for a long, long time to come." She tapped her goblet to Alex's, then drank.

Alex took a sip as well. The liquid was honey-sweet, with the sting of hard alcohol and the slightly thick texture of a liqueur. Alex swallowed, then lifted his own goblet in salute. "To my father," he said softly. "May his mistakes be forgiven, and his soul be at peace."

Again Alex drank, deeply this time. "This is very good," he said. "What is it?"

"Your father's special blend," Elizabeth told him. "He called it ambrosia."

"Nectar of the gods, huh?" Alex drained the glass, set it beside him on the slab.

She smiled, nodded, and turned to walk away, muttering, "Now where is that light switch?" She wandered into the shadows beyond the candlelight.

Alex waited. "Elizabeth, did you work for my father before I was born?"

From the darkness she answered, "Yes. I've been with your family for a very long time."

"I'd really . . . I'd like to know more about my mother."

"Your mother?" she asked. "What do you want to know about *her*?"

Alex blinked. Had Elizabeth's voice turned suddenly harsher than it had been before? No matter. He had to force himself to go ahead with his questions. "How did she die?"

"How do you think?"

Dizziness hit Alex like a wave hitting the sand. It made him think of the sacred place on the beach behind Melissa's house as he swayed and bobbed with the tide.

"Are you all right, Alex?"

"Yeah, I—" He pressed a hand to his forehead, got his upper body to stop wobbling. "I don't know what that was. That ambrosia must be stronger than it tastes."

"It is. A *lot* stronger. Lie down, Alex. It'll pass."

Alex lay down, obeying without resistance. He kept thinking he should be alarmed, he should be getting the hell out of this eerie basement. He kept wondering why it was taking Elizabeth so long to find the light switch. But his brain was too numb to act on any of it. His bare back pressed to the cold stone slab. He drew his legs up, stretching them out on the slab as well.

"Better?"

"Yes. But you didn't answer my question. About my mother."

"She committed suicide, Alex. Jumped off a bridge. You see, she had taken you from your father. His own newborn child. She ran away with Victor's son and heir. And then she just gave you away, like a stray cat she no longer wanted. Just gave you away, hoping Victor would never find you. You, his own guarantee of immortality. I suppose she couldn't live with the guilt of having betrayed her husband so horribly."

Alex shook his head from side to side, but the act made his head spin so badly that he had to close his eyes. "That doesn't make sense."

"Well, she knew why Victor wanted a son. Needed a son. Victor knew he would die relatively young, you see. He'd foreseen his own demise, dreamed of it. He knew exactly when it would come. Fortunately, he also knew your mother's plans. He found her precious little wooden box with her note to you inside it, and he substituted it with a box of his own, an identical one, with a hidden compartment. Then he spoke an incantation over it, ensuring you would find it in time to come to him before he died." Alex heard the woman sigh deeply. "But the cancer in his brain took an unforeseen turn— or maybe it had help from one of your mother's allies. At any rate, he passed just before his work came to fruition and brought you back to him." Her words seemed to echo, as if coming from within a deep well.

"If he knew her plans, why didn't he just . . . stop her from leaving?"

Elizabeth laughed. "To be honest, he had no intention of raising her brat on his own. Why should he, when he knew he wouldn't need you until much later? He let the nuns keep you. He knew you would come to him when his time drew near."

Frowning hard, Alex let those words sink in, tried to make sense of them. He turned his head slowly, opened his eyes. But the candles on the floor around him seemed to be revolving, and he couldn't blink Elizabeth into focus.

"He . . . he didn't want me?"

"Didn't *need* you. Not then."

Footsteps came closer. Elizabeth was back within his range of vision now but different. She'd donned a dark hooded robe that hid her face in shadows. She came to Alex's side, even as he tried to sit up and found his body completely unwilling to cooperate. She leaned over him, and chains rattled. Real fear crept into his blood, chilling it, when he realized she was locking manacles around his wrists and then his ankles.

She vanished again, and when she returned this time, she was holding a dagger. She muttered words in some language he didn't understand and drew the blade across his chest.

Pain sprang up in a fiery trail that followed the knife point. His back arched, lips pulling away from his teeth, arms jerking against the restraints. He cried out, but he couldn't escape. Whatever she'd given him made him weak, dizzy and confused, but it did nothing to dull the pain.

Again and again she lifted the blade, turned it, and drew another line, as if inscribing a message in his flesh. He could feel the warm blood flowing over his ribs, pooling at his sides.

"Are you insane? Jesus!"

She wiped the blade across Alex's thigh, turned, and left him. He managed to turn his head. "What the hell are you doing to me?"

"I'm sorry, Alex. But your father needs your body. He'd planned to take it before he passed, but he was a powerful magician. He's *still* a powerful magician. He can make it work, even from beyond. Sadly, you can't both fit in there at the same time, so I'm afraid you're going to have to leave."

He wasn't sure what the hell she meant—and when he tried to figure it out, he wasn't sure he wanted to know. But he had to know. "You're going to kill me."

The woman shrugged. "Technically, no." Even as she said it, Elizabeth was wheeling what looked like a defibrillation unit up beside Alex's stone bed. "The minute your heart stops, you'll leave your body. Your father has already left his. But he has trained and practiced with this type of thing his entire life. He is in complete control. He will enter your body. You will go on to the afterlife. And then, I'll restart your heart. As far as the rest of the world is concerned, you'll still be alive."

Alex shook his head weakly. "You're insane. It won't work. It will never work."

"Nonsense, Alex." A sharp stabbing pain at his wrist made Alex jerk his arm against the chains, but he couldn't pull clear of the pain. Elizabeth had returned, and she was leaning over him now, adjusting the intravenous line she'd just stuck into his wrist. The tube that led from his wrist hung down, and he lifted his head to see what was on the other end.

Nothing. The tube ended abruptly at an open end that dangled over an empty pail.

He slid his gaze up to his wrist, saw his own blood filling the tube, up to the point where the former nurse had it clamped. "Whenever you're ready, Victor," she said, to no one in the room.

And inexplicably, Alex heard a man's voice whisper, "Begin."

She removed the clamp. To Alex's horror, a stream of blood began flowing through the tiny tube, into the pail on the floor.

CHAPTER 10

MELISSA pulled her car into the driveway of the ancient-looking house. Storm clouds had gathered overhead, almost as if conspiring to block morning from coming to this desolate place. As she and Marinda walked to the front door, thunder rumbled in the distance. But to Melissa, it didn't sound like thunder at all but more like the menacing growl of some cosmic cur, warning them away.

She hesitated. Marinda closed a hand on her arm. "There's no such thing as a deity of absolute evil," she whispered, her voice close to Melissa's ear. "There's only energy. Victor has mastered his ability to tap into it, but the choice to use it for evil was all his. He was just a man, Melissa. Only a mortal man."

Melissa nodded.

"Center yourself, Witchling. We can tap into the same source, the same energy, and direct it against him. His spirit is working against nature. Nature's on our side."

Nodding, Melissa closed her eyes, drew a deep breath, curled her toes inside her shoes as she let the mighty force of the planet, the Mother, flow up and into her. She tipped her head back and opened her eyes, letting the endless energy of the Sky, the Father, pour down into her. She even tapped the power of the storm, and knew, when the wind whipped harder against her face and the lightning flashed, that it was real.

The power of the universe was real, and she was a part of it and a conduit for it.

Lowering her head, she stared at the house. "I'm ready."

The two of them marched side by side up the front stairs, to the door. Melissa was surprised to find it unlocked. She opened it and stepped inside. But she saw no one. The house was silent and brooding, and it felt abandoned.

"Victor's temple room is in the basement," Marinda said.

"How do you know?"

"My daughter lived here, for a time. She told me many things. This way, come on."

She led the way through the massive house, and Melissa followed, struggling to hold on to her connection with the Source of all power. They came to a door, which hung open, went through it and down a steep, long set of stairs into the bowels of the place. It was eerily lit with red-globed bulbs, and the energy that filled it was toxic. Melissa felt it around her, prickling her skin and raising goose bumps on her arms. Marinda never hesitated. She walked through the basement and up to a large door, carved all from one slab of wood. She tried the knob, careful not to make a sound as she twisted.

"Locked," she said.

"Wait." Melissa dug in her bag, pulled out a long, heavy hairpin. "I expected the place to be locked. I'll try to get it open." Marinda moved aside just slightly, and Melissa inserted the pin into the keyhole, twisting, feeling, willing the lock to open.

Marinda pulled something from her pocket, a dry brown flower on a tall, nearly leafless stem. "Maybe this will help." She held the blossom against the lock.

Immediately Melissa felt the tumblers turn against her hairpin and knew the lock had opened. Whether due to her own efforts or the other woman's weed, she couldn't be sure.

Marinda whispered, "Chicory cut with blade of gold, midnight or midday at the height of Sol, clears the pathway to your goal, against it no man's locks will hold." She shrugged. "Hold on to the stem, dear. Folklore claims it grants invisibility as well."

Melissa dropped her hairpin back into her bag and closed a hand around the bottom of the stem the other woman held. "Hell, it can't hurt."

Melissa turned the knob and pushed the door open. The scene laid out within the circle of dancing black candles in the room she entered shocked her right to the core. Alex was on a stone table, chains on his arms and legs, his chest covered in blood that ran in rivulets down his sides. A tube in his arm ran with more blood that was collecting in a pail on the floor.

"Alex, my God!" She let go of the weed and ran to his side, yanking the needle from his wrist and closing her hand over the wound, to halt the blood flow.

"So you've arrived," a woman said.

Melissa jerked her head up sharply, so focused on Alex that she hadn't even noticed the woman standing in the circle. She wore a hooded robe that shadowed her face, and stood between the table on which Alex lay and a machine of some kind.

"You broke the circle," she whispered. "But it's not going to matter." The woman lifted a dagger and came slowly toward Melissa. "Back away from him. Now."

Melissa looked down, and her stomach convulsed when she saw the amount of Alex's blood in the pail. She clenched his wrist tighter, refusing to let go. "You can't kill us all."

The woman looked up, surprised, and only then did she seem to notice that Melissa hadn't come alone. Marinda stepped out of the shadows, into the light cast by the dancing flames of the candles.

"You," Elizabeth said, her voice louder than before.

"That's right, Elizabeth." Then she looked around the room. "Do you hear that, Victor? I'm not going to let you murder my grandson the way you did his mother. What kind of spell did you use to make her jump off that bridge?"

Elizabeth smiled slowly. "Oh, it was nothing so complicated for a man of Victor's power, Witch. A mind control spell, some posthypnotic suggestion, and it was done."

She moved toward Melissa again. Melissa flung up a hand, projecting all the energy she could muster. "Halt, damn you!"

Again the woman stopped.

Melissa focused on Alex then. "Mother Earth, goddess strong, stop this blood by witches' song. Mother Earth, goddess strong, stop this blood by Witches' song. Mother Earth . . ."

Marinda joined in the chant, coming closer, standing right at her side, placing her hand over Melissa's. Melissa felt the wound tingling against her palm.

"Stop it! Dammit, stop right now!" Elizabeth cried. She raced forward again, swinging her blade at Melissa.

Marinda yanked Melissa aside, pulling her hand from Alex's wrist as she did. The blade hissed by, doing no damage. And as Melissa stumbled, regained her balance, and glanced back at the wrist, she saw no further bleeding. Either the charm had worked or Alex was already dead.

Elizabeth stood crouched, blade aloft, ready to attack. But there was something beside her. Some dark, shapeless form that pulsed with evil.

"He's here," Marinda whispered, leaning close. "Open the Western Gate, Melissa. We have to send Victor back through, it's the only way to end this."

Melissa nodded, but she didn't want to leave Marinda's side with this mad knife-wielding woman so close by.

"Go!"

Melissa went. Elizabeth moved to come for her, but Marinda was ready. She snatched the bag from Melissa's shoulder and swung it, catching the other woman upside the head and knocking her to her knees. The dagger clattered to the floor as Elizabeth scrambled to her feet, and then the two women were locked in a struggle, hitting, punching, clawing each other. Melissa knew Marinda had a blade of her own, but she would never use it. Not to do violence.

Melissa located the western point, partly by instinct and partly by the symbols inscribed on the floor in red paint and the large bowl of water that stood at the circle's edge. She stood with her back to the life-and-death struggle, to Alex, and it took all her willpower to do that. Every part of her practical, mortal mind was telling her to turn, to fight, to drag Alex out of here. But the Witch in her, that impractical, intuitive part, knew this was far bigger than a physical battle, and told her to do what had to be done.

She focused, centered, envisioned the great pouring sea, the womb of the Earth mother, the place of transformation, the gateway between the worlds. When she saw it so clearly that she could feel the spray and hear the crashing waves, she pushed her arms straight out in front of her, then slowly opened them wide, parting the mystical waters.

"Guardians of the Western Gate, open the portals wide! Beloved ancestors, come, come, come to us now! Come to gather the soul that awaits its rest. Come to gather the wounded heart of this lonely spirit, whose time on this plane has passed!"

She paused, waiting. She could still hear movement behind her, the grunts of pain, the impacts of hands on flesh. And another voice, a dark voice, Victor's voice, moaning, "No. No, God, no!"

"Sisters of the Moerae, Weavers of the Web of Fate, come! Clotho, Lachesis, Atropos, come!" Melissa cried, her voice gaining strength and volume. "Bring with you the Keres! The hounds of the Underworld! Two men lie at your feet. Two souls hover between the worlds. You alone know which is meant to pass at this time and which is destined to live on in the mortal realm. Come, Sisters! Weave the thread of life into the web of your grand design. Come!"

Melissa paused only long enough to draw a ragged breath, then went on, not even thinking about her words. They came from somewhere deep within her. "Hecate! Lady of the Crossroads!" Melissa was shouting now, and her voice filled the room and reverberated from the walls. "Come, triple goddess! Claim the soul that is your own and spare the innocent from further harm!"

Melissa was jarred from her state of intense focus by a

blast of wind and a crashing sound. The pot of water that had been sitting at the western edge of the circle lay on its side, its contents flowing over the floor. She hadn't touched it; she was sure no one else had, either. It was a moment before she realized the water was flowing toward the center of the circle, and she turned to see it racing toward the table where Alex lay, the dark shape hovering closely over him.

Above the water there was a blur of white. Or was it a trick of her eyes and the candles?

Elizabeth broke away from where she was locked in physical combat with Marinda and ran to Alex's side. Her feet slapped down into the stream of water, and it splashed up and into that dark form.

And at that very instant, the dark form vanished.

Marinda looked up from the floor, her face cut and bleeding in places and bearing angry red handprints in others. Her hair was a wild tangle. Elizabeth was babbling now, weeping, shaking Alex's body as if trying to wake him. "Victor? Are you there? Did you make it?"

Melissa hurried to help Marinda to her feet. "It's over, now, Elizabeth," she whispered. "It's done. Victor's gone."

"No!" the nurse cried. "I only have to wake him in his new body."

Melissa snapped her head around. The woman had grabbed the defibrillator machine's paddles and hit its power buttons.

"He has to be all right! He has to." She leaned over Alex, even as Melissa lunged forward. "Come back to me, Victor!" Elizabeth cried, lowering the paddles.

"No! Wait!" Melissa hit Elizabeth hard, knocking her away from Alex just as she hit the buttons. Elizabeth stumbled, the paddles turning and touching her own body. A charge of electricity surged from the paddles into the woman who held them and who was standing with her feet in a puddle of water. She spasmed there for an instant, like a marionette on quivering strings, and then collapsed to the floor, dropping the paddles.

Melissa hurried to her side, bent over her, checked her

pulse. There was nothing. Her hair was smoking. So was the machine. Melissa lifted her gaze to Marinda, automatically seeking the older woman's wisdom.

Marinda shook her head. "The Fates wanted her. They took her. Let her go." Then she looked past Melissa and smiled. "And my grandson is awake."

Melissa ran to Alex, lifting his head, running her hands through his hair, kissing his face. "You're all right. Oh, God, you're all right."

He tried to embrace her, only to find his arms couldn't reach, because of the chains. "Melissa, Elizabeth was . . . she tried to—"

"I know. It's all right now. It's over." She leaned in, pressed her lips to his, felt the life in him, strong and steady.

"Close the gate, young Priestess," Marinda said, coming to join her at Alex's side. "You've done well today."

Alex was struggling to sit up. His grandmother helped him, freeing him from the manacles and whispering to him to wait, to be still for just a moment. Then he sat there in silence, watching as Melissa turned slowly away, facing west. She pictured that sea again, saw herself on its shore, opened her arms wide.

Then she paused, because she saw . . . something. That woman, that same woman she'd seen before. Jennifer, standing on the shore. Melissa turned quickly to see if the others saw her, too. From their stunned expressions she knew they did.

"Jennifer?" Marinda whispered.

Alex said, "What . . . who . . . what am I seeing?"

"That's my daughter, Alex," Marinda said gently. "Your mother."

"My mother?"

The apparition seemed to smile. Melissa heard, not out loud but in her mind, Jennifer's voice. Her message.

Thank you, Melissa. Thank you for saving my son. Thank you, dear Mother, for helping her.

The rest seemed to be addressed to Alex: *Don't worry*

about Victor, my darling child. This is a place of healing and transformation, not punishment. Now, for the three of you, I have only one request. Love one another, as I love you all.

And then she faded, growing smaller and vanishing altogether.

Tears flooding her eyes, Melissa opened her arms again. "Thank you, Jennifer, for bringing us together, for giving your own life to save that of your son. We love you and we will forever honor your memory." The tears spilled over. "Thank you, Hecate, goddess of the crossroads. Thank you, Sisters of Fate, Clotho, Lachesis, Atropos. Hail and farewell."

"Hail and farewell," Marinda echoed.

"Good-bye, Mother," Alex whispered.

Melissa drew her arms down and together, closing the veil between the worlds. Then she turned and went to Alex.

He was pale, none too steady, as she and Marinda helped him down from the table. "Alex, this is Marinda Simone. She's your grandmother."

He smiled weakly at the older woman. "Hello, Grand-mother."

"Hello, Alex." She leaned close, kissed his cheek. Then she sighed, all business. "There's no reason to open up your father's private life and all his mistakes to public scrutiny. I'll ground the circle energy. Then we'll clean up down here and move the body upstairs. We can throw a hair dryer into the bathtub with poor Elizabeth. The world can believe her death was accidental electrocution. It's close enough to the truth."

"But what about Alex?" Melissa asked. "He needs a hospital."

"No." Alex touched her face with his palm. "Look at the pail. I can't be more than a couple of pints low. The cuts on my chest are shallow. I'll be fine."

She stared at him and she imagined her heart was in her eyes, but she didn't care. "Are you really all right?"

He leaned closer, kissed her mouth, and probably tasted

the salt of her tears, she thought, as she clung to him. When he lifted his head, he said, "I'm all right. From now on, everything is going to be all right."

ALEX let Melissa pull his arm around her shoulders, but he refused to lean on her as she led him through the darkness of the great below, up the stairs, and into the great above. The sun was streaming through the windows now, and the house seemed almost . . . cheerful.

He sat in a chair and allowed Melissa to wash the blood from his chest and his sides, while his grandmother was in the kitchen, brewing what she called a healing tea.

"What did that insane woman cut into my chest?" he asked Melissa as she ran the cloth over the shallow wounds. It stung, but he didn't care.

"Victor's name, in Theban script." She applied salve she'd found in the medicine cabinet, then wrapped his chest in soft gauze and taped it in place. "He thought he could steal your body, basically make himself live again."

"I know. Elizabeth said as much while she was carving me up." Melissa had a clean shirt in her hands, taken from Alex's room upstairs, but she paused now, staring at him with her huge, beautiful eyes. "Do you think that it's possible this thing could have worked?" she asked.

"I don't know. I just . . . I don't know. I think he's been—haunting me sort of. Maybe preparing for this. I've felt him in my head more than once—but not anymore." He shook his head.

"I suppose just about anything is possible," she said.

He reached out, took the shirt from her, and set it aside. Then he took her hands in his. "What about forgiving me, for being such a stubborn idiot about all of this and nearly getting you killed? Do you think *that's* possible?"

Her eyes seemed to search his—and he felt to his core they were doing exactly that. Searching for some reassurance that he hadn't absorbed his father's twisted values and negativity.

Licking his lips, knowing what he had to do, he got to his feet. "You sit. I want to tell you some things I figured out while I was lying down there being drained into a mop bucket."

She did as he said, but she never took those potent, all-seeing eyes from his. God, he loved her. He'd loved her from the second he'd set eyes on her, he thought. She sat in the overstuffed chair, but only after pulling another one closer, so he could sit facing her.

She knew he was still weak and dizzy. She seemed to know more about him than he did, most of the time. She had from the start.

He sat in the chair facing hers and took her hands in his. "I realized down there, when I was pretty sure I was going to die, that you were right. He's built up a lot of negativity, or bad karma, or whatever you want to call it. I figure, since I lived through all of this, I have the opportunity to make things right. Take that negative energy and redirect it into something positive."

"Really? How are you going to do that, Alex?"

"For starters, I'm going to sell this house and everything in it and give the money to St. Luke's School for Boys."

She smiled a little. He liked that, knew he was on the right track.

"Do you think you have to do that for me, Alex? Because you don't, you know. I've been falling in love with you since the first time you said my name. That's not going to change."

He smiled fully. "You think I haven't figured that out already? Hell, woman, you came charging in here unarmed and laid your life on the line for me. I kind of guessed that might mean you cared."

"Not overconfident or anything, are you?" she asked, her tone teasing.

"Not even close." He got to his feet, tugged her to hers. "Melissa, you are—you're *good*. You're so good that I feel like I want to be better. I want to be the kind of man who's worthy of loving a woman like you." He slid his arms around her waist, pulled her close to him.

"You already are, Alex," she whispered, resting her head on his shoulder. "I promise, you already are."

EPILOGUE

"Shhhh!" Melissa hissed. "It's starting!"

She sat in the arms of her husband, in front of the television in the living room of their beach house. There were people all around them. Bowls of popcorn, open pizza boxes, and lots of icy soft drinks covered every surface. The director was there, along with the two beautiful starlets and the new head writer, a woman who was a practicing Witch herself. Marinda was there as well, beaming with approval at her grandson and his wife and hinting about the great-grandchildren she hoped wouldn't be too far away.

The season finale of *The Enchantress* began with the Witch as a guest at an authentic Wiccan wedding, with the bride and groom being played by none other than the creative consultant and the show's producer/creator.

The ceremony was built around Melissa and Alex's actual wedding, held in a grove of oaks, the guests forming a circle around them. Every flower and color and gift had a special spiritual significance, and the officiating minister was a Wiccan High Priestess by the name of Marinda Simone.

Of course, in the script the ceremony was interrupted by some ill-intentioned demon and the Enchantress was forced to vanquish him, but at least she didn't accomplish that by a deadpan recitation of a rhyming couplet from a book. Thanks to the new writing team, the poor, overworked Witch was forced to do research, determine the best astrological timing, find and gather appropriate herbs, stones, and candles, call on the Divine, and channel her power from the elements of Earth, Air, Fire, Water, and Spirit. Also thanks to the new writing team, the show's ratings had climbed through the roof. Every episode dropped a tiny bit of Witchlore or ancient wisdom, all wrapped up in a damn good story, and the viewers couldn't get enough.

When the credits rolled and everyone inside was celebrating, high-fiving each other, cracking a few beers, Alex took Melissa's hand and tugged her with him, through the sliding doors, and down onto their special place on the beach.

"I need you with me for this," he told her. Then he pulled something from his pocket: the gold pentacle that had belonged to his father.

"Alex?" She searched his eyes. "Honey, I thought we were going to keep that put away?"

He nodded. "We were. But I don't think keeping it in a locked box in the back of the closet is really good enough. Not even after all the cleansing you've done on it. I think . . . I think it's time to let it go."

"But it's the only thing you have left of your father."

He shook his head. "No. I've only just begun to realize all the other things he left me. Because of him, I found you. And Grams. And my mother. My family. I have all of that. I don't need a hunk of metal. Besides, I think it makes a great offering of thanks."

She smiled. "And just what are you giving thanks for?"

"Everything I just mentioned. Plus the success the show is enjoying. And most of all, for the little one that's going to be coming into our lives pretty soon."

She frowned. "Honey, I'm not—"

"Yes, you are. Have been, since that first night on the beach."

"How do you know?"

He smiled down at her. "My mother told me, in a dream last night. It will be a little girl, and we'll name her Jennifer." He pulled her close and kissed her. Then he turned to face the sea and hurled the pendant as hard as he could.

It splashed into the water, just as the sun went down. Melissa closed her eyes and whispered, "So mote it be."

A WULF'S CURSE

RONDA THOMPSON

CHAPTER 1

England, 1820

THE impatient stamp of a hoof. The *jingle-jangle* of a bridle. The leather creak of a harness. All sounds of the caravan preparing to leave. Elise Collins stood in the shadows, the wagons barely distinguishable through a thick London mist. She clutched her valise in a white-knuckled grip and kept repeating the phrase, *I am an adventurer,* over in her mind.

A loud roar split the night. Elise jumped. Good God, what roamed the mist?

"Beast Tamer!" a voice thundered. "Come see to Raja. He's in a surly mood tonight."

The door of the wagon closest to Elise swung open. A figure stepped outside. She couldn't see his face, but unless the mist and the shadows played tricks with the night, he was very tall. Moonlight danced around him, illuminating him in a spiritual light. His shoulder-length hair nearly gleamed silver. A low curse floated to her upon the chill, dismissing his saintly image.

"Raja is spoiled for my company!" the man called. "I had hoped to sleep, since Nathan said he'd drive for me."

"Unless you keep the tiger quiet, none who have sleep duty tonight will get any!" the big voice boomed. "Leave your wagon empty and ride a while with Raja."

Tigers? Elise swallowed the lump in her throat. Danny, her uncle's groom and an accomplice to her daring escape, hadn't mentioned that there were wild animals among the traveling show. Perhaps she shouldn't have sent Danny off so quickly once he'd delivered her safely to the outskirts of London. But no, Elise had made her decision. She must follow through with her plans.

Her gaze strayed toward the now empty wagon. With her dark cloak covering her, she should be able to steal inside without being seen. Her uncle would never think to look for her among such people. The caravan was her best hope of escape. Gathering her courage, Elise darted toward the wagon.

STERLING Wulf paused before the sturdy bars of the animal wagons. One dark shape paced inside each wagon. Leena, a black panther, had gotten up in years and seldom gave him trouble, but Raja, a Siberian tiger, was ill-tempered most of the time and needed coddling.

"Want me to ride with you, do you?" Sterling asked. "You're nothing but an overgrown kitten." As Raja paced nervously before him, Sterling related to the tiger's unease. He'd been on edge since they'd reached the countryside of London and begun their nightly performances. London brought back too many memories, and it had been dangerous for him to be seen. What if someone had recognized him? And the temptation to seek out his brothers had almost proven too great. He'd feel much safer as soon as the troupe put London behind them.

Raja rubbed his great hulk against the bars. Sterling shook his head and stuck his hand inside, his fingers rumpling the animal's fur. "All right then. I'll ride with you, but only for a short while."

"I wish you would pet me as nicely as you pet him."

He turned to find Mora, the snake charmer, watching him. "You should be in your wagon," he said. "Philip will call the signal to start moving at any moment."

Mora sashayed toward him, her silver jewelry flashing in the dark. "I had hoped to ride in your wagon tonight—had hoped we could do more than sleep."

Sterling shrugged. "Maybe another time."

She placed her hands upon her ample hips. "You always refuse my offers. Do you not like women?"

Women were a nice distraction, Sterling admitted, but some said they were, for the most part, a curse to man. How well Sterling knew the truth to those words. However, Mora posed no threat to him, at least to his heart. She was older than he was, and she didn't smell all that good, but she held a certain appeal. It had been a while since he'd given in to his baser urges. Sterling found himself tempted, but tonight the cats demanded his attention.

"Raja is upset and I've been asked to calm him so the others can sleep. As I've said, maybe another time."

The snake charmer made a sound through her nose, not unlike the horses that pawed the ground in readiness to be off. "You cannot avoid me forever, Beast Tamer. I am curious to see if the big bulge in your tights is really you, or if you enhance your charms with a sock."

Sterling laughed. He was long past blushing over vulgar conversation. And he hated wearing the blasted tights while he performed. Philip, the caravan master, had insisted, assuring Sterling that not only men liked to ogle the troupe members. He supposed Philip was right. He did collect more than the rest of the performers, and the coin wasn't always tossed by men.

"Time to move!" Philip shouted.

Dismissing Mora, Sterling climbed up beside Taylor, an older man with a hump on his back who saw to the caravan animals, horse and beast alike. The man flicked the reins and moved the wagon forward. Raja growled in protest.

"Enough of your tantrums!" Sterling called down to the tiger. "Sleep, Raja. Heaven knows I'd rather be settled in my cot than feel this hard bench pressing into my ass."

· · ·

THE gentle sway of the wagon seduced her. Elise could barely keep her eyes open. She had sworn not an hour past that she'd be too frightened to relax, but nothing had happened to her. The man had not returned to the wagon. Her back hurt and her petticoats did not sufficiently cushion the hard wood beneath her bottom. Now that her eyes had adjusted to the darkness, she made out the shape of a cot.

What harm would there be in resting there for a moment? Just long enough to ease the stiffness settling into her bones? Elise crawled forward and hefted herself upon the bed. There were warm blankets and a soft pelt to snuggle beneath.

Her eyes trained warily upon the door, she stretched out. She would not sleep but merely rest. The bedding had a scent about it. A male scent. Beast Tamer. What sort of name was that for a man, anyway? And was he really as tall as his shadow? Was his hair silver? Maybe he'd be a very old man, this Beast Tamer.

The last thought comforted Elise. Perhaps he'd be a kind, grandfatherly figure who'd be happy to take her beneath his wing and see her safely to her aunt's door in Liverpool. The sway of the wagon, the steady clip-clop of the horses' hooves as they plodded along, combined to soothe her. She was safe, at least for the time being.

STERLING eased the door to his wagon shut. No need to bang about and wake those sleeping inside the other wagons. He stripped from his clothes and slipped into his cot, only to find it smaller than he remembered. A soft moan rose from the space beside him. He was not alone. Mora, the snake charmer, Sterling assumed. He supposed most men would feel flattered to find a woman waiting in their bed, but he wasn't all that certain he even liked Mora.

Her sweet scent drifted up to him. He didn't recall the snake charmer ever smelling particularly fetching. In the darkness, he touched her hair. Silky beneath his fingertips. Mora appeared as if she seldom took a brush to her tangled mane.

Had she made such effort to please him? Because he *was* pleased. His blood heated in his veins. Lust stirred to life inside of him. Sterling sought her mouth in the darkness. Again he was surprised. Her lips were petal-soft beneath his, and her breath did not reek of garlic. She sighed, opening to him. He took full advantage of her invitation.

SUCH a strange dream. Elise had never been kissed before. It was pleasant. Whoever her mind had conjured seemed to know what he was about, which struck her as odd. Shouldn't her dream include only her own experience in such matters? He swirled his tongue inside of her mouth, something she had never considered a man might do. His lips were firm, warm, demanding, but demanding of what, she wasn't certain.

A response, she realized a moment later, but only because she felt one. Heat flooded her body, settling between her legs. Her breasts suddenly ached, her nipples standing erect against her stiff chemise. And then his hand was there, cupping her through the fabric of her frock. Elise came awake with a start. She suddenly understood that the man kissing and fondling her was no dream phantom. Her first instinct was to scream, but then she recalled her circumstance.

"Kindly remove your hand from my person," she said against his lips.

He immediately pulled back, but his hand still rested where he had left it. "Mora?"

His voice was as deep and rich as she remembered. "That is not my name, and you, sir, are taking liberties against my will."

"What the bloody hell?" He scrambled off of her. She heard him fumbling about, then saw a flint spark, his obvious intent to light the lantern.

A soft glow filled the wagon. Elise got her first good look at this man called the Beast Tamer. He was not old. He looked nothing at all like a kind, grandfatherly figure. His skin was not loose and wrinkled, but firm and smooth. And there was a lot of skin bared for her innocent eyes. The man stood before her completely naked.

CHAPTER 2

THE woman in Sterling's bed was not, by a far stretch of the imagination, Mora the snake charmer. Her eyes were huge and as green as a spring field. Her hair, a silky mass of auburn curls, hung in wild disarray around her pale oval face. The cut of her gown, even be it a simple frock, the delicate kid slippers he saw peeking beneath her hem, told him the tale easily enough.

"Have had a change of heart, have you?"

She swallowed loudly. "W-What?" she whispered.

He shook his head. He'd had this happen before, on several occasions, in fact. Sterling had a rule about women in his bed. Only the common, like himself, and never one he could come to care for. Young women such as the one sitting upon his cot were dangerous to a man cursed. And he was dangerous to her, as well.

"You're not the first proper miss who's longed for a night of adventure in my wagon," he said. "I'll tell you what I told the others: I'm a performer, not a man who can be bought for a night's pleasure. Find your amusement elsewhere."

Her big eyes blinked up at him, then lowered before they widened. Sterling realized that he stood before her naked. Well, hell, like the other women, she probably wanted to know about the tights. Now she could plainly see that he didn't stuff them to enhance his manly assets.

"Oh my God," he heard her choke, which pleased him to a degree. "I'm afraid you don't understand. I did not sneak aboard your wagon; that is, I did sneak aboard your wagon, but not for the reason you have arrogantly assumed."

Since the young woman appeared as if she might swoon, Sterling snatched the pelt off his cot and wrapped it around his waist. "I hope that your coachman has followed discreetly behind, as has been the case for others like you in the past. Then when I throw you out into the night, you won't find yourself in an even more dangerous circumstance."

"Throw me out?" Her head snapped back up. "You cannot throw me out. I have no protection."

"Bravery and stupidity walk a fine line together," Sterling calmly pointed out, although he felt far from calm. The young woman affected him more than he cared to admit. It had been years since he had tasted innocence, and she reeked of it. Her lips, full and puffy from his kisses, drew his gaze and held it. Her mouth moved, but he had trouble hearing her words.

"Speak up," he demanded. "I cannot understand your hysterical babbling."

Her chin rose. He knew the haughty expression well. The wealthy learned it at an early age. He lifted a brow in similar fashion.

"I am not hysterical," the woman said more forcefully. "I am shocked and sickened that you would steal into my bed and take vulgar liberties with me."

His brow rose higher. "*Your* bed?"

A pretty blush suffused her cheeks. "That is to say, your bed," she corrected. "Perhaps I should explain my presence here."

Sterling noticed the valise sitting upon the wagon floor. "Make it quick. The farther we travel from London, the farther the walk when you return."

Her back straightened. "I cannot go back. I must throw myself upon your mercy."

She didn't pitch forward and land at his feet, and she hadn't lowered the superior tilt to her chin. At least her hands shook as she fondled the expensive lace that made a mockery of the term *work frock*. Sterling resented her immediately. She was a reminder. A reminder of all that he had lost.

"The wagon isn't moving fast. The fall when you jump shouldn't do more than scuff your slippers."

Her tempting mouth dropped open. "You, sir, are no gentleman."

He allowed his gaze to roam over her from head to toe. "You've already discovered that. Get out before I'm tempted to prove it again."

THE man was rude, crass to the core. He stared at her with his unsettling gray eyes as if she were the one who'd taken liberties with him. His hair was not silver, but blond, a few strands streaked lighter than the rest. He was tall, and somewhat intimidating, she'd give him that. But she refused to show fear. Animals, Elise had heard, sensed fear and were prone to act upon the emotion. This man with the pelt draped around his hips, looking for all the world like some Viking, probably had the mentality of a simple beast.

"I have money," she said. "I'll pay you."

One of his dark brows lifted again. "Pay me for what?"

Her mouth felt suddenly dry, her eyes in jeopardy of moving over his muscled flesh. "For safe passage to Liverpool."

He laughed. His teeth were white and straight, she noted. Seeing them exposed on her behalf did not please her. He sobered a moment later.

"How much?"

Elise had pinned the small bag of coins to the inside of her cloak. She fumbled through the folds and removed the bag, then handed it to him. "It isn't much, but it's all that I have."

His long fingers touched hers during the exchange and sent another shiver racing up her spine. He held the bag as if weighing it, then frowned. "I'll wager this isn't enough to pay your expenses even this far. But it is enough to get your throat slit and your body tossed into a ditch by someone less scrupulous." He tossed the bag back to her. "Gather your belongings and leave."

Unbidden, a rush of tears sprang to her eyes. Elise might be frightened of the man, but she was more frightened of being forced into the night. Alone, on the dark roads, she would be an easy mark for thieves, or worse.

"Please," she whispered. "You are my only hope of escape."

The man cocked his head, regarding her thoughtfully. "Escape? Who are you running from?"

Frightened or not, Elise had been schooled in proper manners. "It wouldn't be proper for me to tell you. I don't even know your name."

He laughed. "They call me Beast Tamer, and if you cared at all about being proper, you damn sure wouldn't be here."

His rudeness wore upon her already frayed nerves. "Has no one ever taught you manners?"

The wheels hit a rut and bounced him across the wagon. He landed beside her. Elise scrambled back—away from his nakedness, the heat that radiated from his powerful body. For all his rudeness, he didn't speak with a cockney accent like most of the common lot. His bone structure was good. Straight nose, strong jaw, high cheekbones, and well-defined lips.

"Manners do not put food in my belly, or clothes upon my back." His face was dangerously close. "What is your name?"

Did she dare tell him? It occurred to Elise that he could use her true identity to his gain and her loss. He might turn her back over to her uncle in hopes of receiving a reward, or, worse, kidnap her and demand a high ransom for her return.

"Elise," she provided stiffly.

"Elise."

He said her name as if savoring it for flavor. He said it in a way that made her feel breathless and made her heart beat all the faster inside of her chest.

"The name suits you."

She wished he'd move off of the cot and, for God's sake,

dress himself properly. She could scarce look at him that her eyes didn't go roaming of their own accord.

"Beast Tamer does not suit you. Have you a Christian name?"

"You avoid the subject. Who do you wish to escape, Elise?"

Again, the sound of her name on his lips caused a strange reaction. A fluttering inside her stomach. "I cannot discuss my problems with a man whose Christian name I do not know," she persisted.

He shrugged, calling her attention to his broad, bare shoulders. "If we have nothing further to discuss, it is time for you to go."

When he started to rise, Elise grabbed his arm. It was a mistake. The feel of him shot through her. His flesh was muscled and his skin warm and smooth to the touch. She snatched her hand away.

"All right. I will tell you why I must escape. My uncle has promised me in marriage to a man I do not wish to wed."

His response was a snort of amusement. "Running from a life of spoiled luxury, are you? Judging by the cut of your clothing and the way your nose is pointed at the ceiling, you not only know that it is your duty to secure yourself a prosperous husband, but you have been training for it since you were a little girl."

True, she knew making a good match was the best most women of her station could hope for, the most they could aspire to in life, but Elise wasn't like most women. She'd learned the finer arts of being a lady because her uncle had insisted, but she'd always longed for a more adventurous life. Elise did not have friends like other young women her age. The London ton cared little about her cold, impersonal uncle, and he less about them. They were rarely invited to the best parties, and if someone sent them an invitation out of duty alone, her uncle had never attended, or allowed her to attend, either. Her uncle hadn't even given her a proper "coming out," but instead had gone behind her back to settle her future.

"The man he wishes me to marry is old," she whispered. "And very unattractive."

"The richest ones usually are. The young, handsome dukes are snatched up fairly quickly, you know."

He made sport of her. The man refused to take her situation seriously. "Four wives," she said, lifting her chin a notch. "Four wives he's had now, and all of them dead."

The information brought another lift of his brow. She wondered why his brows and lashes were so dark when his hair was the color of ripened wheat. "Unfortunate for them, but not so unfortunate for you, if the man is wealthy and titled."

A rush of heat flooded her face. "Fortunate? Did you not hear what I said? I fear the man is a murderer!"

He ran a hand through his overlong hair, then stood. "And I think your imagination has led you to this folly." He grabbed a board that ran the length of the top of the wagon and stared down at her.

The pelt he wore wrapped around his waist could certainly fall away without much provocation. Elise realized, were that to happen, she'd be staring right at . . . Well, good Lord, why couldn't the man find something decent to wear while they conversed?

"You haven't seen the way he looks at me," she insisted, and shuddered at the memory. Sir Winston Stoneham had often clenched and unclenched his hands in an unconscious manner while in her company. Elise felt certain he wished her bodily harm.

The Beast Tamer's silver gaze ran over her. "Does he look at you the same way that I am looking at you now?"

As he appraised her, boldly, as if undressing her, another shiver wracked her. The way he gazed at her was the same, but yet it wasn't. "No," she decided. "You look at me as if you'd like to swallow me whole. He, I feel certain, would enjoy chewing me up a bit first."

To her surprise, the man threw back his head and laughed.

"You find a person's ill will toward me amusing?" she asked through tight lips.

He sobered and bent toward her, his hands still wrapped around the board above. "Your mother should have told you that lust always comes first between a man and a woman, then, for a lucky few, love."

She looked away from him, knowing that his vulgar words had made her blush. "My mother is dead, sir. My father, too, or I assure you I would not be in this awful predicament."

"Sterling."

Her gaze met his in question.

"Sterling is my Christian name. Sir is a title given to more privileged and more civilized men than I."

"And your last name?"

"And yours?" he countered.

She pressed her lips together.

"Then simply Elise and Sterling it is," he said.

Curiosity overcame her. "Why did you tell me your name?"

He released his grip on the board above him and turned, presenting her with his strong, broad back. Muscles rippled as he bent to retrieve a shirt from the floor.

"I am an orphan as well," he admitted. "In that regard, there is no class distinction between us."

"Is that why you're here? Among these people? Living this life?"

Shrugging into the shirt, he turned. "I am here because this is where I wish to be, and we are not discussing me. I am not the intruder inside this wagon."

Elise was determined to convince him that her plight was one of honest threat. "My uncle is responsible for making the match. He is aware that by placing me at the mercy of the man who has agreed to pay my bride's price, he is also placing me in danger. The money is more important to him than I am, or ever will be. I am an embarrassment to him."

Sterling's gaze swept her again. "I see no physical fault with you. What is his complaint?"

When a man donned a shirt, even if it was a coarse

garment, he should at least fasten the top three buttons, Elise thought. Sterling's shirt hung open, affording her the same view of his naked chest, only now his golden skin tones contrasted nicely against the light color of the shirt.

"My father disgraced his family by marrying for love. My mother came from a modest home. My grandfather was a tutor. I don't think my uncle ever forgave his brother for causing a scandal, and since my father is no longer available to ridicule, my uncle takes his resentment out upon me."

"A child should not be cursed by the sins of the father." The steely glint in his eyes had softened. Did that mean his heart had also softened?

"You cannot send me back," she pleaded. "Not to that dreadful man, the horrible fate that awaits me."

"What awaits you in Liverpool?"

She saw no help but to be truthful with him. "My aunt. I haven't been allowed to see her since my parents' deaths, but I believe she will take me in. She lives a modest life, I imagine, but I am not afraid of hard work. I have an education. I hope to find work as a governess."

"Governess?" A sarcastic grin shaped his lips. "Yes, that is hard work."

"Will you help me?" she persisted. "Will you allow me to travel with the caravan to Liverpool?"

"And what makes you think we are going to Liverpool?"

"Danny, my uncle's groom, said he overheard one of the players complaining of the long trek ahead, and of Liverpool as being one of the caravan's destinations."

"Well, 'tis true," he admitted. "But the journey is long. If you stay, you must earn your passage."

Hope sprang to life inside of her. "The money, what little I have, is yours."

He shook his head. "Keep your small stash guarded. You said that you were not afraid of hard work. We shall see."

Labor? Did he mean that she would fetch and carry? Perhaps cook and clean? Well, Elise was not accustomed to that type of labor, but she would manage.

"Agreed. I will work for my passage."

She thought a slight smile crossed his sensual mouth before he said, "I need to sleep. Tomorrow I will introduce you to the others. Allow me to do the talking."

Elise nodded, relieved that she would not be pitched outside the wagon into the darkness. But there was a problem. He needed rest and there was but one bed.

"I will sleep on the floor," she decided, although the prospect wasn't appealing. Nor did she imagine she would be able to sleep in the small wagon with a stranger, one who had already taken liberties with her. She started to rise, but he waved her back.

"I'll take the floor . . . for tonight," he added.

"For tonight" held an ominous ring. For tonight and then she would be forced to sleep on the floor? For tonight and then she would be forced to share his bed? He grabbed one of the blankets stacked neatly upon the cot and turned down the lantern.

After she heard him settle, Elise stretched out upon the cot. It would be a long night for her. If she made it through the dark hours until morning without being either murdered or molested, what would tomorrow bring?

CHAPTER 3

STERLING stared at his wagon. He sat around a campfire with the other members of the caravan, eating a breakfast of wild berries and stew. He could scarce pay attention to the troupe's jibes at one another or the occasional arguments that broke out among them. Elise occupied his mind. He hadn't awoken his guest this morning.

Reality would find her soon enough. He hadn't told the others about Elise. Sterling wasn't by nature free with his words or open with his emotions. It had been that way with him since the age of sixteen . . . since he'd lost his parents and learned the horrible truth about his lineage. Worse things existed than having an uncaring uncle who would sell a family member for gain . . . far worse things.

Mora had settled next to Sterling and now lifted a lock of his hair. "You are brooding this morning, my prince. You need a woman to take away the tension I feel coming from your body. A woman who knows how to please a man."

"He's a snake you'll never charm, Mora," Sarah Dobbs, also known as Lady Fortune when she performed, teased. "Our Beast Tamer has all the parts to please a woman, but no desire to do so. A bloody waste of nice equipment."

Her husband, Tom, a sour-looking fellow who seldom bathed or shaved, cast his wife a dirty look across the fire. "I got enough parts to keep ya happy, woman, so don't be looking elsewhere."

"Wouldn't mind his parts so much if he bothered to wash 'em once in a while," the woman muttered.

"Too much bathing ain't good for a body," her husband declared. "Ain't that so, Philip?"

Philip was often called upon to settle disputes among the troupe members. He was the leader of the ragtag group. Wagons and animals alike belonged to Philip. He collected all money from the performances and kept accounts of who earned what. Sterling supposed Philip was as close to a father figure as he would ever have, since his own had chosen to take his life rather than face his curse.

Sterling's mother had quickly followed upon his father's heels, but it was shock that probably killed her. Shock at what she had married, shock over what she had spawned from her marriage. Four sons. All of them cursed.

Sterling tugged his hair from Mora's grasp as the door to his wagon creaked open. Elise stepped outside. To say that the troupe members fell silent was an understatement. If not for the restless sounds of the animals, a person could have heard a bee pass wind.

"Who the bloody 'ell is that?" Sarah breathed.

Sterling almost smiled. "You can see into the future, Sarah," he drawled dryly. "You should already know."

In response, she frowned, then grumbled, "I tell people what they want to hear, which is seldom the truth."

Since Elise appeared as if she might turn and flee, Sterling set his plate aside and rose. "Come, Elise," he ordered, holding out a hand to her. "Meet my friends."

His *friends* were the oddest group of humanity Elise had ever seen gathered in one place. There was a sturdy older man with a noticeable hump upon his back. A dark-haired woman with kohl around her eyes and a snake wrapped around her neck—which was less frightening than the way the woman glared at her. A couple joined the group. Both stopped to gape at Elise, of which she did in kind. They were little people.

"Elise!" Sterling called. He still stood with his hand held out to her. "Come."

Elise swallowed the lump in her throat and joined him next to the campfire. Whatever simmered in a pot over the fire smelled wonderful.

"You must be hungry," he said. "Sit. Eat."

"Wait a moment. Who the hell is she?"

The man who owned the same booming voice Elise had heard through the mist the previous night asked the question. He wore the wildest ensemble she had ever seen. His waistcoat was bright pink, his tights, striped yellow and green. His red slippers turned up at the toes. A dark purple birthmark covered half of his face.

"Philip . . . and all," Sterling added, "this is Elise. Elise, this is . . . well, everyone."

"Where'd she come from? And what's she doing here?" a woman asked, one who, Elise noted with relief, looked perfectly normal.

"Elise is from London," Sterling provided. "She'll be staying for a while . . . with me."

More than one brow rose. Elise supposed she might be blushing. He made their arrangement sound far more intimate than it was . . . or at least than she intended for it to be. She cast Sterling a dark glance.

"She's fair," the man with the birthmark commented. "I can see where you were tempted to let this one stay, but I am the leader of this troupe. I decide who travels with us and who doesn't. The woman looks like trouble, and we all get enough of that without courting it."

A murmur of agreement followed.

"Seen her ilk before," the woman who appeared normal snorted. "You've brought a Miss Nancy among us, Sterling. Her kind don't belong here."

Elise had packed clothing she considered the least conspicuous of her station, but even so, her morning frock was far grander than the apparel those around her wore. Like Sterling with his handsome looks and perfect form, she stood out among these people.

"I-I will earn my way," she stuttered. "I'm not afraid of hard work."

The dark woman who sat on the other side of Sterling reached across him and grabbed Elise's hands. "This lily-white skin knows nothing of labor," she spat. "You do not belong here. Go back to where you came from!"

"Mora," Sterling cautioned, "where she belongs is not your decision to make."

Elise wrestled her hands from Mora's grasp, but couldn't avoid the resentment glaring at her from the woman's dark eyes. Mora. Elise had heard the name before. She recalled where and the circumstances. Now she understood the woman's dislike of her. Mora was the woman Sterling had expected to find in his bed the previous night.

"Mora has an itch for our Beast Tamer," a man who needed a shave, and a bath, by the smell that radiated from him, informed Elise. "She won't like it that he'll be scratching elsewhere."

"Watch your vulgar tongue, Tom," the little woman finally spoke. She nodded to a wagon where a young girl had exited, moving toward them. "I'm trying to raise a decent daughter, not an easy chore among the likes of you."

The girl captured Elise's attention. She would have expected that if two small people had a child together, the child would be the same as the parents. That was not the case. The girl appeared to be around the age of twelve, and she already towered above her mother and father.

"Elise has expressed a desire to take Marguerite's former position," Sterling said. "I thought she would do. Don't you agree, Philip?"

Elise's attention returned to the group. Philip's gaze ran the length of her. "She will do," he admitted. "And do nicely, if she can be taught—"

"I will teach her," Sterling interrupted. "If she is my responsibility, and she earns her keep, what harm is there in allowing her to stay?"

"Who is she?"

The child had reached the group and asked the question. Elise stared into the girl's curious blue eyes and smiled.

"Dawn, this is Elise," Sterling said.

Elise would have given a polite hello, but the man with the birthmark spoke.

"Elise is our newest performer."

Performer? Sterling had said nothing about her performing. She had assumed she would earn her way by doing menial tasks.

"What does she do?" the girl asked.

Curious to hear the answer, Elise glanced at Sterling.

"Elise will perform the veil dance," he answered.

Dawn's face darkened a shade. "Oh," she said softly, then turned and headed toward her parents' wagon.

"I had hoped we would be rid of that bit of indecency," the mother complained, then went after the child. The father followed the mother.

"Indecency?" Elise mumbled. She leaned toward Sterling and whispered, "What exactly is a veil dance?"

She enjoyed, for a brief moment, the scent of him, the same one that clung to the bedding upon his cot.

"It is a belly dance," Mora answered. "Like the concubines do to arouse the passions of the sultans in the harems of the East."

Elise felt certain her mouth dropped open. Sterling smiled.

"Could I have a word with you?" Elise narrowed her gaze upon him. "In private."

CHAPTER 4

"LAST night, you said nothing about me performing," Elise said as soon as they entered the wagon.

"I said that you would earn your passage, and you agreed to do so," Sterling reminded.

"But I thought—"

"Which was a mistake." He leaned close to her. "First rule in the world outside the protective care of which you are accustomed: Never assume anything."

Elise made a startling realization in that moment. Staring into Sterling's silver eyes, she saw his resentment toward her. "You don't like me," she whispered. "You judge me before even knowing who I am."

He didn't deny her accusations. Instead, he shrugged. "It is the way of the world. The way of this world anyway. Do you think any of us here are welcomed with open arms wherever we travel?

"No," he answered for her. "We are sneered at, laughed at, accused of any petty theft that occurs while our wagons are camped close by. We are judged because we are different. Why should we behave any differently than how we've been taught?"

Ready words of defense did not spring to life upon her tongue. Elise knew she had reacted to the people outside as most would, certainly most of her station. She'd been afraid and leery of them. Why should she expect more from Sterling than she was willing to give herself?

"Tell me about them."

Her response brought an unguarded look of surprise to his handsome features. A moment later he scoffed, "You don't care about them. All you care about is your own problems. Why pretend otherwise?"

"Make me care," she challenged.

He settled upon his cot and ran a hand through his long hair. "Wish that I could. Unfortunately, humanity only sees what is first visible to them. They seldom look beyond the skin of a man, or a woman, to seek what might truly lie beneath. Philip was born in Paris. Born with the mark of the devil, or so his parents believed. They took him into the city slums and left him to die."

Elise gasped.

Sterling nodded. "A poor hag found him crying at her doorstep and took him in. She was a witch, some said, dealing in potions and magic. She raised him as best she could, but she was old even when he was born. Once she died, the townspeople burned her shop. Philip was left with nothing, except a loud voice and a talent to juggle. He joined a troupe, saved his money, and formed his own traveling show."

"And the others?" Elise settled beside him.

"Philip found Iris and Nathan, they are the small couple, on display as freaks in a circus in Europe. He took pity on them and asked them to join his troupe. They tumble about and make people laugh. I suppose because being laughed at for acting silly is easier than being laughed at because they are different."

"Their daughter, Dawn, is lovely," Elise said.

Idly he plucked at the sleeve of his shirt. "Yes, and Nathan and Iris love her and try their best to do right by her. But Dawn is ashamed of them. It breaks Nathan's and Iris's hearts to have their own flesh and blood turn away from them in shame."

Elise swallowed a sudden lump in her throat. "Doesn't Dawn realize how lucky she is to have parents at all? And ones who love her so?"

His silver gaze met hers. "Few realize their blessings until they have them taken away."

She wasn't certain if he referred to the loss of both of their parents or if he meant that she would soon regret her decision to run away from her uncle and a marriage not of her choosing.

"What about the man with the . . . ah—"

"Hump," Sterling provided. "Taylor. Kindhearted to animals, which don't see his deformity, or don't care about it as long as he takes proper care of them. He's the only one besides myself the cats will allow close to them."

"The cats?"

"Leena and Raja. I will introduce you to them."

A shudder raced through her. "No introduction necessary."

He laughed. "See, you also judge them before knowing them."

"Tell me about the woman, Mora." She noted the distaste in her own voice.

"Mora is a strange one," he said. "Mysterious. She says she is from the East, where she once lived the pampered life of a concubine within a sultan's harem. Marguerite, the dancer who ran away with a merchant two fairs back, shared her wagon for a time. Marguerite once confided to me that she believed Mora had unleashed her snakes among the harem. A ploy to narrow her competition for the sultan's favors."

A cold hand gripped Elise's heart. "You mean, she murdered the other women?"

He shrugged. "Who knows? As I said, she is mysterious. She seldom talks about herself. If I were you, I would keep my distance from her."

"What about the other woman?"

"Sarah Dobbs, and the stinky fellow is her husband,

Tom. Sarah tells fortunes, although she is not truly blessed with the sight. Her husband, Tom, fixes the wagons when they break down and has a skill with crafts. Sarah discovered some time back that if she dressed like a Gypsy and told people what they wanted to hear, she could make more than she did working in a factory."

"Oh, I see," Elise clipped. "She deceives people to earn her way."

"I prefer to believe that she entertains people to earn her way," Sterling said dryly. "But that is the difference between your thinking and mine."

"Which brings us around to the reason I wanted a private word with you." Elise rose from the cot and stretched her legs. "I did not agree to perform, and certainly not to do anything indecent, to earn my passage."

Sterling rose as well. "I knew Philip would not allow you to stay unless he saw some gain to be had by doing so." He stared down at her. "We all pitch in to do our share of the work. You are unnecessary unless you have a talent. Can you sing? Perhaps play a musical instrument?"

Singing was not her strong suit. She could pound out a tune or two upon the piano, but certainly that wasn't an instrument she either was in possession of or could easily cart around with her.

"No," she admitted.

"Then the way I see it, you have no choice." He reached out and tugged a lock of her hair. "Now might be a good time to come to your senses and return to London. We'll reach a coach inn soon. You can use your money to hire a hackney to return you to your uncle."

Sterling's forward action had momentarily startled her, but Elise quickly regained her composure. She would under no circumstances return to her uncle. She'd wanted to be an adventurer. Now was her chance.

"All right," she said.

He sighed. "Good. You'll do better back where you belong."

When he started for the door, she realized he had mistaken her answer.

"I meant I will perform."

STERLING thought he knew how far he could push a proper English miss before she turned tail and ran, but he'd obviously been mistaken. He glanced back at Elise. She stood straight, her chin held high. He might have misjudged this particular young woman. He thought he knew a way to convince her further.

"Wait here," he said. "I'll be back shortly."

The troupe members had abandoned the fire, leaving Sarah to clean up. "Where is Mora?" he called.

"Stormed away to her wagon," Sarah answered. "Had the look of the devil in her eyes. Don't want to make that one jealous."

He dismissed Sarah's concerns with a wave of his hand and headed toward Mora's wagon. Raja growled at him from inside of his cage as Sterling passed. Sterling growled back. He needed to exercise the cats, but first he would make certain Elise knew exactly what type of a performer she had agreed to become.

At his soft rap, Mora opened her door. Her brow lifted. "You tire of the pasty-faced girl already?"

It took effort to keep from rolling his eyes. "I have come for Marguerite's costumes."

The snake charmer motioned him inside of her wagon. "Her basket uses valuable space. Take her things."

Sterling had never been inside of Mora's wagon and felt hesitant to enter now. Did she allow her snakes to roam about freely? Most of Mora's "pets" were harmless, but she had a king cobra that could kill a man with one strike of its deadly fangs.

"Are you afraid?" she goaded. "Is the big, strong Beast Tamer only a kitten in disguise?"

He stepped up into her wagon.

"I did not believe so," she purred, then trailed her fingers across his chest. "I sense something wild beneath your skin. Something dangerous. I could bring him forth, this beast that lives inside of you."

Sterling snatched her hand. His heart speeded a measure over her prophetic words. Maybe Mora had the sight that Lady Fortune did not. Could she see the beast slumbering within him? "I don't think you really want to see him," he said. "In my country we have a saying: Do not play with fire unless you wish to be burned."

She smiled, her lips turning up seductively. "I charm snakes. I enjoy the danger. I will charm you in time as well."

"The basket," he reminded. "I have other duties to attend to this morning."

Her smile faded and her dark eyes narrowed, then she pointed to a basket stacked on top of several others. "The top one. It holds Marguerite's costumes."

Sterling was forced to brush up against Mora in order to retrieve the basket. She smelled of garlic and body odor. He should have known that she wasn't the sweet-smelling, soft woman in his bed last night. After grabbing the light basket, he squeezed past her and hurriedly exited the wagon. Mora laughed softly at his back.

When he entered his own wagon, Elise wheeled around. Her face flushed and he imagined he'd caught her snooping. He set the basket on the floor. "Here are your costumes."

She frowned. "The basket is rather small to hold clothing."

He held back a smile. When she bent to remove the lid, a thought occurred to him. "Stop!"

She froze.

"Stand back," he ordered. "I will remove the lid." The basket might not hold clothing at all. With Mora, one couldn't be too careful. Once Elise stepped back, he eased the lid from the basket. "It's all right. The costumes are indeed inside of the basket."

Elise stepped forward, glanced down into the basket, and gasped.

Sterling tensed, afraid he'd missed seeing a snake hidden within the basket's skimpy confines.

"These can't be costumes," Elise said. "There's nothing here but a pile of sheer scarves."

He relaxed, allowing the smile to surface that had threatened his mouth earlier.

CHAPTER 5

An hour later, Elise still sat inside of Sterling's wagon, staring down into the basket. He was touched in the head if he thought that she would dress in nothing but transparent scarves and dance around in public. She was an adventurer, not a woman of loose moral standards.

Sterling had left, saying he had chores to attend to. Elise mopped the perspiration from her brow and glanced toward the closed wagon door. During the daylight hours, the wagon certainly heated up. There wasn't much room, although it was tall, built in similar fashion to the brightly colored caravan wagons of the Gypsies.

There was the cot, a trunk where Sterling kept his clothing. A sturdy washbasin and pitcher, which he wrapped and put away when the wagon moved, and a couple of lanterns. She wondered what else his chest held besides clothing. She would snoop if she weren't so blasted hot.

Elise smoothed her hair, rose, and brushed the wrinkles from her frock. She decided that she wouldn't hide herself away in Sterling's wagon but venture outside. A bustle of activity took place around the camp. No one took time to stop and stare as they had earlier. In the process of skinning a rabbit, Sarah Dobbs nodded to her. The woman's smelly husband worked on a wagon wheel. Elise saw Mora in the distance gathering wood.

The hustle and bustle surprised Elise. She'd heard that

people like these were lazy and that that was why they preferred their roaming ways. She didn't see Sterling but noticed Dawn, the small couple's daughter, carrying a heavy bucket of water in each hand. The girl struggled with her burdens. Elise decided she would help as well. At least until she figured out her next plan of action.

She joined the girl. "Let me help you."

Dawn didn't protest. She merely shrugged and offered the bucket in her left hand. Elise took it, surprised at how heavy it was, and plodded along behind the girl. They reached a large pot and Dawn dumped her bucket.

"We'll be doing wash as soon as we get the pot filled and Mora gets a flame beneath it," Dawn said. "We may be beggars, but we're not dirty beggars, as my mother says."

Elise smiled. "Your mother seems like a very nice person."

Again the girl shrugged. "She's a dwarf, as some call them. So is my father. But as you can see, I'm not like them."

"You have the look of your mother."

Dawn glanced away. "I need to fetch more water." She left.

Elise went after her, reclaiming the empty bucket the girl had taken from her. "Since I'm at a loss as to what to do, maybe you won't mind if I follow along."

"If you wish."

They walked in silence. She felt Dawn's regard.

"I suppose your parents are normal?"

Her first instinct was to answer to the affirmative . . . but then, that wasn't completely true. "No. Not by society's standards, anyway. My father came from a grand family, and my mother's family was a modest one at best. My father saw her in the market at Liverpool one day, and he fell in love with her on sight. She fell in love with him that very day, as well. They married in secret, and when my father's family found out that he had wed beneath him, they disowned him."

"What does it mean to disown someone?"

"My father's family refused to acknowledge him as one of their own," Elise explained.

"Can a person do that?" Dawn's eyes widened. "Just up and disown their family?"

Elise didn't care for the intrigue she read in Dawn's expression; she liked it less when she caught sight of the girl's mother picking berries. The woman smiled fondly at her daughter, then resumed her work.

"I think it's a horrible practice," Elise said. "Love between families should be unconditional. I wasn't much younger than you are when I lost both my parents to an accident. I still miss them terribly."

They reached a small stream and Dawn dipped her bucket into the water. "At least your parents didn't look different from everyone else. When we stop to perform and I get a chance to play with other children, they laugh and tease me once they realize who my parents are."

Elise squatted beside Dawn and dipped her bucket into the water. She had reacted to the sight of Dawn's parents in a way that made her feel ashamed now. She'd seen the love shining in Iris's eyes a moment ago when the woman had looked at her daughter.

"It's the other children who should be embarrassed . . . to be so shallow that they only judge a person by what they first see. On the inside, your parents aren't any different from other parents. Even though I've only just met them, it is obvious to me that they love you very much."

"They do," Dawn agreed, then stood, struggling with her full bucket. "But sometimes love is not enough."

Elise glanced up at the girl. "Love is everything," she said, and realized she truly meant her words. How she longed to be loved and cherished by someone. When her uncle had agreed to Stoneham's offer for her, Elise had realized that he truly did not care about her. She felt certain that Dawn's parents would never give her in marriage to a monster solely for the sake of gold.

The girl moved away, lugging the heavy bucket toward camp. Elise stared down at her own reflection in the water. Another image appeared.

"Do you really believe that?"

Sterling gave her a start. She hadn't seen or heard his approach. "What?" she breathed, glancing at him.

"Do you really believe that love is everything?"

How long had he been listening to her conversation with Dawn? "I suppose I do," she admitted. "Don't you?"

He reached down and retrieved her bucket from the water. "Love is a curse for most. Just look at Iris and her husband, Nathan, their big hearts full of love for a girl who cannot forgive their small bodies. Few people possess the ability to love unconditionally. Nowhere on earth can you learn that lesson as well as here."

"Dawn will see what is most important," Elise insisted, rising from her crouched position next to the water. "She's young and hasn't yet learned the value of love."

He reached forward and brushed a curl from her forehead. "You are the innocent. Even an animal will turn on one of its own if it senses a weakness, something different."

Flustered by his closeness, Elise said, "People are not animals."

His silver eyes stared into hers. "There is a thin line, I think."

Since he now held her bucket, Elise started back toward camp. "Maybe you spend too much time with your wild beasts and not enough time with people. I didn't notice you working among the others."

"I took the cats out for exercise."

Elise drew up short. "You let them out?"

He laughed. "They are not as dangerous as you might believe. Both have been raised by humans. Leena is fairly harmless. Raja takes more caution. He has his moods."

A shudder skidded up her spine. "My uncle wouldn't allow me to have so much as a hound for a pet. I'm not certain I like animals . . . or that they would like me."

"Why don't we see?"

A hint of teasing glinted within his silver eyes. Elise couldn't very well call herself an adventurer if she backed down in the face of every challenge he issued. "All right," she agreed. "Show me your cats."

STERLING wanted to do more than show her the cats. He wanted to taste her full lips again—wanted to introduce her to the darker side of lust. She affected him strangely, had from the moment he first saw her. She was beautiful, but there was more to her than met the eye.

He'd heard her earlier conversation with Dawn. Elise had touched his heart with her innocence, with her sweetness. Something inside of him had stirred. Something so far dormant. This slip of a girl from London might be more dangerous than his cats.

They entered camp and he dumped the water he carried into the washing pot. He took Elise's hand and led her toward the animal wagon. She only allowed the contact for a moment before she snatched her hand from his.

"I cannot wear the costumes," she said as they walked. "I think you knew that when you fetched them for me."

"It's just as well. You don't belong here."

She drew up. "I don't belong with my uncle or the horrid man he would have me marry, either." Her green eyes flashed with fire. "I'm searching to find my place, and you are doing everything in your power to dissuade me."

Sterling's resolve weakened. He could talk to Philip, reason with him to let Elise come along without having to earn her way . . . but would that be fair to the young woman? The life she had chosen would not be easy. She might as well learn that from the beginning.

"A man, or a woman, born to the common lot has to make their place in life," he said, resuming their walk. "Life is hard, and it's unfair, and sometimes people have to do what they don't want to do. That's a lesson you're better off learning sooner rather than later if you truly plan to leave your uncle. You won't be having everything handed to you on a silver platter."

Her chin lifted. "I don't care about being wealthy, or

having fine things. All I want . . . all I want is to be happy," she finished bravely.

Again, something stirred inside of him. He swore he heard the sound of ice cracking—the protective barrier that surrounded his heart. He stopped, staring down at her. "Even happiness has a price. That is something you'll have to fight for as well. Do you have the courage?"

"Do you?"

The question unsettled him. As innocent as she appeared, he feared Elise might see down to his dark soul when she looked at him. Happiness? How could he be happy when a curse followed him? A curse linked to his very name.

He didn't answer but turned and walked the short distance to the animal wagons. Raja greeted him with a growl. Leena merely yawned.

"They are beautiful."

Elise had been brave enough to follow but not brave enough to stand close. Which showed she had common sense, if nothing else about her seemed common.

"Yes, they are beautiful," he agreed. "But even beautiful things are not always all they appear to be on the surface. Beneath the skin, these animals are still wild." Raja rubbed against the bars of the cage and Sterling reached inside to scratch behind the tiger's ears. "I must always remember that however docile they might appear, they could turn on me at any moment. I must respect them."

"C-Could I touch one?" Elise stammered. "Pet one, the way you are doing?"

He motioned her forward. "Best to let them catch your scent first and see how they react."

She stepped up beside him. Raja sniffed at her. The tiger didn't growl, as Sterling expected, but rubbed himself against the bars. Leena, the panther, found the guest interesting enough to rise from her lounging position and join Raja in vying for attention.

"Odd," Sterling mused. "They don't usually take to

strangers. Give me your hand." She slid her hand into his and Sterling guided her fingers to the tiger's fur.

"He's very soft," she whispered. "It saddens me that he must be locked inside of a cage. I wonder if he ever dreams of running free?"

"Raja cannot miss what he has never known," Sterling said, baffled that she would wonder such a thing. All the snooty misses he recalled from his youth never thought of anything, or anyone, other than themselves. "He and Leena both have lived most of their lives behind bars. Neither could survive if they were set free."

Elise pulled her hand from the cage. "I'm glad that they have you to look after them. To love them."

Sterling ruffled Leena's fur so she wouldn't feel slighted. "A person cannot love a wild animal."

A distraction suddenly drew his attention. Philip came charging into camp, riding one of the wagon horses. "Gather round!" he shouted. "The coach inn up the road has given us permission to perform for their patrons. Make ready!"

CHAPTER 6

ELISE hid inside of the wagon. Would someone at the coach inn recognize her? Would her uncle be there, asking about her? He surely knew she was missing by now, and a man could travel by horseback much faster than by wagon. What was Elise to do? She'd told Sterling that she would not wear the ridiculous costume and perform with the troupe. He'd suggested that she use her money to hire a hackney and return to London, but she couldn't return to her uncle.

The door suddenly swung open and Sterling climbed up into the wagon. "I've brought you breakfast since you were sleeping so soundly when we arrived."

"Are we at the coach inn?" she asked, gratefully accepting the food.

"Not far. The proprietor doesn't mind us entertaining his patrons, but he doesn't want us too close to the inn. Says a man's personal belongings have a way of walking off when our sort come around."

Elise didn't know what to say. She turned her attention to the meal.

"I suppose you'll be going to the inn. You probably have enough coin for a night's stay and a hackney to carry you back to London."

The thick stew stuck in her throat. She swallowed with difficulty. "I cannot go back to London. I cannot go to the inn. I might run across an acquaintance of my uncle's or, worse, the man himself."

Sterling sighed. "Then that would be all the better. Your uncle could see you safely home."

Her temper rose. Elise set her plate beside her on the cot and stood. "I have told you before, I have no intention of returning to my uncle, or to the marriage he has planned for me."

Sterling lifted a brow. "Then what are your intentions?"

"I-I don't know yet," she answered. "I beg you to allow me the shelter of your wagon until I come up with a suitable plan."

He stared at her for a moment, then his gaze lowered to her lips. "You don't know how to beg." Sterling traced the shape of her mouth. "You don't even know how to use your womanly wiles on a man to get what you want."

Her lips trembled beneath his fingertips. Elise wanted to jerk away from him . . . and yet some part of her enjoyed his touch, the fire that had leaped to life in his eyes. She remembered the kiss they had shared. He'd made her feel things inside that no other man had made her feel.

"I do not care to practice vulgar or deceptive methods with men."

He leaned closer. "Then you'll never make a veil dancer. You'd have to understand the effect you have on men, understand it and use it to your advantage."

Did she affect him? He certainly affected her. Elise tried to step back, but her knees met with the cot. "I have no desire to become a performer. I explained that quite clearly to you."

Lifting a lock of her hair, he said, "And I explained that in order to stay with the troupe, you must pull your weight. I cannot go back on my word to Philip. I told him that you would dance to earn your way. If you will not dance, then you must leave."

Panic engulfed her, over either his words or how close his face was to hers. "At least let me go to the inn under the cover of darkness. With the hood of my cape pulled over my head, maybe I can disguise myself until I see if my uncle or anyone else who might recognize me is about."

His face moved closer. "A kiss will grant you sanctuary until nightfall. A farewell gesture."

Her cheeks blazed, as well as other parts of her body. She should slap his arrogant face, but this was not a London drawing room and he was not a gentleman. She had no idea what her plans would entail now that she would be cast from the caravan, but she would in all likelihood never see the Beast Tamer again. He waited, his mouth hovering ever so close to hers, and she sensed that he expected her to flee—run from the wagon and to the inn, as he wanted her to do.

Elise could be shocking as well when the mood suited her. The mood suited her at the moment. She closed the distance between their lips.

The slight pressure of her mouth against his ignited a fire that Sterling had never felt burn so intensely. Her scent wafted up to him, sweet, like the soap she washed with each evening. Her lips were soft—her innocence inflamed his very soul. He loved the taste and smell of her, the feel of her when he pulled her against him. He could never have her, cursed the way he was.

He should frighten her away . . . send her back to where she belonged. Danger lay in wait for a tempting young morsel such as Elise. Better he prove that to her now, while she had the chance to return to her uncle. With her best interests in mind, Sterling forced her mouth open beneath his. He was not gentle about his probing. He expected her to struggle, but she did not. Instead, her arms went around his neck and he felt the shy touch of her tongue against his. The jolt traveled all the way to his toes.

"Kiss a man like that and you're begging for trouble," he said against her mouth.

"You said that I don't know how to beg," she reminded. "And you will not frighten me away . . . not until I am ready to leave."

"You do not fear me, and you should."

She stared into his eyes thoughtfully. "I believe that you intend for people to be afraid of you. That way, they keep their distance. Why don't you want anyone close to you? What are *you* afraid of?"

This was not going at all as he had planned. Her bravery and her insight had begun to annoy him. "We can get closer if you desire." Sterling tumbled her backward onto the cot. "Is this close enough?"

Elise's large eyes blinked up at him. "T-This is indecent," she sputtered. "Let me up at once!"

"I am not a gentleman. I fear that you may try to stow away with another man, and feel obligated to show you the probable outcome. Never trust any man. On the inside, we're all beasts."

He expected her to struggle beneath him, to recoil from him at the very least; instead, she reached up and touched his face. "What has happened to you that you should view the world as such a dark place? Has there never been any sunshine in your life?"

She might as well have struck him. There had been sunshine . . . once, before he knew the truth. She was sunshine, and it sickened him that he would treat her no better than a whore who'd come sniffing for trouble. He rose from the cot and straightened his collar.

"Forgive me," he said, and realized he'd never asked anyone to forgive him for anything. "You are right. I spend too much time in the company of beasts." He turned toward the door, wanting to put distance between them, but only because he felt the distance shrinking. "If you need a disguise, ask Sarah Dobbs. She will help you."

CHAPTER 7

ELISE wore the disguise of a Gypsy girl. Sarah Dobbs was a master at transforming Englishwomen into Gypsies. Sarah wore the same disguise in preparation to tell fortunes. The woman had explained to Elise that no one took an English fortune-teller seriously and that was why she darkened her skin with grease, her eyes with kohl, and wore a bright scarf tied around her head. The cockney accent was gone, and Elise stared in wide-eyed wonder at the crystal ball Sarah had placed on a small table inside of her wagon.

"Would you like your fortune told?" Sarah asked, her voice thick with another accent, a foreign-sounding one.

"Sterling said that you can't really see into the future," Elise responded. "Besides, I believe a person decides his or her own destiny."

Sarah lifted a brow and glanced down into the ball. "I see that you are running from someone. Someone who has not treated you kindly."

Elise gasped. "How did you . . ." She promptly closed her mouth. The woman could have found out from Sterling, or Elise supposed it was easy enough to guess her situation. "You are wrong," she clipped. "Good eve, and I guess good-bye. I am leaving the caravan." She turned to exit the wagon and heard Sarah laugh softly.

"You are not going anywhere. Sterling is your destiny."

The fine hairs on Elise's arms stood on end. She jumped

down from the wagon. What did the woman know? *Nothing,* Elise assured herself. Sarah's fortune-telling abilities were all an act. Making certain the scarf covering her hair was still in place, Elise wandered through the wagons. A crowd had already begun to gather. Several torches lit the area. Elise saw that a cage of sorts had been erected. Sterling would no doubt perform inside with his cats.

"Gather round and witness sights to tantalize your senses." Philip, resplendent in one of his strange outfits, stepped into the circle of light. He began to juggle three balls, all of which caught the light from the torches and seemed to glow in the coming dark.

"I bring to you an exotic flower from the desert. A woman who can charm even the deadliest of snakes. The king of snakes. I bring you . . . Mora."

While Philip distracted the crowd with his juggling, Mora had stepped from the shadows and now stood in the circle of light, snakes draped from her neck and arms, a large basket at her feet. She lifted a strange instrument to her lips and began to play. The lid to the basket teetered. It fell away and the crowd all inhaled a breath at the same time. A large black snake rose from the basket. The snake's head suddenly expanded. His tongue slithered out and he hissed, but still Mora played.

The tune changed and the snake began to descend into the basket. Once the crowd could no longer see the cobra, Mora walked over, placed the lid upon the basket, and gathered it up. She bowed to a burst of applause, and coins were suddenly being tossed upon the ground. Dawn scrambled forward and began gathering the coins.

"Now to lighten your mood, the antics of Nathan and Iris!" Philip boomed.

The couple tumbled into the circle of light. They were dressed in wild costumes that immediately brought a smile to Elise's lips. She laughed out loud at their silliness and marveled over their skill at tumbling. The crowd did indeed laugh and applaud their efforts, all oohing when Iris did a triple somersault in the air and landed upon her husband's shoulders to end their performance. A shower of coins followed. Again Dawn moved into the circle and collected the bounty.

"Now, the bravest man in the world!" Philip stepped forward. "A man who can tame the savage beast, turn even the most ferocious animal into a loving house cat. I bring you the Beast Tamer!"

Torches suddenly leaped to life around the cage that had been erected earlier. Inside, Raja and Leena paced. The crowd went wild. A tall man stepped from the shadows. The firelight danced upon his golden head. He wore tights that hugged his muscled contours to the point of indecency, and two leather straps crisscrossed over his broad naked chest. Heat rushed to Elise's head, among other places. She heard more than one woman among the crowd sigh appreciatively.

Elise did not like it, the way the women ogled Sterling. He cracked a whip and made her jump; then he opened the door to the cage and stepped inside. The crowd grew deathly quiet. Sterling cracked his whip again, issued a command, and the cats took their seats upon two stools that were arranged inside of the cage. Raja growled and pawed at Sterling when he passed, causing Elise to suck in her breath.

Sterling shouted something and the cats sat up on their haunches. The crowd roared. He turned his back on the cats and bowed, which Elise thought was a frightfully stupid thing to do. The crowd appreciated his bravery, however, and coins flew to the ground. Since Dawn did not scramble forward to collect them, Elise assumed the performance had not ended.

Indeed, there was more to follow. Sterling commanded his cats to do all manner of tricks, from lying down on the ground and rolling over, to an impressive feat of jumping through a hoop that was on fire. Sterling also jumped through the hoop, which brought a spray of more coins. Elise felt like her heart was in her throat, but she couldn't deny the excitement that also coursed through her veins.

What she hoped was his last act of bravery was to open Raja's mouth and stick his head inside. The man was insane! Sterling emerged with his head, and more coins showered the ground. Again he turned his back upon the cats and bowed to the crowd. Raja suddenly attacked from the rear. Elise screamed. The tiger knocked Sterling to the ground. Man and beast wrestled and all Elise could do was stare on in horrified fascination. A moment later they were both up and Sterling hopped on Raja's back, riding the tiger.

The applause was deafening; the glitter of coins made the ground appear as if it were paved with gold. The torches around the cage were extinguished, and the crowd roared for more.

Philip stepped into the circle of light. "The night has not ended!" he boomed. "Know your future, find your fortune, or maybe discover if your wife has been unfaithful. Lady Fortune awaits you in her wagon."

The crowd grumbled, but many moved toward Sarah's wagon, which was now illuminated by bright torches. Elise stared at the darkened place where the cage had been erected, wondering what Sterling was doing. She noted that a few women also stared in the same direction. Would they seek out his wagon? No wonder he had thought she was there to find amusement with him that first night. He was handsome, devastatingly handsome. He would draw women like moths to the flame.

She would not stay and witness the fawning. Elise thought it was a perfect time to slip to the inn and secure a room. Most of the patrons were still milling about. She needed her valise, however, so she moved toward Sterling's wagon. She had only stepped into the darkness when a hand grabbed her arm.

"Hello, Gypsy girl," a voice slurred. "I saw you in the crowd and thought we might have a roll together."

She couldn't see the man, but his breath reeked of liquor. "Unhand me this instant," she snapped. "I do not wish to share your company."

The stranger yanked her up close to him. "Whether

you're willing or not makes no difference to me. Who cares what happens to thieving scum like you?"

"I care."

The voice belonged to Sterling, and Elise was never so happy to hear it.

"Go about your business, man, and leave me to mine," the stranger said.

Elise tried to twist away from the drunken man's hold, but his fingers dug into the soft flesh of her arm.

"Let her go."

Sterling did not raise his voice, but his tone was deadly. A low growl sounded in the darkness and rose the hair on the back of her neck.

"Say, who's there?" the man asked, a tremor audible along with the slur. "Be you a man or a beast?"

No answer. Another low growl. The man released her and ran away. Elise might have relaxed, but the growl? What was it?

"Sterling?" she whispered. "Are you here?"

The silence stretched. Her heart began to beat at an alarming rate. She lifted a hand to her throat. A tall shadow suddenly stood next to her.

"Are you all right, Elise?"

"Sterling," she sighed. "Yes, I'm fine. The man . . ." Her voice trailed off. It was impossible, but when she glanced up she swore she saw the glow of an animal's eyes staring down at her. She shivered in the chilly evening air, blinked, and when she looked again, all she saw was Sterling's tall shadow against the night.

"What about the man?"

"He's run away," she answered. "I was trying to make my way to your wagon in order to fetch my valise."

"So, you are leaving?"

She had no choice in the matter. She'd paid for the privilege of sharing his wagon until nightfall, and night had fallen. "Yes. I am leaving."

He took her arm and guided her toward his wagon. "Best

you go now while most of the patrons are still gawking at the sights and having their fortunes told."

"That's what I thought, too," she said. "Now I'm not so certain I want to make my way to the inn alone."

"No, I will escort you," he assured her.

"You are a noble man beneath the skin," she teased. "Even if you refuse to act the part."

"You have no idea what I am beneath the skin. But I won't see you molested."

They reached the wagon and Elise scrambled inside. She grabbed her valise; then they went off into the night, toward the muted glow of the inn.

CHAPTER 8

As they walked, she said, "Must you stick your head inside of Raja's mouth? You nearly took ten years off my life."

Sterling chuckled. "You didn't find my performance thrilling?"

"Well, yes," she admitted. "But really, Sterling, you should be more careful. The tiger attacked you tonight!" She felt his regard and asked, "What?"

"It's been a long while since anyone has fussed over me, and Raja attacking me is part of the performance. He loves to wrestle."

"Oh," she sighed. "You could have told me. I was frightened for you."

"It's been a long while since anyone cared what might happen to me, too. It's . . . nice."

A rush of pleasure washed over Elise. It had been a long time since she'd been allowed to fuss over or care about anyone. But Sterling was not the proper man to bestow her feelings upon. They were ill suited for each other . . . she supposed as were her mother and father. Of course Elise had closed a considerable amount of distance between their stations when she ran away from her uncle. She kept forgetting that she was now free to become anyone, or anything, she wished to become.

They reached the inn. Saying good-bye was more difficult than Elise had imagined. She suddenly felt at a loss for words. "Thank you for all you've done on my behalf," she blurted. "I wish you a happy life."

He reached out and brushed the stray curl that forever crept across her forehead. "And I hope you find what you're looking for."

For a dreadful moment, tears burned her eyes, and she feared she would embarrass herself. "Good-bye then." Elise turned away, only to find herself wheeled about and in his arms the next instant.

His lips found hers. She opened her mouth beneath his. Their tongues touched, danced together, spreading delicious heat through her chilled bones. She explored his mouth, the taste and depth of him, uncaring that her actions were bold. She would never see him again.

He made a low sound in his throat; then she felt the rough wood of the inn cutting into her back. She hardly noticed the discomfort, for the tight press of their bodies wiped logical thought from her mind. She burned for him, ached to feel more than his mouth fused with hers. What would it be like to lie with him? Skin against skin?

Her thoughts frightened her, along with the feelings he stirred. Primitive desires that she had never experienced. Her life had been a sheltered one. If her uncle hadn't been generous with his affections, he'd been overly protective of her virtue. He never allowed her in a man's company without a proper chaperone. Elise hadn't been so much as kissed before, and here she was, rubbing up against a man she hardly knew, like one of his great cats, begging to be stroked.

His hand closed over her breast; then his fingers brushed her sensitive nipple through the fabric. She moaned against his lips, hungry for more. As if he knew her needs, he stroked the other breast in kind, the friction of his fingers against her nipples sweet torture. His hand strayed to the top fastenings of her gown. He suddenly broke from her.

"Go inside," he commanded. "Go inside before I forget myself and drag you back to my wagon, toss you upon my cot, and make love to you as if there is no tomorrow."

If it was a threat, she did not respond correctly. Instead of her being frightened, all manner of indecent images suddenly took shape within her mind: images of tangled limbs and glorious golden naked skin. The night air clashed with her heat-flushed body and made her shiver.

"You should be afraid," he misinterpreted her response. "Now go inside while I still have the conscience to allow you to escape with your innocence."

He turned and walked away from her, which didn't leave Elise with many options. Now that her head had cleared, she understood how foolish it would be to run after him. Not to mention degrading. She imagined he was well used to women dogging his heels. The memory of the women sighing over him earlier brought reason when her body wanted to make a fool of her.

Shaken, Elise slipped inside of the inn. Thankfully, there were few patrons eating in the common room or partaking of spirits. Two men stood across the room, one with his back to her and the other studying a ledger. She assumed the man with the ledger was the proprietor. Something about the other man struck her as familiar, even though he wore a long cloak and high-crowned beaver that hid him from her. As if the proprietor felt her regard, he glanced up. He immediately frowned.

"You're not welcome in here!" he shouted across the room. "Take your thieving ways back to your camp!"

She'd forgotten that her disguise would jeopardize her chances of securing a room for the night. Elise supposed coin might sway the proprietor. The man who stood with his back to her started to turn. She caught a view of his profile. Her heart jumped up her throat. The man was her uncle.

Wheeling around, Elise scrambled back through the inn door. Had he seen her? She hoped that by the time his head had turned, all he'd seen was her backside rushing through the door. Her heart pounded wildly. Fear gripped her insides and twisted. Elise ran in the direction of the caravan wagons. The torches were still lit at Sarah's wagon, which greatly aided her sense of direction.

Seeing her uncle had been a shock and a reminder of how badly she wanted to escape. She might feel a tug of conscience had she believed for one moment that he searched for her out of fear for her safety, but she knew what drove him: the bride's price from Stoneham.

When she reached Sterling's wagon, Elise didn't pause to knock. She flung herself inside and pressed her back against the door, gasping for breath. Sterling stood poised over his washbasin, his face dripping. He grabbed a cloth and blotted the moisture away.

"Forget something?"

What could she say? If she told him the truth, he might try to sway her to return to London with her uncle. Or worse, he might inform her uncle of her whereabouts, thinking he did the right thing on her behalf. Elise had no choice in what she must do, and tonight, hadn't she been caught up with the performances? Hadn't a small part of her secretly longed to be a part of the troupe, to belong . . . somewhere?

"I've changed my mind," she answered. "I will dance."

STERLING bit back a groan. Although part of him had not been happy to see her go, the rational part had assured him that her leaving was for the best. The best for him, leastwise. He had feelings for Elise. Feelings that might become dangerous were he to allow them full rein. Better her temptation had been taken from him.

"It would be wiser for you to follow a different plan," he advised.

Her chin lifted. "We had an agreement. Will you go back on your word?"

Yes! the rational side of him mentally shouted. What was his word compared to his heart? What was honor compared to a curse that would turn him from a man into a beast?

"And you would stay?" he asked. "Even after tonight? Even knowing that I want you? Even knowing that you are not safe with me?"

Her cheeks flamed within the soft lantern light. She

chewed her full bottom lip, then answered, "Better you than the murderer my uncle would sell me to for the sake of lining his pockets. You have more honor than you will admit. I am not afraid of you. Only of the strange emotions that you stir within me."

He turned his back on her to keep from crushing her in his arms. She was so trusting, so honest, to admit that she felt stirrings of desire for him. If the man her uncle insisted she wed was truly as bad as Elise said, Sterling could not allow her to be forced into the marriage. He would not allow any man the right to abuse her. But she was not safe with him; he was not safe with her. What could he do?

"Please," she whispered. "Take pity on me. I promise to do as I've agreed, and cause you little hardship until we reach Liverpool."

How could he refuse her? At least he would know that she had reached her aunt safely. Everything inside of him cautioned him that allowing Elise to stay would be a grave mistake.

"All right," he agreed, turning to face her. "You may stay." When her eyes filled with tears and she took a step toward him, he lifted a hand. "But things must be different between us."

She drew up short. "Different?" Elise moistened her tempting lips. "Are you suggesting . . . that is, are you demanding that I—"

"I'm demanding that you keep your distance," he cut her off. "I am not the man you believe me to be, Elise. I am not honorable or trustworthy. You must think the worst of me and act accordingly. Understand?"

A frown settled over her mouth. "Of course. I would hate to become bothersome to you." Fire had leaped to life within her eyes. "I assure you, regardless of what you obviously believe about yourself, you are not irresistible."

He nearly smiled. This was serious business, however, and Sterling would allow Elise the sanctuary of the caravan, and his wagon, but he could not allow her inside of his heart.

"We will be off again come morning. We'd better both get some sleep."

She glanced at the cot. "Am I to still use the bed, or would you prefer that I sleep on the floor?"

"Take the bed." He turned toward the door. "I'll check on the cats before I turn in."

"About the cats." Elise's brow furrowed. "You didn't have Raja with you earlier tonight, I mean, when the man grabbed me and you intervened?"

"Of course I wouldn't have a tiger with me running loose while the camp was filled with patrons from the inn. Why do you ask?"

She shook her head. "It's nothing, I suppose. I heard growling, animal growling, and it sounded so close to where I stood."

An uneasy feeling settled over Sterling. "Sound carries in the night. I'm sure you did hear Raja complaining, but he was in his cage."

"That would be the logical explanation," she responded. "Good night."

Sterling left her. Outside, he inhaled deeply of the crisp night air. The moon above looked huge against the night sky. He stared at it for a long time, helpless to look away. Growling? He'd been beyond anger when he saw the drunken lout trying to molest Elise. Sterling recalled thinking he'd like to rip the man's throat out . . . with his teeth. Had it begun then? Was the curse upon him? *No*, Sterling assured himself. He did not love Elise but was merely infatuated with her.

What he wanted to give Elise was still a long way from his heart. Desire, lust, he had suffered those feelings for women before, and he had remained safe from the Wulf curse. As beautiful and desirable as Elise was, he could resist her. He *would* resist her. The consequences were too horrible to face if he did not.

CHAPTER 9

STERLING was seated for dinner. His father had claimed his rightful chair at the head of the table. Sterling's three brothers were also in attendance, laughing and teasing one another. His mother flitted about, making certain all was to his father's satisfaction. Sterling knew that his parents' marriage had been arranged, and that the agreement had suited them well, if there was no great love between them.

But then something happened. As Sterling's mother poured his father a glass of wine, he took her hand and brought it to his lips—an affectionate gesture, and affection was something Sterling rarely witnessed between his proper parents. A soft glow entered his mother's eyes. After twenty-five years of marriage and four sons, all born with scarcely a year between them, had the marriage finally become more than an arrangement?

The candles in the huge candelabra gracing the center of the table suddenly flickered, flared, then dimmed. A chill crept into the room. His father's face became different. Hair sprouted from his arms, thick and dark—and his teeth, good God, they were sharp, like the teeth of an animal. Sterling's mother screamed.

Sterling's father clawed at his high collar, his fingers now long and bony, his nails like claws. He howled, a sound that raised the hackles on the back of Sterling's neck. Then his father disappeared, and in his place sat a beast.

The huge wolf leaped onto the table, growling and snap-
ping. Sterling's brothers had all risen from the table, their
faces ashen, their mouths hanging open.

The creature leaped through a nearby window, breaking
the glass. Sterling's mother now lay in a dead faint upon
the floor. He sat frozen in place, unable to comprehend
what had just occurred.

The horrible image of his father's transformation played
over and over in Sterling's mind, squeezing his head until
he thought his brain would burst. He glanced down and
saw his own hands covered in dark fur. No!

"Sterling," he heard Elise's voice from a long distance
away. "Sterling, wake up. You're dreaming."

He bolted upright. Sweat coated his body, and he could
scarcely catch a breath.

"Are you all right, Sterling?"

Her blurred image came into sharp focus. Worry creased
Elise's brow. A long braid fell over her shoulder, and the
nightgown she wore, although modest to a fault, was still
arousing, maybe due to the fact that he wondered what, if
anything, she wore beneath it.

"I'm fine. Only a nightmare." Due to her presence in his
wagon, Sterling no longer slept naked. He threw his blanket aside and struggled to his feet. Elise rose and sat upon
the cot.

"You've had them before," she said quietly. "Although
usually you only moan a couple of times and drift back to
sleep. Maybe if you talked to someone about the dreams—"

"I don't want to talk about it!" he snapped, then immediately regretted his harsh tone. Sterling ran a hand through
his hair. "I apologize. I had no call to lash out at you over
a poor night's sleep. I need some fresh air."

What he needed worse was to get away from the tempt-
ing sight of Elise sitting upon his cot in her nightgown.
How intimate a picture she portrayed. How easily he could
become used to such a sight to greet him each morning.
Sterling pulled on his boots and bolted from the wagon.
The cook fire had already been started, and stew left from

last night's meal simmered over a pot. Only Mora and Sarah were still seated around the fire.

"Best hurry up!" Sarah called. "There won't be much left once they all gather round!"

Sterling grabbed a plate and dished up his breakfast. Elise would be a while, since she wasn't yet dressed. He grabbed a plate for her and filled it as well. That brought a lift of Sarah's brow.

"I told her she wasn't going nowhere," she said, a grin stretching her mouth.

Mora tensed. "You should have made her go," the snake charmer complained. "It is not safe for her here."

"She's safe enough under my protection." Sterling cast Mora a warning glance. "And she'll only be with us as far as Liverpool. Then she will go about her life, and the rest of us will go about ours."

Sarah placed a hand against her head and closed her eyes. "I do not see her leaving in the future. I see a wedding, and children. I see—"

"Stop it, Sarah," Sterling commanded. The last thing he needed was visions of a life with Elise planted inside of his head. "I don't find your predictions amusing."

The fortune-teller opened her eyes and sighed. "I'd hoped she might help you find your sense of humor, but you're as surly as ever. Just like that great beast of yours, always growling and snapping at everyone."

He liked Sarah's comparison less than her predictions. Sterling took Elise's plate and headed back toward the wagon. An older man dressed in clothes befitting a gentleman suddenly stood in his path. The man kept glancing around, as if in search of someone or something.

"Can I help you?" Sterling asked.

The man's gaze swept him coldly. "I'm looking for a girl."

Sterling appraised the man as well, using the same cold tone with him: "You're looking in the wrong place. We don't offer the kind of sport you seek."

Removing his hat, the man brushed the dust away. "I'm

looking for my niece, you idiot. The ungrateful chit has run away. I thought you might have seen her along the road somewhere. Maybe lying in a ditch with her throat slit."

One of the plates Sterling carried nearly slipped from his fingers. This man had to be Elise's uncle. Her change of heart last night made perfect sense now. She must have seen her uncle at the inn.

"I've seen no young women lying in a ditch," Sterling said. He didn't like the man. Elise's uncle, if this was the man, seemed more annoyed by the thought of finding her dead than concerned. "You must be worried if she's taken to the road. No telling what might happen to her."

The man sniffed, then pulled a handkerchief from his pocket, pressing it to his nose. "God-awful animal stench," he muttered. "Makes my eyes itch and my nose drip. I'd leave her to her own sorry fate and gladly be rid of her nuisance, but her bridegroom has already paid a handsome price for her. I don't intend to give him his money back."

Sterling wanted to strangle the man. How could he act so unfeeling about a woman as sweet and gentle as Elise? "If she's taken to the road alone, you won't find her unspoiled," Sterling said, barely able to keep his voice civil. "Her bridegroom might not want her back."

The man waved a hand as if it were of no consequence. "Stoneham won't care. Just another reason to punish her. He likes to punish his wives."

Stoneham? It had been years since Sterling had rubbed elbows with London's social set, but he remembered hearing his mother speak of the man in hushed tones. It was rumored that Stoneham liked to torture his women. Sterling didn't recognize Elise's uncle, though, and obviously the man saw nothing in him but a vagabond.

"What is your niece's name, in case I stumble across her in the future? And where might I deliver her if I do find her? I assume you would be willing to pay for her return?"

The man wrinkled his nose and stuffed his handkerchief back into his pocket. "Collins," he provided, "Elise Collins, and all you need do is ask after Lord Robert Collins in

London and someone will direct you to me. A small reward can be arranged."

Lord Collins. The name rang a distant bell. Sterling tried to recall anything he might have heard concerning Elise's uncle. Nothing immediately came to mind. It was dangerous to ask the questions screaming inside his head. He'd tried to put his prior life behind him, sworn that he would not look back, but he did wonder what had happened to his brothers.

"Long ago, I groomed horses for a family by the name of Wulf from London. Do you know them?"

Lord Collins pinched his lips together and frowned. "The wild Wulfs of London? Disgraceful family. The parents are dead. The sons run wild, wreaking all manner of havoc upon polite society. They are rumored to be mad, and dangerous, which of course only has the mindless society misses all chasing after them. Would serve some stupid chit right if she managed to catch one."

Collins smiled, a chilling smile. "I am not personally acquainted with the family. But I hear things. . . . Supposedly the Wulf brothers have all taken a vow to remain bachelors until death."

Sterling didn't respond. At least he knew his brothers were alive and obviously of the same mind as him. Guard their hearts, save their humanity. "Well, if I run across your niece, I will bring her home and collect the reward."

"Perhaps I should ask some of the others as well." The man glanced around. "Maybe someone has seen something that you haven't."

"We're preparing to leave," Sterling said. "I wouldn't bother them. We all see the same things along the road, and no one has mentioned a young woman lying dead in a ditch."

Collins sniffed again, cursed, and pulled his handkerchief from his pocket. "Too many animals roaming about here. I must return to the inn. Do keep a look out for my niece. I trust you could use the reward money." His gaze swept Sterling's coarse clothing and dusty boots in an insulting manner. "Good day."

The door to Sterling's wagon creaked. The man's head turned toward the sound. A vision draped in gauzy scarves stood outlined against the darker interior of the wagon. A moment later he heard a feminine gasp, and the door slammed shut.

"HEAVEN help me," Elise whispered. Her uncle had found her. She expected Sterling to lead the man directly to her, only because Sterling had never taken the threat hanging over her head seriously. He believed, like most of his class would, that she was throwing a temper tantrum over a marriage that was, in fact, well suited for her.

She scrambled to the back of the wagon and sat on the floor, trying to make herself as small as possible. Why, she had no idea. Sterling and her uncle both knew she was inside of the wagon. There was only one door and no windows. A moment later she heard the door creak open. She covered her eyes.

"It's all right, Elise," Sterling said, his voice coming from above her. "He's gone."

Slowly, she lowered her hands and glanced up. "Gone?"

Sterling set two plates upon the cot and extended his hand. "Yes. I sent him away. He didn't recognize you. He was too busy looking at . . . well, he never looked at your face. I told him you were my wife."

Without thought, she slid her hand trustingly into his. He pulled her to her feet. "You sent him away? I thought you would tell him I was here."

Sterling didn't respond for a moment. His eyes roamed her and he drew a ragged breath. "Good God, what are you doing in that costume?"

She knew she blushed, and over her entire indecently exposed body. "I thought that if I couldn't come out of the wagon wearing the costume in front of the troupe members, I certainly couldn't perform in it for complete strangers."

"Your reasoning makes sense," he agreed. "And if you hadn't been wearing it when you opened the door a moment ago, your uncle would have recognized you. Then I would have had to fight him over you."

"Fight him?" Her blood warmed. "Over me?"

He released her hand and turned from her. "You were right about your uncle. He doesn't care about anything but the coin he will get for you. That woman-abusing monster, Stoneham, will not have you."

As relieved as she felt over the turn of events, Elise was also confused. "Stoneham. I never told you his name."

"Your uncle mentioned his name."

Sterling still stood with his back to her. Although embarrassed by the skimpy costume, Elise also felt self-conscious for different reasons. "Do you not like the costume?"

"I've seen the costume before," he answered. "On many occasions." He turned and his eyes were full of heat. "But I've never reacted to the sight the way I do when I see you wearing it." His gaze ran over her, sending tingles dancing beneath her skin. "You are a vision."

Elise should feel shame for the rush of pleasure his words delivered, but she did not. She liked the way Sterling looked at her. "You said you'd teach me to dance," she reminded.

He groaned and turned his back on her again. "Later. Now I have to help the caravan get under way. You had better stay inside, out of sight."

"Sterling," she stopped him when he moved toward the door. "Thank you. I owe you a debt greater than I can repay."

"You owe me nothing," he said, then hurried out.

CHAPTER 10

His hands were on her hips, and due to the costume she wore, she felt the heat of his palms against her skin.

"Allow my hands to guide your movements. Gyrate your hips."

He tried to guide her, but she felt too self-conscious to follow his instructions. Her hips did not move. He released her.

"What is the problem?"

You, she wanted to say. His closeness affected her. She couldn't concentrate on anything but the feel of his hands on her, the male scent of him, the whisper of his breath against her ear. She stepped away from Sterling and turned to face him.

"I think it might help if you were to show me, rather than tell me."

"I would look ridiculous."

She smiled over the slight blush that darkened his cheeks. If she could bring herself to parade around in front of him barely dressed, he could certainly suffer a little indignity on her behalf.

"I believe demonstration is part of teaching, and you did agree to teach me."

"Men and women move differently in the lower regions," he explained.

She lifted a brow. "How so?"

He reached out and pulled her around, positioning Elise as they had been a moment earlier. "Men move front to back, like this." He pressed against her in a disturbing manner. "Women move from side to side." His fingers found her hips again, and this time she followed his movements or, rather, the movement of his hips against hers.

Gradually, Elise noticed more than the rhythm of their bodies moving in perfect accord. His heat penetrated her back—wrapped around her. Although they were not overly exerting themselves, his breathing sounded labored, and so did hers. Something pressed against her. Something hard.

"As you dance, remove the veils," he said. "This way."

He plucked a transparent scarf from beneath her breast. Elise did as he instructed, plucking away first one scarf and then another until her entire midsection was bare. The costume beneath the scarves was hardly anything: an upper portion that pushed her breasts up and out, held in place by slim straps, and, below, trousers of sorts that hung below her belly button and were sheer from the top of her legs to the bottom, where they gathered at her ankles. Scarves were attached to the thin straps of her shoulders, and she understood those should be removed as well. Although her hands shook, she reached up.

"Slowly, sensually, like this," Sterling whispered, then took her hand in his and ran her palm up her stomach, over her breast. Her nipples hardened. A flush spread from the tips of her toes to the top of her head.

"Your body was made for a man's caresses," Sterling said close to her ear, then nibbled upon her lobe. "You have no idea how desirable you are, how tempting."

The heat seeped to a place between her legs. Elise knew she was not unattractive, but she'd been innocent about desire, her own, and the ability to make a man want her. And she did want a man to want her: Sterling.

"Touch me," she whispered.

He groaned, a low, animalistic sound; then he cupped her aching breasts. His fingers slipped inside of the low-cut costume and grazed her nipples.

"I want to put my mouth on you." He brushed her long hair aside and kissed her neck. "On every part of you."

A throb joined the heat burning between her legs. She wanted that—wanted his mouth on her and more.

"I don't even know your last name," she suddenly realized.

He snatched his hands from her as if she'd suddenly scorched him. A moment later, his hands were back, but only upon her shoulders, pushing her forward. The cot, she assumed. Surely they wouldn't perform the act standing up. He pushed her down upon the cot, but rather than join her, he moved to the door.

"Where are you going?" she asked.

"Out," he snapped. "Away from your sorcery. You have made me forget our agreement. Forget myself."

She blinked. He seemed angry with her. "I thought our agreement was that you would teach me to dance."

"You will have to learn on your own, which I don't believe will be a problem."

"Why won't you look at me?" Elise demanded, her temper clashing with her embarrassment. "You started this business, and now you're acting as if I've done something wrong."

He turned. "You shouldn't tempt me. I told you that things must be different between us. You must heed my warning, Elise."

A shiver raced up her back, not because of his words, but because in the soft lantern light, his eyes looked strange again. The same as they had looked last night. As if they were glowing, like the night eyes of an animal.

She blinked, hoping it was an illusion and that if she looked again, his eyes would appear normal. When she looked again, he was gone.

STERLING'S emotions were a jumbled mess. Desire, red-hot and rampant, clawed at him. He wanted Elise more than he'd ever wanted any woman. But she wasn't *any* woman. She was an innocent, and he had no right to make her his when he could offer her nothing . . . nothing but a life on the road . . . a life with a man who felt his humanity slipping away.

He ran his tongue over his teeth. Was it his imagination, or were they sharper, more canine than human? "No," he insisted, moving toward the animal wagons. Talking with Raja and Leena always soothed him. Sterling had allowed fear to play with his mind. He hadn't fallen in love with Elise Collins. He barely knew the young woman. He found her attractive, desirable, sweet, kind, with every trait a man would want in a woman, but he did not love her.

Upon reaching one of the animal wagons, Sterling wrapped his hands around the bars. "I do not love her."

Both animals were dark shapes hunched in the corners of their cages, their eyes glittering in the darkness. Raja growled low in his throat. Sterling was used to the tiger's moods, but then Leena also growled. Sterling glanced behind him. The caravan was quiet; all had retired for the night.

"What do you see?" he asked. Oddly enough, their glowing eyes seemed trained only upon Sterling. He laughed. "It's only me."

But even as he said the words, he knew they were not true.

CHAPTER 11

ELISE'S mood soured by the day. Sterling avoided her whenever possible. He acted as if she had the plague, and it had begun to greatly annoy her. What of it if they were both developing feelings for each other? The rules of society no longer governed her. They were on equal ground now, yet he treated her as if she was either too good for him or perhaps not good enough.

"Arrogant man," she muttered as she quickly made her way to a nearby stream, bucket in hand.

"You shouldn't frown. Sterling won't think you are as pretty, and he won't like you."

She glanced down to see Dawn staring up at her. Elise hadn't noticed the girl squatting beside the water. She bent beside Dawn.

"How a person looks on the outside is not as important as what kind of person he or she is on the inside," Elise told the girl. "If you truly love someone, you must love everything about them."

Dawn pinched her lips together. "This is about my parents again, isn't it?"

"It's about everyone," Elise countered. "I've known some very attractive people who were ugly on the inside. And I wouldn't want Sterling to like me only because he thought me pretty."

The girl lifted a brow. "Isn't that the reason you like

Sterling? I mean, because he's so handsome to look at?"

"Of course not," Elise chided. "Sterling is more than a handsome face. He's good-hearted, considerate most of the time, and honorable, well, most of the time."

"Most of the time?" Dawn looked as if she expected explanations.

"He did promise to teach me to dance, and he hasn't fulfilled that obligation." Annoyance washed over Elise. "Philip says we are to perform at a fair in three days' time and I'm not ready."

"I can teach you." Dawn's voice was very small.

"What?" Elise questioned the girl.

Dawn glanced around the clearing. "I used to watch Marguerite practice. I can teach you, but my parents mustn't find out. They like to believe they've sheltered me."

"I see." Elise lifted a brow. "So this would be a secret, just between the two of us?"

Cocking her head to the side, Dawn considered. "Yes," she answered, then grinned. "I've never had my very own secret before."

Elise laughed. "Everyone should have a secret or two, all their very own."

"Do you have secrets?"

Yes, she had secrets from the caravan troupe. They did not know about her uncle. And if she was honest with herself, she had another secret. Elise strongly suspected that she was in love with the Beast Tamer. She had never felt so miserable over someone ignoring her before, not even her uncle.

"If you dance like Marguerite used to dance, Sterling will like you again, I promise you that," Dawn assured her.

Elise frowned at the girl, but on the inside, she admitted that she very much wanted Sterling to like her. In fact, she very much wanted ignoring her to become impossible for him. Maybe the child knew more about these matters than Elise did.

STERLING lost himself in the crowd. The fair was good-sized and should line the troupe's pockets well, but he would not earn his keep tonight. He'd told Philip that he didn't feel up to a performance, the truth being, the cats now regarded him differently. They were uneasy with him, with what they sensed lurked beneath his skin. Philip hadn't pressed him, deciding instead to partition the animals off and charge a fee for anyone brave enough to have a look.

Although Sterling couldn't fault Philip's enterprising genius, he didn't like the thought of people gawking at his cats through the bars. Raja and Leena were performers, not freak attractions. If any among them should be locked up and gawked at, it was he.

"I have been waiting for you to slip into my wagon at night now that you have tired of the pale-faced woman."

He hadn't noticed Mora's approach. "I do not care to share your wagon, Mora, or anything else with you," he said.

She grabbed his arm. "Now that you have tired of her, why not take what I offer? She is nothing but a pasty-faced English girl. Nothing but a silly child who could not please you beneath your pelts. She is—"

"Do not insult Elise in my presence again," Sterling warned, tugging his arm from the woman's grasp. "She is a lady and has not shared my bed."

The snake charmer's dark eyes widened. "All this time, she slept in your wagon and you did not take her? Why would you deny yourself?" Now Mora's eyes narrowed. "Unless she has bewitched you. Unless she has stolen inside of your cold heart and claimed it for her own. Only a man who cares for a woman would treat her with respect."

He didn't deny Mora's accusations. What was the point? A man could lie to himself, but he could never lie to his heart. Elise had stolen it, maybe from the very first moment he'd lit the lantern and seen her sitting upon his cot. Denial. He thought it might save him, but in the end, he knew that it would not.

"She is a fool who wears her love for you openly, but you are an even bigger fool. You are not like her. . . . You are like me."

He shook his head. "No. I'm not like you." A sarcastic laugh slipped past his lips. "I'm not like anyone you know of, or ever will. Stay away from me."

Sterling walked away from Mora, mingling with the crowd. He felt women watching him as he moved, but he didn't give them a moment's notice. Only one woman ruled his thoughts. Would she dance tonight? Could he stand to watch her? Could he bear to stay away?

ELISE's stomach twisted. Her skin felt cold and clammy. She stood in the shadows, too dazed to listen to Philip's introduction of her. Philip motioned her forward into the circle of burning torches. An expectant hush fell over the crowd.

She drew a deep breath and stepped into the circle. Loud catcalls almost sent her scrambling for the safety of Sterling's wagon. Elise forced herself to remain where she stood. Her gaze roamed the faces flushed by the torchlight, seeking one face in particular. Disappointment settled over her, but then she saw him. Even with him standing at the back of those gathered around, his height made the eye travel to him easily. But she could not see him clearly, and she needed to, wanted to dance, only for Sterling.

Lifting her hands into the air, Elise gyrated her hips in a slow and, she hoped, sensuous manner. Her gaze remained fixed upon Sterling. He took a step toward her. She turned a circle, body swaying, and when next she faced him, he stood at the front of the crowd, right before her.

His eyes were intense, with a hint of a glow about them. They ran the length of her, then slowly made their way back up to lock with hers. Elise plucked a veil from her skimpy costume. Coins showered her feet and male voices shouted appreciation. Elise cared nothing about the coins or the other men present. She danced neither for payment nor to stir the passions of any man save one.

She wanted Sterling, and she wanted him to want her in return. Her fingers slid up her stomach, as he had taught her. She plucked another veil, and again coins tinkled from the sky like snowflakes in winter. Sliding her fingers over the full rise of her breasts, she plucked another scarf, revealing the expanse of her cleavage. A fire ignited within Sterling's silver eyes. He drew a sudden breath.

For the first time, Elise understood her power over men, her power over Sterling. Her pulse quickened, and so did her steps, her gyrations bolder now. His gaze lowered to her hips, stayed there as if she'd cast a spell over him. Innocence floated away like the brightly covered scarves that now littered the ground at her feet. Elise understood what held him enthralled. The mating dance. The thought of her hips moving beneath him, keeping a rhythm as old as time.

The roar of male voices grew louder. Taylor was suddenly there, walking the circle to keep the men restrained. Elise hardly noticed. She only had eyes for Sterling.

ELISE would start a riot if she continued to dance as she did, Sterling thought. She had worked the men into a fevered frenzy, him included. He wanted to growl at the men, warn them off. Elise belonged to him. He would take her, make her his, and to hell with the consequences.

Without ceremony, Sterling stepped into the circle, snatched her arm, and pulled her along. The crowd erupted behind him. Sterling knew Philip and Tom could handle them. He heard Philip shouting something about a jealous husband. Loud groans of disappointment from the men followed, and then Philip turned the crowd's attention toward the animal wagons.

Elise did not fight him. He reached their wagon and pulled her inside. She sat upon the cot, lifting a brow in question.

"You will not dance again," he told her. "Not for those crazed men who drool all over themselves like village idiots!"

"All right."

Sterling was taken aback. He had fully expected some sort of argument.

"I will dance only for you, as I did tonight."

It appeared as if she was dancing for him and him alone tonight, Sterling admitted. "So we agree that you will dance only for me, and only inside of this wagon?" The thought pleased him.

"No."

His brow shot up this time. "No?"

Elise stood. "You told me that if I wanted to ride safely with the caravan to Liverpool, I must earn my way. Then you told me that manual labor would not suffice. You insisted that I learn the veil dance and perform for my supper, so to speak, and that is exactly what I intend to do."

"Things were different between us then," he reminded.

"They seem to be different between us daily," she huffed. "You will have to swallow your simpering male jealousy, Sterling, and allow me to do my duty by Philip. You lay no claim to me."

He stepped closer, his temper rising. "You are mine!"

Instead of backing from him, Elise closed the distance between them. "You have not made me yours. And even were you to lay claim to my body, to my heart, I have spent my life being ruled by my uncle. I will not trade one prison for another. I ran away in search of freedom. All else I give you gladly, I give you with a trusting heart, but my will belongs to me."

She had come a long way in a short space of time. Sterling admired her spirit, had from the moment he'd met her. Did he really want to clip her wings? She had only just begun to fly. And how could he take what she would give with a trusting heart when she didn't know the horrible truth about him? When he could not bring himself to tell her?

"You should not trust me, Elise," he said softly, reaching out to caress her smooth cheek. "I am not all you think I am."

She clasped his hand against her face. "Then tell me your secrets, and I'll tell you mine."

"My secrets are dark. Too dark for one as sweet and innocent as you. We are as different as night and day, Elise."

"The night and the day cannot exist without each other,"

she whispered. "Why do you fight the feelings you have for me? Do you count me unworthy of them?"

He shook his head, pulling his hand from her grasp. "I don't want to fight them, but for your sake, and my own, I must. I cannot love you, Elise, and you deserve that from a man."

Her brow furrowed again. "Do you mean that you . . ." She blushed. "That you are incapable of performing the act of love?"

He laughed. Sterling couldn't help himself. He was still aroused from watching her dance, aroused from just being near her. "No. I am perfectly capable of performing. It is my heart that I cannot surrender to you."

The softness faded from her eyes. Her gaze filled with hurt. "Why? I have surrendered mine to you."

How sweet those words were to his ears. He had to get away from her before he did surrender, and surrender all. Before she saw him for what he truly was. Sterling pushed past her and reached for the door.

"I apologize," he said. "Stay inside of the wagon. I will be close by if you need me."

In a gesture as daring as her earlier dance, Elise flung herself in front of the door, barring his way. "I do need you, Sterling. I need you tonight."

CHAPTER 12

ELISE stared at the empty place where Sterling had stood. What was he afraid of? Did he think she could never be happy living the life he lived? Did he believe she'd prefer a dull life with a man of wealth? She riffled through her valise and retrieved her nightgown.

Although she'd been frightened of the troupe players when she'd first met them, she'd come to realize that regardless of their differences, they were ordinary people. All but Mora, leastwise. Elise still considered the snake charmer as dangerous as she had the first time she'd met the woman. Regardless, Elise could be happy among these people, if Sterling would only surrender to his feelings and open himself to her. She could truly live the life of an adventurer as she had always dreamed of doing. And she could dance for many if, in her mind, she only danced for the man she loved.

Elise slipped off the skimpy costume, tugging her modest nightgown over her head. There was a soft rap upon the wagon door. She heard a child's voice on the other side.

"I have your veils!" Dawn called.

Swinging the door open, Elise frowned down at the girl. "I thought you were supposed to be in bed."

Dawn handed her the veils. "I had to see your first performance, and you did very well. I heard my mother tell Philip that you brought in the most coins this evening." She glanced behind Elise, as if looking for someone. "Where is Sterling? I thought for sure he'd be here with you."

The girl really was exposed to more than a child her age should be, Elise decided. "Sterling has gone out for a while, and you must go to bed. It isn't safe for you to roam about after dark."

"You sound like my mother," Dawn complained. "I-I thought we were friends."

Elise smiled. "We are friends, and friends care about each other. I'm concerned for your well-being."

Dawn blushed. "All right. I'll hurry back to my parents' wagon. I'll be quiet as a mouse and as fleet as a deer."

And she was. The girl disappeared. Elise shut the door, turned out the lantern, and crawled into the cot. She felt a certain elation that she had danced tonight and, she supposed, well enough. But Sterling had stolen her joy. Why was he so stubborn? She knew he desired her. Elise was ready to give herself, but he kept promising one thing with his eyes and denying that promise with his lips.

The door creaked. She held her breath. Would he come to her now and make her a woman, make her *his* woman? The door softly closed and she sighed, not with relief but with frustration. Well, perhaps he at least battled the desire to surrender to her. Maybe he would lose before the night's end.

Elise snuggled deeper beneath her blanket and closed her eyes. She'd nearly drifted off when she felt a presence—an intruder in her bed. Her heart nearly stopped beating. What had crawled beneath the covers with her did not caress her with warm, gentle fingers but slithered against her legs.

STERLING paced beside the animal wagons. Raja and Leena were once again huddled in their corners, warily watching him. He could not get Elise out of his head. He wanted her, wanted her more than he'd ever wanted anything in his life, but the curse stood between them.

"I know what you're thinking," he said to the cats. "You're thinking that it's already too late, but you're wrong." He clasped the bars of Raja's cage and stared at him. "Look at me. I haven't changed." He held out his hands. "Skin, not fur. I am a man, not a beast!"

Raja rushed forward and slashed at him, his sharp claws connecting with Sterling's hand. Stumbling back, Sterling swore, then brought the injured hand to his mouth. He tasted blood. He'd forgotten his own rules concerning the cats. Lowering his guard with them for even a moment had cost him a nasty scratch.

He glared at the tiger, heard an animalistic growl of warning rise from his human throat. Raja slunk back into his corner. The scratch stung. Sterling knew he must tend to it, but that would mean returning to his wagon for the necessary supplies. That would mean facing the temptation of Elise again. He tore a piece of cloth from the hem of his shirt and wound it around his hand. His gaze cut toward the moonlit shape of his wagon. No light shining from beneath the crack of the door. Elise had gone to bed . . . alone.

As if he had no will of his own, Sterling was drawn toward the wagon—helpless to resist. He eased open the door and climbed inside, careful to close it softly. Elise did not speak to him. He listened to the thick silence. She was asleep. Sterling unwrapped his hand and used the basin to clean the scratch. It stung slightly. He started to leave but couldn't resist standing over Elise, staring down at her. To his surprise, he could see unusually well.

Elise's eyes stared up at him. Her face looked like a pale moon in the darkness. He could not hear her breathing . . . but wait—he swore he heard the sound of her heart pounding frantically inside of her chest. Or was it his? He started to touch her, but her eyes widened. Then he sensed it . . . a cold and deadly presence.

Something moved beneath her blanket, winding a path upward. Sterling held his breath, stood very still. Once the snake's head appeared, frightfully close to Elise's neck, Sterling snatched the reptile, kicked open the door, and flung it outside.

. . .

ELISE wanted to scream, but her throat felt frozen with terror. She turned her head to see Sterling outlined against the doorway, his hands pressed on either side, looking as if he was having trouble catching his breath. She owed him her life.

"Sterling," she managed to whisper.

He turned slowly to face her. Her breath lodged in her throat and her heart lurched again. In the moonlight spilling through the open doorway, he looked different. His eyes had an unnatural glow about them, and his features seemed distorted. His nose appeared longer, his teeth gleamed white, but they were pointed. She closed her eyes tight, hoping that when she opened them, he would appear normal.

She heard the door close and felt him settle next to her. "Elise, are you all right?"

Forcing her eyes open, she glanced up at him. The moonlight was gone, and so was her ability to see him clearly. "Light the lantern," she demanded in a shaky voice.

A soft glow filled the wagon and chased away the shadows. Sterling rejoined her. She ran her gaze over him. He looked like the same handsome man she knew. "Sterling," she sobbed, then threw her arms around his neck. "I was so frightened."

He ran a hand over her hair. "It's gone. You're safe." His fingers tightened around a thick strand. "I will strangle Mora for putting your life in danger." He started to rise, but Elise clung to him.

"Don't leave me. I need you."

His muscles were tense, but as she held him, he relaxed. Elise pressed her head against his solid chest. The steady beat of his heart calmed her. Once her terror began to fade, she noticed the heat and strength of his body—how safe she felt in his arms.

She lifted her head to look up at him. Their lips were a breath apart. The soft lantern light bathed them within a cozy glow. Sterling stared down into her eyes. She silently begged for him to kiss her. Tonight had shown her how short life could be. Elise realized that there was no one in the world whom she would rather spend her time with than Sterling.

Slowly, his head lowered and his mouth brushed hers. She moaned over the gentleness of his kiss, marveled that a big man, strong as an ox and as tall as a tree, could be tender with her. He gently nudged her mouth open, his tongue slipping inside, and thoughts of sweetness faded. Elise knotted her fingers into his long hair. She hadn't known that the touch of tongues, the wetness and warmth of two mouths joined, would heat her blood and make her ache for more.

He touched her through her nightgown—cupped her breast, his thumb rubbing her nipple through the thin fabric until it hardened. She wanted closer contact. She wanted skin against skin. As if he knew her thoughts, he gathered her nightgown, pulling it up past her hips and over her head. Elise now sat before him naked. Some small part of her chastised her lack of modesty with him, but in truth, she felt no embarrassment, only excitement as his gaze ran the length of her and he sucked in his breath.

"My God, Elise," he rasped. "You are perfect to my eyes."

His praise sent tingles of pleasure racing over her skin. A moment later, his hands followed their pathway. His fingertips brushed her breasts, her stomach, hips, thighs.

"So soft." He lowered his mouth to her breasts, traced lazy circles around her nipples; then he gently sucked one inside of his mouth. Her fingers tightened against his scalp. She threw back her head and moaned. Never had she imagined that a man's lips against her breasts could create such delicious sensations. It was as if a tiny string were attached to her stomach muscles and his mouth. The harder he sucked, the tighter he drew the string.

He stretched her to the breaking point. Drove her wild with the flame of his tongue. Sliding her hands through the opening of his shirt, she felt the strong beating of his heart.

"Remove your shirt," she whispered. "I want to touch you, the way that you're touching me."

In one fluid movement his shirt was gone. The sight of his bare muscular chest always took her breath away. She ran her fingers over him. Warm, smooth, hard muscle stretched over strong bones. What would it feel like to press her naked flesh against his? He pulled her into his arms, and she had her answer. A lightning bolt couldn't have generated more heat between them.

"I should go," he said, pushing her down onto the cot. "I should go before I can't leave you be."

She tangled her fingers into his hair and pulled his lips to hers. "I don't want you to go. I don't want you to leave me be."

The lips she offered him in surrender, he took. His kisses grew deeper, hotter, more demanding. She met his urgency, her tongue dancing with his. Then his hand slid between her legs, caressing her in a place that no man had dared venture. But he dared much, her Beast Tamer. He stroked her—long, steady strokes that soon had her gasping for breath and moving wildly against him. It was as if all her thoughts, all her sensation, pulsed beneath his skilled fingers.

She wanted more, ached for what she could not name. When he pressed against her and she felt the hard length of him through his cossacks, she understood what she wanted. The joining. The completion that would make her his, and him hers. Bravely, she fumbled with the drawstring at the top of his breeches, loosening them to the point that she could slip her hand inside. Her fingers found him. They both gasped.

Huge, was the first thought that came to her mind. Frightening, but so warm, hard steel wrapped in smooth velvet. She ran her fingers the length of him, her courage fueled by the soft groans she stole from his lips.

"Elise," he said. "You're killing me. You will be my ruin."

Wicked, she must be wicked through and through, because the thought of being his weakness excited her. The tip of her fingernail glided over the tip of his manhood, and he shucked the cossacks altogether. He and Elise now lay naked together, and she instinctively knew there would be no turning back. Not now. Not ever.

"Do you know about the first time?" he asked, his heated gaze staring down at her. "Do you know about the pain?"

Pain? No, Elise knew nothing about intimate matters between men and women. Her uncle had only told her they were to be avoided at all cost until she went to her marriage bed. He'd offered her nothing else upon the subject. She shook her head.

Sterling sighed and pressed his forehead to hers. "I'll be as gentle as I can. Trust me, Elise."

She trusted him completely. A woman couldn't love a man she couldn't trust. "Make me a woman. Make me your woman."

HER trust should have been enough to shrivel him. But it did not. He wanted her more than life, more than a normal life, leastwise. A beast, whether brought by a curse or nay, lived inside of all men. The beast was upon him now, and having her beneath him, soft subtle skin stretched over womanly curves, he could not deny what she offered him. He could not resist the love shining from her eyes. He wanted that, to be loved. To love in return without fear of what the loving might cost him. Tonight, he would show no fear.

He touched her where he knew her sensation centered. Stroked her until she moved against him, hot, wet, ready for him. He took her to the edge of sanity, and as soon as he felt the tremors begin, he entered her in one great thrust. Her shocked cry of pain mingled with her moans of release and his own deep groans of heaven and hell. Hell that he had hurt her, heaven to be inside of her, buried to the hilt within her tight confines. The force of her release squeezed him until he thought he would spill himself. He grappled for control, then bent to kiss the tears from her cheeks.

"The pain is over, Elise. Now there will be only pleasure."

Eyes bright with tears, she stared up at him, and although her voice trembled, she said, "I could do with more pleasure and less pain. I trust you to keep your word upon the matter."

He smiled down at her. What a marvel. How brave and passionate despite her strict upbringing. She was the type of woman men dreamed about but seldom found. And tonight, she belonged to him and he to her. He began to move, slowly, gently, to show her that the pain would not come again. Gradually, her hips arched against him of their own will. He lost himself inside of her. All thoughts but the feel, scent, and taste of her left his mind. He nibbled upon her ear and whispered, "Dance for me, Elise."

SHE did dance for him. She gyrated her hips against his, gasping when the motion drew him deeper—down into the very core of her. They were slick with sweat against each other, drowning in the moist heat of seeking mouths and tangled limbs. With each steady thrust, he fanned the flame higher and higher. She was consumed by him—by the friction of their joined bodies, the tingling, the building force that sent her ever closer to the edge of madness. When the shudders wracked her, she arched against him, calling his name over and over as she burst, heat and pleasure spreading through her like a slow burn. He thrust deep, paused as if on the brink of his own fall to death, then pulled from her abruptly, his body jerking, his words a jumble of curses and endearments that sent her cheeks to flaming even hotter.

He rolled to his side and pulled her close, their hearts pounding against each other in unison. "I didn't know," she whispered, awed by the force of what had taken place between them. "I didn't know it would be this way. That loving you would make me feel so complete."

Sterling kissed the top of her head. "I didn't know, either," he admitted. "Until you, I had only walked in darkness. My heart and my eyes closed. Now, all will be different for me."

Odd, but he hadn't made his last statement sound as if he found the change appealing. Elise snuggled closer to his warmth. "Would it shock you if I told you that I would like for you to love me again?"

His lips touched her ear. "It would shock and delight me," he said. "I had thought I would be forced to seduce you again before morning. You save me the trouble."

She sighed. "I would hate to be a bother."

"You are a bother," he assured her. "But you are worth it. You are worth everything."

And his lips halted any further comment she might make.

CHAPTER 13

ELISE woke with a man wrapped around her. She smiled, winced at the tenderness of her mouth, tried to move, and discovered she was tender in other areas as well. She glanced at Sterling. He looked almost boyish in sleep. Very much the innocent. She frowned, recalling last night when she hadn't thought him innocent-looking, when she hadn't even thought he looked like Sterling.

Memories of warm bodies moving against each other merged with those terrifying moments when she realized the cobra had crawled into her cot. Elise had no doubt now that the rumors surrounding Mora were true. She would unleash her snakes upon a woman if she fought for the same man's favor.

Sterling would confront the woman, but Elise felt it was her place, not his. If she planned to live a life of adventure with Sterling and the traveling troupe, Elise must learn to stand up for herself. She eased her body from beneath Sterling, careful to be quiet while she quickly prepared for the day.

The group had already gathered around the breakfast fire. Elise marched up to them and narrowed her gaze upon Mora.

"The next time you unleash one of your snakes inside my wagon, I'll chop off its head with a butcher knife! Then, I'll come after you."

Mora rose from her crouched position. "I do not know what you are speaking of, but I do not like being threatened, or accused of something that I did not do."

"Where is your cobra?" Elise demanded.

The snake charmer shrugged. "He must have gotten out at some time last night. I no longer have the snake."

"What is going on here?" Philip asked, stepping between them. "*I* settle disputes among the players."

"She turned her snake loose inside of my wagon," Elise informed Philip. "If Sterling hadn't come in and thrown it outside, I would most likely be dead."

The caravan leader frowned. "Did you do this, Mora?"

"It is her word against mine," Mora challenged. "The Beast Tamer would say anything she tells him to say. She has cast a spell over him."

Philip said, "No, Sterling is good for his word. Fetch him, Elise. I want his confirmation of your accusations."

Elise stood her ground. "It is my word that I ask you to trust, Philip. I danced last night to earn my way, will continue to dance. I ask you to accept me as one of your troupe, and judge me as a separate person from Sterling."

"Elise wouldn't lie," Dawn cut in. "She's my friend. If she says Mora tried to kill her, then it's true."

Elise smiled fondly at the girl, then turned her attention back to Philip.

He scratched his head and eyed Mora suspiciously. "You have never fit in among us, Mora. You keep your secrets and your company mostly to yourself. We are a family, and family do not try to kill one another."

The snake charmer hissed at him. Hissed like a snake, which made the hairs on Elise's arms stand on end. "She has cast a spell over all of you. It is her you should send away! If she is gone, I will have the Beast Tamer as my man."

"Which I'm sure was your intent when you slipped your cobra inside of her wagon last night." Philip glared down at Mora. "Get your things and be gone. I will not have one among us as cold-blooded as her snakes."

Again Mora hissed at them all, making more than Elise shudder in the early-morning chill. She cast Elise a threatening glance, then stalked from the fire.

"Thank you, Philip," Elise said. "Thank you for trusting my word."

"Never did care for her," he muttered.

"Good riddance to bad rubbish, I say," Sarah Dobbs joined in.

"Figured if I didn't keep an eye on my Dawn, she'd try feeding my girl to one of her snakes," Iris chimed in.

Sterling chose that moment to exit the wagon and join them. Elise caught his eye and felt a blush of pleasure run the entire length of her body. He turned to Philip.

"I want Mora banished from the troupe," he demanded.

"You're too late," Sarah said with a laugh. "Your woman has already sent the wench packing."

Elise smiled at Sterling and he smiled back, pride shining in his eyes, but only for a moment. Then it was as if a curtain fell over his features, blotting out all emotion. "I need to see to my cats."

And he walked away from her—left her as if nothing wonderful and magical had happened between them last night. Emotion closed her throat, threatened to send tears streaming down her cheeks. Elise wouldn't embarrass herself in front of the troupe members. Without a word, she hurried back toward the wagon.

STERLING had managed to avoid Elise throughout most of the day. He couldn't avoid her forever, and he couldn't avoid what was happening to him. He stared at the hand he'd unwrapped a while earlier. There was no scratch. It had disappeared. How could that be possible? Only one way he knew of—it had begun. The curse was upon him. He'd given his heart for his humanity.

But maybe it was better to have loved once and lost everything than to have continued his life as it had been for the past ten years. Hiding from the truth, hoping to hide from the inevitable. Elise bravely displayed her own emotions. She wore her love plainly for all to see. But that would change. His change would kill all the love she felt for him. She'd be as terrified of him as she was of the cobra last night. More so, because he was an unnatural being. A thing she would not be able to understand or accept.

There was nothing to do now but wait . . . and he did wait, out in the forest until darkness had almost fallen; then he moved toward his wagon. He must tell Elise that he was leaving the caravan, and he must try to explain why.

Elise had already retired, but she'd left the lantern burning. She turned to look at him when he entered. Her cheeks were stained with teardrops. His heart twisted at the sight.

"I am a fool," she said softly. "I thought I had grown up, but I am still a child. I thought that because I love you, you must love me in return. I thought that last night meant as much to you as it did to me."

Her honesty never failed to amaze him and endear her more to him. It also made him feel all the worse for deceiving her. She would never keep secrets from him; this he knew about her. Elise wasn't capable of lying. Shamed, Sterling went to her, settling beside her upon the cot.

"I do love you, Elise." He gently wiped a tear from her cheek. "I have tried not to, but I have failed. I have shielded my heart for the past ten years, and yet you came into my life and, in the space of moments, crashed through all the barriers I had erected around myself. You will cost me my humanity, but you were worth it. Every moment spent with you will be worth the lifetime of loneliness I am forced to endure."

"You love me?" she whispered, and he realized she hadn't heard anything else he'd told her. "You honestly love me?"

"Yes," he answered. "But—"

She sat and threw her arms around him. "Oh, Sterling. You will not be alone. I want to stay with you always, be a part of your life, be a part of this life. The troupe members and you are the family I have longed for. My aunt will surely understand, and I will have the adventurous life I've secretly dreamed of. I—"

"Elise." Sterling felt a lump form in his throat. What a wonderful picture she painted, if only it could be. "You are not listening to me. We cannot be together. We are not suited for one another. There are things about me—"

"Don't." She placed her fingers against his lips. "Don't spoil my happiness with talk of social positions and a past that I care nothing about. Give me another night to simply be loved by you. Tomorrow is soon enough to discuss realities."

Was one more night with her too much to ask for all that he must sacrifice? His question was answered when she pulled his lips to hers, offering him his heart's desire. To be only a man in her eyes for a while longer. Sterling lowered her to the cot. He took what she offered, and took it greedily. He savored every human emotion she stirred within him, and later, while she slept, he slipped outside to berate himself for being a coward.

The moon hung full in the sky. Sterling stared, mesmerized by the glowing sphere. Stark loneliness rose up inside of him, and for a moment, he felt tempted to throw back his head and howl. The snap of a branch alerted him to another presence. He sniffed, strangely capable of identifying the intruder as Sarah Dobbs. She came upon him a moment later.

"Sterling." She placed a hand to her heart. "Gave me a fright. Thought everyone was abed. Couldn't sleep myself, so I took a short walk, which sometimes helps. What . . ." Her voice trailed off. The fortune-teller's eyes squinted at him through the darkness. Her face paled.

"What is wrong?" he asked, but his voice sounded strange. Garbled and deep.

Sarah opened her mouth and screamed. The woman kept screaming until he heard the sounds of the troupe members hurriedly fumbling inside of their wagons. Elise stumbled outside, clutching a blanket around her nakedness.

"What's happening?" she breathed, staring at Sarah Dobbs. Elise turned to look at Sterling and stumbled back a step. "Good Lord," she whispered. "Your face."

Sterling lifted his hands to his face. He felt tufts of thick hair covering his cheeks. He ran his fingers over his teeth. They were long and sharp. Pain ripped through him, and he doubled over.

"Sterling!" Elise cried, and she was there a moment later, touching him.

He jerked from her grasp. "Don't come close to me!" he warned. "It's the curse. My family curse. To give my heart, I must sacrifice my humanity."

"You're talking nonsense," she insisted. "Let me help you."

"You can't help me!" he shouted, and another pain ripped through him, sending him to his knees. The other troupe members were now gathered around him, their eyes wide and their mouths hanging open. "I should have told you," he rasped. "Forgive me, Elise. I only wanted to love you, to be yours and have you for mine for a short time. Our time is over."

"No!" she cried again, and took a step toward him. "Sterling, allow me to help you. You're obviously sick with some disease."

When he held up a hand to warn her away, he saw that the hair had now spread to his hands. His fingers were bent and misshapen. "This is a Wulf's curse, Elise. Wulf is my family name. This is what I have been running from since I first saw it take my father ten years ago. The witch who cursed us took perverse pleasure in turning all Wulf males into our namesake. She loved one of my forefathers, but he would not acknowledge their love. He married a woman suitable to his station instead, and as punishment, the witch cursed him with this affliction, cursed all males of his bloodline, then and future generations."

CHAPTER 14

ELISE shook her head in denial. Curses were not real. What she saw happening could not be real. As Sterling knelt before them, he began to change. His clothes fell away, exposing strips of thick hair where there once had been skin. She could not bear to watch him lie in the dirt, his body contorting with pain, but she could not look away. The metamorphosis took place in a short time, and yet it seemed to her as if time had ceased to exist. One moment a man had knelt before them; the next, a beast, a great wolf, stood in the man's place.

There was nothing of Sterling left, nothing except the eyes, and as he stared at her, she knew he saw the fear, the repulsion, she felt inside. She also knew instinctually that he not only saw her emotions but also understood them.

The wolf howled, a heart-wrenching sound of despair mixed with rage; then he disappeared into the night. Elise didn't realize she trembled so badly until another blanket was suddenly thrown around her shoulders. Dazed, she turned to see Philip standing beside her.

"Sarah, take her inside and stay with her through the night," he said, but even his booming voice had lost its strength. "We've all had a shock."

Elise felt as if her wits had deserted her. She allowed Sarah to help her back into the wagon, even allowed the woman to dress her in nightclothes and settle her back onto the cot. She lay awake for a long time, staring at the ceiling. It became blurry; then darkness finally claimed her. She awoke with that first wonderful lack of awareness, the sleepy lull before the storm of remembrance jolted her fully from sleep.

She sat, looking around the wagon. All appeared normal. A nightmare? Elise breathed a sigh of relief. Yes, she'd had a horrible nightmare. She dressed for the day, all the while her stomach tied into knots and a feeling of unease riding her emotions. She stepped outside, certain she would see Sterling gathered around the morning cook fire with the others. The others were present. Sterling was not. As all faces turned toward her, she understood that she had not been dreaming last night. Even Dawn appeared as if she'd aged a decade overnight.

Philip rose and came to Elise. He helped her to the fire and Sarah shoved a plate into her hand. "Here, eat something to help you find your strength."

Elise's hands shook as she held the plate. "What I saw last night cannot be," she finally whispered. "It is not possible."

"Maybe not in the world you came from," Sarah said. "But out here, on the road, among the caravans, anything is possible. These old eyes have seen far worse than what we all witnessed last night."

Tom grunted his agreement.

"Sterling's different now," Taylor muttered. "Like the rest of us."

Elise couldn't fathom their calm acceptance of what had taken place last night. "Sterling is cursed," she said. "He is a wolf! We must help him!"

"There is no help for him," Sarah said. "He knew the curse was tied to his heart, but he gave it anyway. He made his choice."

Angry, Elise threw her plate to the ground and stood. "I will not accept what has happened to Sterling. I cannot. I love him. I want him back the way he was!"

"If you love him, then you must love him the way he is," Sarah countered.

"Will you disown him now?" Dawn asked softly. "Will you disown us all?"

Elise's heart constricted. She was the one who had told Dawn she must love unconditionally, and yet Elise was suddenly unsure that she could follow her own order. Sterling should have told her about the curse. God, she'd been chasing him like a fool since the night that she met him, and he'd been running . . . but not from her, from what would happen if he dared love her.

Confused and sick at heart, Elise returned to the wagon. She threw herself upon the cot where Sterling had made love to her, and cried at the injustice of life. As the shadows lengthened and night approached, she wondered if Sterling would return to her. She wondered if he did, if he would come in the form of a man or a wolf.

A voice inside of her head, one she wanted to ignore, suggested that she did not want Sterling to return in either form. It would be simpler on her heart and her mind if she were to find her aunt in Liverpool and forget she'd ever met Sterling Wulf.

His name stirred a memory. Whispers of the Wulfs of London. He was one of them, she realized. The youngest, who had mysteriously disappeared years ago, after his parents' deaths. Not privy to much gossip, Elise had heard little about the family. She'd dismissed what little she had heard. Men could not change shapes. Or so she had thought. Now she understood why Sterling spoke elegantly despite his coarse appearance. She understood all too much.

Shame scalded her from the inside out. She'd once thought him secretive and unfeeling, but he was the bravest of men. He had risked everything, his very humanity, for her. Could she abandon such a man? No, she could not. Would not. She would love Sterling unconditionally. She would love him, curse and all.

Rising from the bed, Elise washed her face, ran a brush through her hair, and left the wagon. The cooking fires had long been extinguished and she imagined most of the troupe had retired to the comfort of their wagons. They would move soon. They always did. She must find Sterling and convince him to come back to the caravan.

The woods were full of shadows. Elise moved through the trees, trying to ignore the pounding of her heart. She hadn't gone far when a voice stopped her.

"You shouldn't be out here alone."

"Sterling," she whispered, turning to face him. With relief, she noted it was the man she confronted, not the beast.

"What are you doing here?" He stepped from the shadows.

"I wanted to talk to you," she answered. "Convince you to come back to the caravan."

He laughed, his teeth flashing in the coming dark, but at least his teeth were not pointed, she noted. "Come back to what?"

She lifted her chin. "To me, to those who consider you family."

"Do not pretend that you are not repulsed by me, by what you saw last night. I know differently."

Again, shame washed over her. "I was taken aback by what happened last night. I believe I am entitled to that first reaction."

He stepped closer. His hair was tangled and he still looked half-wild to her. Elise would not retreat in fear. She knew Sterling would never hurt her, regardless of what form he took.

"What are you saying?" he demanded.

Staring up into his eyes, she answered, "I love you, Sterling. And because I love you, I accept you as you are."

SHE would be the death of him. Sterling's heart soared with hope, even as his spirit plummeted with the reality of their situation. Brave words from her now, but Sterling could not allow her to love him, to waste her young life upon a man cursed.

"I will not have children," he said. "I will not pass this curse to my sons." Sterling gently touched her cheek. "If we could not abstain from the pleasure we find in each other's arms, I would have to be ever mindful of the risks involved in loving you as you deserve to be loved. You deserve children. You deserve a normal life, which you will never have with me."

"I deserve to be with the man I love," Elise argued. She sighed. "I do love children, but a life on the road is not what I would wish for them. It is a life I could be happy with." She stared up at him with hope shining in her eyes. "Please allow me what I deserve most in life, Sterling. To be happy, and I can't be happy without you."

Again, he imagined these were brave words that would soon fade away. As much as he longed to believe her, he could not. He took her slender shoulders between his hands. "Elise. I am cursed by the moon. Whenever it is full, I become a beast that roams the night like other beasts. I have no recollection of what I did last night, but I woke naked and shivering this morning in a man's body."

Instead of recoiling from him, she said, "Well, it's not so bad, then. We've only a few days each month to deal with your curse. The rest of the time we can live a normal life."

He supposed his mouth dropped open. "Are you mad? There is nothing normal about me now, Elise. I want you to find your aunt in Liverpool and forget about me. Find yourself a governess position somewhere and a respectable man who can give you all that I cannot!"

"I don't want that," she insisted. "I want you."

With a growl, Sterling released her and turned his back. Night would soon fall. He felt the change already upon him. "You cannot have me!" If he must be a brute to convince her, then he would. "I don't want you, Elise. I want to live out the rest of my miserable life in peace! I don't want to worry about you, or the people of the caravan! I just want to be alone!"

"Sterling," she pleaded.

"Go!" he shouted. "Darkness falls and the wolf comes. I am lost to him, Elise. I am lost to you."

He left her before she could protest further. Sterling

bounded through the trees, waiting for the awful pain that would soon tear through his body. But before he allowed the beast to take him, he would circle around and make certain that Elise reached the safety of the wagon.

He saw her a few moments later standing before the animal wagons. He crept closer.

"What am I to do?" he heard her ask the cats. "I love him for all that he is, but he does not love himself enough to accept what I offer him. How do I make him see that nothing on earth will make me stop loving him?"

The urge to go to her was overwhelming. His love for Elise in that moment became stronger. But he loved her too much to ask her to share his curse. He would make her believe that he had gone. But until she reached the safety of Liverpool, Sterling would be watching.

CHAPTER 15

IN the month it took Elise to reach Liverpool, she learned to cook, drive a wagon, and become independent. She danced when they found an audience, and always she danced only for Sterling.

She knew he watched her from somewhere in the night shadows. They were connected in a way only lovers understood. Mind, body, and spirit. Today Dawn rode with her as they approached the outskirts of Liverpool.

"Philip says you will leave us now," Dawn said, her young face solemn. "I will miss you."

Elise blinked back a sudden onslaught of tears. "I will go, but only because if I leave, Sterling might return. He needs a family to watch over him."

"I promise to love him unconditionally," Dawn said. "As you have taught me to do. My mother says that you are a good example of humanity."

"Your parents are good examples of humanity," Elise pointed out.

"Yes," Dawn agreed. "I will try to be more like them."

Dawn's admission lifted Elise's spirits. The girl had found the value of love, just as Elise told Sterling she would do.

"I predict you will be a fine lady someday," Elise said. "I have the sight, you know," she teased.

"I'm going to be a veil dancer like you," Dawn whispered. "But I haven't told my parents yet."

Elise would like to be around when Dawn did. She smiled; then her smile faded as Liverpool came into view. Her valise was packed, and she still had the coin to hire herself a hackney to take her to her aunt's address. Her adventures were over.

Once the wagons halted near an inn, Elise steeled herself for the sorrowful good-byes. Sarah actually cried over her. Philip told her that if things did not work out with her aunt, she always had a home among them. Dawn had disappeared, and Elise was thankful. She couldn't bear to say good-bye to her.

Sporting her best outfit, Elise waved good-bye. It was strange to again be in a city, where life teamed along at a fast pace, where people passed on the streets with no time to look around. The house the driver stopped in front of was in need of repair. Elise vaguely remembered it from her childhood visits. The woman who answered her knock did not look familiar.

"Aunt Silvie?" Elise ventured skeptically.

The old woman shook her head. "You'd be looking for Silvie Preston. She's been dead now for going on five years. I bought the house after her passing."

Elise was shocked. Her aunt dead? Elise had hardly known the woman, but still, she'd kept fond memories of her throughout the years. Her uncle must have surely known her aunt had passed, and he hadn't told her. He'd kept the truth from her as if her aunt's death were of no consequence. How she hated him in that moment. He truly was heartless.

With tears streaming down her cheeks, Elise walked back to the waiting hackney. There was only one thing she could do: return to the caravan. She couldn't say that she wasn't pleased to see her family again or that she wasn't welcomed home with open arms. But Elise still worried about Sterling. He'd no doubt be wondering why she had left, only to return. But would he have the courage to confront her for answers? Yes, she believed he would.

While she waited, Elise prepared for the coming performance. She dressed in her costume, then sat to wait for

Dawn to come fetch her. The door suddenly opened and
Sterling appeared. Her heart leaped with joy to see him. He
did not look all that pleased to see her.

"Why aren't you with your aunt?" he demanded.

So much for warm reunions, Elise thought. "I have
learned today that my aunt has passed away. Five years now
she's been gone, and never a word of it from my uncle."

Sterling's expression softened. "I'm sorry."

"Sorry for me, or for yourself?" she challenged.

He smiled slightly. "You were never one to mince words,
Elise."

"No," she agreed. "And I won't start now. Why are you
here?"

He closed the door behind him. "To see you safely into
another life."

She lifted a brow. "In this world, or in the next?"

Sterling threw back his head and laughed. It was good to
see him laugh. It warmed Elise through and through. He
needed her to lighten his darkness. If only she could convince him. He sobered a moment later.

"The road is no place for a woman without a mate to
protect her."

Her arms ached to hold him. Her lips longed for his
kisses. She had learned to be brave, to go after what she
sought in life. "I have a mate," she said. "Even if he refuses to make an honest woman of me."

"Elise." Her name was half-sigh, half-caress. "You and I
both know we could never live a normal life together."

She took a step toward him. "I never said that I wanted
a normal life. I want the life of an adventurer, remember?"

"Don't," he warned when she took another step toward
him. "You know that I cannot resist you, and tonight is not
the night to tempt me. The moon will be full."

Ignoring his warning, Elise stepped up close to him. "I
am not afraid of you. I know that you would not harm me,
or any person that you care about."

"But *I* do not know that, Elise," he stressed. "I won't
take that chance. I cannot."

Gently she touched his face. "You must trust in yourself, Sterling—in your goodness."

For a moment their eyes held and she thought he would kiss her; then a knock sounded upon the door. Elise peeked out and saw Dawn.

"Philip says I'm to rouse everyone," she said, then stretched her neck to see past Elise. "Is Sterling with you?" Her eyes brightened. "He is here."

Sterling smiled at the girl. "Hello, Dawn."

"I knew you'd come back to us," the girl said. "Philip says no matter how different we may seem to the rest of the world, when we're together, we are a family."

Elise swore that Sterling's silver eyes misted over for a moment. "Philip is a good man," he admitted. "But aren't you afraid of me, Dawn?"

She shook her blond head. "Not if Elise isn't. She and I are best friends, you know?"

"Elise is a good friend to have."

Again Elise's and Sterling's gazes locked.

"I hope you'll stay with us," Dawn said, breaking the spell. "You and Elise together, as part of our family."

Sterling reached out and mussed the girl's hair. He did not commit to staying. Still, Dawn smiled, then scampered away.

"I must go," he said abruptly.

"Not yet," Elise pleaded. "Stay and watch me dance. I'll tell Philip I want to perform first, before night falls."

"I like to watch you dance," Sterling admitted. "I always feel as if you're dancing for me alone."

"That's because I am," she said, and kissed him.

He resisted, but only for a moment. They melted into each other, a fusion of warm, seeking mouths and bodies straining against each other. Elise was breathless and dazed when he broke from her. By the time she roused herself, he was gone.

She sighed, then said a prayer that Sterling would come to his senses and realize that he belonged with her and the caravan members. The crowd was small, and Elise was more self-conscious because she danced when night had not yet fallen. She felt eyes boring into her and wondered if Sterling had stayed to watch her. Hoping that was the case, she danced her most sensuous dance. A dance to inflame the passions of her own sultan. She became so caught up in the dance, she hadn't realized that a man had stepped into her circle and stood arguing with Philip. The stranger's voice stopped her dead in her tracks.

"Unhand me, you idiot! That is my niece parading herself around like a whore for all to see!"

"Uncle Robert," Elise gasped.

He marched forward and grabbed her arm. "How dare you embarrass me in this manner? Your future husband will have to beat some sense into you."

Fear paralyzed her for a moment, but Elise dug in her bare heels. "My future husband is not Sir Winston Stoneham," she snapped. "Take your hands off of me!"

"Ungrateful brat," her uncle sneered. "I took you in even though you were an embarrassment to my family name. I gave you fine clothes and an education. You belong to me, and I will have the bride's price for all my trouble!"

"Release Elise this instant," Philip warned her uncle. "She obviously has no wish to accompany you."

The troupe members now stood in the circle, rallying to her cause.

"I can make trouble for you," her uncle warned. "For all of you," he added, his gaze running coldly over the ragtag group. "My name and my influence will see you all hanged for kidnapping."

"No one kidnapped me," Elise protested. "I stowed away upon one of their wagons in order to escape you. They are guilty of nothing but kindness to me!"

Her uncle's grip tightened around her arm. "If you care about what happens to them, you'll come along as you've been told to do."

The last thing Elise would do was cause trouble for the troupe members. "I'll go with you," she agreed. "But leave these fine people alone."

Her uncle smiled coldly over his victory and jerked her toward the crowd. A tall figure suddenly blocked their exit. Elise's heart flip-flopped inside of her chest.

"You, sir, are not taking Elise anywhere," Sterling said. "Least of all back to the monster you sold her to."

"You," her uncle snarled. "You led me to believe that the woman I saw outlined inside the wagon that day was your wife. I should horsewhip you for lying to me!"

"Try it, if you're brave enough," Sterling goaded. He stuck his face close to her uncle's. "But know this: There is nothing short of killing me that will make me allow you to take Elise with you. She belongs here, among people who love her."

"Get out of my way!" her uncle shouted. "I'll not stand here and argue with a vagabond. That handsome face has given you airs, boy. You have no right to tell me what I can or cannot do with my own flesh and blood."

Sterling suddenly grabbed her uncle by his collar. "I love her. And I am much worse than a vagabond. Now, release her!"

Elise might have felt a wonderful warmth spread through her when Sterling publicly declared his love for her, but now she went cold with dread. Sterling's eyes glittered dangerously in the coming dark. In a matter of moments, the moon would rise and her uncle would have far more to deal with than an angry man.

"Sterling," she warned, glancing up. "The moon. You must go!"

He ignored her, his silver gaze locked with her uncle's haughty one. Then he did something that wiped the smug expression completely from Lord Robert Collins's features. Sterling growled low in his throat. The sound was that of an animal, defending his territory, defending his mate.

Her uncle's grip loosened upon her arm and he stumbled back a step, allowing Elise to twist free.

"Sterling," she tried again. "Go now, before it's too late."

But even as she spoke the warning, she saw Sterling changing. Thank goodness the crowd had slunk away into the shadows, wanting no part of a nobleman's personal squabble with a troupe of performers. The more who witnessed Sterling's curse, the more danger he placed himself in.

"What the bloody hell," her uncle whispered, still backing from Sterling. "What have you gotten yourself involved with, Elise?"

Sterling was still enough of a man to register her uncle's words, because he glanced at Elise, sudden hurt shining within the glowing depths of his eyes.

"The man I love," she answered. "Regardless of what he is." She glanced around to include the troupe members. "A man we all love."

"He's a monster," her uncle croaked.

Sterling's teeth had become pointed and now hair covered his cheeks, but Elise felt no fear of him. "No, Uncle, you're the monster. You have no heart. You care for no one save yourself. It is the heart and the ability to love that makes us human."

Elise expected the pain to rip through Sterling as it had the last time she saw him change, but the transformation came within the blink of an eye. She supposed because he did not fight it, but seemed to embrace it under the circumstances. His clothes fell away and the great wolf appeared in his place.

The beast bared his fangs and stalked toward her uncle. Elise knew Sterling's intent. He planned to rid them of Lord Collins once and for all. Her uncle had backed up until he'd tripped over his own feet and lay in the dirt. He clutched his chest, gasping for breath, his eyes huge.

Elise stepped between them, the man she loved and the uncle who had raised her. "No, Sterling," she said. "He has no heart, but I do. I cannot allow you to kill him. He is my flesh and blood, my father's brother, and out of love for one man, I must ask you to spare this one."

The wolf with Sterling's eyes stared at her for a moment, glanced at her uncle, and growled again, but made no move toward the fallen man.

"Leave while you can," Elise instructed her uncle. "And

never come looking for me again. Next time, I may not have the heart to stop him."

Her uncle needed no further prodding. He was up and running for his coach in an instant. Elise watched him go, saddened that their relationship could not have been more than it was. The coach drove away at breakneck speed. She felt certain that she would never see her uncle again.

The wolf stood staring at her. Elise didn't know if Sterling understood her while in animal form, but she said, "Go now into the night, but come daylight, return to us. We love you. I love you."

For a brief moment, their eyes held and Elise felt that Sterling could understand her; then he was gone. An arm went around her waist and she glanced down at Dawn.

"He'll come back," she said, then motioned for her parents to join them, and the girl slipped an arm around her mother's small shoulders. They formed a circle, the ragtag group of misfits. They stayed that way for a long time; then, as if all understood that, due to the night's events, they could not stay, they began to pack up their wagons.

MORNING broke in a display of pink and purple, a glorious day to be alive and traveling the road. Elise stood by the wagon, her insides twisted, heart pounding. She stared at the woods, silently praying.

The other members joined her. A blond head appeared, a man wearing the clothing Elise had left in the woods for him. He glanced up at them and smiled; then his eyes found hers and his smile widened.

"Hurry it up, Beast Tamer!" Philip boomed in his big voice. "We need to get down the road!"

Raja and Leena both growled a greeting to the approaching man. Elise felt that the cats had come to accept their changed master, even as the troupe had come to accept him. Nowhere on earth could Sterling fit in among humanity more than with his troupe of misfits. The others melted away, and then it was only Elise and Sterling, staring into each other's eyes.

"Have you come home?" Elise asked.

Sterling reached forward and pulled her to him. "If a man can love and be loved in return while cursed, is he really cursed at all?"

She smiled up at him. "I would say we are blessed. Few find what we have found together."

"Will you stay with me, Elise? Be my love? Be my life?"

In answer, she leaned forward, brushing her lips over his. "Yes, Sterling," she whispered. "I will have you by my side until we are old, and I will have my adventures, and then some."

Theirs lips met, sealing the bargain.

Read on for an excerpt from

KISS OF THE NIGHT

by Sherrilyn Kenyon

Coming soon from St. Martin's Press

CASSANDRA'S mind was on the Dark-Hunter who'd come to her rescue. Why had he bothered to save her life?

She had to know more about him . . .

Before she could think better of it, Cassandra ran after him, looking for a man who shouldn't be real.

Outside, blaring sirens filled the air and were getting progressively louder. Someone in the bar must have called the police.

The Dark-Hunter was halfway down the block before she caught up to him and pulled him to a stop.

His face impassive, he looked down at her with those deep, dark eyes. Eyes so black that she couldn't detect the pupils. The wind whipped his hair around his chiseled features and the cloud from his breath mingled with hers.

It was freezing out, but his presence warmed her so much that she didn't even feel it.

"What are you going to do about the police?" she asked. "They'll be looking for you."

A bitter smile tugged at the edges of his lips. "In five minutes no human in that bar will ever remember they saw me."

His words surprised her. Was that true of all Dark-Hunters? "Will I forget, too?"

He nodded.

"In that case, thank you for saving my life."

Wulf paused at her words. It was the first time anyone had ever thanked him for being a Dark-Hunter.

He stared at the wealth of tight, strawberry blond curls that cascaded without order around her oval face. She wore her long hair plaited down her back. And her hazel green eyes were filled with a brilliant vitality and warmth.

Though she wasn't a great beauty, she held a quiet charm to her features that was inviting. Tempting.

Against his will, he reached his hand up to touch her jaw, just below her ear. Softer than velvet, her delicate skin warmed his cold fingers.

It had been so long since he had last touched a woman. So long since he had last tasted one.

Before he could stop himself, he leaned down and captured those parted lips with his own.

Wulf growled at the taste of her as his body roared to life. He'd never sampled anything sweeter than the honey of her mouth. Never smelled anything more intoxicating than her clean, rose-scented flesh.

Her tongue danced with his as her hands clutched at his shoulders, pressing him closer to her. Making him hard and stiff with the thought of how soft her body would be in other places.

And in that moment, he wanted her with an urgency that stunned him. It was a desperate need he hadn't felt in a long, long time.

Cassandra's senses swirled at the unexpected contact of his lips on hers. She'd never known anything like the power and hunger of his kiss.

The faint smell of sandalwood clung to his flesh and he tasted of beer and wild, untamed masculinity.

Barbarian.

It was the only word to describe him.

His arms flexed around her as he plundered her mouth masterfully.

He wasn't just deadly to Daimons. He was deadly to a woman's senses.

The *Awakening*

A VAMPIRE HUNTRESS LEGEND

L.A. BANKS

Spoken word artist Damali Richards never thought that the fate of the world would rest on her shoulders. She certainly never wanted to be the Chosen One, the Slayer. Although she had always been aware of her amazing strength and of an unseen evil surrounding her, she ignored it for the sake of a normal life—if growing up in foster care and then later being raised by the streets could be considered a normal life. And yet, when Marlene took her off the streets, explaining that she was a Guardian sent to train Damali for her destiny, Damali knew she could deny it no longer. Rapper by day and Slayer by night, she has now come up against her greatest challenge yet: the undeniably sensual and powerful vampire Fallon Nuit, who wants more than just a taste of her blood—he wants to own her, body and soul.

"If you enjoy Anne Rice, Blade and Buffy, then *Minion* is the novel you have been waiting for."
> —Tananarive Due, bestselling author
> of *The Living Blood* on *Minion*

"*Blade* meets *Buffy the Vampire Slayer*."
> —*Kirkus Reviews*

AVAILABLE WHEREVER BOOKS ARE SOLD
FROM ST. MARTIN'S GRIFFIN

TA 6/03